Reader Reviews:

"...a richly woven tapestry of fascinating, lovable and very real characters enlivening a story that brought me to tears and laughter. And not all the characters are humans. Hold onto your heart. This is tender, heartfelt and wise." —*Andrew Elliott*

"Animal lovers will adore this book. It gets to the heart of loss and the uphill climb toward release, healing and opening up to honest, intimate, no-pretense love. I hated to let the characters go. An engaging and very satisfying read." —*Amazon Customer*

"...There is a delightful cadence to the storytelling and it's populated by characters that ring true-to-life. Skye shows us that the complicated human spirit is capable of growing stronger from dealing with loss and unexpected tragedy, and that love is the balm." —*Elise Kimmons, verified purchase*

"I was hooked immediately. The characters and situations are very real. While Zephyr was the first to win my heart, I found the humans so wise and caring that I hated to part with them when I finished the book. Great read. Can't wait for the sequel." —*Kay*

"...Skye Blaine is an exceptional storyteller. Her characters are fully realized, and her understanding of animals, her empathy, is breathtaking. Highly recommended." —*Wordchaser, verified purchase*

"From the beginning I could not put this book down. Skye's characters, people and dogs, are deep, courageous and lovable with just enough tension in her story to keep me fully engaged." —*Amazon Customer*

"Once I started reading this book I could hardly put it down.... The characters are very real and interesting and the inclusion of dog characters and animal communication added another dimension. ... I experienced the story visually and I definitely think it should be a movie." —*Mo*

Unleashed

book one, *The Pensing Connection*

Skye Blaine

Unleashed is a work of fiction. Is is book one of *The Pensing Connection*

ISBN: 978-0-9779483-6-9

Author's websites and contact information:
    www.skyeblaine.com
    www.theheartofthematter-dailyreminders.org
    skye@skyeblaine.com

Published by:
    Berkana Publications
    Sebastopol CA 95472 USA

Cover image: Balnagown Maybe, photographed by Thomas Christ
Book layout: Berkana Publications

Printed in the United States of America

Dedicated to all the dogs who have graced my life: Baron, Arthur, Nisa, Kylemore, Jesse, Seer, Dancer, Emma, and Maggie.

Baron CDX, a German shepherd, was sweet, highly intelligent, and very obedient.

Arthur, a rescue and shaggy dog, sported big black and white patches. He came with the name Bonzo, but we renamed him to provide dignity.

Nisa came from my friend Shelby. Nisa was reputed to be golden retriever, dingo, and herding dog, but I'm convinced she was a mixture of smooth collie and golden. She rode in the car with her head on my shoulder, and remained a precious companion for ten years.

Kyle, my first Irish wolfhound, chose me when he was ten days old by crawling in my lap. He was bred by Carol Gabriel. A sweet, goofy boy, he died of osteosarcoma at age five. A crushing loss.

Jesse, a herding dog mix, was Kyle's best friend. We were blessed with her alert, smart presence for thirteen years.

Seer, a whippet as large as a greyhound, came to live with us at age eleven. He was a refined and poised gentleman. A friend asked, "But where is his smoking jacket?"

Dancer, an Irish wolfhound, also came to us from Carol Gabriel, but as a young adult. She had a more serious personality than Kyle, but welcomed Emma the puppy in such a generous and loving way.

Emma, a smooth collie, patrolled for wildlife and told us when anything with fur showed up. She was independent and clever.

Maggie, a Scottish deerhound, came from Judy Shaw at Rowanlea. Both elegant and silly, Maggie fulfilled my request for a "soulful" dog. We lost her far too soon. I still grieve for her.

All nine dogs were unique and special, but the four sighthounds own my doggie heart.

Acknowledgements

Boudewijn Boom for his steady support and endless proofreading.

My trusty weekly critique group, BigRig who went through the manuscript three times: **Patrice "PH" Garrett, Beth Mathews,** and **Laura McHale Holland.** They hold my hand and light my way.

Marie Judson Rosier who used to be a member of BigRig, and helped edit the first draft.

Monica Kamsvaag for her kind contribution to the front cover.

Karen Kieffer and Thomas Christ for the gorgeous cover photo of Maybe. I knew the moment she sent it to me I wanted to use it.

Robbi Sommers Bryant for her developmental edit and inspiration. Her website is: https://robbibryant.com

Katie Watts for her encouragement and detailed line edit.

My beta readers Brian Lowe, Denise Jessup, Katie Watts, Mary Ann Rose, Lori Walker, Jennifer Anderman, Tui Wilschinsky, Asha Greer, Rabi'a Laurie Neeno, and Shelby Dunn. Thank you!

Annie Andreson a broker at Coldwell Banker in Sisters, Oregon who helped me locate Moss's imaginary ranch, Bender's Ridge.

Karen Miner at the California Department of Fish and Wildlife who provided valuable information on cougar behavior.

Dr. Nicole Canon, DVM, MPVM who reviewed the chapter that takes place at Francine's veterinary clinic.

Dr. Julie Griffith, neurologist, who had lunch with me to talk about cortical blindness.

I'm sure I've missed some kind soul who assisted me along the way. Contact me, and in the next printing, I'll happily make the correction.

This is wholly a work of fiction. I have retained the true names of the businesses in Sisters, Oregon. However, all characters are invented except for Mary, the owner of Sisters Motor Lodge. When my husband and I stayed there on a research trip, I was touched by both her openness and friendliness, and asked permission at that time to include her in my novel. She probably thought it would never happen!

Chapter One

Sisters, Oregon—July 2005

Stiff after weeding, Moss straightened up and mopped his face with a faded, red bandanna. Two hens dead, probably that fox again. Their torn remains took him back to war—the stench of blood, the abrupt void of premature death. The past remained an open wound; dwelling there was destructive. Worrying about the future sucked the present away—at least that's what his mindfulness teacher said. The guy's recommendation kept him from sinking into the quicksand of despair.

After feeding the girls for months and collecting their warm, colorful eggs, he'd grown fond of them. It wasn't like having a dog, not like Sherlock— damn, he missed him—but breathing creatures, nonetheless. They helped. He had to get out of bed to take care of them. In the morning, he'd drive to Sisters and get more chicks at the feed store. It was late in the season; they might have to special order them.

He walked over to the porch, tilted his head, and listened—too early for evening frogs, but he recognized a couple bird calls—a Pacific-slope flycatcher, he was sure. His tattered *Sibley Guide to Birds* lay on the step, and he instinctively reached for it. He stuffed loose pages back in, including his lifetime birding list. He held the broken binding. *Time to replace this.*

Tonight, he'd sit on the front porch and soak up the sunset. Last evening, beered-up yahoos tracking cougar stomped through his property. He took care to respect boundaries and land ownership, and expected fellow hunters to do the same. In his experience, men who pursued cat were a different sort altogether from deer and elk bowhunters like himself. Cat hunters sought only to overpower the creature, kill for the thrill of killing. Resenting their attitude, he'd gone on a little expedition, shot off some cherry bombs, hollered, and scared the shit out of them. They wouldn't be back, and maybe they'd pass the word on to their cronies.

Moss's focus shifted to the clearing. The bees busied themselves collecting honeysuckle pollen. The plant's sweetness reached all the way to the porch. In search of carcasses, the peace eagles—he couldn't call them vultures, such an ugly name for birds that mostly cleaned up—floated on higher drafts. A black-tailed doe and her fawn foraged a hundred yards away.

He liked the stillness. No one around to blather or bother him. Not wanting to startle the grazing deer, he moved slowly, closed up his chickens for the night, and limped inside to pour a full glass of merlot. No beer or hard stuff. Not anymore. The smells swamped him with war flashbacks. Even though his hard-drinking service buddies chided him for kicking back a woman's drink, he wasn't about to tell them why.

None of their damn business.

Chapter Two

Zephyr cowers beneath the clothes and tucks her paws under. She wraps her tail around her body and up over her nose. She feels safe inside the house—even safer in the closet—but fear still tracks her down. The monster garbage truck rumbles outside. Zephyr remembers clouds belching out the back end—it stings her eyes and eats at her throat. Like the truck that carted her to the shelter, it growls. Its mouth gulps giant-sized buckets—big enough to swallow her.

As the garbage truck lumbered near their house, Rowan brought a picture to mind of the two of them, the boulder in the field, warm from the blazing sun. Lying nearby, she and the pup laze in the shade. Once the images were firmly set in her mind, Rowan concentrated, then hurled them toward Zephy like whizzing arrows.

Under the clothes, Zephyr receives Rowan's mind-pictures one after another. It's like watching a rabbit jump from spot to spot to spot. Boulder. Field. Sunshine. Companionship. She raises her head, listens as the monster moves farther away, and cautiously crawls out to find Rowan. Her girl comforts her and says, "Good dog! Biscuit?" They walk to the utility room where the box of goodies is stored, and Rowan gives her one. Zephyr swipes her hand with her tongue.

Truck gone, Zephyr and Row bounded through the kitchen almost knocking down Rowan's mother, who grabbed the counter edge for balance. As Rowan charged past, she snatched a warm brownie from the stack on the plate and giggled, "Yum! My favorite! Thanks, Mom."

"Outdoors, both of you," Carolina ordered, her frown as deep as her tone was mild. "Our home is not a racetrack."

They blasted outside, leaping over Stormy—Mom's old shepherd snoring on the front porch—flew down the two wooden steps, out the path, and into the field. Zephyr bolted ahead, then made a wide, looping circle back. Zephyr panted and Rowan huffed as they stood together in the recently mowed weeds. Rowan knotted her fingers in her dog's fur. It was too hot to hang out near their favorite boulder. In her mind, she created the new picture she wanted to send—lying in the shade, soaking in the love they felt for each other.

Zephyr abruptly sat and stared at her. Rowan sent the picture and feeling again. This time, her dog took off across the field, and Rowan burst out laughing before following her at a trot. Zephyr received the vision, for sure, because she plopped down in the cool of the old oak and waited for her. Only one ray of sun illuminated her.

Rowan knew she was the alpha-dog in their pack of two—it needed to be that way—but she always thought of Zephyr as her equal. She slowed to a walk, taking in her beautiful four-legged friend who was tall enough to snare goodies from the kitchen counter if Mom wasn't careful. Her wiry, gray-mixture coat glowed reddish in the sunlight, and she sported eyebrow furnishings Rowan had to trim to see Zephyr's dark almond eyes. The dog's one-and-a-half inch goatee could carry a lot of water right after she drank— she'd sopped Rowan often. Zeph had been so small when they found her at the Humane Society that Mom hadn't visualized what "giant breed" *really* meant. Thank heavens, her mother had grown to love the pup, too.

Rowan lay down and put her head on Zephyr's chest, listening to her heartbeat. Her favorite place.

Zephyr awakens and shifts to lick her paw, her tongue curving between her toes as she searches for a sticker lodged in her fur. If she can't find it, Rowan can. Her girl knows how to ease a burr out.

She understands only a few of Rowan's words, like "dinner," "wait," "walkies," and "biscuit," but when her girl makes mind-pictures, she sees them clearly. They play games, and Zephyr loves this most. Rowan makes her "stay," hides in the woods, sends an image, and Zephyr must find her. But even stronger than pictures, she can feel her girl. It's like water ebbing and flowing between them.

A half hour later, as Carolina unloaded the dish drainer, Rowan and Zephyr returned to the house and settled on the couch—her daughter with a book, Zeph with her head in Rowan's lap. Carolina heard a fly zip past as it zoomed from the kitchen into the living room. Zephyr startled, jumped down, skittered around the corner, and slunk toward the master-bedroom closet, her safe hidey-hole. Again.

The pup, for all of her restorative qualities, shied from visitors and, in addition to the garbage truck and house flies, was so terrified of the vacuum cleaner, they had to put her outside until the loud noise was over. Carolina prayed Zephyr would develop some backbone, but neither puppy socialization nor obedience classes had bolstered the dog's confidence. Rowan insisted Zephyr communicated her fears, but the truth was—communication or not—they were living with a huge wimp of a dog. Carolina sighed, put the last cup away, and headed downstairs for a karate workout.

Tired and sweaty, Carolina walked back upstairs to a quiet home. Zephyr slept upside down on the couch, legs splayed in the air, Rowan beside her. Her daughter was rereading *The Bridge to Terabithia* for the umpteenth time, one hand fiddling with the pup's oversized toenails. Hand and glove, those two. Nearby, Carolina saw Rowan's word clipboard and dictionary.

Dark wouldn't fall until after nine, but outside the light was already changing. The late afternoon with its golden slant of sun was her favorite time. She hung up her *ghi* and black belt and took a quick shower.

Afterward, with Stormy snoozing at her feet, Carolina flipped open the road atlas on the kitchen table. It was time to figure out how to manage a car vacation with this unique family of four. She stretched to reach the radio on the counter and turned off the six o'clock news so she could concentrate. Using her toes, she played imaginary tunes on Stormy's back.

She couldn't separate dog and daughter any more than Stormy could be pried away from her side. Her shepherd had aged so much in the past six months that Carolina refused to kennel him. And no museums or city stuff—Zephyr needed long walks every day. Carolina turned to their own state of Oregon. She ran her finger eastward from their home in Eugene. They could try Malheur Wildlife Refuge; she'd long wanted to go there. Her travel book said the wetlands drew a multitude of bird species and lots of waterfowl. A birder's paradise. She shook her head. Fat chance— Zeph would scare away every winged creature in the place. Other birders would complain.

Earlier, Rowan suggested going to the mountains. Camping *was* the best idea this year. They had the needed equipment, so the vacation would be inexpensive—a huge plus. They could head for higher altitudes, maybe Little Three Creeks Lake? She'd been there once, fifteen years ago. Climbing would serve them, muscle them up. Stormy could stay at camp if hiking stressed him too much. She'd find a campsite in the deep shade so he could hang out in the van.

If they were lucky, they might glimpse wild horses, which would thrill Rowan. Well, to be honest, she'd be thrilled too. How would Zephyr respond to the sight of running mustangs, perhaps a whole herd? Lunge or cower? No doubt she'd be a handful. But they couldn't let her off leash, not in the wild. If their dog saw game like elk or deer, or horses for heaven's sake—if either breed description told the truth—she would roar off with her nine-foot strides barely touching ground and land in California before she stopped for breath.

Carolina glanced out the window. This fall, the front field would come alive again. The browner summer landscape held a beauty of its own, but nature's full range of greens bolstered her spirits. The pasture was rimmed by fir and oak woods, Rowan and Zephyr's favorite place to hang out.

Carolina jotted a to-do list: library, bookstore, Bureau of Land Management for maps. She'd put off planning too long; they were leaving in a few days. It was clear why she'd procrastinated. This camping vacation without an adult companion didn't appeal. After her husband died—but before they'd adopted Zephyr—she boarded Stormy and they headed for Seattle, Victoria, or Portland—a different city each year. There was so much to do with a child in metropolises.

In moments like these, Carolina grieved for Rafe. She'd slammed the secret chamber of her heart shut after the blunt-force trauma of losing him. Rowan missed him too. If only he could see his daughter now, four years older. Carolina rested her head in her hands. How could a strong, young man, only thirty-two, just up and die of flu? Sighing, she stared out the window but saw only her own despair.

She pressed the palms of her hands on the table. Okay, five-minute pity-party limit reached. Today was today—each new moment unknown and fresh, blossoming with possibility. Yesterday was gone like crumbled, desiccated leaves carried on the wind.

Time to start dinner. Afterward, she faced a long evening of sewing. Clients waited impatiently for equipment to be repaired—tent tears, broken sleeping bag and jacket zippers—and those packages, plus invoices, had to get shipped if there were to be any vacation.

She smacked the atlas closed, rubbed her eyes with the heels of her hands, held them there for a moment, then rose to rinse the sprouts greening on the window sill. She opened the fridge. "Sheesh, stinky. Bad dairy," she muttered. Rafe had always cleaned the refrigerator, and whenever it needed wiping down, she ached for him, for how he had willingly and lovingly tended their home. It was one way he'd shown his devotion to their family. Doing it herself was an emotional chore.

Shifting containers around, she found tomatoes, avocado, green onions, the last batch of sprouts, cheese—and the soured milk, which she poured down the sink before returning to study the tortillas. Good, not moldy. She didn't have time to go to the store. Tonight would be a this-and-that burrito night.

Carolina smiled at her three charges. Stormy had climbed on the couch with the others, white muzzle plunked between her daughter's bare feet. Rowan slept with her head on Zephyr's hip, the paperback upside down and open on the pup's chest, which rose and fell with every breath. Ten legs among them.

∞

The next day after lunch, Rowan swiveled on a kitchen stool and scribbled her story idea before it got away. Her heroine and the dog sent mental pictures back and forth like she did with Zephy. Rowan stopped and tapped her pencil on the table. What word could she use to describe this image exchange? The more she considered it, the more she realized that no one word fit. I'll just make it up, she decided. That's when it came to her. She'd call it *pensing*—after the word she had learned just a few days before: pensive.

"I wouldn't want to interrupt the creative process," Mom said, her tone wry. "But will you help with the dishes, please?"

Rowan groaned and stashed her journal. "Okay." She jumped up and stepped over Zephyr. "I found five new words this week. My fave is 'honeyfuggle.' It means to cheat or … what was the other word?" Rowan squinched her eyes. "Swindle, that's it."

"Swindle is a wonderful writerly verb. It sounds just like its meaning. I hope it's on your list, too."

Rowan grinned and jotted it down. Then she went to the sink and filled the dishpan with hot water. "I'll try to work those into my back-to-school essay. Not the cheating words though; I'll have to save those for a short story later. English teachers are so dorky—they always use the same prompt: 'What did you do during summer vacation?' Plus, we have to read our papers out loud in class. Most of them are super boring. Mine's going to be good this year—probably about our camping trip."

"Your writing's great. It's inventive." Carolina tossed Rowan the dish towel. "You're thinking about sixth grade already? It's only July."

Row caught the towel with one hand. "I love school more than anything, Mom. And if I want to be a vet, I *have* to like it. Except it's awful to be away from Zephy for hours and hours."

Suddenly, the young dog jerked up, ears alert. Stormy lifted his head, then plopped it down again as Zephyr launched herself through the utility room and out the garage. Rowan heard the flap-flap of the ginormous dog door, big enough for a human to crawl through. Still surprised by how much ground the dog could cover in a few strides, Rowan watched Zephyr tearing across the yard.

"Row, did you check the electric fence this morning?" Mom sounded worried.

Rowan clapped her hand over her mouth. "I forgot!" Not even stopping to shut off the faucet, she raced to the garage. The monitor warning light on the fence box blinked red. Her body went cold.

Zephyr was loose.

Her heart pounded as she hollered for her mother. "It's off! We've gotta find her!"

"Meet me at the van! Bring her leash. The silent whistle, too." Carolina turned off the water and grabbed her purse.

As Carolina drove up and down the nearby country roads, Rowan anxiously scanned the rural landscape. She pensed the dog a picture of home and her kibble dinner—a biscuit neatly placed on top—along with her own longing and worry. They pulled off to the side four times so Rowan could scream Zephyr's name. Her throat hurt and her voice grated from yelling. Guilt and terror ran through her belly in waves. She turned to her mother. "Where is she? It's like she teleported or something." A large lump by the road lay in the distance. She pointed and whimpered, "Mom? What's that?"

Carolina peered over the steering wheel. "It's a deer. Poor thing, but thank God. Try the whistle again."

Rowan blew and blew until her cheeks ached.

"Let's head home and call the neighbors," Carolina said.

Rowan covered her face with her hands. This was her stupid fault. What if Zeph got lost in the next county? All because she'd forgotten to switch on the fence. *My fault. My fault. My fault.* What if they never found her? What if she was gone forever?

Fat tears spilled onto her cheeks.

She felt Mom's hand on her arm. "Honey, she's microchipped. If someone picks her up, they'll likely take her to the pound. Shelters scan dogs now."

Sometimes it seemed like Mom could read her mind just like Zephy did.

They pulled to a stop in the driveway, and before her mother turned off the engine, Rowan dashed for the house. Crying hard, she dropped on her bed, pulled the pillow over her head, and rocked from side to side on the now-damp sheet. *How could Zephyr have run off like that? Was she chasing something and now, lost and all alone? It's all my fault. I was careless.*

A few minutes later, something cold and moist touched her hand. She lifted the pillow and turned, assuming it was Stormy coming to comfort her. Coffee-colored eyes, partially obscured by wiry, gray fur, peered back. Zephyr bumped her hand again, and Rowan's tears turned to gulping laughs. She hugged her dog, then covered Zephyr's ears and hollered, "Mom! She's here! She must have snuck in while we were searching for her." But secretly, she knew the truth—Zephy had gotten her message.

The next morning, Rowan ran down the stairs and through the rumpus room to the sewing studio. Mom was puzzling over a sleeping bag zipper repair. "Zeph and I are headed to the woods. I gotta wear her out," Rowan said.

Carolina smiled. "Great. Make her stretch those powerful legs. Be back by noon so you can help with lunch. I'll ring the gong."

Rowan pulled a face, but nodded and ran upstairs. She whistled for her dog, and they galloped down the path into the front field, dry grasses swishing as they ran. She set the tennis ball and launcher on a knoll where she could find them later. Now, to locate new hiding places.

"Zeph, down," Rowan said in a firm tone. "Stay." She gently pushed her dog's head to the ground between her paws and said "stay" again. Then she walked behind Zephyr and headed into the woodsy area a few hundred yards away, squeezing under a large rhododendron bush. Focusing, she created a mind-picture of the bend in the nearby creek. Then she sent a clear visual image to her dog of where she was hiding, and in her mind called out, "Find me!"

She heard and felt Zephyr's thunderous strides. With no hesitation, the dog scrambled under the bush to Rowan's hiding place and nudged her. Then, tongue lolling, she sat with a sweet doggy smile.

"Smart dog! Good job!" Rowan crowed. She slipped a small biscuit from her pocket to treat her. Three more times she hid, finding new and more challenging locations. Zephyr never once scented the ground. Rowan even crossed the stream. Zephy was definitely getting better at this. Or maybe she was getting better at pensing her dog, she wasn't sure which. Probably both.

Rowan hadn't told her mom exactly how they played together or that she was sure Zeph received her mental snapshots. When she'd first met Zephyr at the pound, she was surprised how the pup stared as though drilling information right into her brain. Mom was way too practical to believe in doggy ESP, so Rowan kept it private.

Enough of this game—it was important to have training variety. Dogs get bored easily. So they ran, Zephyr galloping large circles around the girl. Rowan could barely keep up when Zeph trotted, much less running full out. Gasping, Rowan bent, hands on knees, until her breathing slowed. Then she picked up the launcher and pitched the ball at least twenty times until Zephyr dropped at her feet, panting. Rowan lay perpendicular to the dog, head tilted so she could snuggle against her furry back. The warm sun soothed them both into a short nap until the lunch bell called them home.

As they walked, her fingers entwined in Zephyr's fur, Rowan remembered how, at the Eugene Greenhill Humane Society, and against her mother's advice, she had chosen the wolfhound-deerhound mix that stared straight at her, begging for attention. How could she not? When she walked up to the pup locked in the cage, their connection flared as vivid as orange poppies on a cloudy day. At least, that's what she saw in her mind—she and Zephyr running in their field at home. Summer-green grass. Flowers sprinkled like gems. As Rowan concentrated on the image, the dog's demeanor changed from, "Please choose me. C'mon, c'mon, me, me, me" to a relaxed sweetness. Her mother was impressed with how calm the puppy became that day—she even lay down in the cage.

Mom had mentioned they needed to talk about their camping trip. She patted her dog and encouraged her into a trot. She was hungry. They'd talk over lunch.

Chapter Three

Moss's heart thundered. Gulping breaths seared his lungs. He begged his muscles to ramp up, to drive his legs faster. The terrorist, waiting to detonate, nipped at his heels—so close Moss heard the labored breathing of death. Tears burned his eyes. The explosion, deafening. He screamed as if that could stop the horror, but shrapnel sliced everything in its way.

Pain and shock suffocated him, and his chest heaved as he tried to suck air. *Oh, God, am I dead?* The crashing boom came again, and he jerked up in bed. The rank iron scent of blood swamped him—as it always did—though there was no blood here, not now. Fear-sweat sopped the sheets.

Another sharp bang, but it was only wind smashing the casement against the wall. He dangled a leg over the side, then white-knuckled the mattress. *Fuck.* Even screaming didn't stop the dreams that stalked him. Could he ever break free of the torment? For the rest of his life, he'd need sticks to take a simple piss in the middle of the night. Every step reminded him there was no escape.

He stroked the empty place on the bed, the spot where Sherlock once slept. His heart hurt for his old Blue Tick hound. If only he'd gotten home from leg rehab four days earlier, he would have been with his dog in his final moments.

Only showering gave temporary reprieve. He fumbled for his crutches, latched the window, and headed to the bathroom. Sitting on the pot to pee made him feel less a man. He smacked on the shower. It took steaming water to bring him back here, now—not Afghanistan, not then. He sponged off the fear and prayed that this time the pounding stream would wash away his guilt.

It did not.

A few minutes later, toweled dry, he sat on the bed and pulled on a clean thigh sock and then the prosthesis. He glanced at the clock and grimaced—his usual witching hour, just after 3 a.m. He slipped into sweats, stripped the damp sheets, and remade the bed. Better now than after a couple of drinks.

In the kitchen, he poured a generous serving of wine and downed it. He grabbed the bottle and stuffed it between arm and body so he could carry his laptop, too; if he could get some writing done, the night wouldn't be a complete loss. The wind might clear his head. He limped to the front porch, set down the stuff, and went back for his glass.

Clouds scudded across the night sky. Gusts cooled his face. This place had a unique mix of sage and juniper—the scent of home. He sank into his beckoning recliner. The moon, already past full, slid each night toward another little death.

Cheery thought.

The merlot comforted him and kindled a friendly warmth in his belly. He'd woken up cursing again. During his two years in Afghanistan, that's all he heard. The guys couldn't speak without multiple "fucks" and "shits." Initially, they razzed him hard because he didn't cuss. He eventually gave in. Now, it was hard to break the nasty habit. To him, swearing was a lazy way to express his feelings.

Moss topped off his glass and took a long draw. The recurring dream seemed outlandish—no suicide bomber would chase an individual down; they'd want to inflict large-scale mayhem. Then why did this haunt him? Would he be running for the rest of his life?

In the distance, coyotes yipped. Slashing the mournful night, their melancholy wails sparked Moss's agonized yearning for companionship. Their falsetto always startled him; they were big enough that he expected a lower pitch. A hard lump lodged in his throat. Other than an occasional romp with his Army buddy, Jessie, he just couldn't cope with people.

Not yet.

Come to think, he better call her before settling in with another glass of wine. A few more sips and he wouldn't want to talk—and with his inhibitions lowered, something might spill out that he'd regret later. He liked her—she was hilarious, raw, ruthlessly blunt, unsophisticated—in every way the opposite of Sophie. Maybe that's why he'd hooked up with her so soon after Sophie.... *Don't go there.* Because Jessie had been a nurse in Afghanistan, he didn't have to explain anything about his war experiences—much easier than with women who hadn't served.

He sighed and walked over to his desk calendar. When had he visited Jessie in Ashland last? He thumbed back. The weekend of June 17th. Over five weeks ago. If she was available, he could head over there the first weekend in August. When had they talked last? He paged forward day by day—there. It'd been three weeks.

They never had much to say. She neither read for pleasure nor had similar music tastes, so it was hard to develop conversation. Neither of them liked talking about war experiences. They shared battlefield PTSD, were both amputees, and enjoyed hot sex, although her preference leaned toward faster and meaner.

He dug the phone out of the closet, stretched the cord into the living room, and slumped into his recliner. Punched in her number. "Moss here," he said when she picked up.

"Moss! Shit, it's great to hear from you."

He could hear her intake of breath. What was that? Excitement? Was she getting attached? Too attached? He didn't want that. Couldn't handle it. Not now, not yet.

"Are you coming to visit?" she asked. "It's been so long."

The lift in her voice. That excitement again. It really was there. How can I derail her without breaking off entirely?

"Yeah, okay by you? I've been wildly busy with the garden."

"Ha!" she said, a bit of sarcasm in her voice.

"Seriously though, I was thinking the first weekend in August. Will you be around?"

"Maybe. Should be."

"I'll confirm closer to the time." He glanced at his calendar. "By Monday, August 1st. Does that work?"

A pause. "That's fine."

Now she sounded blasé again. The old Jessie. *That's a relief. I must have read her wrong.* They said their goodbyes and hung up.

He'd picked a load of plump blackberries in the cool of the morning. Dumping some into a bowl, he spooned sour cream and sprinkled brown sugar on top. Back out on the deck, he ate the fresh, tart-sweet bursts of flavor as he enjoyed watching the evening roll in. Just to be sure, he'd clarify things with Jessie when he visited her. No expectation. No commitment.

He brought in the bird feeders. He didn't want to attract bear this close to the house. Dragon-sized mosquitoes would be out any time now. Lighting the citronella lamps, he settled back in his recliner. Wow, he was tired. Now a gimp, it never failed to surprise him how much more energy he burned just to get around. It had been two years since the IED blew off his leg and he still wasn't used to it.

Chapter Four

The sun pulsed overhead as Carolina and Rowan packed the van, loaded the dogs, and settled in for their trip. Carolina looked forward to leaving the soon-to-be-blistering heat, the air-conditioned drive, and the cool relief of the higher altitude at Little Three Creeks Lake where they would set up camp tonight.

Carolina thrilled at the broad smile creasing her daughter's face. Rowan's eyes were bright and engaged. Since the addition of Zephyr, she had perked up. Their gigantic pup turned out to be a drugless solution for Rowan's ongoing grief and depression since her father's death.

The dogs groaned as they settled in the C-shaped beds they loved; Rowan was already listening to a book on her new iPod. Reading in the car made Row nauseous, so when they drove any distance, audio books were the only way to go. Carolina wondered which novel her daughter had chosen for the trip. She seemed content.

A little over an hour later, they approached the cutoff for Highway 242—the scenic route to Sisters. Carolina made the turn, planning to stop at McKenzie Pass to show Rowan the extensive lava flows. She turned off the air conditioning and buzzed down the windows, but only one-quarter of the way, enough that curious dogs could only poke their noses out to sniff the fresh, piney air.

Satisfied her charges were comfortable, Carolina focused on driving. The highway teemed with recreational vehicles. Nothing longer than thirty-five feet was allowed on this road which eliminated semis, much to her relief. But in the summer, Friday afternoons on the highway were crowded with families heading to favorite weekend spots. Fortunately, she had made reservations.

As they crowned the pass, Carolina pulled over for a bathroom break. Rowan jumped down from the van and stared open-mouthed at the lava boulders stretching as far as she could see.

"Mom," she whispered. "It looks like the moon! Imagine the power that made all this!"

They took the dogs out on leashes. After searching for non-existent grass, Stormy and Zephyr made do and peed on the pavement.

Next, they walked up the path to the small, stone building to read about the lava flows that had created the place. Inside, slits had been cut in the granite wall so sightseers could view each of five mountain peaks. Carolina grunted as she lifted Rowan to see out the highest one. Her daughter was growing so fast, soon she wouldn't be able to heft her anymore.

Mother, daughter, and dogs walked back and loaded into the van. Carolina started the engine, and they headed down the other side of the pass. Mountain driving was stressful. She squeezed her shoulder blades together to relieve the tension. Hopefully, they'd reach the campground in a little over an hour. The road flattened out and bent around a corner. Turning her head from side to side, Carolina tried to ease the stiffness. She should never have canceled that chiropractor appointment.

In a flash, a huge shape lunged at the edge of her vision.

Rowan yelped, "Mom!"

Carolina gasped as the windshield pulverized. She jammed on the brakes. Something hard skewered through and slashed her forehead. Blood gushed into her eyes. Unable to see anything except blood and a broken, flailing form, she jerked her head back, trying to avoid what had struck her.

Oh my God—a deer!

Just then, a car plowed into them from behind, catapulting Carolina against her seatbelt. The dogs slammed against the front seats. Carolina fought the steering wheel; Rowan panicked and grabbed her mother's leg. They sheared right and pitched off the road. Dogs, bowls, equipment upended. Rowan screamed; Zephyr keened in terror. The van flipped on its side—gravel grating metal—kept rolling, and came to rest upside down. Glass rained. Dust billowed.

Both airbags hung limp. Carolina's heart pounded double-time. Holding her badly wrenched neck, she turned toward her daughter. Rowan seemed asleep, her head pillowed against the side of the van.

Not my baby. Please, not my baby! "Rowan!" Carolina shrieked, switching off the car. Hands shaking, she tried to unclasp her seatbelt, but the latch wouldn't budge. She stretched to reach Rowan's belt, but it stuck too. She heard shouts and craned her neck to look. Hanging upside down made it impossible. But she could see out the side—one more inch and the steel edge of the mile-marker sign would have shattered Rowan's window. She shuddered and turned back to her daughter. Her stomach roiled. She grabbed Rowan's shoulder and shook her. *No! Her neck. I must protect her neck.* Instead, she rested her hand on her daughter's heart. *Beating! Thank you, God. It's beating!*

Brakes squealed. The sound of rending metal pierced the air. People screamed.

"Call 911! Jesus, we've got a mess out here," a man hollered as he yanked open the van door and reached in with a beefy arm. "I'm a retired Army nurse. I'll help you out."

She gripped the man's forearm. "My girl!"

"It's okay, ma'am; we'll get to her."

Another squeal and then a thud.

He turned back. "Aw, Jeez. Some poor dog just got creamed on the road. Here, I can cut your belt, but you need to stretch your hands out to catch your weight. Don't want you to injure your neck."

"Dog? Oh no!" Carolina latched onto the man's shoulder. "Not me! My daughter! Rowan!"

"Other door's jammed. Got to get you out to reach her, take her vitals," he said firmly. "Think you can support your weight on your hands?"

She nodded and put her arms above her head, resting her palms against the roof, which was now the floor.

He cut through the belt and she eased herself down.

"Here, let me protect your hands. There's a lot of glass." He steadied her, helped her crawl out, then wrestled his bulky body through the door and over to Rowan.

Carolina trembled so hard she could barely stand. Parallel to the road, the van lay like a huge, dead beetle, its wheels little squat legs. Nearby, a pickup and its long travel trailer lay jackknifed. Three other cars were crumpled in the roadway, smoke pouring from one.

The doe lay grotesquely strewn, glassy eyes wide, staring as though surprised. It's fractured, twisted leg still stuck through the windshield. Carolina tried to peer around the medic to see Rowan, without success. Holding onto the side of the van, she staggered toward the back. She had to get to her daughter.

The back hatch had sprung and lay flat against the ground. *Oh God, no dogs! I can't think about this right now.* Carolina crawled into the upside-down van until she touched Rowan's shoulder. She carefully smoothed her daughter's forehead. No response. Fear pulsed through her. "Is she dead?" Her words pushed from her hollow chest.

"Ma'am, it's okay." The man's voice, calm and reassuring, continued. "Your girl's alive. Unconscious, though. I can't move her. We need them Jaws of Life to get her out. Don't see bleeding, not on her. Only you—that's a nasty gash." He pulled a bandana from his pocket. "Here. Put pressure on it."

Instinctively, Carolina reached up to touch her temple, which was sticky with blood. "The deer's hoof grazed me. I'll be fine." But she took the handkerchief. Trying to push through disorienting dizziness, she dropped her head until the fuzz receded. *Why isn't Rowan waking up?* Carolina suppressed the urge to shake her again and rested her lips against her daughter's ear instead. She felt warmth and prayed Rowan would be okay. "Mom's here," she croaked.

A woman knelt, reached through the shattered window, and patted Carolina. "Help's coming real soon. Your girl's knocked out cold, but she'll be okay. Here's some ice for your forehead."

"Thanks." Carolina registered spiky pain as she pressed the cubes to her temple. Taking in her surroundings, she squinted at a bloody heap on the other side of the road and recognized the color of his coat. Stormy. Gone. Her throat thickened with grief for her companion of fourteen years. "Our old dog," she whispered.

"Saw it happen. He didn't know what hit him." the woman said. "Shepherd, maybe? The other, big gray mop? Looks okay. It's lying near the dead one."

With a rush of hope for Rowan, Carolina struggled to see. Rowan absolutely could not lose Zephyr. She'd lost so much already.

"Shall I grab him?" The woman rose. "He won't bite, will he?"

"Let her be!" Carolina wailed. "She'll run if you go after her."

A siren split the air.

Thank God, help for Rowan.

She felt, more than saw, Zephyr turn like a shadow and slip toward the trees. Carolina hollered her name, but it came out a barky shriek. The dog swiveled—ears pricked—and moved forward a step. For a moment, Carolina thought Zephyr would come to her, but as the squeal of the siren grew closer, the dog wheeled and fled for cover. Tears streamed down Carolina's face as she hauled herself up to meet the ambulance.

The next half hour passed in a blur. The firemen stabilized Rowan's neck and set up an IV. The Jaws of Life stripped away the door and the mile marker to free her. After strapping Rowan to a board, the paramedics loaded her into the ambulance. Next, they made a cursory examination of Carolina's head wound.

"You'll live, but you need sutures," the pockmarked medic said, dabbing antiseptic on the laceration.

She winced. "Rowan—?"

"We'll ride you in with your daughter. She's stable for now." He supported Carolina's elbow as she climbed into the ambulance. She rested her hand on Rowan's arm.

The man who helped her earlier plodded over, belly hanging over his belt. "Hey, lady," he said, hitching his pants up for emphasis. "Gotta wait for a tow. You want I should search for your dog? Bring it on to the hospital if I find it?"

"Heavens, I forgot. Please, yes. Her name's Zephyr," Carolina said. "There's a bag of biscuits in the van. It's a mess. Everything is upside down in there."

"It's okay, ma'am. I don't mind."

"She's jumpy, so move real slow," Carolina muttered. "Thanks," she said, a heartfelt afterthought as the man lumbered away. She held little hope—the guy moved like a truck himself; he would frighten Zephyr for sure.

Zephyr huddles, quivering in the bushes. Scanning for danger, she listens carefully, scents the air. Her body aches. She hears the heavy-pawed man call "Zephyr" again and again. Her heart pounds fast. She's tempted—he knows her name—but fear glues her body to the ground. He climbs into a truck and leaves. She tries to send pictures to her girl, but gets no response.

She waits until the sun shines flat in her eyes. Safe to come out now. The pavement isn't so hot on her pads. She limps slowly back to Stormy, now a hump by the road. Her leader is gone; he smells wrong, and when she bumps him, no growl or moan. Lying down by the silent form, Zephyr sticks her nose next to his. Everything is strange. *Where are my people? Dinner? Water bowl?* She remembers the word Rowan says: "Wait." Something good happens after. Rowan says, "Walkies." "Dinner."

Hopeful her pack will return, she settles herself more deeply into the gravel until a roaring monster barrels by, and once again, tail tight between her legs, she slinks into the nearby trees. Frightened, lonely, she sits and watches the road. Now and again, she tries to send images to her girl. Whimpers. Waits.

Chapter Five

With a weighted heart, Carolina peered down at her still-unconscious daughter. They'd been airlifted from Bend to Portland's Doernbecher Children's Hospital for state-of-the-art head trauma care. "Oh, please," she whispered. "My sweet girl, please wake up. I can't handle losing you."

After tests and an MRI, the nurses settled Rowan in the pediatric intensive care unit. They plugged her into so many machines; Carolina took them in now: heart monitor, oxygen level, pulse, intravenous drip. Nothing looked wrong on Rowan's outside—no blood, no visible wounds—even her color seemed relatively normal. She was limp, though, and looked small and vulnerable in the hospital bed. Carolina's thoughts repeatedly dragged back to the accident. She should have been able to prevent this. Somehow. Had she gotten distracted? Dizzy and aching, she wrapped her arms around herself.

After making sure Rowan was taken care of, she filled out endless paperwork. Her own wound was stitched. Now, her head pounded. She hated to leave her daughter for even a minute to make a phone call, but her brother Sam lived in Portland, and she needed his support. It was crazy—he and Stephanie were barely two hours from Eugene, but they hadn't seen each other in months, although Rowan and her uncle chatted on the phone regularly. She glanced at her watch. He should be home from work. She stepped into the hallway and dialed. It rang and rang, then went to voicemail. A few minutes later she tried again. He picked up.

"Sam, it's Carolina. We're in Portland, at Doernbecher."

"Doernbecher? What's wrong?" Concern made his voice ragged.

"Car accident. I'm okay, but Rowan's not. She's in a coma, and I'm a wreck." She sniffled, trying to stem her tears. "I can't stop shaking."

"Rowan? Oh, my God." Silence. "Are *you* hurt?"

"Only a deep gash on my head. The van's totaled. I've gotta figure out some things, and I'm not thinking clearly. Shock, I guess. Can you come?"

"On my way. The drive'll take twenty minutes. And then, parking. Sorry, thinking out loud here. Can I bring anything? Do you want me to call Mom?"

"Yes, call her, but tell her *not* to come. I can't bear her hocus-pocus right now. She'd get here and cast an astrology chart for the time of the accident. Or use those damn cards. She can't afford the flight anyway." Carolina squinted at the sign. "I'm in the Pediatric Intensive Care Unit. If you ask, they call it the PIC-U. Steph and I are about the same size— could you bring a change of clothes and a toothbrush? I'm bloody from the head laceration, and my gear's in the van."

"Good Lord! You bet. Steph's waving at me—sends her love and prayers. Forty minutes or so, then."

Carolina saw Sam's stocky form striding down the hall towing a little suitcase. She hurried toward him, welcoming his strong, male hug, the familiar hint of aftershave.

He pushed his glasses up his nose. "Sis," he said, his voice cracking. "Jesus, look at you." He reached to touch her face but pulled his hand back. "All beat up. This is awful. Is Row awake yet? What happened?"

Carolina had avoided the mirror. When the doctor stitched her forehead, she stopped counting at eighteen sutures. "We were in a multi-vehicle pileup on the way to Sisters for our vacation—we creamed a deer and started a chain-reaction accident."

She smoothed him on the cheek. "I'm awfully glad you came. Let's go see Rowan and talk to her a bit. They say including her in conversation will help her wake up." Rowan adored her uncle. They'd been much closer since Rafe died; Sam had stepped in as a temporary father figure.

"Here," he said, indicating the suitcase. "Steph packed some other stuff too. You know her. It probably includes makeup and perfume—you can ignore those. At least there's a fresh change of clothes. I told her no dresses. She packed a couple of things for Row, too."

"Thanks!" Stephanie had never absorbed that Carolina was a wash-and-wear woman—always in jeans with no makeup. Still, the little overnighter felt like manna.

Carolina signaled for Sam to follow. "I'll spend the night on a pullout bed; you're allowed to visit until 8 p.m." She rolled the suitcase into the PIC-U wing and slid it under her daybed near Rowan. "How'd Mom handle my request for her to stay in Chicago?"

"She was okay, but you nailed it. First thing, she wanted to know the time and place of the accident."

"Sheesh. I don't like her influence on my daughter. Rowan already talks about ESP and I don't want Mom encouraging her."

Sam stood, focused on Rowan. "She looks fine. But check this out—there's a bruise developing." He pointed to her temple. "Here, see? What do the docs say?" He leaned over his niece and stroked her curls. "Hey, buddy, Unc's here. I want to see those bright eyes of yours."

Carolina teared up for the umpteenth time since the accident. "They don't have answers; head injuries are tough. This could be from the air-bag, or whacking against the door—we'll never know. It's just a waiting game."

"Easy for them to say. Waiting's the worst." He tucked the covers around Rowan. "I brought the *Blue Book,* so we can look up the value of your van. It'll give an idea what you'll get from insurance."

"I forgot! I have to call them. You think they'll pay? I hit the deer."

"Like you could have avoided it, right? Wrong. This was a straight-forward accident. They'll pay. You're going to need help on your next van. Stef and I talked before I came and agreed we want to give you the cash. You've got enough going on."

Carolina teared up. "I'm so grateful. Thanks. I'll try and pay you back when I get out from under." Woozy, she lurched and grabbed Sam's arm. "Will you sit with her? I need to lie down. Right now."

"I'll talk to her and watch over you both," he said. "But I'll have to wake you after a bit. You got smacked on the head, too."

∞

Thirst drives Zephyr to leave Stormy's now-cold body and the road where she last saw her pack. She limps off the pavement and travels a few hundred feet, darting glances here and there before raising her nose and sniffing the air. There's water, she can smell it; she licks her mustache. Powerful craving draws her to move. But first, she gives one long look back at Stormy. Zephyr then sends her fear and misery to Rowan, but like the last few times, she feels no return bump. Where *is* her girl?

She hears some other creature's yipping caterwaul. Not her kind. She sits down, points her nose upward, and calls her distress. The cry pours out of her throat, rockets across the hills.

Her forlorn echo returns. She howls again and again. Listens. No response. Again.

After a while, dejected, she climbs wearily uphill. She feels torn leaving familiar smells, but her need for water pushes her, afraid and lonely, into the unknown.

Two days later, Zephyr stretches and yawns in a patch of sun. For a moment, she is disoriented. Where is her pack? She lies down again and crosses her paws in front of her. She grieves for Rowan, the one who touches her and gives her food. She remembers her girl's scent—like a puppy, fresh—and lifts her nose to find it. No humans here. She focuses on memories of her girl. Flashes of being thrown around, horrible screeches and thuds flood her. Her body still aches, and she hasn't been able to sense Rowan since the tumbling.

Thirsty, she returns to the spring where she laps carefully, stopping every few seconds to listen for danger and scan for possible prey. The air is laden with smells. The little ground thing she snags, rips apart, and devours, no longer fills her. Her belly rumbles and groans. Drooling at the memory of the warm, raw taste, she bends her head to the water and slakes her thirst. Then, taking a different path, she limps along the ridge.

She startles a small animal which bounds ahead. Taking off in hopeful pursuit, she lengthens her strides to catch up. She snaps at its long ears, but the quarry darts to the side, then under her, and off in another direction. In her effort to turn fast, she stumbles—rolls over—and loses sight of the prey. Panting, she shakes off dust and pine needles. Her body complains.

She limps back toward a fire pit in the woods. It smells of human food. There's a garbage can nearby. Zephyr knocks it over, dives into the brush as the crashing sound tears the silence. The gnawing in her belly emboldens her, and she creeps forward to nose around. Nothing more than a crust. She wolfs it down and slides into the cover of bushes.

In mid-afternoon, Zephyr heads back to the road where she last saw her pack. Cars and trucks whiz by. Today, like before, she lies hidden, watching, listening, and reading the scents. Here, it's easiest to remember Rowan—her smell, her voice, the soft touch of the girl's hands brushing tangles from her fur. Zephyr flattens her head down between her paws and whines. Images of days before the crunching metal, before the death of her pack mate, Stormy, flash through her: racing in the field with Rowan, dozing with her on the couch, the mother making rich, meaty scents in the food room. Zephyr salivates.

The first drop in temperature is her signal to move. She trots on a deer path heading closer to water and toward the sun-warmed rock with her sleeping nest at its edge. The sound of crashing in the underbrush draws her attention, and she pauses, alert. Something is racing her way. It moves like the meal she missed, this way and that, as though it's being chased. She skirts off the path and crouches. When it's even with her, she leaps ahead and pounces, nails it to the ground. She rakes her teeth through its throat, marveling at the rich taste of blood.

The creature in pursuit abruptly pulls up, snarls, frustrated its meal has been lost. Startled, Zephyr stands tall and backs up, the carcass dangling from her jaws. The fox lunges, tears away Zephyr's prize, and leaves her with only a mouthful. She rumbles deep in her throat as the thief melts into the brush with its stolen meal. Sinking to the ground, Zephyr devours the small piece left, gulping flesh, just enough to make her belly clamor for more. She lies there, puzzled by what just happened. No one has ever snatched food from her before.

Making her way back to her nest, she keeps close watch for other prey. Her stomach feels tight. She licks and savors the creature's blood still on her paws.

Chapter Six

It had been four tedious, endless days since Carolina's van collided with the doe, and Rowan still hadn't regained consciousness. Sam visited each evening after work. Steph came twice, too. Every day, the doctor's countenance seemed grimmer. Carolina continuously touched her daughter as if physical connection might awaken her. She did everything she could—chattering, singing, reading out loud, praying—to invite Rowan back.

When she spoke, though, Carolina was careful not to mention Zephyr. How could she? Zephyr was Rowan's lifeline, and now the pup—already skittish, thrown around, and pitched from the van—was out there in the wild, alone. For sure, knowing Zephyr's character, she must be terrified and cowering. The dog was likely injured, preyed upon, or—Carolina squeezed her eyes shut—dead. She'd read accounts of dogs getting lost after an accident like this and never being found. She should have searched. But she had to stay with Rowan. *Impossible choices.* The pup had pulled Rowan from depression after her dad died. What would happen to her daughter without Zeph?

And now? Carolina had no idea what they were in for. She willed her mind back from future-tripping. Those were bad, bad projections, always picturing the worst possible nightmare scenarios. Anyway, sometimes events turned out worse, sometimes better—but never the way she imagined. So why pay attention to her future-tripping thoughts at all?

Out the window of Rowan's room, sunlight filtering through maples in a courtyard area below caught her eye. She felt desperate for a breath of real air, fresh, un-recycled, with no medicinal taint—and craved a few minutes for herself. A repeating thought plunged her downward: Rowan's injury was her fault; surely she could have swerved and avoided the poor doe. She deserved nothing.

Still, she had to get away. Whispering to Rowan, "I'll be back in a few minutes, sweetie," she dropped a note at the nurses' station so they would know where she was and fled for the elevator. After impatiently waiting the eight floors down, she slammed out the front door toward a vivid patch of grass. Sun blazed. Carolina lay spread-eagled and let the rays savage her—no sunblock, and she didn't give a damn. Rolling over, she buried her face in the lawn. As she drank in the healing scent of moist earth, the pent-up tears came, and she allowed herself to weep.

Next thing she knew, someone was shaking her shoulder.

"Ms. Graham? Wake up! Come quick! Your daughter's calling for you."

"Rowan?" Wincing at her aching forehead as she rubbed her eyes, she tried to stand but stumbled.

The nurse's aide caught her elbow. "Careful. You're not fully awake yet, and you have a head injury, too."

"She's out of the coma? Really?" *Oh, my God. Prayers get answered.*

As they rode the elevator, the aide was trying to explain something, but Carolina couldn't focus. *I should have been with her when she woke up. I should have paid attention on the road. I should have looked for Zephyr myself. I should have—*

Carolina heard Rowan's wail as soon as she stepped off the elevator.

"Mommmm! Mommo!"

The desperation in her daughter's voice, the toddler nickname she hadn't heard in years, steamrolled her heart into overdrive. She flew down the hall, almost colliding with the efficient gray-haired nurse. Swinging around the corner, she rushed into the room, which was alive with humming and beeping.

"I'm here, sweetie, right here," she said, gasping for breath. The room swayed up and down like a teeter-totter. She shouldn't have run, but how could she not? She grabbed Rowan's hand and lowered herself into a chair by the bed.

Her tear-streaked daughter faced her. "Mommo, turn the lights on! I can't see!"

As she made appropriate murmurings to soothe Rowan, Carolina wheeled toward the nurse hovering by the door, demanding an answer to the question she could not bear to voice. Her body felt like it weighed five hundred pounds. As if she'd been dropped from a plane, a sick, empty feeling engulfed her. Rowan, facing a dark world void of images and color? This was too much loss.

"I've paged the on-call neurologist," the nurse murmured, her mouth turned down with concern. "We didn't foresee this."

Carolina stroked Rowan's brow. Despite her quivering insides, she spoke in her most reassuring, motherly voice. "Apparently, your eyes aren't working yet. We'll figure this out, sweetheart." She put her face closer to her daughter's and looked at her intently.

Rowan hiccupped from crying. She tried to wrap her arms around her now-bent legs. The intravenous line prevented her from completing the maneuver. "Why can't I see? And I have a horrible headache."

"A deer smashed our windshield, and you hit your head. You're in the hospital. You've been asleep for a few days since the accident."

"Hospital? Asleep?" Diverted for the moment, Rowan rubbed her tear-stained cheeks and frowned. "Accident?" She grabbed her mother's arm in a vise grip. "Mommo, I can't see *anything*. It's all dark." Each word came out snipped off.

With effort, Carolina smiled at her daughter. "I can see you; I'm looking at your beautiful face." She took Rowan's hands and placed them against her own skin. "Here I am."

Rowan's fingers rested for a moment, then felt around Carolina's cheeks and nose with the lightest touch. When her daughter's fingertips passed over her mouth, she put her hand on top and kissed them. Then, maneuvering between intravenous line and monitor wires, she drew Rowan into her arms and held her lanky, too-big-for-her-lap girl. She rubbed her back and made soothing, untranslatable mommy sounds.

Carolina's mind swung between relief and consternation. Rowan was awake and talking in sentences. Her arms and legs worked. Thank

God! Her eyes appeared uninjured. Was she actually blind? Could this be permanent?

The neurologist *had* to know, right? But instinctively, Carolina suspected he wouldn't have an answer. Not today. They had entered a new and more treacherous patch. She held Rowan tightly, as much to comfort herself as her daughter. This was a loss she could not have imagined.

Rowan heard her mom stand up.

"Sweetheart, my voice has gone hoarse reading out loud, and I'm exhausted. I'm going out to the waiting room to be quiet for a while."

Rowan felt the covers tucked snug around her. "I'm tired, anyway."

"I bet you are. Sleep tight. Here's the buzzer." Her mom put it in her hand.

Rowan wanted to ask what had happened to Zeph and Stormy. Mommo had been avoiding the subject of their dogs altogether. Wouldn't she have said something if they were okay? Or dead? Rowan squeezed back tears. *Why wouldn't Mommo say anything?* Not having the nerve to ask yet, not willing to hear the words spoken, words that could not be taken back—Rowan tightened her fists as if that alone could somehow keep these horrible thoughts from assaulting her. But they stampeded anyway. *Was Zephy hurt? Stormy? Oh God, were they dead?*

She tried pensing her dog, but couldn't form images. She cupped her hands over her ears and pressed hard to stop the throbbing that felt like a nail being hammered into her brain. Sharp stabs of pain sliced through her head at unexpected times. *I probably couldn't see even if my eyes weren't hurt. Now I know what "blinding pain" is.* She rolled on her side and dragged the covers over her ears.

Zephyr trots along. Her nose lifts at the tang of blood. Is there food nearby? She tests the air, circles back, walks forward again. There! She scans the area but sees nothing. Sniffing, she follows the smell through a small stand of trees and into a clump of bushes. The rich bouquet strengthens. Salivating, she slows her steps. The ground is disturbed, and leaves and debris cover a large lump.

There's another odor here, too, a rank scent reminding her of something she recognizes, but can't quite place. She casts a cautious eye around before nosing through the detritus. A deer is torn open under the ribs. She rips hungrily at the flesh and bolts it down. Just as she severs another chunk, she hears a deep snarl. Dropping the bite and twisting toward the sound, she faces an enraged cat almost as big as she is. Its mouth is open, and the size of its sharp fangs—Zephyr's heart booms in her chest.

Never taking her eyes from the creature, Zephyr growls and bares her teeth. Her hackles rise. Tentative, she backs away, then whirls, hoping to escape. But the cougar lunges, catches a claw in her neck, and gashes the length of her shoulder. Squalling, the dog spins, finds her balance and leaps, each stride lengthening until she runs flat out.

When she is well out of sight, panting, she flops to the ground and listens. Nothing follows her. Blood flows down her leg. She makes quick tongue swipes to clean her injury, but urgency and fear force her up and farther away. She limps toward the shallow hole she scoured near the water. First, she drinks her fill, then slumps in her nest, dejected. Why hasn't her pack come back for her? She penses an image of the immense cat, unsure whether Rowan receives it or not. She wants her girl to come. *Now.* She needs her. Her torn shoulder aches fiercely, and she delicately licks what she can reach.

Zephyr bolts awake. She tries to stand but sinks back down. Her shoulder is hot and stiff. The wounds throb. She feels for Rowan now. Wait. There's something ... there she is! Her girl. But she sees pictures of dark clouds. Rowan is distraught. Where is she? Zephyr sends an image of her hiding place and tries to get her attention, but her girl doesn't answer.

Chapter Seven

T hree days later, Moss limped across the crown of Bender's Ridge. The afternoon heat, already sweltering, rose a notch. He dripped sweat. His leg ached. Even the bushes drooped, and sage perfumed the air. He squinted at the sun—close to 4 p.m. Up two hours in the middle of the night, torn from sleep by bloody dreams, now he was plumb beat. He rubbed his scalp with his fingertips: gritty—in need of a second shower. This morning, while shaving, he'd noticed gray hairs—going gray at thirty-eight? Pa's hadn't turned until fifty. Damn stress of war.

He crouched as best he could, sticking his leg out in front of him on the dry hillside dotted with aspen, manzanita, serviceberry, and sage. Though superior to the old one, his new prosthesis still made certain leg motions awkward, if not impossible. He couldn't move as quietly as the tracker he'd trained to be as a kid—not anymore. No matter how much he worked to smooth his gait, a permanent limp remained. He rubbed his stiff thigh and squinted toward a stand of aspen, leaves rattling tick-tick-tick in the barest breeze. A darting movement below caught his eye and, heart hammering, he pushed up, grabbing a sapling for support. Maybe the eight-point stag he'd glimpsed last month had come back.

Raising his binoculars, sounds, smells, textures fell away, and he focused on what he could see through the small apertures. No rack, not a stag. A doe? He re-focused. Shaggy? My God, this was no deer. It must be the dog he'd been looking for. It was surprisingly tall—like a colt—and mostly gray, rough-coated. Its ribs showed. The dog skittered nervously, eyes darted to the hill; Moss guessed it heard him shift position. It was injured, guarding a front leg. With these new binocs, he could make out oozing around caked blood on its shoulder. He squinted and refocused. The leg looked infected.

So he'd been right. Here was his howler that had amplified his devastating nightmares. The newspaper article about the multi-vehicle pileup on this side of the pass was more than a week old. The rumor he'd heard—there might have been a second dog ejected from the van—wasn't a rumor after all. The critter likely had little idea how to hunt and, from the look of it, was slowly starving. For a moment, he thought about heading back for his bow and finishing the dog off, ending its obvious suffering, and his.

No. He had to keep the promise he'd made with his buddy, Frank. Only kill for food. Period.

When he looked up, the dog had melded with the shadows and was gone. With a mixture of frustration and relief, he turned and limped toward home. Where was the stag he'd seen a few months ago? The freezer had been empty of deer meat for a while. He'd been eating only bunnies, the occasional 'coon, and relying heavily on his veggie garden. Thinking about roasted venison, Moss salivated. His favorite. He couldn't take one now—it wasn't deer hunting season—but he could dream.

As he hitched his way down the ridge, he mused about his connection with this property. He missed feeling like an integral, living part of this high desert land—as precious to him as his own beating heart. He spent his childhood summers here in central Oregon, hiked most of the ranch's 1,700 acres. Now, climbing around for a couple of hours with a breather in the middle was the most he could handle. Some days that chafed. Today, it weighed him down, a heavy grief.

That night, soon after dark, the howling litany began afresh. It was a repeated calling that crawled inside Moss's bones. It had taken twenty-four months to rediscover a thread of sanity in his sweet, private valley—now, that was shattered. The dog's misery rekindled his own. *He* was shattered. Worsening nightmares, too. He was torn from sleep, overcome with gripping anxiety that haunted him most nights.

The next afternoon, Moss drove the half-hour trip to Sisters, population 1,174 souls. Advantages and disadvantages of a small town: it had no city vibe; the inhabitants were friendly and relaxed—which he liked—but people thought they knew you, a huge downside. Well, some *had* known him since he was a baby.

He parked his Toyota 4Runner near the Deschutes Library. After dropping off a stack of books and waving at Gladys, the librarian, he drove the few blocks to the market. As he scooped bulk almonds into a bag, he overheard two gossiping women.

The heavier of the two finger-punched a newspaper she pulled from the bottom of her cart. "Did you see this? That horrible accident out 242 a week ago? Here's a follow-up article."

"The one set off by a van hitting a deer? 'Mayhem,' my neighbor said. A dead dog too." This from a skinny older woman.

"My Robert said there's a rumor another dog ran off. Some man helped out, then went looking for it, but no luck. Poor creature. Poor family. It won't last long out there. Probably dead already."

His suspicion confirmed, Moss said nothing. He didn't want to draw attention to himself or rouse interest in the dog.

After he finished food shopping, he headed to Sisters Feed & Supply and sorted through the bags of kibble and boxes of large biscuits, picked the healthiest, and grabbed one of each. At the last moment, he tossed a sturdy leash and adjustable web collar onto the counter. Then, remembering what he'd come for, he walked back down the aisle, grunted as he hoisted a bag of chicken feed onto his shoulder, and set it alongside the other items.

Bob, the octogenarian who'd run the place forever, looked over his purchases. "You getting a dog? About time. It'd be smart to have a companion out there at the end of the road. A dog'll keep the vermin away, and they're real good company."

"I'm thinking about it." Word of his purchases would get around this small, gossiping town.

"Well, you're buying food and gear; you must be thinking pretty hard."

Moss just grinned at him.

As an afterthought, he stopped at Paulina Springs Books and purchased a thick, hardbound volume on dog breeds with luscious color photographs. As he turned to leave the store, he noticed a stack of brand new *Sibley Guide to Birds*, grabbed one to replace his five-year-old falling-apart copy, and went back to the register.

By the time Moss returned home, it was close to dinnertime. He hadn't eaten since breakfast, and his stomach growled in protest. He methodically stashed his purchases, washed lettuce, and put last night's rabbit stew on the stove. While it heated, he hitched out to the garden to pick a scallion, red bell pepper, and tomato to add to the mix of greens. He missed the pea pods he'd eaten every day for a couple of weeks, but they were finished, wasted by the hot weather. Then, as the sun dropped behind the hills, he lazed in his patio chair on the deck with dinner and a glass of wine.

He didn't understand what was driving him. Hadn't he achieved some measure of peace? Yes, the dog's nighttime ceremonial aggravated his nightmares; yes, the animal's loneliness bothered him for reasons he didn't care to examine. Not yet. He felt uneasy, jumpy, uncomfortable inside his skin, and he needed—at a gut level—to find this creature. He realized he was both drawn and repelled. His ache for the secretive dog haunted him during the day and spoiled his sleep. His whole routine had shifted. He wasn't able to focus on writing other than his journal, which upset him. *Clearly, I'm obsessed.*

He stretched, picked up his binoculars, and scanned the far hillside. He'd found scat he figured belonged to the dog—it was too big for raccoon and wasn't cougar or coyote. With a stick, he'd picked it apart to see what it was eating. Not much. Wild fruit pits, stubs of greens, and weird garbage. Two days before, he'd discovered tufts of rabbit fur a few hills over; something about the lay of the kill made him connect it with the dog. Enterprising critter—probably a pet. It seemed like it had taught itself to hunt. So, they'd been competing. He'd stop eating cottontails, leave them for the poor thing, especially since he now knew it was injured. He wondered what the dog had tangled with. Most likely a big raccoon. They could be fierce when cornered.

40

As he ate, he thumbed through the dog book to see if he could find a breed similar to his quarry. He'd only gotten one brief view through his binocs on the far side of Bender's Ridge. He passed by the toy breed section and tried working dogs. Nothing there, not even close. The rough coat—a terrier, maybe? That group yielded zilch. Frowning, he started at the front and perused every page. His heart knocked when he got to Irish wolfhounds. He squinted at the picture. Similar, but the head seemed too broad. He'd been right about the size, though. Enormous. He marked the page and kept going. Near the end, he found Scottish deerhounds. Another possibility. Flipping back and forth between the two, he couldn't decide. The descriptions were similar, both from a group called sighthounds. Never heard of them. He ran his finger down the page. They hunted more with their eyes than their noses, and they could run like the wind. *Interesting.* He took the dog book to bed with him and continued to read.

Later, a sudden and unseasonable rain pounded the roof, waking Moss. "Shit," he muttered. "My new *Sibley's.*" It was on the outside table. Thinking of the effort it would take to leg up, he rolled over, imagining the now-soaked guide. "Too late. Spoiled," he muttered. Crazy weather, he thought, and snuggled deeper in bed, hoping sleep would reclaim him.

A howl split the night air. He pulled the pillow over his head, but the dog's aching loneliness snuck inside him again, ate its way down, and lodged near his heart—no more sleep for a while. He rolled to a sitting position and slipped on the fleece jacket he kept by the bed. The dog's petition continued, but closer to his house than ever before. He crutched to the front door, opened it, and tried to locate where the dog might be lurking. It sounded like the critter was on the near side of Bender's Ridge. Had it come down into his valley?

He'd hike around tomorrow and plant the goodies he'd purchased, figure out some sort of caching system. *Might as well bring in the bird book.* Rain had chilled the night. He hitched outside anyway, stuffed the ruined, dripping thing between arm and crutch, and went back in.

Moss set the book down and shook off his jacket before hanging it in the entryway. Drops flew everywhere. He made his way to the wood-burning stove, first turning on the lamp near the rocker. He couldn't balance and stoke the fireplace at the same time, so groaning, he leaned his crutches against the wall and sat on the floor. Opening the squeaky iron door, he stirred the embers and added two more logs. He rubbed his hands together near the warmth and waited until the logs caught. When the flames roared, he damped down the fire and hauled himself up and over to his desk. Pouring another glass of merlot, he woke up his laptop and opened his journal. Again. This was becoming a 3 a.m. routine.

"The caterwauling drives me wild," he typed. "Each howl inflames memories I've worked so hard to bury—the forlorn sound rips open old, crusted wounds." He paused, took a long pull from his glass. He waited until the rich warmth spread through his cells, then picked up the thread. "Probably because I'm supposed to feel, not suppress. That's what the doc says, anyway." He took another sip of wine. "Damn. The shrinks have done what they can. I'm on my own now. They were right. Burying feelings doesn't work for shit. The hurt just hangs out down there, undigested, waiting to snag me again.

"Somehow, the critter mirrors my loneliness, my fear of the unknown." He drummed his fingers on the wooden arm. "I've gotta try goddamn excavation, instead. A pox on whoever said 'the only way out is through.' A pox on them for telling the truth." He preferred to pace while he stewed and brewed, but that meant legging up. Stomping around with crutches didn't satisfy—too much damn work.

He leaned back. Story lines used to rise up and flow out of him; he missed the ease. He hadn't written a word of fiction since Afghanistan, which frustrated Sarah, who like any reliable agent, noted deadlines and bugged him regularly.

He reached across his desk to a small group of books and ran his finger along the spines: *American Heritage Dictionary*; *On Writing* by Stephen King; the two novels he'd written; *The Elements of Style* by Strunk and White; *Pilgrim at Tinker Creek* by Annie Dillard; and *The Synonym Finder,* his favorite thesaurus by Rodale. Old friends. The dictionary and thesaurus supported the books between. He grabbed his novels, slapped them in front of him, and slid them apart so he could see both covers. Critics had labeled them "fast-moving literary fiction." *Canceled* was his first, but *Drive-by* earned three months on *The New York Times* bestseller list. He liked *Canceled* better—just goes to show there's no telling what strikes readers and what doesn't. Maybe it was his favorite because it came first, and he'd discovered the profound satisfaction of completing a manuscript. Sales on *Canceled* rocketed after the second novel got so much attention.

He shoved the books away. Now, his writing seemed meaningless, just tripe. The characters didn't dig deep enough, or at least it didn't feel like the penetration he'd aimed for could be found on the page. He and his characters had become intimate friends—but he'd somehow failed them in the end. That realization had flooded him the day after Andrea died. Grief for his cousin wedged through his heart. Trying to relieve the hard lump, he knuckled his chest. Almost four years and her loss could still take him down. War had burned through his fury at her death, but it turned out rage solved nothing—a lesson he was forced to assimilate.

He picked up the wine bottle again. *Is this my third glass tonight?* He poured it anyway and took a slow whiff of its bouquet. He clicked open the current manuscript; it sported the tentative name *Daymares*. Jesus, writing a war memoir felt like an assault. The onslaught exposed his savage, most personal pockets of experience.

Sarah was hungry for it; she regularly phoned from New York to ask how the manuscript was going. Recently, she'd called to plead with him to get it done. Her entreating made the process worse. He'd buried the annoying telephone under a pile of clothes on the floor of his bedroom closet. He suspected one day she might just show up on his doorstep.

The next morning, still unable to work on *Daymares*, Moss wandered the flat part of the valley, whistling and calling. Even with his binoculars, there was no sign of the dog. He left little piles of kibble here and there. When he got home, he sat at his desk and drew a rough map of his land, cross-hatching the part covered today. Tomorrow, he'd head up Bender's Ridge.

Chapter Eight

Rowan awakened slowly. Her body felt the same, and she still had a crushing headache, but something seemed different. She patted around the hospital bed. Nothing weird there. Not seeing the window, the bed, or the table flared her anger. It made her want to knock things off the bedside table. She wished she could cry.

After a few minutes, not finding anything changed on the outside, she looked inward—that didn't take sight. She tried to puzzle through what might have shifted. This didn't seem to be a physical change. Instead, it was … she searched for the right word. *Knowing.* An inner knowing. It felt strange and big, like when you see something awful—maybe a squirrel getting squished on the road—and then can't ever unsee it. But this wasn't terrible; it was exciting. Rowan tucked the covers under her chin. It was like she was watching herself think. That sounded dumb. For the first time in her life, words failed her.

Right before falling asleep, her scary thoughts tumbled and crashed. She steadied herself by remembering what the Orientation and Mobility specialist had told her. She hadn't even known such a job existed. The woman, Lisa, had neat suggestions about getting around buildings. She made Rowan practice. Even though she'd start crying—purely from stupid frustration—the specialist helping her seemed to have endless patience.

Lisa told Mom, "First thing, when you get home, find a cane teacher for your daughter. She'll need the independence." That had gotten Rowan worrying about the gazillions of unknowns ahead. *I just can't think about the future. Too scary.*

When she rolled over to sleep, she trembled with anxiety and only dozed off by playing a trick on her mind. She imagined a beautiful little cottage with only one room, filled floor to ceiling with file card drawers—like old libraries she'd seen in movies. She picked just the right drawer, dropped a thought in, shut it tight, and told herself she could come back for it any time she chose. She repeated this for everything that haunted her—Zephy, blindness, the future. When she was finished, she closed the inner door to the room and locked it with an imaginary old-fashioned key, then the outside door. After dropping the heavy key in her pocket, she walked away.

Later, Rowan woke up from a dream about Zeph so real it seemed her dog was breathing next to her hospital bed. The dream had no story, but Rowan felt her coarse fur, smelled her doggy scent, and stared into those aware, dark-chocolate eyes. *Zephyr's alive, I'm certain of it. Lonely and frightened.* She tried to pense a picture to let Zeph know she was okay too, but her head knocked hard, and she wasn't sure if she succeeded.

The door creaked open, and someone came in—she could hear shoes making a familiar sucking sound on the floor—nurses' shoes.

"Hi missy, you awake?" The night nurse took Rowan's blood pressure and guided her to the bathroom. "Hon, the toilet is to your right, and the paper's on the left."

Then Rowan felt her hand placed on a wall button.

"Press this to call me when you're done, okay?"

A few minutes later, as the nurse helped her back to bed, Rowan asked, "What time is it? My head hurts like crazy. Where's my mom?"

"It's a quarter after three—in the morning. Your mama's sound asleep in the waiting room two doors down; I gave her a pillow and blanket."

Rowan could hear her fiddling with equipment in the room.

"She was exhausted but said she didn't want to take a chance of waking you by coming in here to the pullout bed. She's a special mom, isn't she?"

Rowan nodded.

"I'll get meds for your headache. Back in a few."

After a while, she returned. "Here's a pill and some water." She steered Rowan's hand to the cup. "You sleep now. Good girl. I'll check on you later."

After the nurse left, Rowan went back to watching her mind—staying in that place felt much safer. She noticed how thoughts exploded out of nowhere, already whole. Then, almost as fast, they vanished. It was like they weren't really hers, yet they erupted in her head. Strange. She yawned. Tomorrow, she'd think about this more.

To doze off, Rowan opened her imaginary cottage and stored yet another batch of scary thoughts, but her body wasn't afraid anymore. She was sure her dog had survived. Somehow, they had to find her. She had to convince Mommo to search.

The next morning, Carolina paced, waiting for Dr. Spanner to finish examining her daughter. Rowan had been out of the coma for four days and still no vision.

"I'll call this post-traumatic cortical blindness," the neurologist said, after peering into Rowan's eyes. "Her optic nerves are normal. Her pupils respond to light." He turned to confront Carolina. "I have no explanation for your daughter's loss of sight. I'm not sure if it's going to be temporary or permanent or if it's physical or psychological. It was most likely caused by the blow to her occipital lobe. The bruise tells us where she took the hit."

Rowan snapped, "I thought doctors were supposed to figure stuff out. I've been here eight days, and you can't come up with anything!" She turned toward her mom and tears spilled. "I won't be able to run with Zephy."

"Sometimes we don't have answers," the physician said. He sounded genuinely sad.

At the sound of their dog's name, Carolina froze. She couldn't get a breath. Her lungs simply wouldn't work. Oh, God, she had explaining to do. Her skin went cold, then hot, then cold again, and she broke into a sweat. For the briefest moment, she was relieved Rowan couldn't see her reaction.

"Take her home," Spanner urged. "There's nothing more we can do for her here. I'll sign the paperwork. You can leave this afternoon."

At the very mention of leaving the hospital, Carolina's heart contracted. She could no longer hide the truth from Rowan. She shoved her thought to the back to finish her conversation with the doctor. "What about the migraines?"

"The MRI showed nothing wrong with her brain or her eyes. In other words, no cause we can diagnose. I'll prescribe medication for the pain."

"Home? How, exactly, am I going to do home?" Rowan's voice sounded small and scared. "I can't see anything."

"Time and love may heal this," Spanner continued. "It happens occasionally. My nurse can provide information for the Oregon chapter of the National Federation of the Blind."

The specialist handed Carolina a packet.

Carolina glared at the doctor—outraged he had mentioned permanent blindness in front of her daughter—and sputtered, "We'll wait. Wait and see." She stuffed the packet into her suitcase without mentioning it to Rowan.

He shrugged. "Okay. Think about it. I'll go sign the release papers."

After tucking Rowan in, Carolina ducked into the bathroom, leaned on the sink, and struggled to come up with a plan. Her daughter, already upset by the loss of her sight, would fall back into depression when she understood Zephyr was missing. Carolina's throat caught and thickened. The floors at home were strewn with dog toys—that would be upsetting for Rowan. No—she couldn't see the playthings anymore. Worse, she might trip. Maybe her neighbor, Sue, could pick them up before they got home?

She faced the daunting task of introducing her daughter to a sightless world. How in heaven's name would she do that? She desperately wanted an instruction manual to negotiate this new, strange territory. Spanner and Lisa had both been smarter than she'd realized. The Federation they mentioned undoubtedly had resources. She needed guidance.

Now.

How would they get home? Even though Sam had talked about renting a van, she'd been so worried and involved with Rowan, she'd forgotten to call. A vehicle was essential for her work, in addition to carting around kids and dogs. Her hand flew to her mouth. *No dogs. Oh God.* Blind child, beloved hound gone missing, totaled car, sweet Stormy dead on the road, and she hadn't even said goodbye. Sobs choked out of her, and she allowed herself a few moments of grief. *Nothing's the same. It won't be, ever again.* It was like the awful agony she had to swallow when Rafe died—the taste of never being able to go back, never making time stop.

She had to figure this out. Now. Straightening her shoulders, she grabbed a tissue and mopped her nose before opening the bathroom door. Time to face the music. What a dumb expression, she thought. Where did it come from, anyway? Military bands, or something? Music for firing squads? That's what it felt like she was facing.

Rowan had dozed off, so Carolina had a few minutes to decide how to break the news to her daughter. As she walked into the hall, she closed the door so quietly there wasn't even a click. She paced. Wiping her eyes, she pulled out her cell and punched in Sue's number.

"You're back? I didn't see the van. How was your vacation?" Sue asked. Her voice was filled with the playful lilt Carolina loved.

"We never got there," Carolina said. "We were in a terrible car accident."

Sue gasped. "Where are you?" Are you okay?"

Carolina updated her friend and broke the news Rowan couldn't see. There was a long silence.

"My Gawd, Carolina." More silence. "I can't imagine. I don't know what to say. You two are going to need support. Heavens to Betsy. What can I do? Meals?"

"There's more. It's bad." Carolina's words caught in her throat. "The dogs are gone. Stormy's dead, and Zephyr's missing."

She heard Sue's sharp intake of breath. "Oh, dear. This just gets worse and worse." Another long pause. "I'm so sorry. Row must be completely freaking out."

"I haven't told her yet. That's next, right after we hang up. You know where I hide the key, right? Could you and Seth pick up the dog toys, box them, and stick them somewhere? I'm terrified Rowan will stumble on them. Maybe set them on the dryer? I bet she'll want to hold them at some point." She paused. "I will too," she whispered. "Stormy—fourteen years. And Zephyr…." The lump in her throat swelled so big she couldn't speak.

After clearing her throat, she went on. "Supposedly, we'll be back late this afternoon. The doctor just signed the paperwork. Sue—dinner would be great. Keep it simple. And thank you so much."

Next, she called Enterprise Car Rental and arranged for a van to be dropped off at the hospital.

Now, the talk with Rowan.

She prayed Rowan wouldn't blame her; she was doing enough rebuking for them both. Filled with dread, Carolina walked back into the hospital room, their home for the last four of eight hospital days. She sat on the chair next to her daughter and touched her arm.

Rowan turned toward her. "I've got to tell you something before you pack our stuff, Mommo," she said. She seemed unusually intense.

"I do, too, sweetie. May I go first?"

"I guess. If you have to."

Carolina swallowed hard and patted Rowan's hand. "Remember the dogs were with us, and we were headed to the mountains to camp?"

Rowan nodded.

"In the accident, the van rolled over, and the back hatch flew open."

"I have to tell you my dream now! It's about Zephy."

"Wait, please. I need to finish. By the time the guy helped me out of the van and checked on you, Zephyr went missing—you know how she is; she was terrified and ran off. Stormy dashed into the highway—and got hit. Killed."

"Mommo. No!" Rowan swallowed hard. She reached for her mom's face and touched her. Carolina knew her daughter felt the streaming tears.

"My earliest memories are of Stormy," Rowan said. "Like when I was three." Tears spilled down her cheeks too.

"He ran in front of a big camper. He didn't know what hit him." She said this mostly for herself. Believing it kept her sane.

Rowan was quiet for a minute, then swiped her tears away. "But I *know* Zephy's alive. My dream showed me!"

Carolina looked at her daughter, glad for the second time this day Rowan couldn't see her expression, now filled with heartbreak. "Oh, sweetie, I'm delighted you had a nice dream, but we can't be sure what's happened to Zephyr. It's an awful thought, but she may not have made it. We have to face the possibility."

"No," Rowan said, firmly. "I'm sure she made it. You'll see. As soon as we get home, we need to go look for her. Oh!" Her hands went to her face. "I can't search. Mommo!" Her voice rose in a wail.

Carolina hugged her daughter. "I'll search, sweetheart. I'll search for both of us. Of course, you'll come with me. It's your voice she needs to hear."

Chapter Nine

The next morning, Moss fit a water bottle, sandwich, power bar, a big, zippered bag of kibble, and some biscuits into his backpack. He whipped up a nourishing breakfast—three-egg omelet, whole wheat, seeded toast—and considered the best way to place the kibble. He knew any animal could find it; that's probably what had happened on the valley floor. The most important part was to get the caches close to where the dog bedded down. Pile it near a tree trunk? He'd figure something when he saw the lay of the land.

After finishing his meal, he rifled through the recycling bin, pulled out some yogurt quart containers, stacked them together, and added them to his pack. At the least, he could stash food in them for easier cache refilling.

This uphill hike would be tough, but even more taxing would be heading downhill again. He'd best take it slow. He wondered if he would ever accept his limitations in country terrain. The hike would probably be worth it, though; the dog was on the ridge last night, Moss was sure of it. A spring puddled there, even in summer. In this dry climate, wild animals frequented any available water. He knew it would draw the dog, too.

On the way up, he traversed the hill across and back, looking for signs. He'd need the ease of the worn deer track on the way down. Squeezing a sage bush, he sniffed his fingers, inhaling the tart incense.

Reminding himself to be appreciative he could walk at all, he stepped carefully. It would set him back to take a spill. Near the top, he grabbed a boulder to swing around it. The moment he put weight on his bionic foot, he heard the rattle. *Holy shit!* His heart slammed in his chest. Shifting as quietly as he could, Moss eased back on his good leg. *Where the hell is it?* In that second, the snake lashed out.

Fuck!

Moss heard the ping as fangs hit metal.

Shit! Close call.

Slowly edging away, Moss held his breath. He saw the snake slithering into the underbrush. He didn't move again until the last brown diamond and tail rattles were gone. Taking deep breaths, Moss waited until his heart stopped thumping. Pacific rattlers were generally not aggressive; he must have frightened it. Worse, he'd neglected to bring the snakebite kit. Lesson learned. From now on, the kit must live in the daypack. He patted his fake leg—for the first time ever, he was truly grateful for the metal apparatus. He blew out a thankful breath and headed up the steep, final pitch of the hill.

He admired a small stand of manzanita bushes and ran his hands along the smooth, sensual bark. Then he spotted Oregon grape sporting dusky bluish-black berries. Just two days ago, he read the root made a fine tincture to fight infection. Moss marked the location on his hand-drawn map; he'd come back in late fall or winter to dig roots.

Cresting the ridge top, he limped to the spring, eased down and splashed cool water on his face. He was beat—burned a chunk of calories on this climb. He dug around in his pack for a power bar. When his breath came more easily, he devoured the snack, then clambered up to scan the area for his first cache site.

Fresh scat. He picked it apart with a stick. Yeah, the dog's. Just as he'd thought. It smelled the same as what he'd found before. This was the right spot. He pulled out one tub, poured kibble in, and laid it on its side under a nearby serviceberry bush. Whistling mindlessly, he placed biscuits a foot apart until he reached the spring; if the dog came to the water first, the treats would lead to the larger stash. Locating three more sites within a forty-foot radius, he placed additional hoards. When the dog returned, it would find the goods.

Settling back onto the ground, he took out his sandwich and munched. The view always astounded him. When he shaded the sun from his eyes, he could see the corner of his vegetable garden where large heritage tomato plants fruited. It pleased him. Did the dog watch him work in the garden from here? He chuckled. Who was spying on whom?

What was that rustle? The hair on his arms rose. In war, on patrol, soldiers cultivated a sixth sense when someone was nearby, when they were being observed. Either they developed this ability or died. Somebody or something scanned him now. Spooked—it was an old, creepy feeling—he peered in different directions. Nothing.

The birds hadn't gone silent. A positive sign. He was on edge, that's all. Maybe the dog was around? He surveyed his surroundings. Nothing. Relatively sure he wasn't in *real* danger, he stuffed his belongings into the pack and shoved up to standing, always an awkward motion. The knee joint wasn't the same as his own knee had been, and he had to push off the ground in a different way. It made him feel vulnerable.

His project done, he hitched slowly down the deer path. He glanced behind him—that same feeling that he was being watched hounded him. It was the dog, he reasoned—even though a small part of him flashed on Afghanistan. That instinct for survival flared and crashed, leaving Moss in freefall depression. The blues descended through the top of his head, invaded his mind like a brain bleed, then sank to his solar plexus where it sat like a twenty-pound tumor.

There didn't seem to be a pattern to their arrival, at least not one he'd been able to puzzle out. Sometimes the dark feelings were triggered by a dream, a flashback to war, or nothing at all. Sometimes, they left as quickly as they arrived; sometimes they hung around for days, even weeks. Then he'd tackle the mindfulness exercises—especially when he didn't have the inclination or juice. This time, he knew the blues stemmed from that burst of fear that always plunged him into loneliness. And *that* issue, he didn't know how to fix.

Not true. He knew damn well how; he just wasn't willing. When he acknowledged the weight of this lonesomeness, memories flooded back and took him further down. Flashbacks of Sophie welcoming him home, her beautiful blonde hair covering her shoulders, soft mouth curved in an inviting smile—that is until he unlegged and slipped into bed next to her. Her fingers slid over his chest, making him ache with desire. But when she touched his stump, she yanked her hand back. She'd known about his injury, but in the flesh it seemed to repulse her. She rolled over, and the luscious moment bled away.

"I can't do this, Moss," she'd said. "I'm too weak; I don't have it in me."

His heart had flailed in his chest. "You'll get used to it," he'd answered. "I have." *But is that true?*

She'd slid out of bed. "It isn't going to get better; this is my failing. I'm really sorry." She'd twisted off her engagement ring, plunked it on the bedside table, and left for good. Five years invested, gone. If she couldn't deal with his leg, she sure wouldn't have been able to handle PTSD nightmares and moodiness. He was better off alone.

He enjoyed the occasional visit with Jessie at her place. They had similar service disabilities, and liked fooling around on occasion. Since they both were missing a leg, they'd played around and figured out how to make one-legged sex work.

He'd chosen to settle here, on land his family held for generations— his childhood summer territory—where he didn't have to deal with issues like people. He planned to keep it that way.

Zephyr hears something break through the underbrush below. Trying to bear weight on only three legs, she hobbles a distance and crawls under a large bush. Every motion sends bolts of agony through her. She hears a rattle, a loud intake of breath, then silence. Moments later, she senses a human walking. The rhythm is odd. She scoots further under cover, flattens down, and places her head between her paws. She blinks and watches.

He comes into sight. Zephyr presses even closer to the ground, but he doesn't come her way. He's near the water, and she's thirsty. Splashing it on himself, he gets up—like he's hurt—and pulls out a bag, pours something that sounds like dinner and places it nearby. She scents kibble and drools. Her stomach rumbles; it's so hollow it hurts. He eats a cookie. It smells like ones Rowan gives her bites of, but she forces herself to stay in place. She needs to lick the wound on her shoulder, but not until he's gone. He gets up, moves away, and she relaxes just a little. She hears him put more dinner on the ground near the bushes. She longs for food but stays exactly where she is.

He heads down the hill. Creeping out of her hiding spot, she limps to a bush and sniffs carefully. She drinks in both his dense male smell and the familiar scent of food. Her body trembles as she bolts dinner. Zephyr follows the biscuits, crunching each one on the way to the water, then laps her fill. She prowls the knoll until she finds every stash. Then she returns to her hidey-bush and, safely concealed, stomach satisfied, rhythmically cleans the oozing wounds.

Chapter Ten

Rowan fiddled with the clothes her mom laid out on the hospital bed. She had to find the labels to keep from putting them on inside out or backward. Tricky. *It would be, like, so embarrassing.* Checking the label at her neck to be sure she got it right, she felt around for socks and shoes, got those on, and tied. Double knots, just in case.

She heard someone come into the room and two little strange squeaky noises.

"Hi there. My name's Jake. I'm wheeling you down to the front door so you can split this joint. I've just put the brakes on so your chrome chariot won't spin out of control."

"I don't need it. I'll look stupid in a wheelchair," she said.

"Hospital rules, sorry. Everyone complains." He gently touched her arm. "Pretend it's a throne, Princess Rowan."

The guy's voice was deep with a southern accent, and he made her giggle. He helped Rowan shift into the wheelchair and set her bag on her lap. As they went down the hall, Rowan asked to say goodbye to the nurses, so he stopped at the station.

"Please tell Betty, the nighttime nurse, a special goodbye," she said. "She was a rad nurse. Super kind."

"Rad, huh?" The nurse gave a quick laugh. "I'll pass on the message; she'll be pleased. Good luck to you."

Jake pushed Rowan to the elevator. The feel of it dropping and not seeing unsettled her stomach. As he pushed her out the hospital's front doors, Rowan was overwhelmed by cars whooshing, people chattering, horns blasting, and doors slamming. The one relief: the stinky medicine smell of the hospital was gone. Now, only city scents—Chinese food and bus exhaust.

"Ready?" her mom asked. "Think how good home will feel. Your own bed."

"I'm not ready," Rowan muttered. "It's noisy, and I can't tell what is where. I'm scared, Mommo. I'm terrified to live like this."

She heard her mom sigh.

"How about, each day, we'll pick one new challenge to explore together? I guess the name of the game is to be really curious, sweetie."

"But what about my fear? It's bottled up here." Rowan pointed to her belly.

"I can imagine. Deep breaths work the best. Try one with me now."

Rowan took a slow, full breath. Her stomach didn't seem so tense anymore. She heard the van's side door slide open and somebody get in. Her mother was standing next to her; who else was here?

"Slip your hand in the crook of my elbow. I'll guide you," her mom said.

Wobbling, Rowan pushed out of the wheelchair. She took her mother's arm, felt around for the car door, and managed to climb into the front seat. She fumbled for the seat belt and eventually got it buckled.

"Good job!" Carolina said. "The rental car guy is with us. We have to drop him off."

Tears trickled down Rowan's cheeks. She dashed them away. This was too exhausting, and for a moment, she wanted to run back into the hospital where everything felt familiar. *But I can't run, can I. I can't even walk by myself.* Again, overwhelm enveloped her, and she took another deep breath.

This van had a fresh vinyl smell, not the familiar doggy scent of their old one. The slider jarred shut. A male voice spoke from the back. Startled, she jumped. When the engine turned over and they pulled away from the curb, she grabbed the seat. The sensation of being in a moving car without watching the road made her feel like she was racing toward a brick wall. Every time she felt the van brake, she pressed her hands against the dash.

"I feel sick, Mommo. This reminds me too much of the accident," she whispered.

"Carsick?"

"Bad."

"The nurse sent us home with one of those little throw-up containers." Carolina called into the back seat, "Sir? See that flowered bag? Hand me the pink, curved dish, would you please?"

Rowan felt it placed in her hands and fingered the edges to get a sense of the shape. Making sure it was right side up, she gripped it, white-knuckle tight. The car turned and then stopped. She heard the man get out.

"Good luck, kid," he said. "All the best to both of you." He slammed the door.

Her mom patted her arm. "You'll do better on the freeway, sweetie. We'll be home in a couple of hours."

After a few minutes of turns and stops, Rowan felt them speed up and heard cars on either side. This must be Highway 5. She trembled. Being in a van again was scary. She was glad to be going home, although nothing would be the same—no dogs, no reading—and she'd have to feel her way around the house. She leaned her head back against the seat, and suddenly jerked forward. A picture burst into her mind—a giant mountain lion with its mouth open showing huge, brown-stained teeth.

Had Zeph just pensed her?

Rowan shook her head. Was that possible? Zephy pensing? At first, a thrill ricocheted through her, but within seconds, it twisted to fear for Zeph's life. They *had* to search. *We have to do it now.* She knew her mother would close down the moment Rowan mentioned the image she'd seen. She'd have to convince her mother to start a search for Zephy in a different way.

She turned toward her mom but decided to wait on begging until they got home. Mommo needed to concentrate on driving now. She tried to convince herself that big cat was just another scary worry, like the ones she'd put in her imaginary cottage drawers when she couldn't fall asleep in the hospital. She firmly pushed the thought away and shifted focus to her future—not Zephy's, not right now. Like, looking up words in her dictionary and thesaurus—how could she possibly do that? Or playing with Zephy. Or… The steady freeway motion rocked her gently until she finally fell asleep.

"We're home, Row." Mommo came around and opened the passenger door.

Rowan woke up disoriented. *"No!"*

"It's okay, sweetie. We're home now."

"I had a bad dream. We were on our way to camp and—"

"That's all over. Today we're happy to be home, right?" Carolina touched Rowan gently. "Let's go in."

Rowan grabbed her mom's arm, and they plodded up the path to their house. As they passed the bushes, she was acutely aware, for the first time, of hearing subtle variations of sound. She stretched her hand to make sure she was correct and felt the slippery rhododendron leaves. The sound texture was different where the bushes grew close to the path, compared to the spaces where there were none. The new sensation startled her, and she stumbled. Her mom caught and supported her as they mounted the stairs to the wooden porch; the hollow space underneath amplified their footfall. Rowan had never noticed sound changes before. While her mother hunted for the key, Rowan felt for the front door and rested her face against its cool surface.

The click of the lock, the creak of the door, then familiar scents surrounded her as they walked in. Rowan's sense of the dogs was clear, but their absence even clearer. It was too much. Her mom walked her to the couch—the very couch where she and Zeph had been eight days before. She remembered fiddling with her dog's long toes, and Zephy's happy groans. Now her dog was lost in the empty lands of central Oregon, howling for her family, she was sure. Rowan covered her face with her hands and sobbed. "Mommo, where's Wubby? Zephy will need her."

"You put him in our car right before we started on vacation, remember, sweetie? I bet we find Wubby when we pick up the stuff from the wrecked van on the way to hunt for Zephyr. The guy at the tow place promised to save the toys, dog beds, everything."

Grateful that her mother had broached the subject first, Rowan's words raced out. "When can we leave? Tomorrow?"

"In a few days. I've got four sewing projects—our having food in the house depends on my work, and my clients have been waiting a long time. I have to purchase a used van—Sam gave me the money, bless his heart. Also, we don't know what's going to happen with your sight, so you need to be assessed by the Oregon Commission for the Blind to set up cane lessons. They'll evaluate our home to make it easier for you to navigate. At least for now."

"You're teasing, right?" Rowan's heart felt as if it had suddenly cracked.

She felt her mom's hand smooth her curls. "Sorry, kiddo. It's going to be at least four days. Then we can head to Sisters and really take time to search."

"Mommmo!" Rowan threw herself back on the couch and bawled. "You should have searched while I was unconscious in the hospital! I wouldn't have known you were gone. You could have found Zephy and brought her home already."

Carolina tried to console her, but Rowan shoved her away. She heard Mom's startled "Wha—?" but pulled a pillow over her ears to block out everything.

Carolina figured Rowan would come unglued at some point. After what had happened to her, who wouldn't? She sat next to her daughter until the explosion wore itself out; it had worked when Rowan was at the tantrum age of two and three. The trick was to remain close by—so Row felt loved—but not engage.

Eventually, the wailing stopped and Rowan snuggled into Carolina's lap. She ran her fingers through Row's hair, stroking her head and neck. The girl dozed.

When she stirred, Carolina whispered, "Hey."

Rowan turned her face up.

"I'm stiff. I need to move," Carolina said.

Rowan sat up, rubbing her swollen eyes. "Whenever I wake up, it's awful. I'm blind all over again."

"I can imagine."

Rowan shook her head firmly. "You can't possibly know what it's like."

"You're right. I can't. But still, kiddo … we need to work with this challenging situation and be kind to each other. I'm sure you know, in your heart, I'm doing the best I can."

Rowan nodded slowly.

"Even though I feel guilty, I couldn't have prevented the accident. The doe came out of nowhere. And there's no way I was going to take off looking for Zephyr while you were in a coma." She rested her hand on Rowan's knee. "Think about it. I couldn't leave you—you're my precious girl. There are just a couple of things we must attend to first—then we'll go to Sisters, I promise."

"I guess I was mean. I'm sorry."

"You're undergoing a huge change. It's understandable. But it's hard to have you shove and yell at me."

Rowan hung her head.

Carolina heard a soft knock on the door. "Come in!" she called. "It's Sue. She's made dinner for us."

Rowan put her face in her hands.

"She loves you, sweetie, whether you can see or not."

Carolina rose and gave her friend a long hug, then she stood back and drank in the sight of her—carrot-red hair thrown up in a ponytail, tight jeans, and sparkly top. "I'm so sorry I didn't call you sooner. I flat out didn't think of it; it's been too chaotic." She took the dishes Sue held and set them on the counter. "This is so sweet of you."

"Not to worry," Sue said. "I wanna help." She sat on the couch beside Rowan. "Hi there. Seth's real anxious ta see you. I sure was, too."

Rowan folded into Sue's arms and cried hard. "I don't know how to be with him. We always do tomboy stuff. I can't anymore."

Sue rubbed her back. "You guys'll figure it out; you're good buddies."

"But I'm so ashamed."

Sue's mouth fell open. "Ashamed? Really? This is just bad luck. There's nothin' you coulda done to prevent it."

"I feel broken. Kind of wrecked."

"Sounds pretty normal to me. I mean, what an accident! But you're the same Rowan as before." She sat silently for a moment, then patted

Rowan's knee and turned to Carolina. "Are you guys hungry? I made your fave, Rowan. Mac and cheese with hot dogs, and salad. There's enough for four. Can Seth and I eat with ya?"

"How about it, Row?" Carolina asked.

Rowan was quiet for a moment, then shook her head. "I'm tired. I just want to eat and crash. Maybe tomorrow."

Sue nodded. "Sure. We'll grill something. You can come over or we can do it here. Whatever's easiest for ya. I'll try to keep Seth away. I can't promise though; he's a sneaky one."

Rowan couldn't help but giggle. "He sure is."

A few seconds later, the boy burst through the door without knocking. "I was outside spying and heard you. 'Not until tomorrow?' Too bad, but I have to see my best bud!" He strode over to Rowan. "You look normal, like your silly old self. Come on, grab my arm, let's go—just a short walk. I want to hear about your nutso adventure."

Rowan ducked her head and fiddled with her hands.

Seth stamped his foot. "Come on! I can't wait."

"Okay, okay. For Pete's sake." She got up. "Let me take your elbow."

Rowan grabbed Seth's arm. "No joking around. You have to be my eyes. Watch out for what I might trip on or bump into and warn me. You have to really pay attention."

"Okay, got it. Here we go."

Rowan felt him hesitate, then he started forward at a slow pace. "Chair three feet to the left, lamp next to it—"

"Too much information! Just the important close-by stuff." When the area rug slipped, Rowan's feet almost went out from under her. She grabbed Seth's arm harder. "Like that!"

"Oops, sorry." He tapped the rug with his toe. "Mrs. G., you need to get rid of this. It's dangerous. Row, stop here, I need to open the front door."

Rowan waited, relieved that Seth seemed to accept her even though she couldn't see. At least today. He'd probably stop coming around once he figured out all the fun stuff she couldn't do anymore.

He talked her across the porch and down the stairs.

"Where are we going?" she asked.

"To sit on our favorite oak branch in the field. Okay by you?"

She nodded, and they continued on. She felt stupid when she stumbled, but he caught her without any jokes.

"Here," he said. "Right in front of you."

She felt for the horizontal branch and carefully sat on it, swinging her legs.

"Okay, tell me everything," he said. "You've had a crazy time."

Although she couldn't recall the accident, she did remember waking up from the coma; the terror of not being able to see; finding out Zephy was lost and Stormy was dead; her horrible disappointment at not being able to search right away. But she avoided telling him she knew her dog was alive. She had no idea how to explain her experience. He might make fun, and she needed every ounce of trust in herself. She had to have the courage to try stuff, and if people teased her—well, doubt could wreck everything. "We won't be able to run or build forts or play hide and seek with Zeph," Rowan confessed. "I don't know what I can do yet. But I know I'm not much fun, 'cause it's sure not pleasant for me."

"How about chess? There must be chess for blind people. And you know I love to read. I'll read out loud to you." His voice sounded anxious.

"Uh … chess won't work because I could feel my pieces, but I couldn't see yours. I'd probably knock them over."

"Hmm. Right."

She could hear him picking at the tree bark.

"We could put Velcro on the bottoms," he said.

"Good idea, but too hard to keep the whole board in my mind. See what I mean? Life sucks now."

"Well, I can still tell you stuff, right? Like, confide? About my stupid mom?"

"Yup, sure. But you'll get bored with me real fast." She picked at her fingernails.

"Won't."

"Will."

"You'll see."

"That's exactly the problem. I can't."

"Can't what?"

"Can't see."

They were both silent for a moment.

"Hey, Seth…"

"What?"

"I'm looking for a word, but of course I can't look it up. What's another word for noticing?"

"Noticing. Hmm."

Rowan could almost hear him thinking.

"You mean, like being aware? What do I know? You're the one who likes words."

"Aware. Perfect. Thanks."

"How come you asked?"

"Chewing on stuff. You know." Rowan didn't want to say anymore. "But would you look up 'aware' in my thesaurus when we get back? I want to know other words that mean the same thing."

"Sure." Seth cleared his throat. "My teacher's really bugging me. Can you help me write better? She says I need to use my imagination."

Rowan snorted. "Like *they* do. Sure, if you want, I'm happy to play around with ideas."

She felt Seth sling an arm over her shoulder and give a sigh. "Thanks. We can help each other."

Chapter Eleven

Carolina set down the telephone. "Unbelievable," she muttered. She walked into the living room where Row lay on the couch listening to her iPod. She tapped her daughter, and Rowan pulled out an earbud.

"We have a tentative appointment in Portland for cane training. Apparently, they don't offer classes in Eugene."

"We have to drive that long way? Mommo, it's over *four* hours up and back, plus the lesson. You need to finish your work so we can look for Zephy." Her voice rose. "Bummer! Isn't there a local person?"

"Eugene would make more sense. Maybe we could find someone. I'll call the resource person back and lean on her." Carolina returned from her office a few minutes later and sat next to her daughter.

Rowan yanked her earbud out again. "It's hard to get into a story when you're interrupting me."

"But you're always plugged in!"

"Because I can't see. This happens to be summer reading for school."

"Right. Sorry. Anyway," Carolina went on. "There's someone who teaches cane use right in Eugene, but he can't get certified because he's blind. Isn't that crazy? The resource lady wasn't going to recommend anyone who hadn't passed their certification, but I insisted on a name. I explained we need to go search for Zephyr and can't travel to Portland." She rubbed her fingers along her chin. "I figure someone who's been through the experience of being blinded and then learned to use a cane would make an exceptional teacher. Anyway, I gave him a call."

"And?"

"His name is Benjamin. He's coming after work today at 5:30."

"Yay—today! He works?"

"He's an attorney."

"A lawyer? How can he do that without seeing?"

Carolina thought about it. "Well, with braille, a dictation machine, and a secretary, I guess. Where there's a will, there's a way."

Rowan giggled. "You sound just like Grandma."

"I do?" Carolina tried to keep her voice even. She was *definitely* not like her mother. Not even close. Her mother's "clairvoyant feelings" about things—it was a ruse as far as Carolina was concerned. "I know you shouldn't go because my intuition tells me so"—her mom's overused excuse for limiting Carolina's social life. She shook off the tension that memories of her mother brought up and said, "I'm headed downstairs to work out on the mats now, so I'll be done and showered when Benjamin comes."

Later that afternoon, the doorbell rang. Carolina was surprised to see an African-American man with long dreads, facial scars, and sunglasses. He wore a business suit and held three white canes. A taxi pulled out of the driveway.

"Hello," Benjamin said, and chuckled. "I'm not exactly what people expect."

"Hi, I'm Carolina. How'd you know you're not what I was anticipating?"

"Your slight hesitation. Don't feel bad. I'm extra sensitive to cues beyond the visual."

"I guess you've learned things that only being blind can teach. When you said you were an attorney, I didn't expect beautiful dreads! Come on in and meet Rowan."

"Since I'm unfamiliar with your home, may I take your arm?" He shifted the sticks to his left hand. "I don't generally use a cane indoors. The spaces are too tight."

"Of course. Here, I've crooked my elbow for you."

He slid his arm through. "As we walk, tell me what you see so I get a feel for your home."

Carolina described the entryway and the living room as they made their way toward Rowan.

"I'd like to sit near your daughter, please, so we can introduce ourselves."

"Howdy!" Rowan called.

Carolina walked him close to the couch. "Directly in front of you, there's a chair with arms. Rowan's to your right, on the sofa. Shall I stay, or not?"

"Stay while we get a sense of each another. Next time, we might do fine without you. Today, I'd like you to watch us work with the cane, so you get the drift of what I'm suggesting."

Feeling the back of the chair, he made his way around it and sat. He leaned the white canes so the grips rested near his thigh. "Hi, I'm Benjamin. I lost my sight when I was twenty-six. Eighteen years ago. Your mom told me it's only been ten days for you."

"Yeah. A deer launched itself in front of our van. Mom couldn't see 'cause the deer covered the whole windshield, so we crashed and rolled over. At least, that's what she told me. I don't remember any of it. They said I was in a coma for four days."

"It must have been scary when you came to."

"Like … awful. Disorienting. My whole world went topsy-turvy."

"I've been there; I get it. How old are you, Rowan?"

"Eleven."

"You have an impressive vocabulary. Are you an avid reader?"

"Major. I used to haunt the library. I'm a writer, too. I haven't figured out how, since the accident. I'm scared to death I won't find a way."

"You'll find a way, for sure. There are quite a few voice recognition programs so you can speak to your computer, and then it'll read your writing back to you."

"What's your accent? Is it British?"

"You're close. I do sound British, but I'm from South Africa. I've been here since entering college; I received a scholarship to Harvard

Medical School. I was a surgical resident walking home after an all-nighter at the hospital when a bunch of men attacked me. One of them threw paint thinner in my face. They beat me up too, but the paint thinner blinded me permanently."

"Wow," Rowan said, her voice quiet. "All those years studying to be a surgeon, and it got wrecked by mean men."

"How do you know they were mean?"

"Well, they'd have to be to cause another person serious pain and injury."

"I think you're partly right. But I don't believe their anger was at me, or even that it was personal. I was in the wrong place at the wrong time. It was hard, yes. Quite difficult. I had to leave bitterness behind to reclaim my life." He rubbed his chin. "It's a different journey than I'd planned, but satisfying. As an attorney, I work with people who've suffered personal injuries."

"Cool, you figured it out and can help people. I can't imagine my future yet. Mostly, I worry about my dog, Zephy—she got thrown from the van in the accident. We're going to search as soon as I learn to use the cane, and Mom makes some money." She paused and thought for a moment. "Of course, *I* can't search, but I get to go. I can holler for her."

"You sure can. She'll hear your voice and come hunting for you. Describe her to me."

"Do you know what a Scottish deerhound is?" Rowan asked. "Or an Irish wolfhound? They're more common. My dog's a mix of those two."

"I've heard they're the tallest dogs, but I don't think I've ever seen one. Are they like Great Danes?"

"As big, but different. They're gorgeous. Statuesque—the newest addition to my vocabulary." Her words rushed out. "They have wiry coats, and mustaches, and fur that hangs over their eyes, and beards, too. Zeph's head can rest on the dining room table. It's hard to imagine how long her legs are, or how huge her strides, until you see her." Rowan made a choking sound. "Oh, sorry."

Benjamin chortled. "Girl, I've been blind a long time. You're brand new to this, so you're sensitive. There's nothing you could say that would offend me."

"Really?"

"I promise. Anyway, blind people use the word 'see' all the time."

"What a relief. Are you black? Since you're from Africa?"

"I am. Almost blue-black. And I have dreadlocks. Do you know what those are?"

"Sure. When hair is wiry and gets all stuck together. It's stylin'."

He laughed out loud this time. "We'll get along just fine. Before we start, what worries you the most?"

"That I won't find my dog. I have nightmares about it."

"I bet you do. But I mean worries about being blind."

"I'm scared about everything. Besides wondering how I'll write, school starts in September, which I dread worse than anything. The kids staring and all. Talking behind my back. Finding my way around. Having to learn to read a different way. Is it hard to learn braille?"

"It takes a while, but you'll get the hang of it. Do you know about Talking Books at the State Library in Salem? They'll mail you books in braille or on tape for free. I'm going to give you a hard truth, though— you may end up repeating a year of school. I lost more than a year, but I switched programs as well, which made it harder."

Rowan gasped. "No, really? I'd hate it; I wouldn't get to be with my friends anymore." Tears escaped down her face. She dashed them away with her hand, glad Benjamin couldn't see them. "And they'd feel sorry for me or think it's because I'm dumb."

"Clearly, you're quite smart. But it's difficult in the beginning. Daunting. It takes a while for the brain to grasp it has to learn by hearing rather than seeing." He cleared his throat. "Now. Will you stand up, so I get a sense of how tall you are? I brought three canes because I wasn't sure." He stood up as well.

"I'm a leggy thing, or so Mom says."

"Well, Leggy Thing, we usually fit the first cane to the height of your armpit. As you develop confidence, you'll want a longer one because you'll walk faster."

"I'm pretty confident."

Yes—I was too until I walked into a light pole and smashed my nose. There is a learning curve."

Rowan shivered. "Oh. That."

"Shall we take it slow at first?" he asked.

"Yikes. For sure."

"I've been listening to your voice since you stood, so I have a sense of how tall you are." He picked up one of the canes. "Let's try this size." He held it in front of her. "Reach out; you'll feel it. Then put it next to your body and see if it's about the height of your armpit."

She fiddled for a moment. "This one's too short by an inch."

"Okay, try this one." He repeated the maneuver.

"It seems about right."

He set the others aside. "Okay. Good. Let's go to your front walk. How do you manage here in your home?"

"I walk slow and keep my hands in front of me at different heights. Also, I count paces."

"Sounds good. You're smart to count. I have more tips for home navigation, too. Interested? We could cover it another time."

"Sure. But I have to figure out this cane stuff so we can go look for my dog."

"Your priorities are clear. Okay, want to direct me to the front door?"

She chuckled. "The blind leading the blind. Now I get the expression. Okay, the door is to your left, and it's eleven of my paces. I have no idea how many of your steps it is."

"I counted as I made my way across the room with your mom. For me, it's nine. I'm six feet tall."

Rowan concentrated and, carrying the cane, walked across the entry to the door. She felt around and located the handle. "I'm here. Can you tell where I am by my voice?"

"Sure, keep talking," Benjamin replied, confidently. "I'm always orienting myself—by sounds, like traffic or voices, by breezes, by the pressure of air near walls—there are myriad ways. I even use my sense of smell. You'll learn them all and discover you're more skillful at some than others."

"What does myriad mean? It'll be my new word today."

"It's a fancy way of saying 'many.'"

"Nice. Myriad. How do you spell it?"

"M-y-r-i-a-d."

"Interesting. I wonder what the word root is." Rowan chattered until Benjamin found his way to her. They went out, across the porch, and down the steps to the start of the concrete path.

"Myriad comes from Greek," Benjamin said. "By the way, we call ourselves 'cane travelers.'"

"Cane travelers? Cool."

Carolina followed to watch them work together.

"I'd like to take your hand and show you how to hold the cane correctly. Okay with you?" Benjamin asked.

"Sure."

"Are you right- or left-handed?"

"Left."

"Then you want to use the cane in your right so your left hand is free to push the button to change the light at intersections and other tasks. Face me, please."

Rowan turned toward his voice.

"I'm reaching out for your right hand. Your cane's made of solid fiberglass. There are many different materials and styles you can test out later, but I like this kind. It's light. Flexible." Once he felt her arm, he directed her to move the cane to her side and helped her fit the grip properly in her right hand. "They can break, though. Always keep a spare at home. Now—you want to swing your cane from side to side about the width of your shoulders and as evenly as you can, keeping the tip on the ground. When your left foot steps forward, swing the cane to the right. When your right foot goes forward, tap on the left."

"Geez, I can't remember all that. How come I need to know?"

"The cane is giving clues for your next step and has provided information about your previous one."

She thrust the cane at him. "This is way too hard." Her arms wrapped tight around her body.

"It's only hard at the start, I promise. You'll get this, and quickly. Picture the freedom this will bring! You won't have to hang on to someone's arm all the time. Come on now, I know you have courage. Try walking. It's about forty of my paces to the driveway."

Rowan took the cane back and moved forward slowly. After a handful of steps, she stopped. "This is weird," she said. "I'm scared I'll run into something. Like the light pole you mentioned."

"You're doing fine. This is a good place to practice—I felt the grass on one side of the path and bushes on the other when I walked up to your home, so you'll be able to tell the difference when you veer off-track. Carolina, are there light poles?" Benjamin asked.

"No. Off to the side, I've put some solar-activated lights. They're set back about fifteen inches in the grass, and are eight inches tall."

"They're not likely to trip us up. Rowan, notice your rhythm is uneven, and try to make your taps to each side exactly the same way."

Rowan kept at it, and fifteen minutes later, Carolina could see she was getting the cadence. Knowing her daughter, she expected she'd be out here practicing often. She was so anxious to search for Zephyr.

"Your tapping sounds good," Benjamin said. "This is enough for your first lesson. I can come again tomorrow. If you practice out here a few times, you may have questions. Do you have any so far?"

"How can I know if something sticks out at me up high?"

"Hopefully, you'll develop a sixth sense; some people are born with it. We can test for that later. At least you can practice here without worrying about getting smacked."

"And how would my sense of smell help?"

"You ask good questions. Maybe you pass a bakery every day, and the smell of fresh baked bread lets you know you're on track—or the lack of the scent might mean you've made a wrong turn. Something like that."

"It's neat to be able to walk without holding someone's arm," Rowan said.

"Exactly. It's a relief to get your independence back."

Two nights later, Rowan tossed in bed unable to fall asleep. Again, she pensed, trying to let Zephy know she was okay. The mountain lion image that had burst into her head a few days before still upset her. Had she pushed it away because it scared her too much? Had her dog *really* faced a Zephyr-sized cat? Worry lodged in Rowan's belly like a hard lump, and she yanked the pillow over her head. The cool fabric helped her relax. She whispered to herself, "Focus. Think only about Zephy. Send her a clear snapshot and then wait." She rolled over, squinching the pillow into a more comfortable shape under her head.

Seth had looked up "notice" in the thesaurus for her, came up with "aware" and after a few more tries, "consciousness." She'd heard the word in the past but never added it to her list. Remembering her experience in the hospital, she first emptied her mind and rested in what she thought of as the "big field"—consciousness. She formed a picture of her room, including lying in bed, her dog's place empty beside her. She added all of her longings to be together and then released the image, catapulting it like a man shot from a cannon toward Zeph. She now sent feelings more than pictures because she wasn't able to leave her emotions out of it. She prayed her dog would understand.

A few minutes later, boom! Her dog was right here with her, in spirit.

"Did you get hurt?" Rowan sent the question filled with love and concern, along with a fierce mountain lion image like the one Zeph had sent her. A minute later, she felt her dog's response: a picture of her licking her wounds, and a sense of her limping, accompanied by a blast of fear.

"Oh, Zephy." Rowan wanted to wail but had to keep her wits about her. "I'm coming, soon. Find help! There must be someone who can help. You have to *trust*." She pictured their first night together when Zeph had met her gaze head on, then crawled into her lap, bending her gangly legs to fit. Once settled, the pup had given a little whimper, sighed, and dozed. Now, Rowan felt a bump and knew Zeph had gotten her message.

Zephyr startles awake, heart thumping. It feels like her girl is near her nest, only the mind-picture shows Rowan at home. The force of longing that comes is new. She sends another call for her girl to come. She needs help. Now. The wounds smell bad, and licking isn't helping. One tear she can't even reach. Her leg aches. It hurts to run, and she needs speed to catch food.

Later, Rowan shows their first night snuggling together. Rowan is asking something of her. She senses her girl tells her to find safety, but safety is with Rowan. Puzzled, Zephyr settles her head between her paws and whimpers.

Carolina stood up from her work table and stretched. It had been a long, successful morning of sewing. She walked over to the door jamb and backed up against the hard edge to ease the chronic tight spot under her shoulder blade. Rocking against the wood to soften the persistent knot, Carolina knew that she couldn't postpone the trip to Sisters any longer. She'd found a seven-year-old van. Her mechanic said it was in decent shape, so she bought it with the money Sam had given her. Rowan had done her part—after three days, she moved around with the white cane fairly well; now all she needed was practice. Benjamin, so dear, had given her two canes.

Rowan began the long process of learning braille. Benjamin brought a workbook and taught her the alphabet. Carolina knew her daughter grieved the loss of her sight, so she hadn't nudged her. Now, Rowan's natural curiosity resurfaced. Carolina saw her with the braille book in her lap several times. Also, Rowan had been good about not bugging her to start the search—until this morning. She seemed much more worried about Zephyr. When Carolina queried her, Rowan said, "I had an awful nightmare about a mountain lion. Zeph got hurt."

"It was just a nightmare, sweetie."

"She's injured," Rowan repeated. "I know it." Then, she clammed up and wouldn't talk.

Carolina looked at her, puzzled. Rowan's unique and powerful connection with Zeph seemed to be growing stronger. How could it be, a human and dog communicating through dreams? Carolina shook her head. She'd always assumed her mother's "connections" with other realms were a hoax. And now this. *No way.* They were dreams manifested by Rowan's fears, *right*? This couldn't be possible. Could it?

Rowan huffed and, hands in front of her, cautiously stomped out of the room.

Chapter Twelve

Moss moaned before he was fully awake. His hips and leg were stiff; even his stump complained when he rolled over. It was imperative he return to the ridge this morning to check his caches, but he'd have to take the time to massage liniment into his muscles. Intuition told him the food he'd stashed would be gone. He was sure the critter had been watching him; he knew it in his gut. But he needed to check—just to make sure he wasn't going looney tunes—and then plant fresh treats. He'd talk more, sing, and whistle too—get the dog familiar and comfortable with his sound.

He puttered around the kitchen, mixing kale, pineapple, yogurt, whey powder, and orange juice in his super blender—twenty ounces of vitality drink. He sipped the smoothie as he checked his backpack, filled a bottle with well water, scoured the pantry for power bars, and poured kibble into a container for the stashes. The small dog food bag was getting low; he needed to go to town for a forty-pounder.

He patted the backpack pocket to make sure the snake bite kit was there. At the threshold of the living room, he turned back to stuff in the dog leash and collar. *You never know.* As Moss headed out past his garden, he glanced toward his destination. Daybreak dawned luscious; soft clouds—tinged pink, then a deeper rose—piled behind Bender's Ridge. He soaked in the beauty. When he'd lost his leg, he learned the importance of balancing life's blows with slowing down and appreciating the good when it came along.

He walked slower today; the cool, dry air braced him as he hitched up the trail. Two hikes in two days were more than he'd tackled since he lost his leg—usually, he allowed three days between hikes—but now, there wasn't a choice. The critter was injured. The wound was suppurating, a bad sign. An injured animal wouldn't be successful hunting. The dog was in serious trouble.

As he walked, a different idea came to him. Rather than lay out the kibble the way he had before, he'd make the first pile a few strides from where he planned to rest. Then he'd drop bits along a path and clump some near his resting spot. If he lay down and seemed non-threatening, the creature might come to him—it seemed worth a try. It wasn't like the dog was feral. He was sure this was the one from the wreck they gossiped about in town.

The hopeful plan buoyed him, and the climb seemed to pass quickly. He followed the same pattern as the day before—stopped for a drink at the spring, splashed water on his face, then slowly turned full circle, humming to himself as he noted the state of the caches from the previous day. The containers were knocked over. No nuggets lay near the puddle of water. Maybe his tactics had worked. He poured some into a pile a distance from the spring. Then he dribbled a trail of kibble to where he intended to lie down. He left enough so if his efforts to woo the dog failed, it would get a full day's ration.

First, he sat, then flattened on the ground, happy for the warm morning rays cresting the ridge. Turning his head to one side, he murmured soft sounds but saw nothing remarkable. He swiveled and looked the other direction. Something caught his attention, and he squinted to bring whatever it was into focus. About twenty feet away, under a thick bush and barely visible, a pair of watchful eyes blinked back at him. His heart thudded. The dog had tucked itself so successfully out of sight Moss hadn't seen it when he first viewed the glen. He turned his face back to the sun and acted as if he hadn't noticed. He crooned in the gentlest voice he could muster. "Hey, there. I have goodies. You need help, people-help, to make you better." He let his fingers play with the kibble nearest his side. "You'll like Francie; she's the best veterinarian there is. Her hands are kind; they know how to heal." He heard the dog lick its chops, but it didn't change position.

He stayed for an hour, singing lullabies, humming, and talking. The dog didn't so much as shift its weight. Moss abandoned his plan and pushed to standing. With as little motion as possible, he shouldered his pack and headed downhill. He'd have to try, yet again, tomorrow.

The next morning, he hiked to the ridge repeating his patterns. He noticed he was getting stronger, a nice side benefit. Again, the kibble from the previous day was gone. The dark brown eyes peered from under the same serviceberry bush and followed his slightest move. He saw the stalemate: the dog got what it wanted—nourishment—but didn't budge because it didn't need to. He had seen blood on the ground where the animal stood while it ate; the wounds concerned him.

Zephyr hears the human's footsteps go from noisy to quiet. His scent thins then fades. Feeling safe, she comes out from under the bush, but before eating the kibble, she sits, listens, and watches. After a while, she sees movement far down on the valley floor. Only then, she turns to search out every bite of food. When she's done, she drinks at the spring and limps back to the serviceberry bush where she swipes at the wounds she can reach on her leg. She gives a plaintive whine for her girl and sends pictures of where she is—her hiding place, the water hole, the limping man, her hurt leg.

When Moss returned home, he called Francine. "Moss here. I've got a problem, and need your help."

He could hear the smile in her voice when she responded. "Do you have a sick chicken? What's up?"

When he explained what was going on, she said, "But the dog's eating all the food?"

"Yeah, I think the moment I leave. I've even heard it swallow from salivating. When I come back the next day, nary a kibble left."

"Well then, he's not desperately ill yet, even if he is injured. Try one more day, max two. If your plan doesn't work, you should dart him. I don't think drugging the food is wise. It could take a while for him to go down, and your beastie could cover some distance." There was a pause on the phone. "Then, he would become prey."

"We sure don't want that. If I need the dart gun, I'll come to town to borrow it."

The next day, he followed the same routine and limped home, discouraged. His stump ached, and when he unlegged, he wasn't surprised to find a rub blister. "Damn," he muttered and pulled antibiotic cream and large adhesive pads from the medicine cabinet. "One more day," he said aloud. "And I shouldn't do even that." His prosthetist would not like this, not one bit.

The following morning, Moss snarled as he readied his backpack. Then, noting his frustration, he sat down to change his attitude before heading out. She'd pick up on his bad mood, and it'd scare her off. *She?* Where'd that come from? On the phone, Francine had referred to the dog as male. He thought back. No clue, really, but he had an inner sense. A *girl* dog. He felt better already. He missed having female energy around, and a dog would be much less complicated than a woman.

On a whim, he pocketed a few extra-large dog biscuits. Whistling, he opened the door and hitched onto the porch. He didn't see the great hound until he caught his foot on her and hopped to avoid falling. She squealed and tried to run, stumbled, picked up her front paw and stood, trembling. He heard her moan, and she dropped onto the deck near the stairs. Sore himself, he leaned against the door and hummed his favorite lullaby. After a few minutes, he saw her body ease. Her eyes never left him.

He talked to her. "You're hurting and came for help. Smart girl! You must have been lying smack against the front door." He fished for a biscuit in his pocket, glad he had one on him. "I'm going to bring you a cookie. I'll take it real slow."

When he moved in her direction, the dog struggled to rise, but gave up and lay quivering. As he approached, he made a slow, wide circle around her so he could sit on the steps and ease his leg. Each time he moved, her body stiffened, and he saw the whites of her eyes. Once seated, he held the biscuit out. She lifted her long, elegant nose toward the scent and after a slow sniff, oh so carefully took it from his hand. She munched it quietly. Her dark eyes peered steadily from beneath furry eyebrows. Her nose flared, checking out his scent, taking him in. He admired her facial furnishings—he'd learned about those from the breed book he bought— eyebrow tufts, mustache, and beard. She needed a good brushing.

When she finished and was licking her mustache, he reached out his hand. She leaned as far from him as she could without getting up but suffered his touch as his fingers ran through her rough, gray coat. In places it had actual mats. He kept up a quiet litany. "We'll make you better, I promise—regular meals, too. We're friendly folk; you can trust us."

Hearing his words, the dog pulled back, dipped her chin, and stared at him.

He wondered what he'd said that got her attention but caressed her with his fingertips, working his way up to her head. She leaned into his touch and curled her lips up. For a moment, he mistook her show of teeth as displeasure. Then, delighted, he realized it was a full-on doggy smile.

With his free hand, he reached into his pocket for another biscuit. The dog's ears perked. She gave his palm a lick and took it delicately, keeping her powerful teeth away from his fingers. Her dignity impressed him. Next, still touching her, he slid his pack off and eased it onto the step below. She tensed at the movement, but stayed put, finishing the biscuit and taking time to lick the crumbs that had fallen onto her paws and the porch. He fished inside for the collar and leash and set them between his legs. He probably didn't need them—she had come to him, after all—but decided it was wise to put the collar on. Besides, then it would seem like she belonged to him. He held it in front of her nose as he talked so she could get a good whiff. Before he clipped it around her neck, he needed to get a look at her other side—where the injuries were—so he wouldn't inadvertently hurt her and spoil the rapport they were building.

Moss craned to see. At the sight of her wounds, he took in a fast breath. He'd guessed she'd tangled with a 'coon, but the claws that had flayed open her shoulder had all the marks of mountain lion. She needed to get to Francie. *Today.* Besides the deep shoulder gashes, she had one tear on her neck. Definitely infected. If he was careful, he could avoid putting pressure on it. Latching the leash onto the ring, he threaded the collar under her neck, around, and clicked it shut on the near side. It was then he realized he'd been holding his breath.

Moss coaxed her up, astonished that her muzzle came level with his hip. She was enormous! Realizing he hadn't verified she was female, he leaned down to look. Yep, a girl. With his support, they made their way into his house. She seemed grateful for his assistance. Panting, she sank down on the braided rug. The open wounds would seep onto the wool, but he didn't care. He hooked the leash loop under the foot of the couch. Giving her a reassuring pat, he rose awkwardly and pushed the front door shut until he heard it latch. Safely contained at last. Then he went back and felt her nose. Dry and too hot. Even without a thermometer, he was sure his girl was running a high fever.

He dug out the phone and stretched the cord as he walked back into the living room. He wanted to keep an eye on his dog.

Six rings. Francine picked up. "The Country Vet, what's up?"

"Moss here. I've got her. It's bad. She needs medical attention now. Got a slot?"

"Of course. I'll make time. Think you can load her?"

"I'll use the van. It has low entry at the slider."

"Can you estimate her weight?"

Moss gauged the dog. "I'm guessing a hundred, give or take five."

"My tech called in sick today. You'll have to help me lift her onto the table. We can trank her first. Can you stick around for the procedure? I could use another pair of hands."

He heard the rustle of paper, probably the calendar on the desk.

"Come in around eleven?" she asked. "I'll clear the late morning."

"I can make it. Sure, I'll stay and help. Thanks, Francie. Ciao."

After he hung up, he stood thinking for a moment. Shit. He'd given the critter two extra-large biscuits. He rang her up again and explained.

"Let me take her temperature, assess the wounds. If we can wait, I'll do surgery in the evening."

"I'm pretty sure she's got a high fever."

"I'll most likely operate early, then. It's not the best of all worlds, having food in her stomach—but you won't sue me."

Moss went back to the hound, sat with her, and stroked her back. She nudged his pocket, and he realized another biscuit was still stashed there. "Sorry girl, no more food 'til we patch you up." She bumped his pocket again, more insistent this time, so using the couch arm, he pulled himself to standing and returned the biscuit to the box in the utility room. He didn't want to tease her. Checking his watch, he saw he had another half hour to acclimate her before taking her into town.

By the time they needed to leave, she had stopped panting and dropped her head into his lap. He unhooked the leash from under the couch leg and encouraged her to get up. The dog was seriously lame and getting worse; she had surrendered to help just in time. He supported her until she found her balance and then slowly walked her out to his vehicle.

As they approached the van, she reared back and almost jerked the leash out of his hand. But even more disturbing was the sound she made—a low, upset, moany whine. Moss shivered with recognition. *Oh my God, poor thing.* The dog had post-traumatic stress; there was no way he could load her alone. A wrestling match would only make the situation worse, and she'd win anyway. He'd once seen Francie and two male techs try to subdue a nine-pound cat and barely succeed. Between claws, teeth, and sheer will, that day he'd learned raw animal power must never be underestimated.

He circled away from the van and quietly encouraged her back toward the house. She calmed and hobbled obediently alongside. Clearly, someone had trained her—even in acute pain, she struggled to meet his requests. She stumbled on the steps up to the deck, so he looped an arm under her belly.

Once inside, he redialed Francine. "There's a complication," he said. "We're quite the pair. This dog's got PTSD, too; hers is around vehicles, probably because of the wreck she was in. No way on God's earth I can get her in the van myself. Can you drive out with a cage and tranquilizers?"

"I'll bring the largest portable crate I have. See you soon."

He went back to hang with his dog. She licked his hand and tears flooded his eyes.

Chapter Thirteen

Moss heard a car pull in the drive but didn't recognize the engine's sound. He checked his watch—thirty-five minutes. It could only be Francie, but where was her truck? He walked to the front window and saw a brown van park near the house. Ah, she'd brought her brother's rig. Dust still settled as she walked up the steps to the deck.

"Thanks for coming," he said, and welcomed her with a hug.

"I brought John's wheels. It'd be too hard to wrestle a caged animal this size into the bed of my truck. She'd be a nervous wreck back there anyway. With vehicle PTSD, she'll need constant human companionship."

Moss nodded, grateful. He opened the screen door. "Come on in. But please—move slow."

She cuffed him on the arm. "I'm a vet. I know important things like that." She smiled. "You're feeling protective, aren't you?"

He grinned. "You bet." He opened the door, and Francine, murmuring soft words, slipped into the living room.

"Wow," she whispered to the hound. "You're gorgeous. Using those feminine wiles, eh? You've already got a boyfriend." Francine made her way to where the giant dog lay on the rug. The dog panted and carefully watched her, eyes clouded with doubt.

Francine knelt and let the dog sniff her hand and then stroked under her chin. Moss could see her taking in information with each touch. The hound lay on her good side, exposing the wounds.

"She tangled with a cougar, no doubt about it," Francine said. "It's amazing she survived. She probably got away because her strides are so huge and, with the adrenalin rush, she didn't feel the slashes until later." Moving slowly, careful not to startle the dog, she lifted a lip to check the color of her gums. "She's pale and, you're right, really hot." She looked up at Moss. "Shove my bag over here, will you? Before I explore more, I'm going to give her light sedation. I don't want to bring in the crate until she's dozy."

Francine opened her case and, squinting to estimate weight, filled a syringe. She rubbed alcohol on the hound's good front leg and slid the needle into a vein. "This will just zone her out, not actually anesthetize her." A minute later, the dog closed her eyes and set her head down.

Francine took her temperature. "You're right, almost 105. No wonder." Then she palpated the long tears on the dog's shoulder and leg. "I'm checking to see if I'll be able to pull this skin together. The wounds aren't as fresh as we hope when we're looking to close. Jeez, what an infected mess. These lacerations need major cleaning, then trimming up." She sat back on her heels and rubbed her low back. "Let's give her five or ten minutes and then load her. With drugs on board, I think she'll tolerate it."

Moss gathered what he needed to take to town for an overnight stay and stuffed his backpack. Then he fetched the cage from the van and rolled it into the room. Francine released a lever and lowered it to the ground. It was lined with a thick blue-plaid pillow covered by multiple layers of washable padding and sported doors at both ends. "This is clever, Francie," he said. "Did you invent the crate?"

"A vet friend did. It's hydraulic. Cool, huh?"

"Very."

They shifted the hound onto an extra-long towel. Using it like a sling, they positioned her butt close to one door and threaded the cloth through that door and out the other. Moss went to the far side and grabbed the other end of the towel. They lifted her, now dozing, a few inches and slid her in.

Moss worked his hound's long tail into the cage and tucked it between her legs. He moved her head into a more comfortable position, gave her a gentle pat, then closed both doors. Francine maneuvered the lever again. The wheels lowered and lifted the crate a few inches off the ground. Moss took the handle, like on a child's wagon, and pulled the drowsy dog through the front door, around the side of the deck toward the ramp—left over from his wheelchair days—and out to the van.

Francine stood by the car's slider and opened the crate door. "Let me check to see if she's sedated enough. I don't want to panic her; she doesn't have the reserves right now." She pinched a little skin on the hound's lower leg and gave a thumbs up. "She barely opened her eyes; she's fine. Bring the rig as close as you can."

They wrestled the cage into the van, and Francine secured it to the floor with thick straps. She pulled the door quietly shut and leaned into it until it latched.

"I'll follow you?" Moss asked.

"Yes—I'm going to keep her in the clinic for a couple of days. She'll need close monitoring. The fever worries me, Moss. I need to clean these wounds, get them closed, and put her on stiff antibiotics." She started the engine. "When you see a cat bite, think snake bite. They infect easily. Thank heavens you caught her. You saved her life."

"I didn't catch her. Remember I hiked to the ridge to coax her with kibble? Last night, she must have tracked me home. I tripped over her this morning. I think she was lying snug against the front door."

"Well, I'll be. After what she's been through, to come off the ridge and surrender to a stranger? Straight-up courage. Okay then, let's get going. I'll see you in town."

In Sisters, both vehicles pulled to a stop in front of the clinic. While Francine went to unlock the door, Moss removed the security straps and worked the crate from side to side to get it close to the slider. They hefted crate and hound onto the ground and rolled them into surgery. Opening both cage doors, they repeated the same method they used at the ranch and eased her out. Francine dropped her hydraulic table as low as it would go. Moss helped her lift the dog, and the vet raised the table to a comfortable working height. "Watch her for a moment—keep your hand on her," she said. She came back with a gadget Moss didn't recognize.

"This is a microchip scanner. The first rule here is to find the owners."

His heart turned to stone. "Aw, jeez, Francie, no. Please! You know how I feel about this dog. I worked hard to save her; she's my dog now."

"I'm sorry, Moss. This is the ethical thing to do."

Feeling powerless and frustrated, he turned away. He knew she was right. *But damn.*

She turned the scanner on and ran it slowly over the hound's sedated body. "The chip is actually a tiny transponder. Chips return a unique number, and then we call the company. Perhaps in the future, they'll carry important medical information, like the animal's allergies."

Each pass that found no chip lifted his spirits. But when Francine ran the scanner across the side of the dog's neck down near her shoulder, she got a hit. Moss crumpled inside.

"The chip would have been injected here." She lifted loose scruff on the hound's neck. "But hers migrated downward. It happens." She copied the number. "Stay with her again; she could come to, and we don't want her falling off the table. I need to phone the company." She touched his hand as she passed by. "A dog like this—you must have known she's special to someone."

As Moss heard her make the call, the blues surrounded him like a shroud, and his chest went thick with grief.

When she returned, she handed Moss a piece of paper. "She comes from Eugene. Her owner is Carolina Graham; here's the phone number. I got the dog's name, too—Zephyr. Grand name for a running hound." When her eyes met his, she said, "Oh, my God, this is hitting you hard."

He nodded but couldn't speak. Instead, he whispered the hound's name, "Zephyr." It felt strange in his mouth, but it was a solid fit. He stroked the dog that was no longer his. The sedation was wearing off. The dog lifted her head to nuzzle his fingers then dropped back on the table. Tears filled his eyes yet again. "I can't do it, Francie. I can't call the owner. Zephyr's saved me. Because of her, something frozen since Afghanistan has softened. I *need* her."

Francine put her hands on her hips. "Moss, this is non-negotiable." Her voice had an edge. "Anyway, we can deal with it later. I don't want to wait on surgery until tonight, not with this fever. Let's make her better now." She crossed her arms in front of her chest. "I'll give you five days to contact the owner, and really, I shouldn't be delaying at all. If you don't call by then, I'll drive out to your place and stand over you until you do. In any case, she's yours for a while. She can't travel until I say so."

Her words didn't ease the painful lump under his breastbone.

Francine set up the anesthesia equipment and retrieved a sterile pack from the supply room. After further sedation, she inserted the endotracheal tube and hooked up anesthesia. She shaved a spot on the dog's front lower leg, inserted an intravenous catheter, hung a bag of saline solution and plugged it in. Then she adjusted the flow. "I'll leave this port in for a day or so after surgery," she said. "It'll make it painless to give her medication. She's been through enough."

When Francine needed Moss's help, she talked him through every step. She set about shaving, then meticulously cleaning the wounds. She used foam soap, scrubbing vigorously. It made Moss cringe; a few times he had to turn away. It brought back raw memories of his hospital stay in Germany after he lost his leg. *Thank God Zephyr can't feel it.* Then Francie trimmed up the skin margins. The long gashes were ready for stitching—first the deeper layers of muscle, then skin.

"At home, you'll need to keep her quiet. Tight-leash quiet."

Moss nodded. He knew she was trying to divert his attention by keeping up a stream of conversation. Sometimes it seemed like Francine read his mind. He guessed that came with knowing someone your whole life. A flush of gratefulness shot through him, and he realized how much he needed her friendship.

After she closed the wounds, she pressed her fists into the small of her back and said, "Those were the major lacerations. Now, I'll search for other, smaller spots." Francine examined Zephyr's body, parting her wiry coat to look for anything she'd missed. Moss pulled the fur back from the ugly tear on the dog's neck, and she went through the same routine of shaving, cleaning, trimming, and suturing. At the end, she gave Zephyr a hefty injection of antibiotics. "Okay, let's get her off the table and onto a towel." They slowly lowered her to the floor.

She reached into a cabinet and pulled out a T-shirt. When she unfolded it, Moss saw it was a well-worn black Trail Blazers' tee with "Rip City" in red and white lettering.

"What's the shirt for?"

"You know those dreadful cone collars used to prevent pets from licking wounds and tearing out sutures? For a dog this size, the cone is humongous—it wouldn't fit through a door. A T-shirt's sufficient to get most giant breeds to leave their incisions alone. Let me show you how I do it." She threaded Zephyr's front legs out the arm holes, then gently pushed her head through the neck opening. Together they lifted her enough to pull the knit shirt down her torso. Francine made a big knot in the tee's hem right on the hound's back to tighten it around her belly tuck so it wouldn't drift forward.

"There. I bet it's enough to keep her from fussing with the surgical areas. I can loosen the knot when I need to look at her shoulder incisions. She can't reach the one on her neck." She stepped back to look at the sleeping Zephyr. "Cute, eh?"

"Stylish. Not sure about cute—she's so darned elegant."

"Elegant shmelegant," the vet said. "She looks silly! Now, we can haul her into the first run in the back. If you want, stay with her until she wakes up. I'll get you some pillows. And don't worry, I'll be with her all night."

"The chickens can miss one meal. I'll spend the night as well," Moss said. "We'll take turns." They lugged Zephyr to the recovery cage. He held onto the chain-link pen and supported himself as he lowered to sitting, adjusting his leg when he reached the floor. "You were right, Francie. Having a dog to care about is good medicine for me."

Zephyr's nose tells her she's at a vet's—she scents her kind, cats, and other animals she doesn't recognize. There's a pungent tinge to the air. She's lying on soft pillows. Kibble Man's hand is on her, which feels comforting. She smells the doctor, too—close by—and blinks her eyes open. The front part of her body aches, but differently than before. She's in a cage—it reminds her of the shelter where Rowan found her. When she tries to lift her head, it feels heavy, and medicine taste sours her mouth. She wants to pense her girl, but can't focus.

Kibble Man strokes her; she sighs and relaxes. She hears him hum. His tone is gentle like her girl's. Even though her shoulder throbs, she shifts so she can set her muzzle on his ankle.

"Zephyr," he says.

Startled, she stares at him. He has never said her name before. His rumbly sound tells her he is pleased with her response.

There's a covering on her body like humans wear. Underneath, her leg feels tight and stiff; she jerks to loosen it up. The doctor comes over and kneels by her.

"Leave it," she murmurs, her tone quiet and firm.

Zephyr knows those words.

Something is taped to her front leg. The vet pulls out a syringe, and Zephyr anticipates a pinch, but the woman pokes the thing instead of her. Her leg goes cool. She's suddenly sleepy and can't hold her eyes open. She rests her head on Kibble Man's leg again and drifts.

Chapter Fourteen

O n their way to search for Zephyr, Carolina turned onto Hwy 242 toward McKenzie Pass. They passed the lava beds at the crest, and she tensed as they headed down the other side of the mountain. "We're about fifteen miles from the accident site," she said to Rowan. "I'd like to stop there. Would that be okay with you?"

Rowan nodded. "For a little while. We have to start searching for Zeph. Will you recognize the spot? How'll you know?"

How could I not know? "It was right at the 88-mile marker," Carolina said. "I noticed it when I waited for the firemen to cut you out." She did not mention how close the sign had come to shattering the window and impaling her daughter. "I want to stand on the ground and acknowledge Stormy." Her voice caught. "I brought a special remembrance rock to leave there."

Twenty minutes later, she spotted the location. Scrape marks scarred the pavement where the van had slid on its roof. Sound memory flooded back and jolted her. "Here," she said and described the area to Rowan as she pulled well off the road. She left her emergency blinkers on. "Do you want to get out?"

"For sure. This is where Zeph took off," Rowan whispered. "Ground Zero."

"The highway folks cleaned up the deer and took away Stormy, too," Carolina said, her voice thick. She shook as she went around the van to help her daughter out.

Rowan threw her arms around her and, for the first time on this trip, cried hard. "I'm so sorry, Mommo, sorry for all of us." Her words were barely audible, and she snuffled. "Nothing is the same."

Carolina struggled not to weep. No matter what anybody said to ease her mind, she felt responsible for the accident. She rubbed her daughter's back and whispered in her ear. "But we survived and have each other. I'm so grateful."

After a minute, Rowan quieted. Carolina opened the hatch and twisted the large river rock back and forth until she got it to the back edge. "I need your help. If you can grab the rock with me, I'll talk us across the ground. It's flat." She guided Rowan's hands onto it, and together they lifted and slowly carried it.

"Too fast, Mommo. I can't see, and don't have my cane to feel the rough spots."

"Right—I'm sorry." As she slowed her steps, guilt threaded through Carolina, but frustration, too. Everything took so long nowadays. She wasn't used to it yet. "We're almost there. Maybe five more steps."

"Let's set it here," she said. "I can roll it under the bushes later. Will you sit with me for a moment?"

Rowan nodded.

They knelt on the ground and put their hands on the rock. "Sweet Stormy, friend for fourteen years, thank you for your companionship," Carolina whispered. "Thanks for loving Rowan, too and being so patient with her when she was a pesky two-year-old and followed you everywhere. I'll see you at the Rainbow Bridge."

Although Rowan gave a little smile, tears leaked down her cheeks again. Carolina rolled the rock into its final resting spot. When they stood, she put her arm around her daughter's waist. "Do you want to whistle and call for Zephyr?"

"She's not near here anymore. We have to go downhill, closer to Sisters, and to the right—the South, I think."

"How do you know?"

"I feel her. It's like I'm a compass, and she's true North. I don't know how to explain it any better."

She gazed at her daughter, amazed at how different they were. Rowan, so invested in "knowing" certain things, once again triggered

Carolina. She didn't like the similarities between her mother and Rowan. This "supposed talent" gave her a quick shot of anxiety. Yet Rowan seemed so certain.

Arm in arm, they walked back to the van. "We'll stop at the tow place next," Carolina said.

"I've gotta have Wubby." Rowan felt her way into the car and fastened her seatbelt. "And the geodesic ball."

"I'd like the dog beds, too. Bowls. All of it." Carolina said. "We'll hope for the best."

When they arrived, Mike, of Mike's Towing, was slouched in a creaky office chair, feet on the desk. He sported a 1950s flattop and a beer belly his T-shirt couldn't hide.

"Yeah," he said after Carolina explained who they were. "Here, in the back corner. The Missus washed the covers. Potato salad spilled all over them and stank pretty bad."

There lay the two C-beds, one red plaid, and one green with black paw prints. The dog dishes. The leashes. Carolina's throat constricted. She guided Rowan to sit on the floor.

Her daughter felt around and tenderly fingered each item. "But where are the toys?" she asked, her voice tight. "Wubby the octopus, and the geodesic ball?"

"My pup must've carried 'em off," Mike muttered.

"You *have* to find them. We're going to search for my dog now; it's why we're here."

Mike looked at the floor. "I figured since I stored your stuff for you, you'd cut me a break," he said. "You know, kind of like rent."

Rowan swung in his direction. "You took things for yourself without even *checking* with us?"

Carolina added, "I'll pay you some storage, but we need those toys back."

He shuffled, still looking down. "My dog loves that octopus, and the wife loves the dog."

"*My* dog loves the octopus—and it's *hers*!" Rowan barked, close to tears now. "Go buy your own! You're stealing!"

Carolina quieted Rowan with a touch that signaled "enough."

"All right, already," Mike said. "Jeez, it's just a dog toy. It'll take me fifteen minutes round trip. Wait here."

"I'm not moving," Rowan said. "And remember the red ball, too."

"I'll never hear the end of this from the Missus." Mike walked out, shaking his head.

"That man," whispered Rowan, "shouldn't run a business if he steals."

The Sisters Motor Lodge comprised four one-story buildings, each with a few rooms in it—sixteen total. Mary, the owner, welcomed them. She sported spiky-blonde hair and a friendly smile. As she handed the key to Carolina, she pointed to the building that housed room No. 9. "We call it 'Victoria,'" she said. "It's two rooms. We have a good selection of DVDs—free to watch. I bet your daughter would love a movie—we've got some great kids' flicks."

"It won't work for us; Rowan's blind. But thanks," Carolina said. "She'll listen to audio books and I'll read."

Mary clapped her hand over her mouth. "I'm so sorry," she said.

"You were just being generous. There's no way you could have known."

Carolina fussed with the key. Finally, the lock clicked, and they walked in.

"The place has a different smell," Rowan said.

"Probably cleaning products or dryer sheets to soften the bed linens. It's a fresh, clean room."

"It doesn't smell like home."

"You're right, but these are nice accommodations." She set down their suitcases. "Oh, look—one of those plug-in air fresheners. That's probably what you smell, and it's got to go." Carolina tugged it out of the socket and put it in the desk drawer. She bounced on the bed—firm, a real blessing. "Want to walk to Martolli's Pizza? It's less than a quarter mile from here. Three or four blocks."

"Okay, but this time, I just want to take your elbow. No cane. Using it is tiring." Rowan felt around for the bed and set down the dog toys.

Later, after they ordered a split pizza, half "Rip City" and half "Porky Pine," Carolina said, "So for the search tomorrow, I guess we'll just—"

Rowan broke in. "Let's go that way!" and pointed diagonally across the room.

When the skinny, boyish-hipped waitress returned, Carolina glanced at her name tag and asked, "Beverly, where can I buy a map of the area?"

"Paulina Springs Books'll have one for sure. They open tomorrow at 9:30."

"Do you know what direction this is?" Carolina indicated where Rowan had pointed.

Beverly planted her hands on her hips and frowned as she considered. "South or Southwest, I'm pretty sure. I'll check with Big Bob in the kitchen. He has a sense of direction better'n a dog headed for home."

Carolina chuckled. "Thanks. We'd appreciate it. Any bulletin boards in town where people leave notes? We're actually looking for a lost dog."

"There's a board in the post office lobby."

The next morning, after checking the post office bulletin board— only one notice about a found cat—they headed for the bookstore. The day was already heating up. "Thank God for the van's air conditioning. It's going to be a roaster," Carolina said.

Armed with a detailed map, they sat in the car while she studied the roads out of town toward the southwest—Big Bob had confirmed Rowan's direction. "We have to take 242—the same road we came in on—west for a mile or two and turn left on Pole Creek Road. Do you want to stop every mile or so and call?"

"Yeah, but not close to town. Let's wait until we get into real country. Zephy would be scared of busy streets and better darn well not go near them, either."

"We should pick up some sandwiches and juice first."

Carolina surrendered to Rowan's need to choose the direction they took at each new intersection. She held no hope of finding Zephyr, but they had to try.

They wandered back roads all day, but no luck. Grumpy, sniping at each other, and exhausted, they drove back to the motel for the night.

Day two went the same way.

After a third tiring day of searching and calling, the back road dwindled to a dead end. Carolina pulled the car over.

"Mommo, why are you stopping here? I wanted to make a right turn back there, off of Pole Creek. You said there was a numbered dirt road."

"Sweetheart, this is close to the end of the line, and I'm beat."

Rowan pounded her fist into the seat. "I don't want to stop yet! We're super close. She's near! I can *feel* her."

"We'll come back first thing in the morning when it's cool. Besides, your voice is almost gone."

"Mommo!" Her daughter clenched her fists and turned away. "You don't believe me," she snarled. "You never have. It's why I don't share with you. And *I know* I'm right. You'll see. Then what will you have to say to me?"

Carolina huffed a sigh. Row was pissed, and right on one count—her mom didn't believe woo-woo stuff.

In stony silence, they headed back early to the Motor Lodge.

Once in their room, and within cell range, Carolina checked her phone. Her heart knocked when she noticed a voice mail. She didn't recognize the number, but it was the 541 area code, same as Eugene. She prayed it wasn't a bill collector. She got them often these days.

Not wanting to worry her daughter, she said, "Row, I'll be right back. I'm going to find ice so we can have cold sodas." She grabbed ice bucket, purse and phone, and walked to the alcove that housed the vending machine and ice maker. Leaning against the wall, Carolina listened to the message:

"Lose your dog? Call me. Name's Moss."

What? *Really*? Could it possibly be Zephyr? She scrambled for a scrap of paper and took down the number. *Hmmm, what a terse message.* She was already annoyed by the guy's snippy attitude. What was it about him? She sensed something—but wasn't sure—his tone? The way each word snapped? She sure hoped he was friendlier than he sounded. Maybe she was overly tired from the search, guiding Rowan, and having to attend to every detail. Fingers shaking, she punched in the number.

"Mr. Moss?"

"Carol?" A man's resonant voice.

All her life, people had mistakenly called her Carol. "No, it's Carolina," she retorted. She hated when people were careless with her name.

"Just Moss, no mister. Have you lost a dog?"

"Yes! Oh my God! Have you found her?" Unsteadily, she slid down to sit on the floor.

"Describe her," he said.

"Is she with you?"

"Tell me what she looks like. I have a right to make sure she's your dog."

"Let's see. She's really tall and skinny, with a wiry, gray coat. Her hair hangs over her eyes. What else do you want to know?"

"Her name."

"Zephyr. Her name is Zephyr. Do you actually have her *with* you?"

"It's your girl. She needed surgery, and I've been nursing her."

"We need to come, right away. My daughter's been frantic."

Pause.

"Daughter?" His voice stiffened. "How old?"

"It's *her* dog. Rowan's eleven."

"Nope." Lengthy silence. "You can't bring a child here." His tone was implacable. And there was something else, something she couldn't quite place.

"What do you mean, I can't bring my child?" Carolina's voice rose. "Are you a pervert or something?"

"No! Jeez."

Now he was clearly irritated. Immediately, she regretted the uncensored words that spilled out of her mouth. "I'm sorry. That was uncalled for. But what *is* it then? Look—my daughter's blind from a car accident last month. She goes where I go; I can't leave her alone. She's desperate to be reconnected with Zephyr."

A longer pause. "I'm not set up for kids."

Carolina sensed the man's unspoken thought—especially not a blind one. She closed her eyes and shook her head. Nothing about this would be easy. The silence—like a black hole sucking energy—went on so long she wondered if the call had failed. She squinted at the phone to see if the seconds were still ticking.

A throat-clearing growl. "Well. I guess I could meet her. Then we'll see."

Seething, Carolina said, "You bet we will. What's your address?"

"I don't have one—not one you could find. You'll have to meet me in Sisters and follow me back. The microchip said you live in Eugene—take you two-and-a-half, three hours? Want to come in the morning?"

"What do you mean, you don't have an address?"

"Carolina," he emphasized the correct pronunciation of her name. "I live in the boonies on a large piece of property. There's no street address. I have a PO box in town."

"I'm supposed to follow you, with my blind eleven-year-old, way out in the country? You could be—"

An impatient sigh. "I know, a pervert. Good God, I'm harmless. You watch too many thrillers. When you come tomorrow, stop at the library—Gladys, the librarian there, has known me since I was born. I keep to myself, that's all."

"But we're not in Eugene. We're in *Sisters*. We've been searching for Zephyr for three days now. Today, we were way out Pole Creek. Do you know the road?"

"Pole Creek? Christ Almighty, that's really … how'd you get so close?"

"Close to what?" *I'll have to ask him not to swear around Rowan. For sure he'll appreciate that.*

"To my property. Are you psychic or something?"

Now, Carolina fell quiet. *Really? We were that near his home? Close to Zeph?*

She wasn't going to try to explain; she didn't have the faintest idea how. Now she'd have to apologize to Rowan. "Luck, I guess. My daughter told me which way to turn. Can't you bring Zephyr to us?"

The slightest hesitation. "She can't climb into cars yet."

"Well, 4:45 p.m. then. You'll find us at the library talking with Gladys. How long will it take you to get to town?"

He chuckled. "I guess I deserve being checked up on. I've got a couple of chores I need to do. I'll be there in forty minutes or so. Neither of us can be late; the library closes at 5 p.m."

"Moss, please don't swear around my daughter."

"I'm going now." The phone went dead.

Shaking her head, Carolina filled the bucket with ice and bought two drinks. *That guy is strange.*

When Carolina walked into the room, Rowan was asleep on the pink, flowered bedspread, Wubby wrapped in her arms. Grubby Wubby, she thought with affection. She sat on the bed next to her daughter and stroked her back. "Hey, Punkin, we have a lead. We need to go over to the library in a little bit." Rowan came to and rubbed her eyes with her fists. "Lead? What's a lead?"

Carolina put her arm around her. "A clue. A man named Moss left a message on my cell. Says he has Zephyr. He's been caring for her."

"*What?*" Rowan bolted up, placed Wubby on the bed, slid to her knees, and felt around the floor for her shoes. "Let's go!"

"Whoa! He won't be here for forty minutes. You can finish your snack and soda."

Chapter Fifteen

After asking directions from Mary, Carolina helped her daughter into the car and stashed the white cane before climbing in front. Rowan held Wubby against her heart. A few minutes later, they pulled in front of a plain building—both shutters and door painted slate blue. She glanced at her watch—plenty of time to grill this Gladys person.

Rowan insisted on practicing with her cane from car to library, so Carolina described the surroundings as they made their way. "The building's beige, and much smaller than our Eugene library. Watch out for the base of this light post. Can you feel it with your cane?"

Carolina pushed open the door, releasing the familiar musty paper scent all libraries have. Only one person, a plump woman with gray hair pulled into a bun, was at the desk. With Rowan at her elbow, Carolina headed toward her.

"Excuse me?" Carolina said.

Gladys held up a finger and pointed to her headset.

Carolina mouthed, "I'm sorry!"

Rowan leaned on the counter and propped her cane underneath it.

Gladys hung up and turned toward them. "How can I help you?" The woman's voice was as low as a chain-smoker's.

"Hi, I'm Carolina, and this is Rowan."

They shared a smile.

"Do you know a man named Moss?"

"Why do you ask?" Gladys focused on Rowan. "Hello there. The children's section is in the corner if you want to browse." She pointed toward the back right of the library.

Rowan's face fell. "I can only use audio books right now. I lost my vision."

"Oh my, I *am* sorry. My, my. We have tapes and CDs. If you're interested, I'd be happy to read the titles to you."

Rowan shook her head. "I haunt our library at home. I have a bunch in the car. Thanks, though."

Gladys turned back to Carolina. Her face was softer. "Again, why are you asking?"

"Moss gave you as a character reference. Apparently, he found my daughter's dog and wants to meet us here and lead us out to his place. Naturally, I'm wary. He seems strange. Bitter, maybe."

Rowan tugged on her sleeve and asked in a whisper, "When will he come? Soon?"

"I've known Moss Westbury since he was born; he's a good man," Gladys said. "I'm friends with the whole family. They're upstanding people. Done a lot of good for this town."

"Westbury?" Carolina thought for a moment. "Why does that sound familiar?"

"They're the owners of Westbury Financial."

"Good God," Carolina mumbled.

Gladys nodded. "Ashton is his father."

Carolina was stunned. The family owned one of the largest investment companies in the country.

Gladys hesitated as though unsure how much she should say. She added, "Moss holds his privacy close. He's a veteran. We hardly see him in town, although he does come here—he's highly educated and a big reader. And—"

They heard a door squeak, and all three swiveled toward the entrance.

"Just in time. Here he comes now." Gladys sounded relieved. "He can speak for himself."

Carolina gawked at the man who walked in. Moss looked about thirty-five or forty, over six feet, and had those craggy, tanned good looks of countrymen who've been outdoors their whole lives. Blue jeans and a black T-shirt. Slim, but muscled. He had curly black hair and nice smile lines, but deep frown crevices too. He limped and seemed uncomfortable in his body.

"Hey, Gladdy," he said. "Has she been grilling you?"

"Yes, sir, she has. As she rightly should," she said with a smile. She came from behind the desk to greet him. "Are you open to a hug today?"

"Okay," he said, and bent down and gave her a warm squeeze. "But I need to greet these folks." He shifted his weight. "You must be Carolina." His lapis eyes lingered on her longer than necessary.

Had he been staring at her mouth? Uncomfortable, she turned to her daughter. "Yes, and this is Rowan. Zephyr is her dog."

She felt Moss contract. It seemed as if he had to gather himself before he could turn and greet her child. *What is it with this man?*

Rowan stuck her hand out. "Hi. What happened to Zephy? Are you sure it's her? Is she okay? Where's she hurt?"

Moss hesitated then squared his shoulders and looked directly at Rowan. He chewed his lip but shook her hand.

Carolina could see how hard it was for him to greet her.

"You have lots of questions," he said. "Your dog will heal up, but she got injured pretty bad. She tangled with a large critter, something with huge claws. It only takes once for a dog to learn; she won't do it again."

"Yeah," Rowan whispered. "A mountain lion."

"How'd you know?" Moss peered down at the girl, seeming more curious now.

"I just know, that's all. I don't think you'd understand."

As he pursed his lips and nodded, he put more weight on his right leg and rested a hand on the counter. "Fair enough. I guess because Zephyr's so tall, she figured she could take the cat and have herself a big, juicy meal. But he ripped her shoulder wide open. She has tears in other places, too. Shaved patches and sutures here and there."

Carolina gasped. Rowan tensed against her, tears flooding her eyes. Carolina turned to Moss and mouthed, "Tone it down!"

Looking from Carolina to Rowan, he hurried on. "The vet stitched her up, a beautiful job. She has to stay real quiet for at least three more days. Doctor's orders. Her wounds should heal completely within a month. Oh, and yes, I'm sure it's your Zephyr. My vet scanned her microchip."

"Let's go!" Rowan squealed. "I gotta see her now!"

Carolina raised her eyebrows and silently queried Moss.

He stood still a moment. Then he grimaced, looked at the ground, and shook his head.

"Rowan, please stay with Gladys." Her voice quivered. "Moss, we need to talk outside." As Carolina marched for the front door, she tried to relax her fisted hands and clenched jaw. *What in Lord's name do I have to say to make him understand?* She threw open the door and sat on the front portico without looking back. She heard the hinges squeak. He eased down next to her. They were quiet for a couple of minutes.

"You can't understand." His voice shook. "This has nothing to do with you."

Carolina whirled on him. "Please, hear me out. I have no idea why my daughter upsets you so, but it's clear the very idea of her does. I'm sorry because she's just terrific." Carolina paused and grabbed a breath. "You found and cared for our dog. We're profoundly grateful. Now, I'm a practical, down-to-earth woman. Do you know the expression, 'The only way out is through?' From my vantage point, it looks like you need to surrender to whatever issue you have." She thought for a moment. "This is my precious daughter I'm talking about and her beloved, severely injured dog. Zephyr pulled Rowan out of a devastating depression last year, before the car accident that blinded her. Gladys says you're a good man. I can't believe you intend to keep them apart any longer."

Moss stared at the ground, his jaw muscles bunched. When he looked up, there were tears in his eyes. "You're right. In fact, I wrote those same words, 'the only way out is through,' in my journal a couple of days ago." He fell quiet.

Startled, Carolina felt beats of time passing but didn't let him off the hook by saying anything. She let the silence hang. *This dude is introspective.*

He sighed. "If you must, you can follow me out to my ranch. No promises, but I'll do my best."

Carolina gave a curt nod and stood up. "Thank you." She walked back in to collect Rowan. "Come on, sweetie, we're tailing Moss to his place."

Gladys flashed a kind smile and a silent thumbs up.

In the car, Rowan built scenarios about how the reunion with Zephyr might go. "We have to move slowly, Mommo. You know how she loves to joy leap when she's excited. But we can't let her, because of the stitches. That guy should go in first so he can leash her."

Carolina kept her attention on the road but patted Rowan's leg. "You need to remember Zeph's been through a scary time. We don't know how she'll react. I wouldn't have expectations about how this might unfold, okay? You don't want to be disappointed."

"Ooooh. Right." Rowan fell quiet.

Carolina concentrated on following Moss's gunmetal gray Toyota 4Runner. They headed in the exact direction they'd gone this morning.

"Like everything has changed for me, too, being blind and all. Big time." Rowan's hand gripped her arm. "Do you think Zephy won't like me anymore, 'cause I can't play with her like I used to?"

"Oh, sweetheart, she adores you! It won't matter to her whether you can see or not. Keep in mind, though, she's been through an ordeal. Consider how you might want to approach her. Or, even better, how she ought to be approached."

Rowan thought for a while. "I guess, when we get to his house, I'd like to go inside and sit on the floor and be quiet. Make myself small."

"Perfect. And then what?"

Another period of quiet contemplation. "I need to let Zephy come to me; I'll talk so she can hear my voice."

"Great idea. Maybe ask Moss if he has a biscuit?"

"Right. Mommo, is he afraid of kids? Or does he hate me 'cause I'm blind? He seems kind of weird; I could feel it."

"I sensed it too. I don't know what his problem is. But the librarian, Gladys, gave us a clue. He's a veteran—he's been to war. That might make him behave differently. When I sat with him outside on the steps, I saw a different side. Vulnerable. Tender, even. I bet he's been kind to Zephyr."

Moss turned onto a dirt road, and Carolina followed. Dust coated the windshield. He pulled farther ahead. She shut the windows and set the car to internal air only.

"Rowan, this is Pole Creek, where we were earlier today. Moss lives off this road." Rowan had gotten them so close. Could she *really* sense her dog like she said, or was this blind luck? Blind luck—good God, where did *that* expression come from?

"Ha! I got us almost there. Told you so."

"Yes, and I owe you an apology. I don't know how you did it, but that doesn't matter."

"Maybe next time, you'll believe me. Life isn't 'the world according to Mommo.' Sometimes you're right, but other times I know stuff you don't."

Carolina swallowed hard. "I suppose that's true."

They made a right turn and rattled their way along the narrowing road, the exact road Rowan had wanted to follow.

"Are we ever going to get to his house?" Rowan asked.

"Eventually. Moss said he lives in the deep country."

About a half-mile farther, they made an abrupt left turn—the opening was hidden between bushes, she never would have found it—and followed the SUV for another half mile on a single-lane, rough dirt road. After a curve, Moss pulled around the circle in front of an elegant log home with an expansive front porch, nasturtiums in bloom along the edge. Carolina described the scene to Rowan as she parked alongside his vehicle.

Zephyr lifts her head and swings—like a compass needle—toward the road. She feels Rowan coming close again, and Kibble Man with gentle hands. Earlier today, she waited patiently, knowing her girl was near. But then the sensation faded away.

After a lonely stretch of endless space and no people, she is caged up like when she was a pup at the shelter. She whines at the strangeness. She pushes her nose against the wire, but it doesn't give way. Her leg pulses; it's stiff. She jerks in discomfort, but sharp jolts of pain stop her. Whimpers spill out. She nibbles at the T-shirt and wrinkles her nose at the medicine smell. Then she remembers the man says with a growl—just like the doctor does—"Leave it." She licks the shirt instead.

Again, she quiets and listens. Truck. The truck is here. Her stomach rumbles. When Kibble Man comes, he gives dinner.

Slamming doors. Talking outside. Her ears prick. Footsteps. Familiar voices! The talking stays outside for a while.

She rises stiffly, stands, stumbles, then bears weight on three legs. Now she catches a whiff of the puppy scent of her girl. Her heart races with memories of the screeching, slams, Rowan screaming, being tossed upside down. Stormy, her pack leader, in the road. Gone. She slumps to the floor again, turns away from the voices and presses against the wire at the back of the cage. Her body trembles.

Chapter Sixteen

L et's sit on the steps first," Moss said. "There's more I need to explain." He watched Rowan cautiously navigate toward his voice using her cane. A stuffed octopus toy dangled from her other hand.

"Sit here, sweetie," Carolina said, slapping the step.

This woman was pretty cool with the girl. She seemed dedicated to her, yet able to give her space to figure things out. That was a unique quality. How do you cope with your child losing her vision?

"I really need to see Zephy now," Rowan begged. "It's been forever."

"Yes, of course, but I want to prepare you," Moss said. "She's been through—well, a lot. I suspect she might not seem like the same dog. Not as trusting. More cautious." He paused, considering how to explain this to a child. "At your school, did they ever mention PTSD—post-traumatic stress disorder?" He'd heard they'd added it to some classes.

"Yeah, they held an assembly about it because some dads coming home from Afghanistan and Iraq have it."

"Good. Well, PTSD doesn't only happen in war. And not just to people, either. Zephyr is suffering flashbacks from the accident. I recognize them." He stopped. He hadn't intended to disclose his difficulties.

Carolina must have noticed it. He felt her gaze focus on him. Almost like she understood something now. Moss quickly shifted his focus.

"But I'm her *person*," Rowan insisted. "She trusts me more than anyone in the world."

"Yes. And that matters. But she may act differently than you expect or hope." He stretched his leg out and mindlessly rubbed his thigh as he pondered what to say next. Then he turned to Carolina. "Remember on the phone when I said she can't get into cars yet? It's not because of her wounds. She's terrified of vehicles; I had to get the vet to come all the way out here to tranquilize her so we could take her in for surgery. She's one powerful girl."

Carolina nodded. "She is."

"Then how will we get her home?" Rowan's voice rose to a worried pitch. "We have to be able to take her with us."

"That's the problem. I'm not sure. I suppose you could sedate her if you had to," Moss said. "But it doesn't solve the issue—she must learn to ride in cars again. You need to build her confidence, specifically around vehicles." He rubbed his chin. "Now, about her wounds. Her right shoulder is the worst. The biggest is an eight-inch incision. There were four long tears there. She has stitches on her lip, too. And neck, also on the right side." He slowly shook his head. "She's one lucky girl."

"So, I can pat her on the left?"

"That's safest, for now. Come on inside, and I'll get her. Oh yes—she has a T-shirt on to keep her from bothering her wounds."

"I wish I could see that," Rowan said. "I want to sit on the floor. Make myself small."

Glancing at Carolina, Moss nodded appreciatively. "That's the right approach." He opened the screen door and ushered them ahead of him.

As he followed, he saw his house through fresh eyes. A manly home, but comfortable. Handy places to stash boots and hang coats filled the entry wall. At the end of the hall, another door opened into the living room, furnished with a ruddy brown leather couch, his padded rocker, and a leather recliner. Lots of bookcases. The efficient woodstove took up one corner. His desk, where his old *Sibley's* lay open alongside his laptop, filled another. There was a traditional fireplace in front of the couch. Light streamed in through a large south-facing window and two skylights. *My place. My energy.* He didn't invite guests. And now…. His thoughts jumped to Jessie as he realized he had never invited her to visit him. *Why not?*

Carolina took Rowan's arm as they negotiated the threshold. "From the door, we're walking through a corridor into the living room. A couch lies from 9 to 11 o'clock. There's a desk at 7. The door to the kitchen is at 2."

Moss indicated a place on the floor near the recliner, and Carolina helped Rowan settle there. The girl sat, octopus in her lap.

"I'll be back," Moss said and headed into the kitchen. Zephyr whined, and he murmured to her. "It's your folks, girl, but you know that already. Everything's going to be all right." He whistled "Home on the Range" softly. She pressed to the side of the crate but pricked her ears at the sound. He opened the wire door and stood back. "Come now, let's be polite and greet your family."

Moss could hear Rowan make crooning sounds and Zephyr responding. She rose, whimpering at the weight she had to bear on her right front paw to get up and out of the crate. Slinking down, she crept into the living room. The dog approached Rowan, making soft guttural sounds and groveling along the floor.

"Mommo, what's she doing? That's a weird scraping sound."

Carolina said in a choked voice, "Crawling, sweetie. You're hearing her nails on the floor. She's crawling across the hardwood toward you."

Watching her progress, Moss teared up again.

Still making throaty noises, the dog reached the rug and then Rowan. Zephyr nosed the octopus out of her lap and rested her head in its place.

I'll be damned, he thought. Look at that. No question whose dog this is. Now tears overflowed and rolled down his cheeks. He swiped them away.

"You okay?" Carolina whispered.

He nodded.

The girl buried her face against the top of Zephyr's head. "Oh, Zephy," she said again and again.

"Watch her muzzle," Moss warned. "The cougar tore her right lip."

Moss could barely look at Carolina. Her expression showed how broken she felt for her daughter and dog—one blind, the other reduced to terrified creeping. Even though he tried to seal it out, the depth of her sorrow lodged inside of him.

Rowan raised her head and whispered, "Could you two please go outside for a while? I can feel you staring at us, and I have things I need to say to Zeph in private."

Moss blinked rapidly before turning to Carolina and shrugging. "How about a glass of wine? We can sit on the deck. Give them space."

As if considering a major decision, Carolina took a moment, then said, "Okay."

"Merlot all right?"

She nodded, grazed Rowan's curls with her fingertips, and headed outside.

Zeph nudges Rowan's leg and sucks in her scent, just to be sure it's her girl. It is, but something about her is different. Now, together again, the tumbling memories—the loud thumps and squeals that haunt her as she makes her way across the floor—quiet. Will they go back to their nest and the place where they play hide-and-find games? She sets her muzzle back down and lets go. Finally.

Moss poured two glasses and limped after Carolina. He saw Rowan lean down and place her forehead against Zephyr's. Were they communicating? He surprised himself—he'd avoided every child since Afghanistan, but he longed to hear the conversation between this girl and her dog.

They sat in two handcrafted lawn chairs angled gently toward his fenced vegetable plot, a few hundred yards away. His orderly, abundant garden. He'd created a verdant sanctuary—one of the ways he'd found to heal himself. He loved the peace pole he'd added. It stood, a bold symbol, in the circle of the drive.

He got up his nerve to look at Carolina as she took her first taste of the wine. She was an attractive woman, slender and athletic. More than attractive. Downright pretty. Too damn pretty. He didn't trust good-looking women. Not anymore. And those lips—he'd noticed them first thing in the library—full, beautiful, and expressive. She wore a teal T-shirt, cargo shorts, and well broken-in hiking boots. Her outfit showed off tanned arm and calf muscles. A boyish haircut framed her face, and the late afternoon sun caught red highlights. An easy-care woman. Gamine, he thought. She must have a sweet side, with all those smile lines. But still, the phone call had irked him—she'd been judgmental and sharp.

"Thank you so much for phoning," Carolina said. "And allowing us to come here. This reunion's huge for both of them."

"Yes, clearly." He hesitated. "But I don't deserve thanks. I didn't want to contact you; I wasn't ready. My veterinarian forced me." *Too much information. What's going on with me?*

"Good for your vet." She frowned at him. "But why? Why the hesitation to do the right thing?"

He looked down at his wine and slowly ran his finger around the rim of the glass. Then he took an appreciative swallow. "I suppose Gladdy told you I'm an Afghan vet. That woman can't keep her mouth shut."

"Just a brief mention. Not even where."

"I lost a leg over there. Did she tell you that, too?" He patted his left thigh, narrowed his eyes, and shot her a look.

She shook her head but seemed to take the news in stride. "I'm sorry. I know it's hard." She paused, then held up her hand sporting a stub for a ring finger. "Minor—but still, it has affected my grip. I can't play racquet-ball anymore, or flute. People respond so differently when they notice, don't they?"

They both chuckled. The amputee club. The strain between them softened.

She took a sip. "Can you talk about it? The war?"

Moss turned his glass, staring at the garnet liquid. "Zephyr can't travel, not yet. It'd be way too stressful, and I'd like my vet to see her through this."

As if she could read his mind, Carolina looked him directly in the eye.

He quickly averted his gaze and pointed to a structure not far away. "See the guest house? It's smallish but fully equipped. Think about staying at least until she gets her sutures out." He took a swallow of wine. "Zeph'll go ballistic if you leave for town without her. She howls when I leave, and she hardly knows me well enough to care."

Carolina tapped her fingers on the wine glass. "Your offer is both kind and generous; I'll think about it and talk with Rowan. But I want to backtrack. Why did you hesitate to call us? That's upsetting."

Persistent woman, he thought. Maybe it's a good thing. Yank me out of my comfort zone. He shifted uncomfortably in his chair. "How about dinner first? I have leftover stew and French bread. I'll make a salad from the garden. If you decide to head back to the motel after it'll still be light for the drive."

She nodded. "I just need to point out you brought it up, about not calling. You wanted it out in the open."

He rubbed his finger along his lip. "Shit—caught. Unconscious, but you're right."

"So, we'll return to this topic. Deal?" She held her glass out to him.

He considered her request—and those damn beautiful lips—before he answered. "Deal." They clinked, and each took a swallow.

What have I gotten myself into?

Rowan stroked Zephyr's coat, avoiding the places Moss had described. She murmured a steady stream of soft words. "I couldn't come. Can you forgive me? I was in the hospital for eight days." She brushed her lips against the top of Zeph's furry head. "Then Mommo took me home, and I bugged her to search 'til she yelled at me. She made me take cane lessons first, while she caught up on work—so we can afford your food." She ran her hand down Zephyr's good leg. "I get bad headaches; I can't pense you pictures right. You sent me one of the mountain lion, and it scared me so much I tried to convince myself it wasn't true." She rubbed her dog's neck on the side that wasn't hurt. "Have you figured out I can't see? I won't be able to run with you."

Tears came, so Rowan fiddled with Zephyr's toenails and paws to distract herself, and the dog groaned with delight. "You've been through awful stuff. Were you terrified? I hope you'll show me your adventures when you're ready." Feeling for Zephyr's left ear, Rowan rubbed inside with her knuckle. The dog leaned into her. "I got us really close, Zephy. We were almost at this driveway. Tomorrow, I would have found you for sure. You did that; you called me home to you."

Carolina sat near Rowan and Zephyr on the floor. Moss was in the kitchen heating up the stew. "I sure am glad to have you back, girl." She stroked Zeph's head. "You gave us quite a scare." Carolina tapped Rowan's hand. "Moss suggested we stay in his guest house until Zephyr's stronger and less scared of cars. He said she'll get real upset if we leave to go back to Sisters. What do you think?"

"Okay, I guess. I don't think he likes me, but it would be cruel to leave her." She stroked her dog. "All I care about is that we're together. I'm kind of stuck anyway since I can't see. What about our stuff?"

"I hadn't thought about that. After dinner, if we're staying, we can go back to the motel and pick it up. I'll go check out the guest house now."

Carolina went to talk to Moss. "Can I help?"

"Nah, I've got it."

"We're considering your offer. Mind if I look at the cottage?"

"Sure, fine. Actually, you could pick some salad fixings from the garden first. That would be a big help. Do you mind?" He stopped stirring and thought for a moment. "There's lettuce, carrots, scallions, lemon cukes, spinach and…." He thought for a minute. "And beets. If you like, I could steam those a bit. Don't forget the tomatoes. The Early Girls are the best. Medium-sized round ones."

He reached into the mudroom and handed her a willow basket, gloves, and scissors. "Sorry, the gloves will be too big. You saw where the garden is?"

She nodded.

Outside, she strolled across the circle past a peace pole and down the path. She appreciated the alone time to ponder this unusual situation. Gladys said Moss—how had she worded it? "Guarded his privacy." But he had just invited them to stay. What was going on? Should she say yes, and move out of Sisters Motor Lodge? It was the cheapest she'd found, but for her, it was costly. It would be fantastic to save money and not pile more debt on her credit card. They'd planned to search eastern Oregon for two weeks; she'd set it up before leaving home. It was hard to be away from her work this long during her busiest season, but she'd wanted to try every avenue to find Zephyr. Now found, the dog needed time to heal.

The garden was surrounded by an eight-foot fence. No way deer would get in. Carolina opened the gate and took in the sight. Spread before her was a labor of love and a serious food source. The beds were weeded and staked. They weren't rectangular but more leaf-shaped. Where one leaf curved, another snuggled into it with bark-covered paths between. She squinted and computed—at least a quarter acre. The mystery surrounding this man grew.

She picked an Early Girl and sniffed it. It had a fresh, acidic tang— to her, the signature of summer. In three bites it was gone, the juice running down her chin. Walking up and down the paths, she admired and picked, particularly enjoying how the carrots let go and slid out of the ground. After filling the basket with sun-warmed vegetables and delivering them to Moss, she walked around the corner of the main house and down the other path.

The cottage was as well-appointed as the house, just in miniature. It had a little porch with two chairs and nasturtiums around the deck. Curious, she opened the front door. The living room, dining area, and kitchen were one open space. It had beautiful hardwood floors that gleamed red. Cherry? She wandered down the hall and found a renovated bathroom with a stone shower—maybe marble—and a nook with a worktable. Across the hall, she saw a good-sized bedroom with a queen and a single. The room had built-in shelves and drawers. Colorful quilts on the beds. She walked over and fingered the queen spread. The design, clearly hand-stitched, looked like a scene from this property. Gorgeous. She'd ask Moss who made it. There must be a woman in his life.

A bell clanged. She guessed dinner was ready and headed back.

Chapter Seventeen

Moss acknowledged Carolina as she slipped into a chair at his old, scarred oak table. It had real character. During summers, previous generations of children had eaten here, himself included. Zephyr rested contentedly near Rowan's feet. A large, fat housefly buzzed.

"Oh no," Rowan said. "I hear a fly, right? Zephy's *terrified* of them! At home, she hides in the closet 'til we kill it."

Just then, Moss saw Zephyr raise her head and track the fly. A moment later, the dog nipped the air and swallowed. "Well, she's not scared of them anymore. She just ate it."

"*Ate* it?" Rowan's mouth flew open. "Wow. She's *really* changed."

"She's been through a powerful experience where she had to rely on herself. I guess compared to a mountain lion, a fly seems minuscule to her now," Moss said. He could see Rowan considering his words.

"Hungry?" Moss asked Carolina. He felt attracted to her but didn't quite trust her or his instincts.

"You bet. Smells terrific. Unfamiliar," Carolina said. "Rowan, how's your appetite?"

"Like a dire wolf," she said.

Moss was taken aback. This was an unusual child. "What kind of wolf is that?" He ladled a bowl and set it in front of Rowan. "How'd you learn about them?"

Rowan explored the bowl with her fingers. "Research. They got extinct like 10,000 years ago, but they were super big and fierce. They roamed North and South America for over a million years," she said, matter-of-factly. "Major predators. I love animals; I read voraciously—until the accident."

"Voraciously—that's quite a word."

"I'm a word nerd. I collect them like some people collect stamps or other special things."

"Wow," he said. He was too astounded to respond further, so he turned to Carolina. "We fed Zephyr. Rowan explained exactly how she does it." He gave a wry smile. "She set me right. What's your take on the guest house?"

"It's cozy. Nice. Beautiful. Who made the splendid quilt?"

"My great-grandmother Nanon. The cottage was the only dwelling on the property and her home. Bessie, my grandmother, lived in it last. It's only been used for visitors since we built this house."

"I think it makes sense for us to stay if that's really all right with you—and Rowan, of course."

"It's okay," Rowan said, "'cause it's best for Zephy. She needs us close." She felt around for a spoon then dug into the stew, but frowned as soon as the food entered her mouth. "What *is* this?"

"Venison."

"Venison? You mean like deer? What store carries deer?"

"I shot, dressed, and froze it."

"You *shot* it? An innocent deer?" Rowan's glare deepened, and she dropped the spoon with the next bite back in the bowl. "How could you do that?"

"Rowan!" her mother said. "Where are your manners?"

"Where is his kindness?" She scowled in Moss's direction. He tried to keep a straight face, but his shoulders rocked with laughter. Carolina shook her head at her daughter.

"Do you eat meat at home?" Moss asked, wondering if they were vegetarian.

Rowan twisted the spoon in the stew. "Yeah. We do."

"Well, how do you think meat gets on your plate? Does it walk there by itself?"

"You shot it with a gun?"

"No. I hunt with a bow. I won't kill with a gun anymore."

He saw Carolina cast a curious eye in his direction.

"It's far more humane than how they kill cows, for God's sake. With the bow, there's not even a loud noise to scare the critter. The deer is living its life in the wild and then it isn't. Much better than being crammed together in a feedlot. Ever been to one? The cows, they know what's coming." He buttered a slice of French bread and passed the basket to Carolina. "I try to grow and hunt most of my food on the land. I prefer to be self-sufficient. Besides, it tastes better."

"Try another bite," Carolina said. "You might like it. Here's some buttered bread, too. I set it at three o'clock. Your milk's at one."

Rowan ate the bread, then dawdled with her spoon again. Pulling a face, she took a tentative, second taste.

"How'd it go down?" Moss asked.

"It's—well, darn. It's yummy," Rowan said. "And I'm ravenous. Poor deer." She fell silent and ate steadily.

Moss smiled but stayed quiet. He thought he'd handled the situation pretty well. More than anything, he dreaded being around children again— but this one, this one was a trip.

∞

"Tell me what's outside the front door," Rowan said. "I need to take Zeph for a pee break."

Carolina hesitated. "How about I go with you, talk you through the territory? You'll take your cane?"

Rowan nodded, pushing her chair back from the table. She counted the steps back to the couch out loud. Zephyr struggled up to follow her. The girl felt around for her stick.

Moss brought the leash. "Keep it as loose as you can. If you tighten the collar, you may squeeze her neck wound."

After a couple of tries, Rowan snapped it on. But the moment she picked up her cane, Zephyr reared back and squealing, strained against the leash. She almost pulled the girl off her feet.

"She's terrified. I can see the whites of her eyes," Moss said.

Rowan grimaced. "Then this time, we'll do without." She patted and comforted her dog. Leaning the cane against the couch, she shortened the leash until Zephyr was right beside her. Feeling with care to avoid the neck incision, Rowan took some of the dog's neck fur along with the lead. "Talk me outside, Mommo."

"The door's at eleven o'clock. About eight steps to get there." Carolina watched how Zephyr seemed to take note of the girl's hesitant gait and leaned into her. Rowan used her other hand to feel for the doorway, and Carolina saw her press against it for a moment when she touched it.

"Great work! The hallway's about four paces long," she called, following behind. She talked them across the porch and down the steps. Instead of going to the grassy circle with the peace pole, Carolina directed them to a weedier area. She watched their teamwork develop. Zephyr understood Rowan needed her, and her daughter seemed to know when her dog finished her business. They made their way back to the porch.

Moss leaned against the door frame, arms crossed, taking it all in. Carolina couldn't read his expression. Was it curiosity?

"You're a stride from the steps," Carolina said to Rowan. Her heart squeezed inside her chest as she remembered dog and girl flying across the field at home. Now, Zephyr had a heavy limp, and her daughter moved hesitantly. But Rowan broke out in a broad smile when they walked across the porch, and Carolina noticed she squared her shoulders. As Zephyr and Rowan got closer to the door, Moss moved out of the way. He favored his leg now.

Once they got inside, Carolina looked at her watch. "We've got to head to town and pick up our gear."

"Shall I go for you? I could drive the road with my eyes closed."

Carolina looked right at him. "You'd best get your prosthesis off and give your stump a rest."

Moss leveled a stare at her. "You sure are direct."

"Yep, I'm known for that. Besides, you're limping."

"You could leave Rowan here with Zephyr," he said. "Then Zeph won't get upset. They can hang with me until you get back. They're both tuckered out; I bet they're asleep within minutes."

Carolina looked from Moss to her daughter who had collapsed on the couch. "Is it all right with you, Row? The trip will take more than forty-five minutes, maybe an hour."

"Go for it, Mommo. I've got to get her used to the cane. And then I need to brush her everywhere she isn't hurt. She still has some tangles." As she spoke, her hand rubbed the top of Zephyr's head. The stick lay on the floor next to the dog who bumped it cautiously with her nose.

Carolina hesitated. Could she leave Rowan here, alone with Moss? He'd certainly shown kindness and generosity. Besides, if he tried anything untoward, Zeph would snarl. It felt all right to go. What a relief to have girl and dog reunited. It was one step toward normality and another away from depression.

She returned from town an hour later with their suitcases, backpacks, dog gear, and a thank you gift for Moss. She hauled them directly to the cottage, stashed the gift for when they were ready to go home, unpacked pajamas and toiletries, and turned down the unfamiliar beds. This place smelled like sunshine.

Then she headed over to the big house to collect Rowan and Zephyr. Tiptoeing in, she saw they were both asleep on the floor. Her daughter was fitted around the dog who had Wubby snuggled between her paws, her furry head perched on top of the octopus. Moss was working at his computer, a glass of wine nearby. She noted with satisfaction that his crutches were propped against the wall.

He looked up and nodded hello. "They crashed early. I didn't have the heart to make Rowan move. She seemed comfortable."

"I wouldn't have either. They have so much catching up to do."

"I'd help you get her to the cottage, but I already unlegged." He pursed his lips. "Sorry. Comes with the territory. Plus, you ordered me to take it off." He winked. "I could leg up again," he added as an afterthought.

Carolina laughed out loud. "Like anyone could order you to do anything. Not to worry; I've been a single parent for four years now. I can manage. May I have a glass of wine? I'm not ready to go to sleep."

"Help yourself." He closed the lid of his laptop and pointed to the nearby table.

"Please don't stop. I'm happy being quiet. There's a lot to absorb."

"I'll just finish this paragraph. I'm journaling right now," Moss said, "a habit I picked up during the war. It's easier for me to journal than write." He opened the lid again and went back to work.

Carolina poured a glass and settled in the rocker, swiveling so she could see the girls and Moss. It amazed her to suddenly have a new acquaintance in her life who felt—well, comfortable to be around, especially after the unpleasant start. So far, he tolerated her bluntness. That was a good sign.

His curls tumbled over his forehead, and he ran his fingers through them. Strong, useful-looking hands. She wanted to know more about him *and* those hands. But the idea disturbed her. Liking him was not part of the bargain she'd made with herself.

True to his word, when he completed the paragraph, he closed the laptop and turned toward her. "Your trip went smoothly?"

"Yes. I was relieved to find the break in the bushes. You know, where your driveway starts?"

He laughed. "Fancy name for a dirt track. Because the opening's hidden and the road's not paved, people don't show up unexpectedly. It's the way I want it." He shifted in the chair. "So how'd you end up a single parent? Are you divorced?"

She shook her head and sipped the wine. "No. Rafe died of influenza. A fluke." Although it was covered with some kind of stocking, she could see Moss's stump now. Amputated above the knee. She'd heard that was a more difficult adjustment.

"Really! What a shock, to be a widow at your age."

"Yes. Sudden. Awful. Rowan was seven. And then, last year, her best girlfriend moved to Indonesia. Row took her dad's death very hard, but when her friend left, she fell into a deep depression—compounded losses. I needed to help her find her way, and the suggestions our family doctor made were anti-depressants and a therapist. The idea of drugs didn't sit well with me. We settled on a dog instead, and Zephyr came to live with our family—a far better solution. Her puppy energy was good for both of us."

Moss gave a thoughtful nod. "What breed is she? She looks like wolfhound, maybe deerhound?"

"I'm impressed. She's a mix of those two. Most people have no idea."

He grinned sheepishly. "I picked up a dog book after I caught a glimpse of her in the brush. I couldn't imagine what she was and didn't even guess the dog group correctly. I had to page through the whole book."

"The breeds were new to me as well. We found her at our local pound. I had no idea how huge she'd get; it's been a shock." She shrugged. "But she's the pup Rowan bonded with, and I wasn't about to say no after I'd promised she could choose." She picked up her glass again—her mind zooming back to her earlier question—why he didn't want to call them. Best not to push; she'd give him the chance to come forward. Instead, she took a swallow and asked, "Have you been married?"

The lines around his mouth pulled deeper. "We got close, but then 9/11 happened. I enlisted and got sent to Afghanistan." He looked down and rubbed his hands.

Carolina could tell she'd touched painful territory. She figured he was considering how much he wanted to say.

"Sophie is her name—she couldn't handle this." He pointed to his stump. "After I got home from Germany, she didn't see me as the same man."

"Oh, my God," she whispered. "After all you must have been through? That's terrible."

"I try not to dwell on it. Not always successfully. I heard she's getting married next month." He pinched his lips together. "FYI, on another topic: sometimes I have nightmares. If the windows are open, you might hear me. I wake up screaming."

She shuddered. "Good to know. Thanks for the warning."

"So, one more question—I'm curious about your short hair. It looks great on you, but how come?"

"I used to wear it long, but a couple of weeks after Rafe died, I was bent over the sewing machine, and it got caught in the seam I was stitching. There I was, my head yanked to the sewing table. I had to yell for Rowan to come cut me loose. It must have been a real sight. Then, of course, after an unglued seven-year-old sawed through my hair, it was lopsided—I looked like a madwoman." She smiled. "I went upstairs and buzzed it to one inch. It was a cathartic move, a response to Rafe's death. I needed a big change. I intended to grow it out again, but people liked it, so I've kept this style."

"Better to sew your hair than your hand," he said.

"Yeah, well I've done that, too. One moment's inattention is all it takes." She rubbed her right index finger.

"About tomorrow," he said. "I write in the morning, so I'm unavailable. Come in the back door and collect what you want here to make yourselves breakfast at the guest house. The dog food is in the mudroom." He pointed through the kitchen.

"You'll be here? No job to go to?"

"Writing's a painstaking job."

"What are you working on?"

"It's about the war. To be honest, I'm having a terrible time writing. Nonfiction. Memoir—authentic experiences."

"I know what memoir is. Rowan writes. What I've seen is good. She's pretty private about it, though."

Zephyr moaned and jerked. Rowan startled awake. "Mommo?"

"I'm here, love." She nodded to Moss, finished the last sip of her wine, and rose to collect her charges.

Moss switched off the lamps in the main part of the house and headed for the bathroom. After leaning his crutches next to the sink, he looked in the mirror—who in God's name was this guy? Inviting strangers to his sanctuary, and one of them a kid? *Really? Am I fucking crazy?* And not just having them come to the property to pick up Zephyr but suggesting they stay a few days? He didn't know this guy.

He looked at his reflection for a while and rubbed his evening stubble. *Tell the truth, Moss.*

He peered at himself. There stood the man from before the war. Until now, he was convinced *that* Moss had died in Afghanistan. As he glared into his blue eyes, he realized his heart was rushing. His hands shook as he gripped the sink. He'd ripped open without even noticing, without the moment of conscious awareness it took to shut himself down.

Sadness and grief scratched at his soul. Raw pain cascaded through him. He pressed his forehead against the hard surface of the mirror and splashed water on his face. Eventually, his heart slowed.

After he washed up, he crutched to the bed, slid under the covers, and grabbed the second pillow. Moaning, he pounded it, hard. Then, realizing the window was open, he hopped over and slammed it shut, threw himself back on the bed, and pummeled the pillow more. Christ, this room—without the giant pup lying by the bed breathing—seemed empty, and worse, lonely.

Sophie was marrying some dude with two good legs. It pissed him off. Irrationally, he wanted her to be someone she clearly wasn't. He didn't yearn specifically for her anymore—he needed gumption in a partner—but he was sick of the empty loneliness that lived inside of him. Now, all he had was a damn feather punching bag and a houseful of strangers. Well, yeah, and his friend-with-benefits, Jessie. It was nice to have sex on occasion, but during their time together, he often felt isolated. They didn't have real intimacy; she was shut down herself.

Today, with Carolina and Rowan, he kept slipping—sharing too much information. *Why did he do that?* He chucked the pillow across the room, rolled onto his back, then kicked the covers off. He was *not* ready to care for other people—he couldn't even handle himself. It was a horrible mistake to have invited them to stay.

Another lie.

He knew damn well this was exactly what he wanted.

Zephyr sighs and settles deeper into the C-bed on the floor next to Rowan. Her shoulder pulls and aches, but the light breathing of the girl is a comfort. Rowan's hand hangs off the bed, and the dog gives it a nudge and soft lick. The girl rouses and responds with Zeph's favorite, an ear rub.

A few minutes later, Zephyr feels Rowan slide off, snug around her, and drag the blanket over them both. The girl's lips come against her ear.

"Don't tell Mommo," she whispers.

The dog sends a pense, a warm blast of love. Contented, soothed by the girl's body so close, Zephyr falls into profound sleep.

Chapter Eighteen

Moss awakened in the pre-dawn, legged up, and slid into well-worn jeans. He made a quick espresso, downed it, and took leftover smoothie from the fridge. He grabbed his daypack and headed for Bender's Ridge. After a rough night, he needed the vista to clear his head and heart; writing would have to wait. He grabbed his walking stick on the way out the front door.

He chose the deer path—the sensible route—to conserve energy. A half hour later, he crowned the ridge and stopped at the spring to drink. Then he sat with his back against a tree and let his heart float with the rising sun.

If Carolina and Rowan came over to pick up breakfast supplies, there would be conversation. He knew he was running away from these strangers who felt like friends, but he didn't care. They were clearly capable folk. This morning, they could fend for themselves. He'd pull himself together by the afternoon.

Two days later, a cloud of dust swirled as a green truck pulled into the driveway. As the vehicle door slammed, Moss called, "Vet's here."

"Yay! I want to meet him! Can I take your arm? I'm too slow with the cane."

"Dr. Steward will check Zephyr right here on the carpet, so her paws don't slip. You don't have to go anywhere." He smiled as the vet clomped up the stairs. He figured this might be a surprise. "Rowan, this is Dr. Francine Steward."

"Francine? *Really?* A woman vet? Hi!" Rowan bounced with excitement as she stuck her hand out. "That was my dream, before the accident."

"Hi, there," Francie said, shooting a questioning glance at Moss. "And what are your dreams now?"

"Nobody would take their dog to a blind veterinary surgeon," Rowan said. "So I'm going to be a writer. Unless I get my sight back. The doctor said there's a chance."

"Let's hope so. Women make great vets." Francie scratched Zephyr's head. "How's our big girl doing?"

Zephyr gently wagged her tail.

"Better, at least I think so," Rowan replied.

"So, Rowan. You're Zephyr's person?" Francine continued to rub Zephyr. "You were smart to have her microchipped."

"The Humane Society insisted."

"She's a pound dog? She looks purebred to me."

"She's a mix of Irish wolfhound and Scottish deerhound," Rowan said, with pride. "She's a lurcher, actually, a longdog. And she's *so* smart."

"Longdog lurcher? What's that?" Francine asked.

"Lurcher means she's a cross between a sighthound and some other breed, and longdog means she's specifically a sighthound-sighthound mix. Most people have never heard the term 'longdog.'"

"And I should definitely know it, thanks. Let's check her out. Come help me, okay?" Francie clucked and murmured to Zephyr. "Hey girl, how you doin'? You must be a happier camper now you're reunited with your family." She unknotted the T-shirt and carefully pulled it off, then ran her hands over the dog.

Moss loved to watch her work on animals.

"Rowan, will you please ask her to lie on the rug?" Francine asked.

Rowan patted the floor. "Zeph, down!" she said with a firm tone.

With a groan, Zephyr obediently settled on the carpet.

"She's still stiff, isn't she," Francine said. "I'd like her to lie on her side. Moss, help me?"

"Wait, I can do it," Rowan said. "Zeph, dead!" The dog obediently flattened onto her uninjured side.

"Good job. Have you felt around her wounds?"

Rowan shook her head. "I was too scared. We're just getting reacquainted, and I didn't want to mess anything up. Aren't they awfully sore?"

"They're uncomfortable, but I think it would be all right," Francie said. "She trusts you. You can tell a lot about injuries by palpating them. I usually close my eyes when I'm feeling with my fingers anyway. May I guide your hand?"

Rowan sucked in her breath. "Okay. I'll try."

"Here. Lightly, now. The pokey ends are sutures."

Moss watched Rowan use only the soft pads of her fingers to move lightly around Zephyr's shoulder.

"It's so long," the girl said, with a shiver. "Right here, what's this? Swelling?"

"Sure is. See how smart your hands are? It's a tiny spot of infection." Francie opened a jar and deftly applied thick medication to the area. "Wounds can get inflamed, particularly when inflicted by cats. Let's put her on Clavamox and nip it in the bud. Can you pill her?"

"Yep. I make her sit, and I stand right behind, so she can't back up. Zephy's pretty good about it," Rowan said. "Watch out for her super big teeth, though."

"Yes, I take good care. I know a couple of vets with one short finger."

Rowan shuddered. "What did you put on her? It smells sweet."

"Manuka honey. It comes from Australia and has significant wound healing properties. I want you to spread it on all her incisions four times a day, okay? I'll leave you a jar."

"Won't she just lick it off? I would!"

"Her wounds are either covered with the T-shirt or in places she can't reach. I've put some antibiotic samples on the small table near you, so your mom doesn't have to run to town. Those will last a few days. Two tablets, twice daily, after you feed her. When we're done, let's give her a snack, and I'll administer her first dose. You need to pill her again before bedtime." She clipped a leash on Zephyr. "I'd like to see her walk. Can you do that for me?"

Rowan nodded. Taking the leash and a scruff of Zephyr's fur, she said, "Zeph, forward." She counted the steps to the door, across the deck, and down the stairs. Zephyr limped slowly, her shoulder at Rowan's left hip, clearly pacing herself to the girl.

"They're doing great," Francine murmured to Moss. "It's almost like Zeph's a guide dog."

"Those two are connected in a spooky way. As soon as I saw them together, it was obvious she's not my dog."

"Any luck getting her in a car?"

"Not yet," he said. "Rowan's working with her. Slow progress." He leaned against the door frame to ease his leg. "At least Zephyr doesn't cringe at the sight of the girl's cane anymore. But the car—she moans and rolls her eyes until the whites show."

Francine looked directly at Moss. "How're you bearing up with company? Where's Rowan's mom?"

"Oh, so you know everything. Gladdy can't keep her goddamn mouth shut," Moss grumbled. "Carolina's weeding and harvesting in the garden. I'm coping; they give me lots of space. Anyway, they're nice."

"Folks are talking."

"Folks can mind their own damn business."

Crouched near the zucchini, Carolina wiped her brow. There was little to do—it was hard to improve on Moss's dedicated work. Still, she wanted to contribute. Carolina had heard the doctor's truck rattle onto the property. As curious as she was to meet the vet, she thought it would be more fun for Rowan if she stayed out of it. Her daughter would tell her about the visit. When she saw them exit the house, she picked up the basket of harvested vegetables and headed toward them.

Carolina was surprised to see a slender brunette standing on the porch talking with Rowan and Moss. An animated, lovely woman. *Had Moss told her the vet was female? And why am I thinking more about the doctor than how Zephyr's examination went?* She shook herself to get a grip and walked up the steps to greet them.

"Ah, you must be Carolina, the talk-of-the-town mystery woman," Francine said, extending her hand. "Pleased to meet you."

"Hi." Carolina set the full basket down and took a moment to collect her thoughts. "Mystery woman, really? How silly. We're just a mom and girl reunited with their dog after a harrowing few weeks. How's Zephyr?"

"Better. She's a great pup. Rowan did a fabulous job training her, which makes treating her much easier. It's so important with these giant dogs." Francine stroked Zephyr's head as she talked. "She's healing nicely, but there's a little infection we're treating now. Her emotional state worries me more than her wounds."

"I agree. Any suggestions about her car phobia? We need to head home soon."

"Has Rowan offered her food in the van?"

"Yes. It didn't work. Each time, Zephyr started bucking fifteen feet away."

Francine rubbed her chin. "You know, she came out of the wild to Moss. That's when her life turned toward normal—human companionship and regular meals again. Moss, you should get in the van; see if you can encourage her."

Moss raised his eyebrows at Rowan. Carolina saw him catch himself and touch her daughter on the arm. "I hadn't thought of that. Are you willing for me to try?"

The girl chewed her lip for a moment. She reached her hand out and rested it on Zephyr's back. "Yeah. I guess so. Okay."

Carolina wanted to hug Rowan. She knew it was hard for her daughter to imagine someone else being able to coax Zephyr, but the reality was Moss saved the dog.

"I'm headed out," Francine said. "I've got another appointment at the Kimmons' place. They have a sick cow." She gave Zephyr a final pat, wrapped her arms around Moss for a prolonged hug, and then spoke to Rowan. "So nice to meet you. Remember the dose of antibiotics tonight."

Then she reached a hand toward Carolina. "Call me if anything changes with the wound. Here's a 'scrip for more Clavamox. I gave your daughter a three-day supply; Zephyr should remain on it a full week."

Carolina took the paper, shook Francine's hand, and smiled goodbye. She politely murmured something appropriate, but her mind was somewhere else—the warm hug Francine gave Moss. Friends? More? Why did she care? She could not let her thoughts carry her away. This was *not* the plan.

The next morning, Rowan and Moss met before Zephyr's breakfast. Rowan talked Moss through placing Zephyr's bed, with Wubby, in its proper place in the van. He brought the dog's full breakfast bowl outside. Rowan settled in the back. Moss sat behind the dog bed and put the kibble on the floor of the van near the slider. He whistled an old tune Rowan had heard him use before. Carolina held Zephyr on the leash—if she bolted, she'd tear out the sutures.

Moss stopped whistling and talked to the dog, a soft conversation with inflection. "Hey, there. Comin' to visit, huh? We've got your favorite goodies here."

He kept up his patter, describing to Rowan everything her dog was doing, but using the same soft cadence. "She started to quiver about five feet from the van. She's not moving another step—in fact, she's backing up, pulling on the lead like a wild horse. We need a different plan."

"I have to try something," Rowan said. "You go take the leash from Mommo and just stand there with Zephy. I need to concentrate really hard 'cause my head's still not right. I'll sit where you are now."

After they changed positions, and Moss held the leash, Rowan pictured happy rides in the car—like when they were getting home from the dog park in Eugene, tired, and played out. She directed the stream of images to Zephyr.

The dog stopped shaking and tilted her head. She took a hesitant step forward, then retreated. Moss kept a loose leash. "Whatever you're doing, keep it up," he called.

Rowan recalled meeting Zephyr for the first time—the rush of connection she'd felt, and then she visualized getting in their car and heading from the shelter to Zephyr's new home. She sent a mind-picture of introducing Zeph to their land with a field so big she could run full speed. Then she pensed riding in their new van back to the same big field where they played together every day.

Kibble Man has her on the line. Her girl is sending pictures—fun rides, the play park with all the dogs, flopping on the floor at home. But her girl wants her to get into the monster again? Her body goes tight, and her heart beats fast. Kibble Man pats her and makes soft sounds. She steps forward. He calls out to Rowan, and more pictures come: sensing the girl for the very first time as she walked toward the cage in the shelter—a human who listens—then riding in a monster to a new nest with a running field. Now, this monster takes them back to that field? She tilts her head.

Moss reported that the dog took three tentative steps forward. She caught a whiff of her breakfast. Soon, Rowan heard her crunch kibble. She grinned. Zephy hadn't gotten in the van yet—that might take a few days—but now that the dog was eating out of a bowl sitting on the floor near the door of the van, she knew they'd succeed.

After lunch, Moss followed Rowan when she took Zephyr outside to pee. "What exactly did you do this morning? To get Zephyr to come to you?"

The girl hesitated, wondering if it was safe to tell him. Would he believe her? Would he rat to her mom? Mom always seemed uncomfortable when she talked about intuitive things, so she stopped sharing them. And the pensing? She definitely kept that private. Considering, Rowan picked her lip, then took the leap. After all, he asked.

"Okay, I'll tell you. I've never even told Mommo. She doesn't like this kind of talk." She sat on the ground. "I made up a word. I call it pensing, from "pensive." How come you're interested?"

"Pensing, huh? Clever." Moss joined her on the grass.

She heard him stick his prosthesis out in front of him.

"I'm interested because the two of you have something special," he said.

Rowan described stopping at every cage at the Humane Society. "The dogs were okay—you know, most were cute and curious. They were nervous and panting. But not Zeph. As soon as we made eye contact, she sat in the cage and contemplated me. She was a little thing back then—didn't have a mustache or beard yet. She met my gaze—the only dog in the whole place who did." Rowan hugged her knees. Zephyr settled next to her. "When she looked at me, I got, I don't know, like a bumping sensation. And then I could feel her. It's hard to explain."

"You're doing fine. Do you think it's why the two of you walk together so well?"

Rowan nodded. "For sure."

"Had you ever felt a bump before? In any situation?"

She shook her head. "Nope."

"Your mom mentioned the day before we met that you got really close to my ranch. Almost to the driveway. Was it the same kind of experience?"

Rowan thought for a moment. "No. It's more like tuning into a compass or something. Like true North lies wherever she is. Does that make any sense?"

"It does. Remarkable."

"You mean you believe me?"

"Why shouldn't I? You're obviously smart and honest. Life is strange, Rowan. I don't think it's anything like we're taught growing up."

"I don't either," Rowan said. "There's more. Now," she hesitated and dropped her voice to a whisper. "We send each other pictures. She pensed me an image of the mountain lion. That's how I knew." She could feel tears welling. "But I never, ever could talk about this, not with Mommo. It's hard not sharing. Only Zephy and my journal know. I think Daddo might have understood, but he died." Tears spilled, and she turned away to hide them.

Zephyr bumped her arm and pushed under her elbow to rest her head in the girl's lap.

"Hey," Moss said. "I've learned tears are a healthy thing. I'll keep our conversation private."

With that, her weeping came in earnest. She threw herself toward his voice, pressed her nose into his T-shirt, and gripped his back. All she could think of was her dad who had listened to her intuitions and unusual ideas. She felt Moss hesitate, then wrap his arms around her. A moment later, she heard him snuffle, and then he cracked open into sobs.

Moss's shoulders shook. His nose ran. He couldn't get a grip on himself. Was he holding Rowan, or was she holding him? He pulled away with a rough, "Sorry," pushed himself up onto his feet, and limped as fast as he could toward the house. *How could I have let this happen?*

Blinded by tears, he stumbled on the bottom step of the deck and smacked into the railing. Pain flared up his stump as he hobbled into the living room. He shoved past Carolina, who was tidying the dining room. "Please, get out." He fled into his bedroom, slamming the door behind him. As soon as he hit the bed, howling overtook him, and he buried his face in the pillow to stifle the sound. He craved to hold someone, but that someone could not be the girl. He keened for the three blown-apart Afghan children who stalked his dreams; he keened for his own lost soul.

Ordered from the house, Carolina dashed across the deck and down the steps. She'd seen Moss, Rowan, and Zephyr on the grass. Something happened, and she needed to know what. Moss was distraught. Her daughter was hugging Zephyr and crying hard, face buried in the dog's ruff.

Carolina knelt down and stroked her daughter's back. "I'm here, love."

Rowan whirled and held her tight, pressing her face against Carolina's chest. Her daughter felt like a coiled spring.

"What happened? Did you two argue about something?"

"No, not at all." Rowan gulped and cleared her throat. "I need tissues."

Carolina reached into her pocket and pulled out a clean handkerchief. "Here you go."

Rowan blew her nose. "We were having a great conversation, talking about Zephy. Then I thought of Daddo and got all teary. Mossy said tears are good, and I kind of threw myself at him." She mopped her eyes. "He caught me. Then he cried too and ran away."

"It's difficult for men," Carolina said. "But why did you call him Mossy?"

"Because he's all soft, but he survived on hard stuff, just like moss clings to rocks. The war must have been awful. He's all hurt and sad."

Carolina marveled at Rowan's insight. "I think you're right. It's almost like you can see into people, sweetie."

"Only a few. And Zephy, of course." She snuggled closer.

"But Moss is one of those people?"

"Yep."

"Are you mad at him?"

"No. Sad for him."

"Me too." She hugged her daughter and patted Zephyr. "Do you think you can get her in the car soon?"

"I'm not sure. I can try."

"Are you ready to go home?"

"And leave Mossy? He'll be crushed. He loves Zeph."

"I know he does, hon, but I think he needs some space. Doesn't it seem like he does?"

"You'd better ask *him*, Mommo. We can't know."

Chapter Nineteen

A few hours later, Moss caught a glimpse of Carolina. She was walking up the path toward his house. The late afternoon sun haloed her hair. He lost sight of her, but by then, he could make out her footfall on the deck. He had to talk to her—he wasn't irresponsible, just broken. His behavior was inexcusable. To fall apart in front of a sweet kid, and on top of that, to be rude to both of them? She'd be forthright—it seemed to be her nature. Probably, she'd blast him. He had *it* coming; he just didn't know what "it" would be.

Better not to have this conversation here, in his private space. Moss hauled himself out of his chair and limped into the living room. His stump still ached from the stumble.

Carolina stood by the door, hand poised to knock on the screen door.

He waved her in. "Hey," he said. Wearily, he passed his hand over his eyes. "Please, come in and sit down. Cheese and crackers? Wine?"

"All of the above would be great."

He headed for the kitchen, relieved to have a few minutes to collect himself. He placed Brie and Cambozola on the cutting board then pulled out seeded crackers and spreading knife. The glug-glug of wine filling glasses, the commonality of it all, steadied him. Two people, talking sensibly—he could do this, except he had no idea what to say, how much to divulge. He headed back into the living room expecting to find her sitting in the rocker.

Instead, Carolina was settled on the couch, and when she heard him, she patted the leather cushion next to her. "Sit here with me."

It threw him off kilter, but he set the tray on the table, sat down, and handed her a glass. Girding himself, he turned to her.

"She calls you Mossy," Carolina said.

Moss's heart clunked hard then rat-tat-tatted. He knuckled the center of his chest. I'll be damned, he thought. Even when I act weird, Rowan isn't afraid of me.

"When I asked her why, her words were, 'He's like moss on rocks.' She said you're soft, but strong, too." She shook her head. "Sometimes that girl stuns me, and I wonder where she came from."

"Does she take more after her dad?" Moss took a swallow of wine; the warmth radiated through his body.

"Yes," Carolina admitted. "She does. And my mom who, supposedly, is psychic. Apparently, I didn't get that gene, thank heavens."

"Not skills you appreciate?"

Carolina shook her head.

"Before you grill me about today," Moss said, "I want to answer your question from the first evening. I haven't forgotten."

Carolina looked startled. "Oh? When I asked why you put off calling us after you discovered Zephyr was microchipped? I figured you'd passed on it." She reached out and spread Brie on a cracker.

"Nope. We clinked glasses. I keep my promises." He rubbed his chin and considered how to proceed. She handed him the cracker she had fixed, which surprised him. "Thanks," he said, setting it on his knee. "After some time wooing the dog, she eventually followed me home. In our own way, we both were wild. Untamed. A bit wary of each other.

"Post-surgery, I nursed her, and she gained strength. Something in me eased." Pausing, he chewed the cracker and took another sip of wine. "I'd walled myself up here without another breathing soul— well, other than my chickens and the native animals. Zephyr broke through. She needed me. Badly. I hand fed her those first couple of days. I learned I needed her as well." He smoothed his fingers up and down his forehead. "Bottom line? I didn't want to let her go." He gave a derisive snort. "Selfish, I know. But Francine set me straight; she gave me five days to call you."

"Five days? Wow. Generous for you. Are you two involved?"

Puzzled, Moss squinted at Carolina. Something in her expression had tightened. "Francine and me? Really?" He chuckled. "No, Francie's gay. She's been partnered for a decade. But we did run loose together as kids. We go way back; maybe that's what you picked up on. She's a dear friend." He kneaded his thigh, trying to ease the soreness. "I owe both you and Rowan an apology. I lost it today, but even worse, I snarled at both you and your girl. Maybe you can handle it, but Rowan—unconscionable. I'm sorry."

"Apology accepted—for me, anyway." She sat silent for a long moment. "I think it's time we head back to Eugene, and let you get on with your life." Her lips barely turned up at the corner. "We're a rich diet, a lot of intense face-to-face for a wild, untamed critter—your words—who's been hanging out alone. Sometime, I'd like to know what happened out there."

Moss shuddered. "I've never talked about it, except with a fellow vet and my counselors. Not even my family."

"I was referring to out there with Rowan, on the grass—today."

"They're connected." He glanced down as he worked his fingers.

"Yes," she said. "I suspected."

"You might have asked if I needed my space back rather than assumed," he said. He allowed his tone the slightest edge.

"Rowan said the same thing. But you did tell me to get out. Anyway, sometimes I jump to conclusions."

He looked at her without faltering or hesitation. "I like your frankness. In an odd way, it's comforting. I know where you stand, and where I stand with you." He hesitated, then leaned over, and rested his fingers under her chin, grazing her lips with his. A sensual, electric shock jolted his body. He had not planned on kissing her.

For a second she leaned into the soft kiss, then pulled back, her fingers jumping to her mouth. "*That* was unexpected."

"Are you sure?" He gave a crooked grin. "If so, why did you invite me to sit next to you?"

Pink lit up her cheeks, and she looked away.

"Anyway, I apologize again. It wasn't appropriate. Carolina…." He touched her on the shoulder. "Go away if you must—I'm sure you have a regular routine calling, but I don't think we're done."

"Done?" She looked back at him, questioning.

"Against my better judgment, there might be something here." He gestured with his hand to include both of them.

She sat quietly for a moment. "I promised myself I wouldn't get involved with anyone until Rowan is in college. It's messy with kids entering their teens."

"You mean because they resent the intruder?"

"Exactly," she said. "And what about Rowan? You were so negative about children on the phone."

"Your daughter is wonderful," he said. His tone came out ragged, almost rough. "I've always loved kids."

"What then?"

"Another time," he said. "I'm damaged goods." He fixed a second cracker and handed it to her. "Most important, I want to heal. Part of that will eventually be talking about my war experiences. But I'm not ready. Not yet. Writing is hard enough. Speaking of them to others— it's too much." He spread Cambozola slowly onto a cracker for himself. "Rowan seems to like me. We had an in-depth conversation today. Until I blew it."

They sat silently, sipping wine.

"Where is she now?" he asked. "I need to talk with her."

"She's napping. Processing a world without sight is still exhausting. She sleeps much more than she used to." Carolina glanced at her watch. "It's been over an hour. If she conks out any longer, she'll be too wired to get to bed at a decent time. Go ahead and wake her."

Even as her shoulder stiffens, Zephyr lies still. The girl curls around her on the floor, asleep. Sensing her exhaustion, the dog doesn't want to wake her. She pricks her ears; Kibble Man is coming. Her two people, together in one place. She sighs with contentment and rests her head on Rowan's arm, waiting. She thunks her tail on the floor.

∽

Rowan stirred as Moss walked quietly into the room. She recognized the sound of his lopsided gait. "You came back!" She heard the creak as he sat down on the single bed near them.

"Of course I did. It was wrong of me to jump up and leave without explanation. I'm sorry, Row."

Rubbing her eyes, she sat up, patting Zephyr as she crossed her legs, Native American style. "I was confused. You said crying is good, and then when *your* tears came, you ran off like you were ashamed or something."

He pursed his lips and blew air out. "Old stuff. In this culture, men are supposed to be strong, especially around kids."

"At first, I thought I'd done something wrong, but I always think that when grownups get upset."

"It was nothing you did, trust me. I'll try to do better. Can we put it behind us?" he asked.

"If you tell me why you were crying." She desperately wished she could see his face so she could read his expression. Instead, she was left with tuning into his energy, which was harder. She tried to rest in the big field, behind her thoughts. It was always easier to sense stuff there.

He groaned. "Your mom just asked me the same thing. I'm not ready."

"That's an excuse," Rowan said. "You're afraid. I know 'cause I do the same thing." She heard the bed squeak, but she could tell he was still there. She guessed he'd shifted his position. Zephyr moved her head into Rowan's lap. She stroked the dog's ears but said nothing. She'd learned if she didn't fill the space with chatter sometimes people added more.

"How do you know these things? You're only eleven."

"What does age have to do with it?" Rowan said. "I'm a person, just like you. We aren't so different."

"Yikes," Moss said. "I've met my match."

Rowan giggled.

"I want to know you and your mom better," he said. "But I'm afraid my experiences will put you off."

Rowan considered his words. "Yeah, I guess it could happen. But Mom and I, we're kind of cool people." She heard Moss stifle a chuckle.

"That's for sure," he said. "Anyway, your mom says the three of you are probably headed home day after tomorrow."

"I don't want to go. It's easier here. People who knew me before, you know, before I lost my sight? Except my neighbor, Seth. The rest, they act all weird."

Moss chortled. "See? It's no different from how I feel about my missing leg. You need some time, right? To adjust to the new you."

"Right. Right," Rowan admitted. "Eugene is noisy and busy. I don't know which way is what without my sight. It scares me." She unfolded her legs and stretched them out.

Zephyr adjusted to fit the new position.

"Here, it's quiet, and everything is kind of the same from day to day. I feel super safe." She put her hands over her face and shook her head. "Each day I wake up, and I'm newly blind all over again. I hate it. Early mornings are awful."

"Yeah. I feel the same way," Moss said. "Mornings *are* the worst. The shock of it. It doesn't ever seem to go away."

They sat in companionable silence for a few minutes.

Rowan gathered her nerve. "Can I feel your fake leg?"

"Whoa, you don't want much! That's pretty personal, don't you think?"

"Yeah, I guess." She frowned and sat cross-legged again, thinking. "But still. We both have disabilities; shouldn't we be able to teach each other?"

"Fair enough."

She heard a shuffle and felt him switch positions.

"I've stuck my prosthesis in front of you. Go for it."

She tentatively reached out and touched his pant leg. Jeans, by the texture. She followed the leg down, lifted the hem, and rested her fingers on the device. It felt like a smooth metal post with more material at the ankle joint, and wider at the calf. "This is different than I imagined. I thought it would look like a leg."

"The foot is shaped like a real foot so it fits in a shoe," he said. "But they don't bother fancying up legs for guys who wear pants most of the time. The ones that look real are for women who wear dresses."

"What's the knee like?"

Moss placed her hand on the knee joint and bent his leg so she could feel the motion.

"Wow," she breathed. "It's weird and wonderful. Kind of a miracle."

"What a good way to think about it. I could do well to adopt your attitude."

"How does it attach to you?"

"A plastic cup was molded to what's left of my leg so they match. Like a hand and close-fitting glove."

"Well, at least they could replace your leg with something that kind of works. There's no way to replace my eyes."

"You're right, kiddo. It's a tough break. Not fair."

"Would you talk to Mom about staying a little longer?"

"You're always welcome to visit here later. Don't you think it might be good for you to go back to Eugene and test out life? Besides, isn't school starting soon? With your love of words, I bet you enjoy learning."

She rubbed the back of her neck, ignoring his questions. "Won't you miss Zephy? I think you should get a dog, a companion. I see how Zephy loves you. And you know just how to be with her. You're great with animals, I can tell."

There was a pause before he spoke. "I'll consider your suggestion. Yes, I'll miss her a lot; you've got a grand dog there. I doubt I could ever find one as special."

"Mossy, you saved her. I'll never forget." She dashed tears away from her cheeks. "She won't either. We're all friends for life. Right?"

She felt his hand on her head, ruffling her hair. His voice was gravelly. "You bet, Row. You bet."

Chapter Twenty

wo days later, Carolina heard a vehicle rumble onto the ranch. As she tied back the curtain, the Country Vet sign on the side of the truck glinted in the morning light. She slipped out of her pajamas, pulled on jeans and T-shirt, ran her fingers through her hair, and hurried toward the main house, just as Moss limped out, his hair tousled.

"Just the two people I hoped to see," Francine said. She turned to Carolina. "I brought some tranquilizers in case Zephyr needs them on the trip home. It's light medication—it'll function more for calming than knocking her out."

"Should we give them to her in anticipation of stress?"

"I wouldn't. Save them. If she manages the car ride without, she'll develop more confidence." Francine handed them over.

"Thanks for taking such good care of her. It means everything to us." Carolina leaned against the porch railing.

"The thanks goes to Moss for bringing her in." Francine turned toward him. "I have a dog who needs fostering for a bit. I thought you might be just the right person."

Moss stepped back. "What kind of dog?"

"She's greyhound and yellow lab, though you can hardly see the retriever part. A good-looking dog, and fun. Her person died."

"I don't know, Francie. Sounds like she doesn't need fostering; she needs a permanent home."

"Well, she's at my house. Stop over and visit this afternoon if you want. I'll be there."

"Yeah. I'll come. But don't get your hopes up."

Knuckling her eyes, Rowan stepped out on the guest cottage porch, Zephyr by her side.

"Morning, Rowan!" Francine called. "Bring her over, would you?"

"Okay." Rowan grabbed some of Zephyr's fur and said, "Forward." They made their way toward the adults, and Carolina stepped forward to give her daughter a good morning hug.

"I want to have one last look to make sure she can travel. I've got to remove those sutures, too," Francine said.

"Today? I don't want to leave." Rowan's voice was both sleepy and irritable.

"I'm just going by what your momma said on the phone. Don't shoot the messenger."

"Sorry."

"Rowan, you hold her collar," Francine said. "I'll loosen the T-shirt to get a clear look underneath." She undid the knot, pulled the shirt forward to expose the hound's shoulder, and gently probed the area. "This is looking much, much better. The honey helped the wounds close, and the antibiotics are clearing the infection. Grip her firmly now, and I'll snip these stitches."

"Will it hurt?" Rowan asked, her tone anxious.

"No. It just pulls a tiny bit."

It took about five minutes to remove the sutures, and Zephyr seemed unconcerned.

"Moss, may I have another of these?" Francine passed off the soiled tee and redressed Zephyr in the freshly laundered one. "She's quite a sight," she said to Rowan. "Her new shirt is dayglow orange."

"Zephyr's cleared for travel. Check in with your vet once you get home. Finish the full week of antibiotics and keep up the honey for a few more days. Here are my number and email if you have questions." She handed Carolina a card. "See you after lunch, Moss?"

"Sure, I'll stop by."

"Good luck on your reentry. I'll be thinking of all of you," Francine said, offering each of them a hug.

After Francine left, Rowan tugged on her mother's sleeve. "I can't face going home. Not yet. Please, please can't we stay a couple days longer? At home—I hate running into people who know us. They feel sorry for me." She chewed on the end of her finger. "I feel much safer here. Comfortable."

Carolina rubbed her daughter's back. "I know, sweetie. But Eugene's where our lives are, and we need to face up to it. More important, it's where my livelihood is." She glanced over at Moss. "Could we visit?"

"I hope so," he said.

Tears rolled down Rowan's cheeks. "Mossy told me that yesterday. I know I sound like Grandma, but I can't bear going home."

"You can," Carolina murmured. "You'll see. We'll get there, and it will all feel familiar. And remember? Benjamin will come over and give you another braille lesson. You enjoyed him. You can show him how skillful you are with the cane, now. You'll see Seth, too. How about getting dressed? Then we'll eat and load up."

Moss whipped up breakfast omelets. Afterward, they all went outside to finish packing the van.

The mouth of the monster is open. Zephyr can see her nest and favorite toy inside. Her girl hugs and talks to her, soft words that have a push to them, too. She sends pictures—the playing field, dog couch, treats. Hesitating, Zephyr walks closer. No roars or rumbles. She steps inside to get a treat.

Zephyr bumped Rowan as if asking, "Now, where's my breakfast?" Rowan felt around and pulled it from behind the seat, and the dog ate with relish. As soon as she licked the bowl clean, she settled in her bed, crossed her front paws with Wubby between, and looked at the people staring at her.

Chuckling, Carolina shook her head. "That dog never fails to astonish me. She's from a unique doggy planet."

"She *is* different," Moss said. "I've never met one like her. She communicates intuitively. It's almost like telepathy."

"No." Carolina frowned at him. "You don't believe that."

"I do. It was uncanny watching how Rowan and Zeph figured out walking together—it can't be easily explained."

"Science doesn't support what you're suggesting," Carolina said. "And I wish you wouldn't encourage Rowan in this woo-woo business."

Moss shook his head. "Your science only reports material facts. We don't know much, not really." He hesitated a moment and said softly, "Your beliefs about how the world works might make things tougher with Row."

"She's my daughter; I understand her better than you do," she snapped. She knew her practical nature was hard on Rowan; she often feared it might pull them apart. *But this? With Moss?* "I can't get into it now. We've got to get going," she said, with the evenest inflection she could muster. Afraid if she met his eyes she might cry, she looked away. Moss was right. He and Rowan seemed to understand each other. In a crazy way, Carolina felt left out.

"Hey." He walked over to her. "Apparently, I hit a nerve. That wasn't my intention."

"It's nothing." She shrugged, but the roughness in her voice made her irritation clear.

"All righty then." He backed off.

Instantly, she was sorry.

"I'd appreciate a call when you get home, so I know you've arrived safely." His tone was measured. "Most likely, I'll be on the land; a message is fine. I'd like to know how Zephyr manages, too."

"Sure, we'll do that."

Moss helped them carry the rest of their belongings, and Carolina stashed them behind the back seat.

Rowan said in a strangled tone, "Mossy?"

He held her tight. "It'll be all right. I'll make sure we see each other soon." He reached in and stroked Zephyr. "You take good care, you brave girl."

Carolina wiped tears away. "Thanks so much—for your kindness and generosity to all of us." She turned and, without looking back, climbed into the van.

Rowan hunched near the passenger window. The car bumped along. She could taste dust as they retraced their way to town.

"Zephyr seems to be doing all right," Carolina said. "I guess she surrendered."

"I wish I could snuggle back there with her." She was quiet for a moment and then added, Why'd you cold-shoulder Mossy? He was so nice."

"I didn't! We just had a rough spot at the end."

"You mean when he said he believed me? That Zephy understands?" Rowan spat the words at her mother. "She does! And you've gone and wrecked everything. He's kind. And fun."

"I don't *not* believe you." Her mom's shoulders were raised around her ears.

Rowan snorted. "So you say."

"He is kind. But he's, uh, complicated," her mom said. "Remember how odd he was in the library?"

"That was before he got to know us. Mossy really likes you, I can tell. Even when you blow it."

Rowan felt the car stop. Then they turned left, and abruptly the ride went from rough to smooth. "I miss Daddo," she whispered.

"I know, sweetie, I do to. And I did enjoy Moss. But these were strange circumstances, wouldn't you say? Not a good start for meeting someone."

"Mommo, life is strange. There is no normal. Like Daddo dying of flu, or Zeph nearly killed by a mountain lion and then finding Mossy. Totally off the wall."

"Or having a daughter as precocious as you."

Rowan hid her giggle; she wanted to stay mad longer. It wasn't Mom's fault she was pigheaded about some stuff—most everyone was. But Mossy was the first person since Daddo who seemed to actually listen to her. She yearned for someone to confide in.

Zephyr lies in her bed in the car, head pressed between her paws. The pictures of home the girl penses from the front seat—the field where they play, the silly, sweet boy who smells of food and dirt—stop coming. Rowan sleeps and doesn't comfort her. Zephyr aches to be home, not here with the rumbling, scary noise. She trembles as big, loud trucks rush by and remembers the car tumble. Stormy in the road, gone. Terror and loneliness. The cat fight, then she isn't running fast, and dinner gets away. Soon, hunger pinches.

The urge to sing her misery comes, and Zephyr lifts her head and whines. Her girl doesn't hear, so she points her nose high and howls. Now Rowan wakes, speaks firmly to the mother in her command voice, and soon the car pulls to a stop.

Rowan comes in back; her warm body snugs around Zephyr. Shaking stops as calming mind-pictures flood—lying on the couch, eating biscuits, long walks. She slurps Rowan's hand; the girl knuckle-rubs her ears.

Chapter Twenty-one

Moss watched Carolina, Rowan, and Zephyr drive away. He paced the deck, unsure what to do with himself. The ranch, which used to be the perfect hideaway, now felt forlorn. The blues dropped on him like a sudden downpour, flooding in the top of his head and streaming all the way down to his toes. Did he take an anti-depressant this morning? So much had been going on, he'd have to count how many pills were left in the container to be sure.

Damn, he'd imagined a different parting than what had unfolded, and blamed himself for the stupid comment he made to Carolina. He knew how practical and down-to-earth she was. Was he unconsciously trying to bait her? No. He was just speaking his truth. Still, he was pissed at himself and annoyed with her, too. Why'd she have to get so arrogant and tear off without a hug?

He marched out to the barn, hefted the ax, and threw himself into chopping wood, finding satisfaction each time the blade cleanly split a log. Working up a fine sweat, he added a layer to the growing woodpile before he stopped, hands on thighs, to catch his breath. Nothing like hard physical labor to soften a troubled heart.

He walked over to the guest house to see what he could put right and was surprised to find Carolina had tidied up. Sheets and pillowcases tumbled in the dryer, and the beds were freshly made with linens she'd found in the closet. The little kitchen sparkled. She'd vacuumed, too—not even a clump of Zephyr's fur lay behind the doors. It was as though Carolina, Rowan, and that venerable dog had never been there.

He sank into his grandmother's rocker and passed his hand across his forehead. Now what? He pulled Great-Grandma Nanon's crocheted afghan from the couch and held it to his nose as he had when he was a child. Through the window, he'd seen Carolina curled in it on more than one evening. Was this her scent? He wrapped it around himself. *I just need to forget about her.*

Zephyr smells home, sits up in the back of the van, and looks out the window. Her body trembles again, but this time, it's delight. Carolina lets her out, and she limps up the path. Now at the door, Zephyr sits and scratches on the wood.

"Leave it!" the mother calls.

Zephyr knows what that means. Quivering, she lies down to wait. She wants in.

Moss startled awake, realizing he must have dozed. He buried his face in the afghan one more time, drew in a breath, then set it back on the couch. Out the window, the sun was high, just past noon. When he rose to return to his house, he saw a gift bag by the cottage fireplace. How had he missed it? He retrieved it and pulled out two bottles of his favorite vineyard's merlot—but this was top of the line—stuff he'd never buy for himself. Carolina shouldn't have; he bet she didn't have extra funds. But she'd wanted to thank him.

He almost missed the envelope tucked flat in the bottom of the bag. Sitting down on the couch, he slid his finger under the lip and winced as the sharp edge sliced soft flesh. Blood flared. As he sucked on the wound, he took in the elegant photo of Zephyr. This woman was so practical and organized, she traveled with a thank you card just in case she needed it. Then again, Row, intent on finding her dog, might have insisted they bring it so they could show the picture around town.

A letter fell out when he opened the card. His fingers trembled. Handwritten and a whole page. Not now, he didn't have the courage; he'd save it. He put card, letter, and wine back in the bag and carried it to the main house, placing it by the fireplace. Later. Tonight. With a sumptuous glass of her merlot.

As he made lunch, he remembered Francine's comment about the foster dog. He heard old man Lynch had died. In fact, he met his dog about six months ago outside the farm store. He vaguely recalled her as being unusual.

This afternoon, he planned to run into town for supplies and stop at Francine's after; if he didn't show, she'd call and bug him for sure. After all, he'd promised. In her hands-off way, Francine looked after him. Sweet of her. In his current mood, he'd better be proactive and keep busy—no sinking back to where he'd been before. It would be easy, but he didn't want to lose the ground he'd fought for these past couple of weeks. Moss lazed in the sunshine on his deck and ate lunch, admiring house finches swooping the feeders. The sounds of nature—bird calls, the breeze in the aspens, bees buzzing—surrounded him.

After taking his dishes back to the kitchen, he picked up the compost bucket and headed to the barn to dump it in the chicken pen. Although his heart wasn't in it, he talked in an upbeat tone to the hens as he spread vegetable remains. They fluttered and picked at the new offering, chattering about it, as chickens do. He hadn't collected eggs yet—he'd tend to that after sprinkling the lettuce he'd seeded five days ago. Maybe tiny sprouts would be showing. The rhythm of farm chores provided a nourishing pastime—but today, he felt the pull to molder with his feet up in the living room. He must keep moving. After watering, he carried eleven eggs back to the house, washed them, and added one from the fridge to take to Francie.

Moss completed his errands and headed to Francine and Clare's home. One block from the clinic, the old Victorian sat on an acre. It was rumored to be the town's oldest house. They'd done wonders renovating it, completing most of the work themselves.

Clare answered the door. "You're so generous!" she said, taking the eggs and hugging him with her free arm.

When he stood back, he appreciated this statuesque woman. She was over five nine in flat shoes. Today, she wore her chestnut hair braided and coiled on her head, making her seem even taller.

"Hey," he said. "Really nice to see you. Is Francie here?"

"Uh huh. Out back, throwing the ball for Jasmine. The dog's been moping without Jack around. Francie's trying to cheer her up. Dogs, they know." She ushered him in. "Jasmine was with Jack when he died."

"Ouch. That's sad. I wondered how it played out. How old is she?"

"According to her records, a year and a half. Sweetest thing. Would you like some iced tea?"

"Sure, but I'll take it to the back yard. Francie's got her heart set on getting me to adopt this critter. She used the word foster, but you and I both know her sneaky intentions. After Zephyr, I don't know if this dog will be a good fit—or any dog, really."

"But she's part sighthound. That's why Francie thought of you since you fell so hard for Zephyr. Come in the kitchen so I can get your tea."

"Right, but this one's half lab, as well. Retrievers are a loyal family dog, but not elegant, if you know what I mean. I got sucked in by Zeph's regal quality. It spoiled me."

"Give this girl a chance. You may be surprised." She set down the eggs and handed him a frosted glass topped with fresh mint. He took a swallow.

"Refreshing. Hits the spot. Thanks, Clare. See you in a bit."

The dog's long, light strides captured his attention, so much that he forgot to greet Francine. The hound flew over the ground, nabbed the tennis ball, and sped toward them. "My God, amazing! What makes you think she has Labrador in her at all?"

Francine chuckled. "Because she has webbed feet like water dogs and loves fetching. Hi to you, too!"

Moss hugged her. "She's a beauty," he said under his breath.

"I knew you'd like her. You'll see she has a different coat than a greyhound, although it's still short and not substantial." She snapped her fingers for the dog. "The Bend Shelter gave Jack the information when he adopted her. The old guy blushed when he told me she was 'pretty as a flower.' That's how she came by her name. He was delighted with her, but apparently a strict owner, from reports I've heard."

Moss sat down in a wicker chair. He pursed his lips and made a squeaky sound. Jasmine turned to consider him then walked over and stuck her head under his hand as if waiting for Moss to pet her. She was blonde, skinny-headed with folded-back ears, and looked directly into his eyes. It surprised him—dogs don't often hold human gazes. Well, that wasn't true. Zephyr did.

This dog's ears were unbearably soft. Something inside of him shifted. "Oh, jeez, Francie. You know me so damn well."

"I recognize two souls who need each other. You've both had significant losses."

He felt Francine smiling at both of them. "She's had an awful lot of change. You think she'll handle yet another living situation?" He stuck his knuckle in the dog's ear. She leaned into him.

"I told her staying here was temporary. Besides, what dog in its right mind wants to live with its veterinarian? In a pinch, my dogs get stuck for blood transfusions. Pretty often." She leaned against the porch four-by-four. "I considered keeping her, but my big guy, Chance, didn't take to her. Gotta have a happy pack."

"How'd Jack die?" Moss asked.

"Brain embolism. His daughter found him on the kitchen floor staring at the ceiling. Jasmine was lying with her head on his chest."

By this time, the dog's nose rested on Moss's leg. She was still looking at him.

"How can I say no to two powerful women?" He patted the dog. "Okay, I'll try her out. Give us two weeks."

Francine clapped her hands. "I knew you'd come through! Chance will be so relieved."

Clare joined them, refilled Moss's iced tea, and the three chatted about old man Lynch's death. Moss was grateful they didn't grill him about Carolina.

Francine gathered Jasmine's gear, set it near Moss's truck, and lifted the dog into the front seat. She stashed food, bed, bowl, and biscuits in the flatbed, leash in the front. Pulling two tennis balls from her pocket, she dropped them through the window. "Jasmine will ride quietly with her head in your lap. You'll see. One more thing: the day after Zephyr's surgery, Jack's daughter brought Jasmine in. She sought Zeph out and lay by her cage most of the time. They got along great." She winked and closed the door of the truck. "Have fun getting to know each other."

Carolina swung the door open. The comforting scents of home—hints of lavender and the faintest trace of dog—swept over her. Zephyr limped in behind, made a turn into the living room, slid on the hardwood floor, and let out a yelp. She crawled onto the couch. Carolina turned to tell her daughter what had happened, but before she got the words out, Rowan said, "She's already in her spot on the sofa."

Carolina was surprised how sharp her daughter's hearing was becoming. "Yes! Obviously, she's one happy pooch to be back in familiar surroundings."

Suddenly, grief for Stormy soaked her. He'd been such a reliable, good dog. Obedient, protective, smart. Patient. Even as an oldster, he'd accepted Zephyr and her puppy antics from day one.

"Go snuggle with your girl, Rowan. I'm going downstairs to work out for a bit—I have to sweat."

"You need to call Mossy. You promised. First thing," Rowan said.

Carolina pursed her mouth, then said, "You call him, sweetie. I'll look up his number. You remember the layout of the buttons, right?"

Rowan squeezed next to Zephyr and felt for the phone. "Okay. Give me the numbers two at a time."

Carolina fumbled in her purse and pulled out a small, spiral-bound notebook. "Hang on; I've almost got it. Westbury." She read the numbers to Rowan who felt for the buttons and slowly punched them.

Rowan listened briefly. "I got a weird squealy sound—a fax tone, I think. Say it again."

"Let's review the keypad."

"No! I've got it. Anyone can dial a wrong number."

She was right. Carolina repeated the digits. Rowan dialed again. This time a big smile lit up her face. "It's ringing! Maybe he'll answer!"

"He said he'd be out in the garden. Wait for the answering machine."

She paid attention as Rowan talked. When her daughter said in a strangled tone, "Mossy, I miss you," Carolina called out, "Time to get off now. That's a long enough message." She'd fulfilled her agreement and let him know they were safe. Best they stop this, right here, right now. After all, they'd been thrown together in an unusual circumstance—not by choice. Time would sort it out, and the intensity would fade.

Moss studied the dog whose lithe body stretched across the passenger seat. Her head did rest on his leg just like Francie predicted. This girl reminded him of California hills in the summertime—her coat radiated like warm wheat. He talked to her as he maneuvered his truck along pot-holed dirt roads. "You're movin' to paradise, sweetheart. The only hard part is me. I'm a tough case; I get the blues. It'd be fantastic if you'd help cheer me up. Oh yeah—I have nightmares, too."

She yawned widely, ending with a little squeak.

The dust grew thicker, and he closed the windows. "Okay, I've told you my worst flaw; now it's your turn." He fondled the dog's ears. "By the way, I don't know about your name—it's awfully frilly. I hope you'll settle for Jazz."

Moss pulled onto his property and turned off the engine. Jazz stood peering out the window. She'd been living on a farm, so he figured this land looked pretty much the same. But when he opened the passenger door, she sat down instead of jumping out.

"Hey, Jazz," he said. "It'll most likely work. Come on, give it a try." He clipped the leash on and encouraged her out. No go. He coaxed and cajoled then dug around for a treat. Jazz pinned her ears back and sat firmly. He reached in to pick her up, but she stiffened and clung to the seat with her toes. He gave up and called Francine. "She won't get out of the truck. Not even a biscuit lured her."

"What was it Jack used?" Long pause. "Try 'free dog!' Like 'go play' intonation, but different words. I think I heard him say that once in the parking lot."

Moss went back to the truck. "Free dog!" he said.

Jazz jumped out, inhaling the scents before squatting. Then she ran back to Moss.

"I'll be damned. What are your other commands? I guess I'll find out."

He walked into the house and busied himself in the kitchen while Jazz poked around. When he went hunting for her, she was lying next to his bedroom reading chair. "Good girl," he said. "I'll put your bed there. We'll keep each other company at night."

He realized he hadn't checked his messages, and sure enough, there was one—a rare event. Hoping to hear Carolina's voice rather than his editor's, his heart sped up as he pushed the button on the answering machine. It was Rowan, not her mom.

"We made it; Zephy's okay—we didn't have to give her any medicine. She howled once, but I made us stop and went in the back to comfort her. Mommo said she ran up to our front door and scratched on it! She wanted in bad. Mossy...." He could hear her take a breath. "I miss you. A lot. Okay, Mom's waving at me. I have to get off now. Bye."

He closed his eyes and held the receiver to his chest. Then he pressed the button and listened to the message again. *Damn. Carolina didn't even send a 'hi' through Row.* He hung up the phone, hesitated, and then saved the message.

Jazz followed as he limped back to the truck to unload her things. When he dropped her bed in the same spot by his chair, she scratched in it before lying down. As he left the bedroom, he thought for sure he caught a soft doggy sigh.

For dinner, Moss reheated lasagna, dumped leftover salad on his plate, and headed for his favorite chair in the living room. Jazz trailed him. After giving the gift bag an interested sniff, she settled in front of the fireplace. "Oh, right—that," he said. "Thanks for the reminder."

He ate his meal in leisurely fashion and cleared his dishes to the kitchen. Then he fixed her food in the mudroom and called, "Jazz, come! Dinner!"

A curious, slender face peered around the corner. She sat.

"What pup doesn't rush for food? Another new command? Let me think." He rubbed his hand on his chin. "Dinner" hadn't worked. "Gusto!" he said. She didn't move. He tried a couple of other words. No luck.

"Francine," he said, after she picked up. "She won't eat. She's waiting for something. I need another command."

"Use 'free chow.' Sorry, I forgot to tell you. But let me get her chart to find other commands for you. Let's pray there's more written down."

"You're still at work? It's dinnertime."

"Yeah, well, you know."

"Don't forget Clare. I hope you treasure that woman."

"You bet I do. Okay, here's her file. We often ask clients about their dog's vocabulary during the intake interview. You'd be amazed how a list of familiar words can help in unexpected situations."

Moss could hear her finger turning pages.

"You'd better email me the list, Francie, and I hope it's long. Otherwise, I'll be phoning you every half hour, although I suppose I can try 'free' in front of everything. Poor dog, didn't she ever get any downtime? Guess I'll have to teach her."

"I'll email it to you now."

"Free chow" released the dog. Jazz gave the dish and food a careful sniff with her long, narrow nose. At last, she delicately picked up one kibble. Piece by piece, she ate. Once finished, she sat and looked at Moss.

"Now what?" he asked.

Chapter Twenty-two

After Rowan went to bed, Carolina tackled the ever-growing mound of medical bills. Sorting through the new mail, she counted more than twenty envelopes that had accumulated while they were away. She fumbled in the top drawer for a knife and sliced open the first, a bill from the hospital. She tried to focus on the bottom line but had trouble absorbing the bold print: $17,925.01. Her body went cold. She nervously tapped her fingers on the counter as she contemplated the remaining three-inch stack. What would they all add up to? This first bill alone would swallow her savings account. She had a small monthly stipend from Rafe's life insurance; it wasn't big enough for what was coming, that was for sure.

She had no idea how they would manage this huge uptick in expenses—beyond paying the mortgage, buying food, and school supplies. Her daughter needed therapies of different kinds, too. Tutors. Braille books likely cost a fortune. Did braille libraries even exist? And, despite all the turmoil, Rowan kept growing, as kids do. She needed new clothes before school started. Her pants were above her ankle bones.

With shaking hands, she drew on an inner reserve and opened the remaining pile. It was important to know the total, then she could develop a plan to negotiate with the medical providers. She shucked off the envelopes, methodically smoothing the bills. Then she ran the numbers on the calculator: $119,672.59. Her eyes brimmed with tears.

Was this amount possible? What about her health insurance? It did have the highest deductible, but still. She looked carefully at the pages more carefully this time. At the bottom, in tiny print, each sheet noted her share. She'd been so anxious she'd missed the small type. She went through the pile again, highlighting her part in yellow. The new total came to only $18,997.44. For a moment, her tension softened. Then, realizing the amount was only small in comparison, she shook her head. It still wiped out everything she'd struggled to put away.

Even if she mailed each provider $20 a month to keep them from sending her to collections, for all twenty-three bills, the total came to a whopping $460—a huge bite out of their monthly disposable income. She'd have to spread the word, take in more sewing. Carolina mused for a moment. Her industrial machine showed signs of wear. The last time she hauled it in for repair, Joe told her it was getting harder to find parts. She counted back. She'd gotten the sewing machine while pregnant with Rowan, so it was more than eleven years old. And it labored hard. She'd need to replace it with a current model soon—before she paid medical bills—while she still had enough cash in the bank.

What other unexpected expenses would compound an already financially devastating situation? For sure, tutors for Rowan. And she needed to make payments to Moss for Zephyr's veterinary bills. The surgery and the ensuing days at the vet's wouldn't come cheap. House calls, too. She better phone Francine and get that total to add to the growing bottom line.

Carolina shoved the calculator away. Then catching herself, she backtracked and tore off the paper tape, clipping its shocking news to the top bill. She wondered if the bank would give her a second on her home. She'd rather have a single amount to pay than a slew of individual ones. If the bank consolidated her debt, maybe the monthly total would be smaller than $460.

Before she went to bed, she tiptoed in to check on her daughter. Both were sound asleep. Zeph lay on the double bed beside Rowan, shaggy head resting on the second pillow. Her daughter's arm was slung over the dog. Carolina had tried, without success, to keep Zephyr off the bed. No luck. In the scheme of things, it didn't matter. She tucked the sheet under Rowan's chin and gave Zephyr a little stroke on the way out.

After dinner, Jazz snored softly by the fireplace. Her nose made a little twitch with each exhale. Moss found it endearing.

He figured since she'd been with Jack when he died, it was a little easier—she didn't have to wonder where the heck he'd gone. Dogs astonished him; most simply moved on. Except, of course, Greyfriars Bobby, the Skye terrier in Scotland who lay on his master's grave for fourteen years. As a boy, the story moved him—sparked his understanding and appreciation of loyalty and patience.

Moss popped the cork, poured a glass, and rolled the wine on his tongue. The aged merlot was perhaps the best he'd ever had. He took a moment to savor it and picked up the bottle: 1995 vintage.

He couldn't avoid reading Carolina's letter any longer. He'd brought the bag close to his chair before he unlegged for the night. Pulling the card out again, Moss set the sheet of paper in his lap. First, he admired the photo of Zephyr and compared her to Jazz. They had the same basic body type, tall and long with a deep chest and tight belly tuck. But Zeph was quite a bit taller and sported a crazy, wiry coat—a Rastafarian greyhound, that's what she was!

Jazz stirred and peered up at him with a quizzical expression. He reached down and gave her a caress. "How do you handle the winters here, girl? You don't have much hair—nothing compared to Zeph." He shook the letter at the dog. "I've put off reading this—afraid of what it might say. I refused to open it until you arrived. I needed your company." He took another sip of wine, put on his reading glasses, and unfolded the letter. Carolina had neat, interesting handwriting; her "Y's" were long, yet snappy. So like her.

> "Dear Moss,
> "Your generosity to the three of us makes me tear up. Thank you! You saved Zephyr's life; Rowan is forever indebted to you, as am I. I know Zeph incurred large veterinary bills—I'll get the total from Francine and send monthly payments to her.
>
> "We met under remarkably odd circumstances, especially that first awkward phone conversation. I'm glad it got easier."

Moss's heart pumped fast, fueled with hope.

"Your kiss remains with me. I recall how soft it was—curious, inviting. It let me know you're sure of yourself, and I find that attractive. But Moss, I made a promise to myself not to get involved, not even a fling before Rowan goes to college— seven more years. I don't want my attention drawn away from her. My daughter needs all of me, especially now, since her blindness. Technically, the accident was not my fault, yet I feel horribly responsible. I must honor my commitment."

His mood plunged. He could understand Carolina's reasoning, but he absolutely did NOT agree. He dropped his head and immediately felt a cold, moist nose. His eyes flew open. It was Jazz, resting her head between his knee and his stump. This girl already sensed his moods.

He stroked her ears as he pondered Carolina's words. Yes, Rowan would get 100 percent of her mother, but Rowan potentially could ... he broke the direction of his thought. No reason to get ahead of himself.

He pressed the back of his hand against his mouth and smelled sweet musky dog. "Okay, Jazz, I'm going to finish the letter," he murmured. She thumped her tail on the floor.

"I'd like to get to know each other better. As friends. Perhaps that's best, anyway. You may not like what you discover. Or vice versa. I don't have any skeletons in my closet, but I can be difficult."

And I'm not? he thought. All humans are challenging with unique proclivities that trigger each other. That's just how it is.

"Besides, Row wants a relationship with you, and I saw how easy you two were with each other. She could benefit from a male role model—I even suggested getting her a 'Big Brother' after her dad died. She wasn't open then, but she really took to you. She told me what you said—that you agreed we're all friends for life. I hope you meant it. Otherwise, her heart will be broken, yet again. She's had enough loss.

"At some point, after we get back to Eugene, I'll call. Of course, we'll let you know we arrived safely, but I'll phone you later to talk.
—Carolina"

Moss rested the letter on his lap. His feelings were difficult to parse. Delight and sorrow, urgency and patience, deep frustration and a strong pull, all roiled inside of him. And then there were feelings harder to name. He concentrated, trying to zoom in on those emotions. He picked up the glass and took another mouthful of wine. Well, there was fear, for one—major fear of opening up again and yet the yearning to do so. And Rowan? Sweet, funny, smart, cheeky Row. He wondered if she was to be his redemption. Then, the grumpy, shut-down way Carolina left. What was *that* about?

When he looked up, Jazz was sitting directly in front of him, focused on getting his attention. What now? Go out? He got up awkwardly, grabbed the crutches, and made his way to the front door. "Free dog," he called. She didn't move. Maybe she was used to getting a treat in the evening; after all, he liked dessert. He walked to the mudroom and dug out a large biscuit. She walked after him, and sat quietly, waiting. "Free chow!" he said and offered her the bone. To his relief, she accepted the goodie, lay down, and with slow care, dismantled and chewed it. He found her attitude about food bewildering, and so un-dog-like.

After Jazz licked the floor and her paws, she walked to the front door and sat. *Who's training whom?* He chuckled. "Go free," he said, opening the door. She tilted her head and contemplated him for a moment but accepted his slight modification and ran outside. He turned on the outdoor lights to follow her progress, making sure she didn't head for Bender's Ridge. After a few minutes of sniffing and doing her business, she bounded back to the house. When he let her in, she darted to her bed, dug in it for a moment and with a groan, settled down.

Moss picked up an apple from the bowl in the kitchen, crutched back to the living room, and relaxed in his recliner. As he chewed the first bite, Jazz showed up at his side, ears perked. On his second bite, she licked her lips and swallowed. The dog was salivating. He finished eating and offered the core to her.

"Free chow," he whispered.

With soft lips, she accepted the gift. It vanished far faster than the kibble had. Then she gave his hand a tongue swipe and went back to her nest.

Moss reread Carolina's letter. The urge to call her overwhelmed him—the pull so strong that he gripped the arms of his chair to keep from getting up. He scanned the letter yet again. His inclination was to question every sentence, word by word, and examine the underlying meaning. "I'm acting like a damn sixteen-year-old," he growled. "Besides, she blew it today." With that, he folded the letter, put it back inside the card, set it on the fireplace mantel, and headed for bed.

He knew he was screaming, but he couldn't wake up. A lucid nightmare, his specialty, flooded him with devastating, repetitive war memories—this time, the children. What startled him awake were sixty pounds of dog leaping on the bed. She licked his face, jumped off, howled, and hopped back up to slurp him again. When he was conscious enough to stop screaming, the howling ended, but the face bath continued.

He swiped a hand across his mouth. "Okay! Leave it. Free stop! What in God's name will you understand?" He pushed Jazz over to the other side. Just as quickly, she crawled back and planted her head on his chest. Then, with a gulp, he realized—she likely thought he was dying. He stroked her head. "It's okay; we're okay, Jazz. Let's get something to drink. I'll have valerian tea, then read for a bit. I always sit up for a while after one of these." He rolled to the side and reached for his crutches. "So sorry this happened the first night you're here. Welcome to my world, girl."

As though nothing had transpired, she followed him into the living room, flopped down in front of the fireplace, and cleaned her already immaculate feet. He'd remember to get a soft bath mat for the spot—not thick enough to trip over, but some comfort for her. The image startled him. They'd only been together for twelve hours and she already was family.

Chapter Twenty-three

R owan awakened slowly. Zephyr's paw looped over her chest, and the dog's big, damp nose pushed against her neck. She used to lie in bed in the morning and stare, taking in how Zephy's wiry eyebrows moved with every breath she took. Loss rolled through her, and her throat tightened. *Yeah, but she's here with me. It could have turned out way worse.*

Every morning, she tried to get out of bed without waking her pup, but she hadn't succeeded. Yet. The moment she shifted, Zephyr bounded off, filled with silly, young dog energy. This morning, she was glad her dog trotted out the door—Mommo would feed her, and she could lie here and think about stuff. Nothing was the same. BB—before blindness—she used to write in her journal first thing. AB—after blindness—impossible. BB, on weekends, after she fed Zephy, she'd go back to bed and read. AB, she couldn't do that either, not until she got super good at braille. Listening to a book wasn't the same. Recorded books had been a special part of car trips, not home. And how was she going to do research? What she missed most of all were the familiar rhythms of her life.

What Benjamin said was true—her hearing *was* better, and she *did* sense when objects were in front of her—not all the time, but she improved each day. Her worries about the upcoming school year loomed. She hated the idea of having an aide by her side; it would make her stick out, draw unwanted attention. But how else could she get along? Even with an aide, starting the school year blind was scary. What was the word Benjamin had used? Daunting.

Daddo had used that word when he wrote her a letter from the hospital four days before he died. She remembered trying to puzzle out what it meant. Mommo was way too upset so Rowan didn't dare ask, and back then, she wasn't very good at using the dictionary.

She couldn't forget that something positive had happened from losing her sight, too: she'd discovered the big field behind her thoughts, where she and Zephy connected more easily. Rowan pulled up the covers, closed her eyes, and rested in that big field.

After Zephyr eats, she yawns and stretches. Her girl's worries translate into jumbled images in her head. She walks back, licks Rowan on the cheek, and penses a picture of slowly walking in the field together, heading toward to a favorite hiding place in the woods. Even though Rowan feels her way around—and stumbles—Zeph knows she can carefully guide her girl. Another lick, but Rowan doesn't stir. Zeph climbs back on the bed and rests her nose on the girl's hip.

A week later, Carolina prepared a mocha, smacking the bottom of the shaker to liberally sprinkle powdered chocolate on the foam. She sat with her mug and looked out the living room window toward the mist hovering above the field—her morning routine.

The mail came early. She was the first stop on Paul's route. They'd gone to high school together. Whenever she saw him slip the letters into her box, she waved. These days, although glad to see her classmate, she dreaded the mail. Even so, she felt compelled to quickly sort through the bad news before getting on with her day.

The white truck with the stylized blue eagle pulled up, but instead of putting the mail in her box, Paul walked toward the front door with a package. She frowned. What could it be? Then she remembered she'd ordered voice-recognition software so Rowan could communicate with the computer without using a screen. It would both type and speak back to her. She prayed it would work. She opened the door and took the parcel with letters on top. "Thanks, Paul. Say 'hi' to Sarah and the kids."

"Sure will," he said. "Sorry to be the bearer of hospital letters." He pointed to the envelopes. "I'm assuming. They stick it to ya'. But at least one isn't a bill. Take care, now. See ya' tomorrow."

She set the package down, took the letters to her desk, and sorted quickly—four from medical providers, two from insurance, and one extra thick envelope. It was addressed not only to her but to Rowan as well. Not recognizing the handwriting, Carolina checked the postal imprint. *Sisters, Oregon.* Her hands trembled as she turned the letter over. The back was stamped: *Moss Westbury, Bender's Ridge, PO Box 2, Sisters, OR 97759.* She blew out a breath to slow her heart, but instead, the rhythm sped up. Why was she having this reaction? The note could be a simple thank you for the wine. But somehow, she knew better.

She sipped her mocha and stared at the envelope. After a moment, she turned it over and traced her fingers along the handwritten address. Picking up the letter opener, she ran it under the flap, pulled out a letter with her name on it, and a CD for Rowan. She set her daughter's gift aside and unfolded the paper. It was typewritten. A sudden pang and a yearning yawned in her belly. She wanted to see more of his handwriting.

"Dear Carolina,
"I think more clearly at the keyboard—the writer's curse. Friends complain it doesn't feel as personal. Know it is. The wine is fantastic. What a delicious gift. When I sip it in the evening, I think of you, Rowan, and Zephyr. You shouldn't have, and thank you!

"I miss you all. You blew into my life and turned it upside down in a remarkable way. I'm grateful. Zephyr opened a door for me—now I know I need other warm-blooded beings around me. More than chickens.

"Consider this: Rowan might benefit from a male role model. Not just an uncle-friend, but someone closer. Perhaps you want to remain open to the possibility for both of your sakes? I understand you made a promise to yourself; I'm wondering if that might be shortsighted. In the war, it became abundantly clear life is too short not to speak my truth.

"Carolina, I have severe PTSD. Mostly, it manifests as nightmares that I have difficulty waking from. As I mentioned, sometimes I awaken screaming. I suspected because my throat is often raw in the morning, so I set up a voice-activated tape recorder. Yikes! It's good I live deep in the country, or my neighbors might have committed me. I'm not sure why, but I'm driven to write about my experience, and it helps. A lot.

"I've been fortunate. My circumstances allow me to hide in a beautiful, quiet place to heal, unlike many of my compatriots who live on the streets. I do not take this gift lightly. I want my life to benefit others. I don't plan to remain isolated forever. I've been alone here for two years, and I gave myself four. I will never give up this property—it's been in the family for generations—but maybe I'll live on it part time or make a center here for other veterans to visit and recover. I don't know yet—I'm not sure I can share the ranch in that way.

"There are adjustments I've had to make since coming home. I can't watch the evening news depicting devastating conflicts in graphic detail or the violence in so many TV dramas. How is this entertainment? Anyway, it's a big trigger for me, so I don't have a television.

"So, if you can bear having a messed-up friend and can accommodate my foibles, I'm good for the challenge. I hope the three of you will come visit for a weekend soon.
      —Moss
P.S. Yes, I meant what I said to Rowan. We're friends for life."

Carolina wiped away tears. Thank heavens Rowan would not suffer yet another loss. She hugged herself and nodded slowly. Moss had shared so much more than she expected. Good on him.

Rowan heard a knock and stirred in bed. She knew from the footfall it was her mother. After all, who else would it be?

"I have a CD for you from Moss," her mom said as she opened the door.

"Really?" Happiness rushed up Rowan's body. "My player's under my pillow. Let Zephy check out the cover, Mommo, and tell me what she does."

Rowan heard her mom put the cardboard sleeve in front of the dog's nose.

"She's snuffling it all over, and her tail is wagging. She smells him, and after two days in the mail. Amazing. You go ahead and listen, and then there's something he wants you to share with me. He says you'll know what it is."

As her mother turned to leave, Rowan fumbled for her earbuds and put the CD in the player. She teared up as Mossy's voice started:

"Dear Row,
"I miss you all. The place seems huge and empty since you drove away.

"You'll be happy to know I have somebody to talk to. Do you remember Francie mentioning she had a dog she wanted me to foster? Get this! She's lying at my feet as I record this. Her name is Jazz—I shortened it because Jasmine didn't fit for me. She's supposedly part greyhound, part yellow lab, but she's mostly sighthound in body style and temperament. Her coat is the color of sand. I guess if she were an Irish wolfhound, you'd call it 'wheaten.' She's quite the character and is teaching me, not the other way around. She has a unique vocabulary of commands. If I try different words, she stares me down as though I'm looney toons. You can bet that I'm encouraging her to mellow out. You should see her catch a Frisbee on the fly. Her leaps are incredibly high. Does Zephyr retrieve? Jazz and Zeph met at the hospital and apparently got on great, so your pup has a friend when you come for a visit.

"I had a nightmare last night, and she woke me by howling and licking my face. A few minutes later she acted like nothing had happened. You were right, Row. I needed a dog and didn't know it.

"I hope your return to Eugene has been relatively smooth. I know nothing is the same without your sight, but I'm sure your place smelled wonderful and felt like home.

"Until next time, and a big hug,
Mossy
P.S. I told you about Jazz because I knew you'd get a kick out of it. Please share it with your mom."

"Jazz is acting like those service dogs the librarian told me about," she whispered. She tucked the CD player against her heart. "A letter just for me. And I get to hear his voice!" She played it again.

Three weeks later, Carolina came upstairs after a hard karate workout. She showered, headed to the kitchen, mixed tuna salad for lunch, and added her secret ingredient—a splash of lemon juice. Rowan perched on a stool at the kitchen island. "That smells yummy. Tuna sandwiches?"

"Yeah, with salad on the side."

"I've figured out something Seth and I can do together—like old times."

"What's that?"

"Wrestle on the mats in the rumpus room. I'll feel the edge of the mat, so I don't hit the wall."

"It'll be good exercise for you. You've been sedentary since you got out of the hospital."

"You mean since I lost my vision."

"Right. You haven't been able to run around with Zephyr, either."

"I miss it something terrible."

Carolina rounded the island and hugged her daughter from behind. "I know, sweetie. But we're so lucky she's here with us. Why don't you phone Seth and invite him for lunch?"

"Maybe we should get another dog, Mommo. For you. And for Zephy, so she'll be able to run. Can we?" Rowan counted steps into the living room and picked up the telephone. "I'll call Seth."

Another dog. How could we possibly afford one?

"He'll be over in ten minutes. His mom is forcing him to clean up his room." Rowan giggled.

"Forcing him?" They had a word game—if Rowan used a word where a more accurate one might serve better, Carolina would throw it back at her. They'd been playing this way since Rowan turned eight. She watched her daughter screw up her mouth and ponder for a moment.

"His mom insists that he clean his room."

"Great choice! Why don't you go pick up yours until he gets here? You know if he says ten minutes, it'll probably be fifteen."

Rowan pulled a face but felt her way down the hall.

During lunch, the kids teased each other and fooled around. Zephyr lay near their feet waiting for crumbs. Carolina saw Rowan surreptitiously drop small bites of bread but said nothing. She was relieved her daughter seemed more like her old self—lighthearted and playful.

It wasn't long before the kids headed down to the rumpus room. Carolina paused at the top of the stairwell for a few moments. Thuds. The occasional grunt. Some thunks and chuckles.

The next morning, Rowan lounged on the living room floor listening to a book while adjusting Zephyr's invisible fence collar. Her mom tapped her on the knee. "Hey, you."

"Look," Rowan said, punching the pause button and pulling out an earbud. "I had to loosen this up a notch because she's filling out. Now, I can slip just three fingers under the collar, so this is the proper fit."

Carolina reached down and tested it. "Good you noticed. I'm going over to Sue's—she's stuck on a sewing project and wants me to problem-solve with her. I'll be back in less than an hour. Maybe sooner."

"See ya. Say 'hi' to Seth if he's there."

"Work on the braille lesson, okay? School starts in a week."

Rowan nodded. She heard Zephyr's toenails click on the floor and knew she went to the window to watch Mom head down the walkway and cut across the yard toward the gate between the two properties.

Zephyr whined.

"Mommo will be back, girl. Don't worry," Rowan said. "She's just going to Seth's." She patted the floor. Zephyr came back, lay down next to Rowan, and nudged her hand. She wanted to be petted. Getting lost had changed her—now, she preferred her people close. But she wasn't afraid of flies anymore. And this morning, when the garbage truck came up their street, Zeph didn't run for the closet. She hadn't even raised her head.

Rowan leaned against the couch. She felt around for the braille workbook and opened it, then remembered, and set the voice-activated timer. She'd put in her fifteen minutes, but no more. Braille books were extra fat because of the thickness of the dots on every page. Her fingertips were getting more sensitive, and she could figure out a few basic words now. It would take a long time to get fast, though. She missed reading with her eyes—the illustrations, the beautiful covers hinting at what was inside. Most of all, the delight of quickly devouring a story.

When the timer dinged, she set the book on the coffee table. "I'm going downstairs to work out. I want to practice my somersaults. Let's go!" she said to her dog. Rowan made her way to the basement doorway. "Come on, Zephy!" As she turned for the banister, Zephyr pushed between her and the stairwell wall. Rowan missed her grip. She tried to catch herself but stumbled on the floppy end of her sock. As she pitched forward, she threw her hands out and scrabbled for anything to grab. She banged her knee, and then whacked her head as she landed. Hard.

Chapter Twenty-four

Zephyr hears a loud thud, startles, and wheels around. Crumpled at the bottom of the steps, Rowan lies motionless. The hound nudges her. No movement. She lies down and worms her nose under her girl's shoulder. Nothing. Puzzled and worried, Zephyr licks Rowan's face. No response. She remembers Stormy lying in the road and bumps her girl harder. Rowan doesn't respond. Zephyr sits and peers at her. This is very bad.

Ignoring her sore leg, she bounds up the steps, through the kitchen and utility room, into the garage, and slams out the dog door. She lopes past the front of the house toward the gate. As she approaches the fence, her collar zings. Zephyr skids to a stop and backs up a few feet. She knows the boundary—when she doesn't pay attention and gets too close, it hurts. *She must find the mother.* Zephyr approaches the fence again; again the collar warns her, and whining, she backs off.

She circles back toward the house then turns and gallops full speed toward the gate—it's lower than the fence on either side. As Zephyr leaps, the shock jolts, and she squeals. Then, up and over, her thundering strides eat up ground toward help. Her neck stings, but she doesn't care. Her paws barely touch the neighbor's front stairs, but a door stops her. Barking, she scratches the screen with her paw.

"It's Zephyr," Carolina says. "How'd she get here? Bad dog!"

Zephyr knows both her name and the word "bad." She hangs her head but woofs sharply, twice this time.

Sue comes to the door and opens it. Zephyr gallops to Carolina and knocks under her arm so hard it flies up in the air. Then she sits directly in front of her and stares.

"She's acting peculiar. Rowan's alone. I'm going home."

As she rises, Zephyr grabs her wrist and tugs.

"Good God, I hope it isn't fire."

"Hurry! Go!" Sue urged.

As soon as they get out the front door, Carolina breaks into a run. Zephyr outpaces her, then catches herself and loops back toward the woman. As they near the fence, remembering the jolt, she pulls up short and sits. Carolina passes her, then trots back and, with shaking hands, unsnaps the collar and takes it off. "Let's go, girl."

Zephyr reaches their front door first and waits for the woman to open it. Rushing inside, Carolina says, "Zeph, find her!"

The dog takes the steps downstairs in three leaps. Behind her, she hears Carolina's sharp intake of breath. "Oh, no. Oh, my God!"

Rowan hasn't moved, and Zephyr flattens herself next to her girl. She licks her face again and makes quick whining sounds.

"Stay with her! 911—where's my phone?"

She hears Carolina's feet pounding upstairs, then fast words.

Sirens. Zephyr remembers that sound. This time, she will not run. Quivering, she leans into Rowan. A fly buzzes over the girl's head. Zephyr snaps, catches it, and swallows.

Deep voices. Carolina's voice, alarmed. Thudding across the floor above. Two men clump down the stairs. Carolina follows close behind.

"Good Lord," one mutters to the other. "Careful, Bob, that's one huge dog. Ma'am, could you get a hold of it?"

Carolina grabs neck fur and tugs. Zephyr pulls back, wanting to stay with Rowan. "Come on!" Carolina snaps. "They need to help her!"

One man opens his case. Zephyr sniffs the air. It smells like the place where her leg is fixed. She goes with Carolina but never takes her eyes off her girl. They huddle together and watch.

The men move quickly. One listens for the girl's breath, then shines a light in each eye. "Decent respiration," the burly man says. "Pupils are equal and reactive. She's out cold, though, and this wrist is broken." The other wraps something around her neck and then her arm. They slide a board under her body and strap her down. "Follow us. We'll get her started on oxygen as soon as we load her up."

Zephyr doesn't understand most of the words but knows the men are helping. Her job is done.

Carolina dashed around the house looking for her purse and sweater. She put Zephyr's invisible fence collar back on, and commanded her, "Stay home. Good girl."

As she headed out the door, Sue called from the gate. "I heard sirens. I'll look after Zeph."

As Carolina ran toward her van, she yelled back, "Rowan fell downstairs. She's unconscious and broke her wrist." She saw Sue put her hand on her heart and then wave.

Carolina stayed right behind the ambulance. The eighteen-minute drive seemed interminable, but eventually, they wheeled into the emergency room parking lot. "Her vital signs are strong," the heavy-set paramedic said, as they unloaded the gurney. "But she took a bad head wallop."

Carolina knew to stay out of their way and headed to the registration desk. Her hands shook as she fished insurance cards and her license out of her wallet. Under any circumstances, two concussions in a lifetime were serious. Two back-to-back were unthinkable. She should never have left Rowan alone. As soon as she assigned self-blame, her sensible self pointed out the same fall could have happened if she'd been close by.

While waiting for a neurologist to see Rowan, Carolina pulled out her cell, punched in the number for the only voice she needed to hear. Damn, the answering machine. At least he had the shortest message in the world: "Moss here; you know what to do."

"Moss! Rowan fell down the basement stairs. She's unconscious. Again." Her voice broke. "I thought you'd want to know." There was nothing more to say. She folded her phone shut.

Disoriented, Carolina glared at the cell in her hand. Did she *really* just do that? Call him? After all the talking-tos she'd given herself? Feeling off-kilter, she shook her head to clear it, stuffed her phone in her pocket, and walked toward the curtained cubicle where Rowan lay.

With Jazz at his side, Moss ambled in from his early afternoon stint in the garden. As he shed a boot at the front door, the dog sat and scrutinized him. Then he wrestled the boot off the fake foot—Jazz always seemed interested in the process. It was curious that she noticed the difference. He gave her a pat and headed to the bedroom to strip and shower.

The answering machine blinked. After his guests had left, he'd hauled the machine out of the closet—where it had been for the last eighteen months—and put it back on the bedside table. He pressed the button and heard Carolina's distressed message. The sunlit day, the sweet tiredness after turning earth, skidded away.

He dropped into coping mode. No question here. Even though Carolina hadn't invited him, his next stop was Eugene. He thought for a moment. What was the name of the hospital? He closed his eyes, reeling his memory back to college days. Something with an "S." Savior? Sacred? Yes, Sacred. Sacred Heart. Poor kid. Poor Carolina. What a bad break.

Jazz could come; she'd keep Zephyr company. He would stay at their house, on the couch, if need be. Payback time. He dialed the library, his real foot tapping the floor. Gladys picked up on the fourth ring.

"Moss here. I need a favor. I have an out-of-town emergency—Rowan got hurt. Will you stay at the ranch? Could be a few days; maybe a week."

"Is she okay?"

"I don't know much more than she fell down stairs. She's in a coma."

"Oh, dear." Gladys sighed. "I'll drive out as soon as I close up. Same watering and chicken feeding? What about Jazz?"

"I'm taking her with me. Yeah, everything's the same. Eat whatever you want; freezer and garden are full. Have a party if you'd like. You're the best, Gladdy."

Moss took a two-minute shower, tossed clothes and toiletries into a zippered bag, and stuffed his cell phone into his pocket. He headed for his truck, dog at his heels. "Jazz! Free load!" She leaped into the front seat.

He hesitated for a moment. For two years, he'd been so focused on himself that he'd become more or less a hermit. This felt like a new step—responding to someone else's needs. His extra pair of crutches was still in the back of the SUV. Then he remembered Jazz needed supplies too, and limped back to get her food, bowl, and bed. Suddenly, his life was not only changing, it was doing so remarkably fast.

The trip up and over Santiam Pass dragged. Moss drummed his fingers to country music the entire trip—a guilty pleasure. He loved Reba McEntire. Although he didn't admit it out loud, he enjoyed Willie Nelson, too. Memories came back—when his roommate at Taft introduced him to this new-sounding music in the ninth grade. It was as though his world had been blown wide open. The sad words had spoken to his teenage heart.

Jazz lay with her head on his leg. From time to time, Moss stroked her velvety ears. Just east of Springfield, they stopped at a park for a restroom break. When they rolled across the bridge into Eugene, he pulled over and fished out a map. It had been seventeen years since he'd graduated from the university, but Moss knew approximately where the hospital was. Near Hilyard and 13th.

He pulled his vehicle into the covered parking structure so Jazz wouldn't overheat. After giving her a drink and a biscuit, he cracked the windows a couple of inches and told her to "Wait." Then he limped toward the hospital door.

Immediately, the medicinal scent smacked him. All hospitals stank in the same way—a mixture of cleaning products and misery. After returning from Afghanistan, he spent long periods of time in these places—they were intrusions of painful familiarity and difficult to reenter. He leaned against the wall to adjust, to calm himself. Slow, even breaths helped him wash out the overwhelm. Sounds were familiar—the hum of equipment, the elevator bells dinging—flat, lifeless noise mixed with stale air. He rolled his shoulders back and headed for the front desk.

"A patient, Rowan Graham," he said. "What room is she in?"

The stout woman behind the desk tapped keys and scanned her screen. "They've moved her to intensive care. Only family can see her."

For a moment he thought about fibbing. "I'm a close family friend. I'll look for her mother in the visitors' area if you tell me where to go."

She nodded, jotted the floor and room number for him, and pointed the way to the elevator.

Moss pushed the UP button. He considered calling Carolina but decided against it. He hadn't made a plan. Then it struck him, he didn't need one—the moment would take care of itself. He allowed the crowd of people to exit before getting on the elevator. As soon as the door closed, his heart rate ramped up. He felt like a damn teenager again. This woman had wormed her way inside of him. All three of them had.

When the elevator reached his floor, he stepped out and tried to reorient himself. Why were hospitals always an unfriendly maze? This one was smallish, but he still got lost twice. Turning a corner, he saw the unit he was looking for and poked around until he found the waiting room.

There sat Carolina, hunched in a chair, her face in her hands. He studied her from the doorway. Her hair was tousled, most likely from running her fingers through it. She was dressed in well-worn jeans and teal T-shirt with a sweater over her shoulders. Even in a hurry, she must have remembered air-conditioned buildings can be chilly. Well, she'd done a long stint in a Portland hospital just a few weeks ago. His instinct was to rush over and take her in his arms, smooth the frown from her brow, but common sense prevailed. He headed in her direction.

Chapter Twenty-five

C arolina disliked the helpless waiting game. Rowan was unconscious and, once again, in intensive care.

"You can be with your daughter fifteen minutes an hour," the nurse had ordered.

Fifteen minutes? It seemed damn unfair. Mothers should sit with their kids.

The neurologist grimaced when she told him what happened five weeks before. "At least the MRI shows no brain bleeds," he said.

Carolina cringed at the thought.

"That's good news," the doctor went on. "And her EEG indicates normal brain activity. To be on the safe side, I want to keep her in intensive care overnight. If she's stable, we'll move her to a regular room tomorrow."

Something yanked her out of the morass of her thoughts. She looked up, unable to process what she saw—out of place and time. Finally, her brain kicked in. *Moss?*

He made his way toward her with that slight hitch. Those eyes, tender smile lines, lanky body—it hit her how much she'd missed him the last few weeks. At first, she'd been annoyed. He hadn't wanted to let them know he had Zephyr. *What kind of person would do that?* And then bringing up the woo-woo business about dog communication just as they left. *How could he encourage Rowan in that way?*

She stood up, shakily. "Heavens, you came? From my message? I didn't expect—" She felt his arms gently surround her. As though she might shatter, he pulled her close.

"Of course, I did," he whispered, his lips against the top of her head. "How is she?"

"They say she's stable for now, but still in a coma. This is a horrid repeat, Moss." She shook her head. "My mind can't accept it. How could this happen? Two brain injuries in a little more than a month? Along with a broken wrist."

He said nothing, offered no bromides.

Carolina was glad. Her questions had no answers. Millions of unfair events occurred around the world, every day. Why should she and her family be exempt?

"They told me I'm not allowed to go in, but can I see her through a window or something?" Moss asked.

Carolina took his hand. "Over here—you can look through the glass." She pointed. "She's two beds to the right."

Moss walked over and watched steadily for a while. Then he turned back to Carolina. "You'll spend the night here?"

"You bet."

"I brought my new dog, Jazz. I thought while we're at the hospital, she could keep Zeph company. They met, you know." He gave her a quirky smile. "Got a guest room?"

"Sure. Do you want directions so you can get Jazz settled?"

"Please. Then I'll come back to be with you."

"You don't have to. Take the night off."

"No way."

"Our property isn't enclosed, not traditionally. We have an underground electric fence. There's a second zap collar; it's on the dryer. Do you think it'll work for Jazz?"

"Yeah. I'll put it on her and walk near the boundaries. She's hyperresponsive to commands. She'll want to hang with her new buddy, anyway."

Carolina took a pad out of her purse and sketched a map. "Here, it's pretty easy. I'll call Sue and let her know you're coming. She's looking after Zeph."

"I'll be back in a couple of hours with something tasty to eat."

She smiled. "You know hospital food. Bless you."

He hugged her again. "We'll get through this."

Carolina leaned into him long enough to hear his steady heartbeat.

After he left, Moss's parting comment flashed through her mind—*We'll get through this."* Not *you'll* get through this." A slip of the tongue? Probably.

She flipped open her phone and called her neighbor.

"I've been pacing. How's Rowan? What's happening?"

Carolina filled Sue in then added, "Moss, our friend from Sisters, just showed up. The one who found Zephyr? He's going to stay with us, and he's headed over there now. He wants to leave his dog with Zeph."

"I'll watch for him. He drove all this way? For you!"

"He really connected with Row," Carolina said, not ready to admit how much she cared for him. "Show him to the guest room, okay?"

"Carolina, are you *sure* that's the message you want to send?"

"He's already gotten the message, loud and clear. Yes, I'm positive."

"If you think so. Keep me posted about Rowan. Any time, night or day. Promise?"

"I will. Thanks." She knew her friend and added again, "The *guest* room, Sue."

Moss returned to his truck. "Hey, girl, that wasn't so long was it?" She gave him a swift lick and thunked her tail on the seat. He reexamined Carolina's directions then started the truck heading south through town, across Eighteenth, and into the country southwest of Eugene. It only took a few more minutes until he turned right onto Gimpl Hill Road and then left on McMorrott Lane. A dead end, he noticed with delight. Her home was on the left. He pulled in the long drive until he got to the modest green house, then turned off the engine. It looked like a ranch, but it must have a flight of stairs. Jazz sat up, curious.

He got out and stretched, sucking in the moister air of western Oregon. Nice. She settled in a sweet, quiet place. "Free dog," he said, and Jazz jumped down. Zephyr appeared from around the corner of the house and bounded toward them. Unsure, Jazz slipped behind Moss and waited, peering around his leg. "Zeph!" Moss called, and the dog skidded to a stop in front of him. Her tail flew from side to side, and she stuffed her big nose into his crotch.

"Hey, girl!" To avoid any jealousy, he reached around with one hand to stroke Jazz while greeting Zephyr. He examined the surgery site as he patted her shoulder. "You've healed beautifully!" The hair hadn't fully grown back, but the incision no longer looked raw. He stepped aside. "Hey, look who's here. Remember her?" The dogs touched noses. Tails carried high, they sniffed each other from nose to tail. Then Zephyr made a pouncing motion, and they were off, flying around the field. Jazz's legs weren't as long, so she cut corners to catch up. What a lovely sight.

Moss saw a woman open a gate on the side of the property. This must be Sue. She was a little thing with bright red hair in a long braid. He waved to her.

"Welcome, Moss! Wish the circumstances were better."

As he shook her hand, he nodded. "Rotten bad luck, I'd call it."

"Awful. Let me show you around the place. Wow, your dog is beautiful."

"That's Jazz. Carolina said you might be willing to look after her as well as Zephyr?"

"As long as they are mellow with each other, which they seem to be. Have they met before?"

"Yes, although not in a situation where they could play. Zephyr was just out of surgery when Jazz showed up at the vet's." He whistled, and Jazz wheeled away from her new friend and ran toward them. She sat neatly in front of Moss.

"Impressive," Sue said, reaching out a hand to stroke her.

"I agree, but I can't take credit. I'm encouraging her to relax." After a brief greeting, Moss said, "Free dog," and Jazz took off after Zephyr again.

Moss and Sue walked to the house, and she gave him the quick tour. "Here's the guest room. The bath's across the hall."

"Great, thanks. Where should I stash Jazz's stuff? I brought her food and bowls. I'll stick her bed in with me."

"Here." She indicated the utility room off the kitchen. "There's a dog door in the garage."

Moss noticed Zephyr's kibble bag on the dryer and set Jazz's next to it. Same brand, different flavor. He turned back to Sue. "I'll feed Jazz before I go back, but when you give Zeph her biscuit tonight, would you mind giving my girl one, too? You'll have to say 'free chow,' or she won't take it."

"I suppose Zephyr should get her biscuit first. Pack order and all that?"

"Good plan," he said.

Before following Sue back into the living room, he scanned the washer and dryer and found the zap collar. He brought it out and set it on the kitchen counter where he wouldn't forget. "Do you know a good restaurant where I can pick up food for Carolina?"

"There's a down-home noodle place on Pearl, just a few blocks from the hospital."

"I want something nicer than noodles."

Sue thought for a moment. "Got it! Chef's Kitchen. They have a takeout window. Don't let it put you off—their food is some of the best in Eugene. It's not far out of your way, either. Call first, though." She put her hand on the door handle. "Thanks for coming, Moss. It's real kind of you. Carolina can use the support." She opened the door to leave and added, "If you like duck? They have the best I've ever tasted."

"Do you think Carolina would enjoy it?"

"For sure."

"That's what I'll get. Thanks."

Sue waved goodbye and headed out the door.

Moss decided to lie down for a few minutes before walking the field with Jazz. First, he wandered around the house, curious to get a sense of Carolina's home. The vista out the back opened to a lovely view of a larger valley. Her downstairs workspace was orderly, even though she'd obviously left a project in progress. He switched off the sewing machine light and walked upstairs to her room. He didn't go in—that required an invitation—but stood in the doorway and sensed her space. He liked it. A sturdy cedar chest stood against one wall. It looked handmade. Other than the beautiful throw on the bed, it was a plain room. He felt relief she wasn't a woman who liked frilly knickknacks. He remembered she'd remarked about the beauty of his great grandmother's quilt and wondered if she'd crafted this crocheted one.

A picture of Rowan with someone sat by the bedside. He craned his neck. That must be Rafe. He wanted to get closer and take a long look at it, but couldn't cross the boundary. Maybe he'd find another photo elsewhere in the house.

He discovered a phone book in the kitchen drawer. Paging through, he found Chef's Kitchen and placed the duck order for two, 6 p.m. pickup.

Moss went back to the guest room, set the alarm on his phone for fifteen minutes, and without unlegging, stretched out on the bed. He'd learned to catnap while serving overseas. It was high on his list of handy skills.

Panting, Zephyr flies back through the dog door to get a drink of water where her food lives then ambles around the house. Kibble Man is in a sleeping room. She pads in, remembering—Rowan at the bottom of the stairs. The sirens. Strange voices. Zephyr can't feel her girl, and there have been no mind-pictures. She flops down nearby on the floor. Worried, she presses her nose between her paws. The other dog tags along and settles in her bed.

As Zephyr dozes off, a sharp sound wakes them all. She hears the man mutter as he swings into a sitting position. Puzzled by the short sleep, she sits up.

Kibble Man talks to both her and the new dog friend. Zephyr hears her name, the other dog's name, Rowan's name, and "wait" a few times. Her ears drop. She doesn't get to go. She glances at her playmate. Apparently, she's not going, either.

Moss splashed water on his face, fed Jazz, clipped on the zap collar and headed outside with her. He walked her around the field. Zephyr bounded along with them but swerved away from the fence before her collar buzzed. Moss made sure Jazz walked into the zone a couple of times. She looked startled and immediately backed away. He was satisfied— she wouldn't test the boundary.

"Okay you two, be good. Zeph, watch after my girl." He remembered what Rowan told him, and even though it felt awkward, he tried sending mind-pictures to Zephyr of the two dogs hanging out together and settling down to sleep in the house. *It couldn't hurt.* He told them to "wait" and headed for his truck.

He figured he'd be staying overnight at the hospital. He'd miss Jazz—after that first nightmare when she'd jumped on the bed howling, she'd changed her behavior. Now she woke him with soft whines, nudges, and face-licking the moment a bad dream started. He'd come to depend on her.

Dense fog pressed Rowan down. She struggled to swim upward, pull herself toward the surface, break through, but it was too thick, like swimming in cold honey. Amid waves of pain, she heard sounds and sometimes her mother's voice. She couldn't process the words but felt her mom's loving touch. *Where is Zephy? Is this a nightmare? What happened? Why does this feel so familiar?*

Chapter Twenty-six

Outside the intensive care unit, Carolina noted the lowering sun. Moss could arrive any moment. The thought of his sweet company—and the decent food he'd promised—cheered her. A part of her felt nonplussed he'd come. Until he showed up, she hadn't realized her unconscious hope he would. She couldn't bear another awful night. Waiting. Alone. Had he read her heart?

She'd already crossed the firm line she'd drawn to stay single. *Damn!* The way the smile lines crinkled around his eyes, showing his kindness; how one front tooth barely overlapped the one next to it, a lovely imperfection; the chiseled cheekbones and tan arms—and he was sensitive and aware—a gentleman, even. She thought back to their stay at his ranch. He'd disarmed her with the willingness to expose his weaknesses. His honesty was a fair match to her own. She needed that.

She heard crepe-soled footsteps and turned to see the charge nurse walking toward her.

"You can go in now, Ms. Graham. Fifteen minutes."

"Thanks for coming to get me. Any change?"

"None yet. You'll be the first to know."

Carolina slipped through the door, back into the environment of beeps and whooshing sounds, and made her way to Rowan. She looked at her beautiful girl and put a hand on her forehead. No fever. She seemed asleep—like any eleven-year-old—if you ignored the cast that went above the elbow. Rowan's puffy fingers took Carolina back to when she'd shattered her own wrist at thirteen. She remembered the excruciating pain as the swelling pressed against her cast. When Rowan woke, she was in for intense discomfort for a few days. *If she woke.* Carolina took a shaky breath.

Rowan's color seemed normal, a good sign. As she brushed her daughter's hair back from her face, her fingers traced the large lump. Row did so well navigating that Carolina hadn't given a thought about leaving her alone. Had she been negligent? She sat next to the bed and took Rowan's hand. "Sweetie," she murmured. "I have a huge surprise for you. Mossy's here. But you have to wake up to enjoy him. Make your way back; you can do it. Zephyr's waiting for you. We all are."

Moss arrived carrying two paper bags. He spoke to the nurse at the station, and she pointed him to a table in a nearby alcove. He laid out tablecloth and dinner and added a battery candle. Bruno, the owner of Chef's Kitchen, suggested he explore the Jiffy Mart next store and its fine wine selection. Moss had uncorked the bottle and put it in unobtrusive containers before coming back—he was pretty sure alcohol was frowned upon at the hospital.

He stood by the unit door until Carolina came out. "Hey," he said. "Any change?"

Carolina shook her head. "Not yet. Waiting is hard."

He put his arm around her shoulder. "Come eat. Dinner's warm and ready."

As soon as Carolina saw the plates, she smiled. "Really? You brought me Chef's Kitchen duck? This is the best food in Eugene. My appetite just rushed back."

"Sue recommended it. Sure smells fantastic. Does Bruno always mound the rice this way, half white, half black? The plates look great."

She nodded. "Yes, he does. I once asked him to give me a half portion of rice, and he refused. He seemed a bit offended and said it ruined the symmetry."

He handed her a napkin and pointed to the takeout cups. "You might enjoy what's in there."

"Decadent?"

"Just a little. Bruno's suggestion."

Carolina admired her plate and, after enjoying the taste of wine, dug in. It relieved him to see her eat with relish. Hospital stays could be marathons; he knew from experience, healthy food was key. He took a bite. The cherry sauce complimented the exquisitely tender bird. He grinned and sipped the wine. It was full-bodied, a nice match.

Eight o'clock and the hospital was winding down. "Why don't you head back to my place and get some sleep? The guest bed's comfortable."

"I'll stay here with both of you—sleep in one of the chairs in the waiting room."

"You don't have to do that."

"I *want* to."

Their gazes met for a long moment.

The next morning, the nurses moved Rowan out of intensive care. She was no longer hooked up to machines, only an IV for nourishment. Carolina and Moss pulled chairs up to the bed. He looked at the girl for a long time before speaking. "Row," he said, and then his voice broke. He swallowed to regroup. "I came the moment I heard about your fall." He touched her cast and smoothed his hand over her swollen fingers. "You've got to wake up and meet my dog, Jazz. I brought her to Eugene. She's playing with Zephy right now."

Had Rowan's finger grazed his or did he imagine it?

Carolina stared at him, her eyes wide open. "Did you see that?"

"I felt it. Rowan reacted to Zephyr's name."

"Moss, she responded to *you*. Your voice." For a moment, Carolina looked stricken.

"Me?" He pointed to himself, surprised. "Would you rather be the one speaking to her?"

"No! Please, think of more stories to tell her!"

Moss kept up a patter—cougar footprints out past Bender's Ridge, a bear sighting, raccoons in the garbage—anything that might interest the girl.

Over half an hour, they watched Rowan fight her way toward consciousness. The excitement in the room rose when Rowan squeezed Moss's hand. Then again. Carolina and Moss glanced at each other and then back to Rowan. And then, as if suddenly roused by a crash of thunder, Rowan's eyelids flew open.

"Rowan!" her mother gasped. "Oh, my God, we've been so worried. Welcome back!" She grabbed the side bar to steady herself and hugged her daughter.

Rowan blinked in rapid succession. "Mommo? Where am I?"

"In the hospital. Right here with us, sweetie."

"Hospital?" She shifted her head and frowned at Moss. "Who are you? You were talking to me; I know your voice. Mossy? Is that you?"

"Yes! Thank God, you're awake."

"Your hair's curly just like mine!"

Carolina's eyes widened, and she gripped Rowan's arm. "Really? You can see him?"

Her daughter nodded. "You're like a character in one of those weird old movies. There isn't any color. You're tall, and you have really dark hair."

"Can you describe the shirt he has on?" Carolina's voice quivered with excitement.

Her daughter blinked steadily. "Plaid. What color is it? To me, it's black, with dark and light gray."

Eyes wide, Moss and Carolina stared at each other. "It's a bloody miracle," he murmured. "Call the doctor." He turned back to Rowan. "My shirt is green, blue, and black. But you can see it!"

Carolina picked up the buzzer on Rowan's bed and trembling, pushed the button.

"My head hurts bad," Rowan said. "It's pounding. And my arm is killing me." She tried to lift it and then noticed the cast. "What happened?"

"You broke your wrist and knocked yourself out," Carolina said. "Do you remember falling downstairs?"

She frowned then shook her head. "What stairs?"

"At home."

"Home? Is Zephy okay?" Rowan seemed frightened.

"She's fine. Playing with Jazz. Why?"

"I can't remember. Something—"

A nurse walked in. "She's conscious! Great. I'll buzz Dr. Franklin."

"I'm hungry," Rowan called after her. "Can I have a burger?" Then she turned back and focused on Moss. "It's spooky seeing again." She scanned the room and set her focus back on Moss. "You're handsome!"

Moss blushed. "I had nothing to do with it."

"Yeah, but lucky you. No wonder Mommo likes you."

He cast a covert glance at Carolina. Now, she was blushing, too.

Fifteen minutes later, the neurologist walked in. He peered in Rowan's eyes. "People with cortical blindness sometimes get their sight back, but it returns gradually, and they see color as well. Her vision came back all at once, but black and white." He shrugged. "I have no explanation. This is a case for the textbooks. Let's be grateful."

"Do you think her color vision will return?" her mom asked.

"We don't know. Research doesn't tell us yet." He glanced around. "No books here. I'll get a magazine from the waiting room." He came back carrying a copy of *People*. "Rowan, read to me."

Moss watched her thumb through and stop at a page with a photo of a dog.

She read out loud, "Jack has been taught a unique group of complex actions he can perform on command. His trainer created special new tricks for his upcoming movie." As she turned to her mom, her eyes flooded. "I can read again! I'll be able to run with Zephy, and school will be normal without some stupid aide."

Carolina, too moved to speak, teared up as she patted her daughter.

The neurologist covered each eye individually. "Your vision is focusing fine. But no running for at least a month, maybe more—you've got to give your brain a rest. Do you want to try getting up now?"

"Okay." Rowan hung her legs over the edge of the bed. "My head feels like it's going to crack open. Can you make it stop? My arm's killing me, too."

"I'll prescribe medication. This is common after head trauma and, unfortunately, a waiting game. With luck, over time, your headaches will go away." He cocked his head as he looked at Rowan. "Your cast requires support. I'll have the nurse pull that IV, too."

When Dr. Franklin returned, a nurse followed and gently fitted a blue sling around Rowan's cast, snugging the Velcro clasps. She carefully removed the tape, the intravenous needle, put a Band-Aid on the small wound, and crooked her elbow. "Want to get up? Take my arm in case you're dizzy."

Rowan hooked her good arm through the nurse's, slid her feet to the floor, and rose unsteadily. Carolina watched as they made it past a couple of rooms and back.

"I need a burger before I try again. I'm wobbly," Rowan said, settling back on the bed.

"Food's on the way. It should be here within ten minutes," the nurse replied.

Rowan turned to Dr. Franklin. "Can I go home? I'll heal quicker if I'm with my dog."

"You have to stay two days so we can monitor you. If you're still stable, I'll sign the paperwork." He turned to Carolina. "She's got to limit her activity level. I'll write a scrip for pain medication now and also when she goes home. Call my office for a follow-up next week."

"I can go to school, right?" Rowan asked. "I *can't* fall behind. Please?"

Dr. Franklin peered over his half glasses. "You love school that much?"

"You bet! I want to be a veterinary surgeon. And a writer."

"Well, try it. But no sports or outside recess. See if the school nurse will let you lie down during those periods. I'll write a note." He pulled a pad from his jacket and looked at Carolina. "She needs to be honest with herself, and if it's too much, admit it." He turned back to Rowan. "The more you rest, the sooner you'll be able to run with that dog of yours."

Rowan nodded. She tucked into her hamburger the moment it arrived. "French fries, too. Yum."

"At this rate, you'll have your strength back in no time," Moss said.

Two days later, all signs pointed to a solid recovery, and Dr. Franklin completed the discharge papers. Moss turned to Carolina. "Why don't I go ahead and run the dogs in the field, so they aren't too bouncy. You-know-who will be excited to have her girl back."

After Moss left, Rowan said, "Mom, my eyesight couldn't vanish again, could it?"

"I don't think so. But you have to avoid head whacks. No more soccer, Row. You can't chance it."

"It's super cool to see again, even if I'm in a black and white movie." Rowan's voice rose in excitement. "Getting around, reading, everything. No more cane. Or snail-braille. It's okay about soccer. I can write in my journal. Oh, boy!"

Carolina nodded, smiling. She moved around the room, packing Rowan's belongings. "I hope we're done with this place forever."

The dogs galloped across the yard to greet Moss—Zephyr in the lead, Jazz not far behind. When the giant hound shoved her head into Moss's crotch again, he broke out laughing. "Don't teach Jazz this trick." He pushed her nose away. "Rowan's coming home!" He grabbed the tennis ball launcher from the back of his truck, clapped his hands, and headed to the front field. They followed. He pitched the ball until the dogs, sides heaving, dropped to the ground. Zeph already knew how to fetch. "Enough? Okay then. Mind your manners when the girls arrive."

He walked into the kitchen and noticed dishes in the sink. Whistling, he washed and dried them, then opened cabinets until he found where they lived. When he finished, he leaned on the counter. Had he over-stepped a boundary? This wasn't his home. Other than a brief nap, he'd never even slept here. He'd spent three nights stretched on a couch in the hospital waiting room. But then, noticing clumps of dog hair behind the door, he reconsidered. *What the hell. She tidied up my place; I might as well vacuum, too.* He found the machine in the utility room and did a once-over on the living room and entryway while Zephyr and Jazz snoozed on the couch.

A few minutes later, the hound whined, went to the window, and watched the driveway. Moss followed. Carolina's van came to a stop. As Zephyr turned to race for the dog door, Moss grabbed her collar and pulled her up short. "Sorry, girl. You have to be a real lady. Be gentle," he said firmly. With a solid grip on her collar, they walked out the front door.

Chapter Twenty-seven

A trill erupted from Zephyr's throat. Rowan dropped to her knees and wrapped her good arm around her dog's neck. She whispered in her ear. "Zephy! You're so beautiful." Tears spilled over. "In a month, if I heal up right, we can play hide-and-seek again." She pulled back and looked her dog right in the eyes. "I see you!" Then dropping her face in her good hand, she burst into quick sobs.

Puzzled, Zephyr sat down and tried to slurp away her tears. When Rowan lifted her head, she noticed the other dog. "This must be Jazz. Wow! She's real pretty." She stroked the short-haired dog, but Zephyr pushed her way in. "Okay, okay, don't be jealous. I'll greet Jazz later."

They all walked into the house. "Can we go to the library now? I'm hungry for a normal book!" Rowan crossed fingers. "Please?"

Carolina checked her watch. "If you promise to nap first, we'll go later. You heard what the doctor said: rest, rest, and more rest."

"Oh, Mom! How boring!" Rowan grumbled. "Okay, I'll nap on the couch with Zephy. And Jazz."

Moss turned to Carolina. "I hope you don't mind, I put dishes away and ran the vacuum."

"Good Lord, I appreciate the help. Zephyr must have flipped out when you turned on the vac. We always have to put her outside."

Moss looked startled. "No, she napped on the couch."

"Well, that beats everything," Rowan said. She contemplated her dog. "Flies, the garbage truck, and now the vacuum, too? What a good, brave girl you are."

Rowan finished hugging and praising Zephyr and walked slowly around the house. She touched the recliner, paused in front of the colored-pencil portrait that included Zephyr and Stormy. She dashed tears away. Poor Stormy. The drawing looked different in black and white, but still, the place felt like home. She moved on, staring into her room, absorbing all she hadn't been able to see for five weeks. She fingered her journal, then clutched it to her chest. How weird to have sight taken away and given back. Had cracking her head again restored her vision?

She longed for color, then caught herself, and remembered to be grateful. Tomorrow, she'd ask Mom for Benjamin's number and break the news he'd lost a student. She liked him—he was fun and kind—but didn't need him anymore. A pang of loss streaked through her. Maybe they could meet once more so she could see his dreads.

Rowan set the journal on the coffee table and went to peer down the stairs. Her heart rate sped up, and she grabbed onto the banister just to steady herself. *What a long flight. I'm lucky to be alive.* She took a deep breath and wandered over to the refrigerator to look at the yogurts. She could no longer depend on the flashy yellow lemon picture to identify her favorite flavor. Grabbing one, Rowan sat in the corner of the couch and ate the creamy snack.

"Here you go, Zephy," she said as the happy dog licked the spoon.

Her mom was right. Time for a nap. Rowan tried to put both hands on the sides of her dog's head, but with her cast, she couldn't do it. She settled on one. She loved Zephy's big, damp nose and the way her nostrils looked like giant quotation marks. "You found your courage all on your own, and I didn't even get to be there." She pensed Zeph the flush of pride she felt for the dog's newfound maturity. The hound gave her a swift lick.

"Can I have a pain pill? My head really hurts," Rowan said. Zeph crawled up, and she felt the familiar weight of her dog's long muzzle settle on her hip. A moment later, Jazz came in. She looked at Rowan and Zephyr, then turned to Carolina with an inquiring expression.

"Go ahead, Jazz. It's fine in this house." Carolina patted the pillow. "Free dog." Jazz scrambled up and settled in the empty corner.

She went to find the medicine and returned within minutes. "Look at you three. Here's your pill. It's probably good you just ate something."

But Rowan was already asleep.

∞

Holding two glasses of iced tea, Carolina joined Moss on the deck. They sat in silence, appreciating the view past the oak and fir woods into the wide valley beyond. Northern flickers, with their woodpecker markings, darted among branches playing hide-and-seek. One, then another, landed on the deck railing, preening and parading for each other.

"Tell me about Gladys," Carolina said. "She's so willing to help out—unusually so. What's that about?"

"We go way back," Moss said. "She and Ma were best friends in high school. Decades ago, Gladys and her husband, Mac, purchased a small ranch a couple of miles from ours. He was the best cutting horse trainer in the state—raised his own quarter horses. Gladdy loved that man and their land more than anything."

He ambled over to the orchid in the window and deadheaded a few wilted blooms. "Mac got ALS—you know, Lou Gehrig's disease. It took him four agonizing years to die, and apparently, it sopped up every penny they had. After he passed, she lost the ranch—not mentioning a word about it to my parents. Too damn proud and stoic. She might have found it easier to tell me, but I'd just left for Afghanistan.

"When I got back and found out, I questioned her until she admitted she had *nothing* left. No savings. She'd rented a room from Francine and taken the librarian job to keep afloat." He sat down. "Pa tried to get the new owners to sell it back, but they wouldn't budge. He wanted to purchase Gladys a small spread—but without Mac, her heart wasn't in it. Pa offered her a comfortable stipend if she'd be available on a moment's notice to help out, babysit our place. It took her a few months to set her pride down and accept. Eventually, she did."

"That seems like a win-win."

"She's quite happy about it now. Ma and Pa asked her to come live at Bender's Ridge when she retires. It gave my parents peace of mind to have her tend the place while I was at war. She's been a big help. For me, it means I can get away, the garden won't shrivel, the chickens won't starve, and the fox won't take advantage. She cares for the ranch like it's her own."

"Will she take over the guest cottage?"

"No. When she's ready to retire, Pa'll build her a little home out behind the barn. She'll need privacy and will want to give our family the same." Moss put his hands on his legs. "I'm going to head out, now," he said. "Row's recovering well. I have a buddy in Ashland—we know each from the hospital in Germany. I'm due by dinner."

Carolina's throat thickened. She forced her words. "I thought you might stay for a couple of days, so I can show you around, introduce you to our lives."

"Not this time, but soon, I hope. Like me, Jessie has PTSD. We give each other support."

"Does he get nightmares too?"

"Jess is a woman. Not bad dreams—anxiety attacks. Loud noises set her off, fireworks, cars backfiring. Especially helicopters."

Carolina's hands trembled so much that she needed to press them against her thighs. Trying to formulate a coherent sentence, it surprised her when all that came out was a low, "Oh." Her heart beat fast. "Are you two involved?" It sounded flat. Dumb. Childish.

"We have been, yes." His tone was matter-of-fact. "We've gotten together every couple of months since Sophie walked out on me. I guess we needed each other's help adjusting to civilian life."

An ugly wave roared up her body. When it reached her stomach, she thought she might throw up. *I can't compete with that.* The wave kept rising. Her throat closed; her face heated. She had no right to be jealous. Or was this reaction the terror of yet again losing someone she cared about?

"Carolina?"

"All the stress of the last few days, I guess." Her voice came out a squeak. She cleared her throat. Looked over at him. "Why the hell did you kiss me and act as if … as if you were interested if you're involved with another woman? What kind of a man are you?"

He sighed. "Come here," he said, rising to his feet.

"I'm fine right where I am." Carolina's words carried a sting.

"Well, I can't kneel. The leg won't do that." He slipped his hand under her armpit, and in one smooth motion, lifted and pulled her against his chest. "You wanted space," he murmured, his lips in her hair. "Then you called me about Rowan's accident. I'll lay bets you stared at the receiver after leaving the message wondering what the hell just happened. Well, I listened to your message, and in a nanosecond—no thinking involved—I knew I was leaving for Eugene. To be with you and Rowan. Something's shifted here—but this has to go slow." He waited until she looked up at him. "We *both* need that."

She flushed again. Her eyes were hot with jammed-up tears. The rhythm of his heart thudded in her ears. Another woman? *Another woman?* Damn him! She wanted to pound on his chest, pick a fight. She hated he was not only right but demonstrating solid maturity.

She felt him harden against her. At least he wasn't immune. "Please stay," she whispered.

He leaned back. "We're not ready."

"You mean, *I'm* not ready."

He grazed her lips with his, the softest touch. "That would be correct. You asked for time; you're going to have it."

Shit! A dose of my own medicine. Is he teaching me a lesson here? Or does he actually care? Her body still quivered like gelatin, and she wanted to wallow in tears. "Be sure to say goodbye to Row," she whispered.

"Good Lord, woman. Give me some credit. Let her sleep for a few more minutes," he said. "I have to pack the truck. I'll let you know when I'm ready to leave."

Zephyr pricks her ears as she hears Jazz race toward the door. What's happening? She pulls herself up and heads to the front window. Kibble Man carries a bed, dish, and backpack to the monster, Jazz following. They're leaving? She loves having a pack buddy to play with. She checks—Rowan is on the couch, sleepy and sad. Zephyr is torn; she wants to go, too, but her girl is here, and where her girl is, that's home. She walks over to Rowan and nudges her arm.

The girl hugs her hard and whispers, "Mossy's going away. We won't see him for a while. Mom's hiding it, but she's upset. I don't get adults, do you? They act so strange."

Zephyr whines.

Moss whistled for Jazz. On his terse command, she leaped into the truck. Chest aching, he climbed in, too. He knew he must drive away, but he wanted to explode out of the vehicle. Fly into the house. Take Carolina in his arms. Instead, he bit his lip, turned the key, revved the engine, and took off down the driveway.

He glanced in the rearview mirror. Zephyr stood, bewildered, just behind the margin of the electric fence. Jazz hung her head out the window, staring back. Even the dogs got along. What the hell was he doing? How could leaving be right?

When they rounded the corner, Jazz slumped down with her nose in Moss's lap. He laid a hand on her head and forced himself to stay on track. Driving through town, he headed past Lane Community College and entered the stream of traffic on I-5 south. Toward Ashland. "Damn!" He swore repeatedly and pounded the steering wheel. Startled, Jazz sat up and stared at him. But soon enough, Moss regained control of himself, and she returned to her favorite position.

He'd told Carolina the truth about Jessie—they shared a ton of common ground. Was it enough to consider a full relationship? Was he willing to let her go? He wasn't sure. Now that he'd met Carolina, he couldn't ignore the feelings she evoked. She was different. Special.

Heading to Ashland, he intended to figure out that difference. The sooner, the better; he didn't like leading women on. Besides, if there were to be any chance with Carolina, she needed to make another move toward him. Previously, she'd been clear that she didn't want a relationship; now, he had to know if she was open to one. That stunt when she left in a snit without saying goodbye had rubbed him wrong. After Sophie, he couldn't face another rejection.

The expression on Rowan's face when he told her he was leaving made his stomach hurt. She scowled and turned away without a word.

No goodbye hug. He prayed he hadn't left a bigger mess in his wake. Still, he drove.

Zephyr sits, ears pricked, long after the truck is gone. Rowan calls her, but for a minute, she doesn't move. She needs to listen. Rising, she plods toward the house—they aren't coming back, not now. She slips through the dog door and laps water before making her way to the living room. She climbs on the couch with Rowan and slumps down with a groan. Her pack mate is gone. Her girl is mad. The mother is restless and upset. The whole house feels wrong.

Carolina paced the deck. Moss hadn't given a clue he had planned on leaving. That hurt. The lump in her throat made swallowing painful. *Rafe had been lighthearted and fun, but he was a better friend than lover. I never realized that before.*

She marched to the kitchen and attacked the refrigerator, yanking out containers so she could wipe the shelves. Moss had been so sure of himself, attractive, maddening. Her so-called friendship with him had charge and she was frightened to open herself to the sparks between them. For the first time, something raw and sexual and womanly was awakening inside of her—and he was behaving like *this*?

Her hesitation had driven Moss to another woman. Or was his relationship with this woman established, and he simply wanted another fling? Was he pissed and acting out because she had left his home without hugging him? Would she lose the possibility of what they might have together? It galled her that he'd just driven off. Pressing her hands on the edge of the sink, tears welled, but she blinked fast, refusing to let them spill. Maybe she should work out, throw her hurt and rage into karate.

No, she had to get hold of herself. Take Rowan to the library. She'd promised.

Chapter Twenty-eight

A s Moss approached Ashland, he smelled smoke. The soot thickened as he drove into town. Scanning the hillsides, he spotted fire high in the mountains, and three helicopters cycling through, dumping water. Coughing, he closed the windows and turned on the inside air.

Before reaching Jessie's little rancher, he pulled onto a side street near her neighborhood and parked. Jazz sat up expectantly. "Not yet, girl. I've got to think a few things through." He patted the seat, and she lay back down.

He frowned. What did he need to know? The last time he was with Jess, he sensed she wanted more—something deeper. It wasn't anything she said, but he noticed her glancing at him slantwise when she thought he wasn't looking. And that phone conversation when he'd called her from the ranch a few weeks ago? Maybe she cared too much. She was dear, another friend for life. They played together, laughed, and healed.

But.

But what?

Clearly, they needed to clear the air. Weird, he was better at sharing feelings than she was. Two years of therapy had made the difference for him. Jessie hadn't been open to the idea. But a simple discussion might crack open the door and help clarify what was going on.

I've come empty-handed. That won't do. He started the engine again and drove to the Ashland Food Co-op to pick up a nice wedge of cheese. He wandered the aisles, dawdling. It dawned on him he was stalling. He paid for the crackers and smoked cheddar, her favorite, and headed to her home.

As he walked up the path, dog at his knee, he saw Jessie at the door. He was always startled by her size—five feet ten in bare feet, and stocky. Her blonde hair, chin length and turned under at the bottom, accentuated her cheekbones. So different from Carolina's spare form.

"I've really missed you," she whispered. She hugged him close and then leaned over to greet Jazz. "She's unusual. Not the dog I'd figure for you."

"What'd you expect?"

"I don't know. A retriever, I guess, since you hunt. Or a short-haired pointer?"

He chuckled. Two months ago, those breeds would have been his choice. "Yeah, well, it turns out she's perfect. We're tuned into each other— she even wakes me before my nightmares get going. Hey, I saw the fire when I got to town. The air's awful. When did it start?"

"Two days ago. Arson, they think—hard to believe someone would do that. The helicopters beating over the house set me off. They're why I called."

They walked inside. With a crooked smile, he handed her his gift, then looked around. Her home sat on a half-acre, and, behind her property, a farmer held another few acres planted in vegetables. Right in the middle of town.

She beamed, her Nordic face lighting up. "Thanks! We'll have some of this right now. Dinner'll be ready in half an hour. Do you want wine?"

"Do you have bubbly water?"

She tilted her head and peered at him. "I think so. That's a change from your regular pattern. Lemon okay?"

"Sure, fine." He shrugged. "A lot has happened. The howling dog I mentioned? Her name's Zephyr. I could tell she was severely injured, so I put out food, and, eventually, she came to me. Francine—you remember my telling you about my veterinarian friend—scanned her for a microchip. That's how we found her family."

She poured his water and a beer for herself and sat next to him on the couch. Jazz settled nearby. For a few minutes, they sat in silence until Moss sliced the cheese and spread a cracker for her.

"Something's different," she said. "You're different."

"It's obvious?"

"It is."

"You know how shut down I've been. My heart opened to Zephyr. She needed me. I needed her. You should see her—she's elegant and sensitive."

"And her owner?"

He nodded, slowly. "Nice folks. A mother and eleven-year-old daughter. Zeph belongs to the girl."

He needed to invite Jess to the ranch, feel her in his space. It might reveal a lot, clarify his unease. "Hey, would you like to follow me back to my place? Spend a couple of days there? We can get out of the smoke tonight and spirit you away from the helicopters, too."

Her smile broadened, turned almost coquettish. "After a year and a half, I thought you were never going to ask. But you've already had a long drive today."

"I'm allergic to smoke. Pretty soon, I'll start sneezing, and my eyes'll water. C'mon, let's head over there."

Did inviting her open a door that might be awkward to close? Even so, he had to know. But in his bedroom? Is this what he wanted? Sophie was the last one who spent the night with him. Lately, he'd been fantasizing Carolina there. Now, for the first time in his life, he was juggling two women who cared about him. Not comfortable. Not comfortable at all.

They ate a quick, quiet dinner, and then she packed some belongings in a small travel bag.

"Bring hiking boots," he said. "And a jacket. The altitude brings cool evenings. We should get to the ranch before midnight."

He fed Jazz, sent her out to do her business, and called Gladys to say they were on the way home.

"Just so you have an idea where we're headed," Moss said as they loaded their vehicles. "We'll take Highway 62 out of Medford, 97 to Bend, and 20 to Sisters. Then you have to pay attention because the road to my place is rough, and you'd never find the turnoff. Your GPS won't register where I live. But first, I'll need to stop for gas."

"Yeah, me too. Don't worry, I won't lose you."

Five hours later, they pulled their two cars in front of the main house. Gladys had turned the small pathway lights on before she left. On Moss's soft request, Jazz leaped from the truck and squatted on the grass. Then she followed them.

"Good heavens," Jessie breathed, as they walked across the porch and in the front door. "This place is classy."

"It's home. Whether I'm here or not, part of me always remains. I'm beat," he added. "All that driving. You can stash your gear here." He pointed to a chest at the foot of his bed. Jazz settled nearby.

Once they finished stump care, they slipped under the covers. He threw open his arm, and Jessie moved against him.

"Thanks," she said. "I didn't realize it at the time, but getting away was a good idea." She gave his chest a lingering kiss. "The 'copters…" As she snuggled close, her breathing changed.

Relief flooded him—she was out. With her PTSD activated, she must not have slept the last few nights.

Moss lay staring at the ceiling for over an hour. Eventually, he slid out of bed and eased into sweats. Jazz sat up, yawned, and followed him. He pushed the door closed so the light wouldn't wake Jessie and crutched to his computer. Opening his journal, he put his hands on the keyboard but hesitated, and shoved back his chair to think. Carolina's reaction that afternoon was the first thing to come to mind. What about his responses over the last few days? The anticipation before greeting Carolina at the hospital, his heart pounding in the elevator, his joy when Rowan came to—he couldn't deny his growing attachment.

But he and Jessie were relaxed together, and that was not a gift to be underestimated. Carolina challenged him which wasn't always comfortable, but it did invite him to look deeper. It encouraged intimacy. Jazz pressed her nose to his knee. He gave her a reassuring pat, reached over to the side table, and poured a glass of wine.

He crawled back into bed at 3:45 a.m. No words written.

Next morning, the aroma of coffee awakened him. A few minutes later, Jessie, wearing sweats and a T-shirt, brought him a mug.

"Mornin'," he said. "Thanks." He sat up, stuffed pillows behind his back, and took the cup. Jazz jumped up next to him. He patted her.

"Welcome to my world," he said to Jessie. "Is that a new leg? You aren't limping the same way."

"Yeah, and it sure fits better. I've stopped having trouble with rub spots, so I went for a short walk. Your place is gorgeous. You must have over a hundred acres here." She perched on the edge of the bed.

"1,700," he said.

Her eyes widened. "You have 1,700 acres? How can you afford it? I can barely manage the mortgage on my little place. This is a fancy spread; the finishes in this home are high-end. There's a guest house over there?"

"It was the original structure on the property. This isn't Ashland, it's the boonies. Land values are cheaper." He looked at her, trying to decide how much to disclose. She'd find out sometime. "There is no mortgage. It's been in my family for generations; I inherited it."

As she gawked at him, he could tell she was reorganizing whatever picture she'd held since they met.

"Moss, are you ... like, rich?"

His insides knotted. "What are you asking? Do you mean, did I grow up privileged?" He thought for a moment. "Family, friendship, home-grown food, companionship." He stroked Jazz. "They are my riches. But I suppose you're referring to money?"

She nodded.

"Yes." He watched her body language carefully.

She looked down at her cup and after swirling it, sipped her coffee. The pressure between them mounted. "I don't know what to say," she muttered. "I'm really uncomfortable I asked."

"Does it matter? Wealth?"

"I don't know. Maybe. Suddenly, I don't know how to be with you."

"That's a problem. You'd better set down your cup." She seemed startled, but when she did, he slung a pillow at her. Then another. She gave a nervous giggle and heaved one back.

"Come on, Jess. Get over it! I'm the same man I was two minutes ago, the same person you got to know in the hospital when you cheered me up with filthy jokes."

"Yeah, but you've been hiding a chunk of yourself. That's why you never invited me here, isn't it?"

"Uh huh. I prefer being appreciated for what's essential. You have to understand—when people find out, they often treat me differently. I thought it was better for us to ground our friendship, for you to get to know me for who I am, first."

Jessie licked her lip. "Riiight. Handsome *and* rich." Her hand jumped to her mouth. "I didn't mean to sound bitter or sarcastic. That came out all wrong."

He stared at her. "Damn right! That's not who I am. What about kind, or generous, or insightful? Those qualities last. Handsome? Temporary. Soon enough, I'll turn into an old dude with age spots. And you never know about money—it can come and go. Shit happens."

He grabbed his crutches. "I'm showering." He headed for the bathroom, slamming the door behind him. He sat on the bench and let the hot water pound him, hoping to wash away his rage and disappointment. He tried to consider her viewpoint, how he might feel in her position. But really—*handsome and rich?* The first words out of her mouth? That didn't sit well. Maybe the choice was being made for him. He needed someone with nuance.

He took his time in the bathroom, waiting until his emotions simmered down. After shaving, he dressed and crutched back to the bed to put on his leg. Bacon tang floated in the air—he was hungry.

When he walked into the kitchen, Jessie was turning bacon strips and flipping omelets. She turned to greet him. "I have a big mouth," she said. "You caught me off guard. I'm really sorry."

"Yeah, I'm sorry, too; I flew off the handle. But I hope you can consider what it's like for me."

"Now, I do. Nothing like sharp words to make me take stock. Hungry?" She tried to smile.

He nodded. "Smells delicious. After breakfast, let's take a walk up to the vista, and I'll show you my garden on the way out. And the chickens."

Zephyr feels Kibble Man. He's back at the big land. She wants to pense him. Her girl is uneasy and restless, then picks a fight with the mother. She wants them to be together again. She tries sending him an image, but has no sense he gets it. She bumps Rowan, sends her a picture of Kibble Man.

"I know, I miss him too," Rowan whispers.

Chapter Twenty-nine

As Jessie accompanied Moss to the garden, she slipped her hand into his. A moment later, he dropped it to swing open the gate, revealing the large expanse of vegetable beds. Jessie stopped in her tracks. "Good grief! With all this, you could feed an army squad, maybe even a platoon."

"Yeah, it's more than I need. I give the excess to the Kiwanis Food Bank in town. They're real grateful for the organic produce."

"It looks like we need to pick and make a run today."

"They only accept food on Wednesdays. I'll take a load in then. But you're right—this is the height of harvest season. We'll wander through and out the other gate. I'll introduce you to my chickens."

"Chickens. Whoop-de-doo." She twirled her finger in the air with mock enthusiasm.

He gave her a look, but she was checking out the beds. They meandered the curved paths, and Jessie admired the eggplants and carrots. He pulled a long carrot from the ground and hosed it off for her. She smiled and bit into it. "Delicious," she said. "What a rich flavor. I'd forgotten. Way better than store-bought."

"Completely different," he said. "That's why I garden."

"Surely someone helps you?"

"No, ma'am. I do it all myself." He held the gate open for her. "Come meet the girls."

"Moss, they're just chickens," Jessie scoffed. "They lay eggs, and we wring their necks for meat."

"No, they aren't *just* chickens," he said, frowning at her. "Each breed has a different personality. Mostly, I keep Rhode Island Reds because they're easy going and great layers—beautiful brown eggs. You cooked them up this morning. But here," he indicated a black and white one— almost a herringbone pattern—with a red comb, "is a Plymouth Rock. Isn't her coloring pretty?"

"Uh, for a chicken, I suppose. I had to muck their nests growing up."

He overlooked her tone. "Yeah, I did too. This girl's a Silkie." He pointed to a fluffy all-white hen. "I know better than to have special ones—the foxes around here are ingenious and take birds regularly. But I couldn't pass her up at the county fair last year. I'm a bit of a sucker."

"Apparently. I hope she lays as well as the others?"

"Oh, yeah. Otherwise, I wouldn't have bought her."

She turned away from the birds. "Can I see the barn? God, I'd really love to have a horse."

He raised his eyebrows. *Uh oh—was she thinking of living here? Away from the helicopters? A horse in the barn?* He showed her the six stalls and pointed out the tack room. "We don't have any stock right now, but when we were kids, we kept horses."

"What's there?" She pointed to a staircase in the corner.

"More guest quarters."

"I want to see!" She turned and headed upstairs before he could respond.

"Okay." He hesitated, set his little pack on the floor, and went up the stairs behind her.

The morning sun poured in through a large bay window—its light brightened a crocheted jewel-toned quilt covering the king-sized four-poster bed. Two carved chests filled one corner. A framed photo of aspen trees graced the wall.

She grabbed his hand again, tugging him toward the bed. "Hey, want to play? It's so beautiful up here. We haven't, you know...." Her voice trailed off.

Interesting, he thought. She can't say "make love." Because we don't. We fool around, we carouse. He hugged her. "I don't think so. Whatever change is happening in me, it's important that I honor it."

She pulled away and looked at him, eyes filling with tears. "This must be big. I was hoping—" She looked out the window as though to collect her thoughts before swinging back. "Over this year and three-quarters, I've fallen in love with you."

He looked at his hands and gathered his courage. "Oh, Jess." He shook his head. "I've met someone. You and I have a wonderful friendship, and for a while, we were friends with benefits, as they say. You've helped me so much." He touched her face. "I hope we'll always be there for each other. But I'm not in love with you, not that way."

Now tears poured, but she made no sound. She glared at him, wide-eyed—an angry flush pinking her cheeks. She choked out, "You've. Met. Someone?" She took a deep breath. "*You've met someone.* Since when have we been dating other people?" she snarled.

"We never said that our … our … connection was monogamous."

"Shit. Why didn't you mention this woman? You've been stringing me along, haven't you? Like a yoyo—pull me in when you want sex and throw me out when you don't."

"I did tell you about her. Right now. The moment I realized it."

He didn't flinch when she pursed her mouth and scrutinized him.

"She must come from the same background as you." Her voice caught. "Is *that* it?"

He reached to wipe the tears from her face, but she smacked his hand away.

"Hey!" He rubbed his fingers.

"You don't have the right to wipe away my tears." She swiped them herself. "Well, is that the reason?"

"No, I think she comes from a modest upbringing. She's a widow and struggles to pay her bills."

"What, then? What is it? What does she have that I don't?"

He went quiet, settled deep inside. "There's no explanation. Chemistry just happens, and when you don't expect it. I wasn't looking; I was too busy healing. When you and I got together, we had a great time. That, and writing, made up my whole world—until Zephyr's lonely howling disturbed my privacy."

"Have you slept with her?" Jessie's tone was sharp as though she expected him to answer "yes."

"No," he said. "I wouldn't take that step without having this talk with you."

"So, you're talking to me now, implying you're planning to?" Tears flowed again. "Is that why you invited me here? You thought it would let me down easier?" She stubbed her foot against the floor.

"Not at all. I wanted out of the smoke, and you needed to get away from the helicopters. It seemed like the obvious solution."

She walked to the window and stared out, but he sensed she was only seeing her own internal landscape. "You expect me to believe this change came about since we arrived last night?"

"Something's been brewing, and I figured it out this morning." He walked toward the stairs. "Come on, let's hike, give this conversation a rest." To his relief, she followed him from the guest room and down the wooden staircase.

Moss grabbed his pack. As they headed out onto the land, he considered threading his fingers through Jessie's, but held back, not wanting to give her the wrong idea. He didn't take her toward Bender's Ridge, his favorite. He wanted to save that for Carolina.

They limped along in silence until they climbed a deer trail behind the house. Then he led the way, and she followed. When they paused halfway up to catch their breath, she whispered, "I hate this, and how I feel now. I should have known better. Stupid me."

"Beating yourself up isn't the answer," he said.

She whirled on him. "You smug, arrogant, rich bastard."

He stepped back as though struck. "Whoa! Harsh. Try and look at what we have—a dear friendship. It's a precious thing."

"Are you *really* imagining we can ratchet this down?"

"That's my hope, yes, for long-term friendship."

She turned away staring down the path they traversed. "Damn, no way. It's just not possible."

"Maybe give it some time. Ready for the next leg of this hike?"

"Yeah, okay. This is tiring. Hope it's worth it."

His only answer was a sad smile.

Ten minutes later, they crowned the top. "Don't look up yet," he said. He guided her to a spot with an unimpeded view. "Okay, now."

A fresh dusting of snow on the South Sisters peak gleamed like a blanket of crystals in the morning sun.

When she lifted her head, she took in a sharp breath.

"Isn't it something?" he said. "I come here when I'm tangled in my little miseries—the vast beauty always changes my perspective. And look." He pointed to a steeper hill. "That's Bender's Ridge. My great-grandpa named the ranch after it."

"Have you climbed all three Sisters peaks?"

"In my early twenties. As a two-legged man. I'm not up to it now."

"This view makes my problems seem smaller. Thanks for *that*, at least. I'm thirsty—you have a bottle in the pack, right?"

He handed her the water container.

After drinking, they struggled to sit on the ground, noted each other's effort, and chuckled. Moss found a power bar in the pack. He broke it in half and handed her a piece.

Something caught his eye, and he swung around. "Look!" He pointed. "A red fox. Probably the one murdering my chickens." He grunted. "Oh, well, she's gotta eat too."

"Why don't you shoot her? That's what we did with varmints when I was a kid."

"She deserves to be here as much as I do—her brethren lived on this land before my family came. Besides, I won't use a gun to kill. Anything. You know that." He took a breath. "Look at her! She's gorgeous."

They fell silent. Then she said, "You're so different from me. I keep a loaded pistol by my bed. I'd blast that sucker." She tapped her fingers on her prosthesis. "Moss, I'm heading home. This is too hard. I need space. Maybe I'll call sometime."

After Jessie left, Moss sat on the porch. He felt as if he'd slipped into a trough. He might have just lost his best friend. He was confused, but also relieved he didn't have to fight her off. He hadn't realized how different they were. Probably, it was for the best she went home. Maybe, down the road, she could accept the dial-back to friendship and make contact. He'd hate to lose his only veteran buddy.

And what if Carolina didn't call? He stood to lose them both. He picked at the webbing on the chair as he thought about Carolina, determined to wait it out, not weaken and call her first.

Chapter Thirty

R owan sat in the corner of the couch, reading *Bridge to Terabithia* instead of one of the library books she picked out. The girl's boldness in the story always inspired her, and somehow, it felt right—after regaining her sight—to return to her favorite novel. Zeph lay nearby. *Almost like old times.* She smoothed her hand over the rich blue book cover. She remembered the color but still saw everything in black and white.

"I'm happy I can see," she said to Zephy. She reached for her favorite picture, Mom and Dad at the beach. She stood in between them; their arms were wrapped around each other. Happiness. Tears filled her eyes as she fingered the frame. Would she ever see the color of her father's sandy hair again? Or the cute, ruffled red bathing suit she wore that day? Or the purple, green, and red beach ball?

"Do you want to know a secret," she whispered to Zephy. "I know I should be grateful. My sight's back, and I am so, so happy, but is it wrong for me to want to see Daddo in color? Does that make me selfish, spoiled? Or unappreciative?" She put the picture back on the bookshelf. And Mossy? Would she ever see the color of his eyes? *Would she ever even see him again?*

Her mom walked into the room. Rowan set down her book and frowned. "Why'd Mossy go away yesterday? Were you mean to him?"

As Rowan scooted over to make room for her mother, Zephyr jumped from the couch.

Her mom sat next to her and patted her on the knee. "I didn't ask him to leave. He had plans to visit a friend in Ashland. You were kind of mean, too. You didn't even hug him goodbye."

"Yeah, after he left I felt bad. Grown-up relationships are so confusing and complicated." Rowan pointed to her heart. "I miss Daddo so much, I ache." She wiped a tear. "More now than right after he died. I know he's never coming back." She paused because her eyes filled up. "But I want family again." She leaned into her mom, so familiar and comfortable. "I love you big—you know that—but there's a giant sucking hole in my life."

"In mine, too," Carolina murmured.

"Daddo would want family for us. I know he would."

"Yes, I suppose so."

"And Mossy's just right. All three of us love him." Rowan felt her mom stiffen.

"Sweetheart, healthy love between adults takes a long time to grow. People need to get to know each other really well—learn about weaknesses and strengths and, over time, see if it's a good match for everyone involved."

"I know you don't like the sixth sense I have for stuff like Grandma does. You think he's going to die of the dumb flu or some stupid accident." She put her head in her mom's lap. "Or get called back to Afghanistan and get killed. Anything could happen."

"Well, not that. Because Moss lost his leg, he won't have to serve again."

"Oh, right!" Rowan whooshed out a breath. "That's a relief! But why can't you just accept Mossy so we can be a family again?"

Her mom fell quiet. Rowan waited, anxious.

"You have sensitive radar, but you can't push us together." She stretched and shifted.

They both found new positions facing each other. Her mom went on, "I know how much you think you want this, but we hardly know him. Moss and I have a lot to figure out. You've got to let it be. Can you promise me? It's important. If you try to force us together, we'll have no chance of finding our way." Her mom fiddled with her fingernails. "I'm really scared. Losing your father was a devastating shock. I guess I'm afraid to love again. There are so many unknowns."

"Losing my sight and getting it back in a second weird accident has taught me everything's unknown."

"And it terrifies me. Can you understand?"

Rowan fell silent for a moment. "Yeah, I guess so." She felt her mom's attention fixed on her.

"Will you promise to butt out?"

Rowan unfolded her legs and paddled Zephyr's paws with her feet. "I'll try. You could make the 'zip your mouth' signal if I forget. You know, the one Daddo used for secrets?"

Five weeks. Not one damn word from Moss. Sunday night, after Rowan went to bed, Carolina huffed with frustration and, on impulse, grabbed the phone and dialed. Zephyr showed up and stuck her nose under her arm. One ring. Two rings. She almost lost her nerve, but then he answered.

"Hello?"

Hearing his resonant voice, she dropped the receiver, fumbled, and then retrieved it. "Moss! I didn't expect you to pick up. It's Carolina." Her hands trembled. She sat down on her bed.

"Hey," he said. "I've been thinking about you. How's it going?"

Irrational anger welled. *Like he didn't know.* Then she caught herself. Actually, he had no clue. Everything she'd been chewing on she'd locked away, not shared with anyone.

"Carolina? Are you still there?"

"Yes," she said, shakily. "I'm here. I could be better." She took a breath. "It's been hard since you left. I care. You knew that, and yet you dashed off to see another woman." She cleared her throat. "I was so damn jealous. And then Row lectured me."

He was silent for a moment. "Thanks for telling me. You weren't forthcoming, you know. You're a challenging woman to read."

"I'm afraid and tripping all over myself. It's not about you. Well, that's not true. Of course, it is about you. And me." She hesitated. It was now or never. "May we come visit?" she blurted.

"Of course, you can! I'm here. It'd make me happy. You're welcome anytime."

Any time you're not with that other damn woman. "This weekend?"

"Wonderful. Make it for Friday dinner."

"Thanks." Carolina paused, pondering how to say what was on her mind. She felt the seconds ticking by. "I know it's none of my business but—"

"The answer is no, Carolina."

"No? You don't even know what I was going to—"

"No, I didn't sleep with her when I left you that day or since then. Yes, I want you to come. Very much."

"But are you still seeing her? I mean, will you be?"

He sighed. "As a friend, maybe, but that's all. We're done."

Carolina took a deep breath. Then another. "In that case, I think I'm ready to try a next step," she said. There was a sound on the other end; it took her a moment to decode. *Really?* The man had the nerve to chuckle. How impossibly irritating.

He cleared his throat. "That's good news," he said, his voice rough.

He offered nothing else. "Did you start to say something?" she asked.

"I did. I reconsidered."

"Want to reconsider again? I'm curious."

He grunted. "Okay. I want you to stay with me."

Did he think we would stay in town? "I was hoping we'll stay at Bender's Ridge like last time. In the guest house."

"With me, Carolina. In the main house."

Oh, my Gawd! She blushed and covered her mouth with her hand to make sure her thoughts didn't spill out in words. She took another deep breath and tried to keep her voice even. "Interesting proposition. Shall we see how it unfolds?"

"Don't do that." His tone was soft, kind, as if he understood—but firm.

"I … I was stalling for time." She rubbed the palm of her hand across her chin. "I've never experienced this kind of pull toward someone before. It scares the shit out of me."

"Me too."

"Really?"

"Yes, ma'am. I've been holed up here, mostly isolated, for two years. I swore off beautiful women when Sophie walked out. Then you came along. You're not only lovely, you're subtle and deep. I suspect what we have is strong and good, but it feels like free fall."

"Free fall," she whispered.

As soon as she hung up the phone, Carolina paced her room, back and forth, back and forth. What was she doing, breaking the rules—rules that had been in place for four years? Four good years. Could this possibly be right?

Zephyr crawls onto the couch next to Carolina, who weeps softly. The dog rests her head in the mother's lap, sensing she needs the company of a pack member. Her girl is asleep, so she's the only one to help. The woman cuddles her and strokes her ears. "Thank you. How'd you know I needed you? It's spooky how you show up at just the right time."

Zephyr raises her head and licks tears from Carolina's face. This human is kind, but she doesn't understand.

The next morning over breakfast, Carolina brought up her plan for the weekend trip.

"Oooooh, I want to go so bad. So does Zephy. But Seth and I have that big snowflake project for Mr. Clarke's class. It's half our grade and due a week from today. We've got a bunch of work left." Rowan twisted her finger in her hair. "I have to rewrite and turn in my summer essay, too."

"It sounds like you and Zeph better stay with Sue so you can get your work done."

Rowan looked crestfallen. "Zephy and me—we *need* to see Mossy."

"Zephy and I," Carolina said. "You'll get to go soon. Moss will make sure of that."

The school bus honked, startling her. "I'll ask Sue. I'm sure it will be fine with her."

Rowan grabbed her books, supported them with her cast, and ran for the door.

"Walk! Doctor's orders."

Rowan slowed. "Love you!" she called over her shoulder. "But I'm still totally disappointed."

"Love you too, sweetheart!" Carolina blew out a breath. Sometimes, events seemed to conspire. She felt like a lamb being shed from its herd and driven in another direction. Driven by life.

After she washed the breakfast dishes, she headed for Sue's property.

"C'mon in," Sue called. "Want a cuppa?"

"Please. I have a favor to ask."

"Lay it on me." Sue waved her to a counter stool and turned on the teapot.

"Rowan and Seth have a joint project due Monday. I didn't remember and made plans last night for us to visit Moss this weekend. Can Zephyr and Rowan spend the weekend with you?"

"That's fine." Sue squinted at Carolina. "You're gonna stay with him?"

"Yeah—Moss thinks we're all coming. Should I warn him?"

Sue gave a wicked grin. "Oh, boy! No, surprise him!"

"Our phone conversation last night? He got underneath—where I'm vulnerable—in such a kind way. And he was unguarded, too. I can't help myself. I really like him, and it's scaring me."

"That heated up fast. I thought you two were just friends. Are you sure about it? What about birth control?"

Carolina blushed. "I started the pill after my last period. Just in case. Another sign that I'm out of my mind. This is nothing like Rafe and me." She picked up a banana from a bowl of fruit and peeled it. "Will I remember how?" She shook her head. "I feel like I'm seventeen."

"What do you mean, 'out of your mind'?"

"Getting involved before Rowan goes to college."

"Those kinds of plans only work 'til they aren't needed any longer," Sue said.

Carolina frowned, uncertain.

"You've grown and moved on." Sue laughed and cuffed Carolina on the arm. "Of course, ya should go. It's about time ya got a break after all that's happened. But—take condoms."

"You're right. About everything."

Sue grabbed a banana, too. "Rowan and Zephyr are family," she said.

Later, Carolina sat in her kitchen, drumming her fingers. She was going to trash her safety net and go to Bender's Ridge. It didn't feel right to surprise Moss, though. She suspected he'd had too many harsh jolts in his life.

At lunchtime, she picked up the phone and punched in his number. She figured there was a chance he might answer. Three rings. Four rings. He must be digging the phone out of the closet.

"Carolina," he said. "Hi."

"How'd you guess it was me?"

"Every once in a while, I sense something beforehand. Doesn't that happen to you?"

"I guess so."

"Well, like that. Intuition—you know."

"Intuition?" She took a breath to calm down. *Not the time to get sidetracked.* "I'm coming alone."

Silence.

"Really? I didn't … that's great!"

"Free fall," she said.

Friday morning, as Carolina cleaned up from breakfast, Rowan set her backpack on the kitchen counter.

"Mom," she said. "Give Mossy a big hug for me. Jazz, too."

Her toddler nickname, Mommo, had slipped away after she got her sight back. Carolina missed it. "I will, sweetheart. I'll call you after lunch tomorrow."

Her daughter put her good arm around her. "You have a fun time, okay?"

"Thanks. I know you two will be thoughtful guests. I'll take Zeph and her stuff to Sue's." She hugged her daughter back, kissing the top of her head.

That afternoon, after she dropped Zephyr off and started the van to leave for Sisters, tingling in her belly started. At first, she interpreted it as anxiety, but it soon dawned on her it was plain old excitement.

Chapter Thirty-one

C arolina pulled up to the Bender's Ridge farmhouse and checked her watch. It was 5 p.m.—she'd made good time. Stiff from the drive, she climbed down from the van. Jazz bounded in front of Moss as he limped out to greet her. His hair was still damp from showering, and he looked crisp in khaki shorts and a black T-shirt. It was the first time she'd seen him wearing his prosthetic leg without long pants. *Cool.*

He welcomed her with a shy smile. "Hey," he said and grabbed her into a long hug. "This feels yummy," he murmured. "And you smell good. You're my birthday present. I turn thirty-eight tomorrow."

"You could have told me; I would have brought a gift." She turned her head to the side to listen to his heartbeat. Then she tilted back her face to be kissed, eyes wide. He bent down and skimmed her lips, then met them full with his. An invitation, she thought. A slow, welcoming solicitation. His quiet pacing intrigued and heated her. Maybe he felt it, too.

"*You* are my gift." He kissed her lightly once more and stepped back. "Come on in. I'm cooking dinner." He took her hand as he opened the door. "I'll bring your gear in later. We're going to eat by the fire."

She realized he was introducing her to the way he lived his life. No fancy table with candlelight. No pretense—smart man.

Jazz came forward and asked for attention, so Carolina knelt to scratch behind her ears. The dog's fur was the opposite of Zephyr's— short, and remarkably soft.

"Do you want to sit down for a few minutes?"

"I've been sitting for hours in the van. I'd love some water."

"Follow me," he said.

At the kitchen sink, he dispensed a glass of filtered water and handed it to her.

She pointed to the island where he'd spread out an array of freshly-picked lettuces and vegetables. "How about I fix the salad?"

"Perfect." He handed her a paring knife and cutting board, then added more ingredients to the stew while she chopped. When she finished, he said, "I'll go grab your gear."

"There's a backpack and hiking boots behind the driver's seat. I'll freshen up in the guest bathroom."

Jazz rose to follow him out.

"She's so attentive to you."

"She's broken through my isolation. I'm going to feed the chickens and lock them in the coop for the night. And bring in the bird feeders. I'll be a little while."

Thinking about what Moss had said about his dog, Carolina washed her face and ran her fingers through her hair. It was awfully remote out here. That was why his initial invitation had surprised her. She thought he liked being that secluded.

Meandering into the kitchen, she gave the stew a stir and returned to the living room. She picked a book from the shelf, settled on the couch, and studied the cover. *The Things They Carried* by Tim O'Brien. The title seemed vaguely familiar, but she was sure she'd never read it. Perusing the back cover, she saw it was a memoir about Vietnam. *Nope, not what I want right now.* She returned it to the bookcase and chose *Early Morning: Remembering My Father* by Kim Stafford. Wasn't that the poet William Stafford's son? This might be interesting. She curled up in a corner of the couch.

When Moss and Jazz came back, he dropped her boots in the entry and set her pack in the living room. "You'll have to decide later whether you want to stay in the guest room or my space," he said.

"Your space it is," she responded, meeting his lapis eyes. "It's probably a good time to say I'm on the pill."

"Woman, you're in free flight! There's a lot of air between you and the ground."

Nodding, she said, "They say to cast your arms wide and enjoy the rush of the wind." She swallowed hard. "Once you're over the terror and shock, that is."

He laughed aloud. "All right, then." He shouldered the bag again and took it into the master bedroom.

When he returned, he said, "After you called, I went to town for an HIV test. Negative. No other STDs, either."

They contemplated each other.

Delight coasted through her. *We've both been preparing. I won't need those condoms after all.*

"I wish you could see your expression," he said, laughing.

Her hands went to her face.

"Ready to eat?"

"I'm hungry. It smells wonderful," she said, grateful for the subject change.

Moss pointed to the fresh salad and stew and handed her a wide bowl. "Farm style." He didn't offer wine. It surprised her, but she accepted the fizzy water and realized she was relieved. Whatever came next, she wanted them unencumbered by alcohol. Apparently, he did too.

She joined him on the couch in front of the crackling fire. The room smelled faintly of wood smoke and dried autumn leaves. Jazz settled on a small rug, happy to soak up the heat. They ate quietly. "You're a fine cook," Carolina said. "Every meal you've made since we met has been unusual and delicious."

"Thanks. I learned out of necessity and then discovered I loved the process—starting with planting seeds. Digging in the earth heals me."

After they finished, Carolina cleared and washed up. When she returned, he raised his arm and invited her to snuggle in. "Beware, my prosthesis is really hard—don't whack yourself. Takes some getting used to. If it gets in the way, I'll unleg."

She leaned into him and rested her head on his chest; the beat of his heart steadied her. He was so … male. Sinewy. And he must have shaved before she'd arrived—lemony scent lingered.

The silence lengthened. A barn-sized chunk hung between them.

Moss cleared his throat. "It's time I shared what went down over there. I'll try, at least. I've only told my therapist and one other friend." His tone was ragged. "It's best Rowan isn't here. This could change how you feel about me."

Carolina shifted on the couch so she could face him. He stared at his hands and blinked fast. "How about introducing me to your leg?" she said. "Rowan told me you showed her. You can work backward toward the other stuff. Slowly. In your time."

"Thanks. You're kind. Okay." He put his hand on the man-made leg. "This is called a transfemoral prosthesis, because I lost my leg above the knee. For a lower amputation, it's called a transtibial. Amputees simply say AK—above knee, and BK—below knee." He bent his leg and rested the foot on the edge of the coffee table. "As I told Rowan, they don't bother to pretty these up for guys since they're usually underneath pants."

"I think it's beautiful. Clean function has a special elegance."

His eyebrows whizzed up. "Yes! I agree." He demonstrated how the ankle joint worked and then the knee.

"What holds it on?"

"This one was molded to my leg. Different models vary."

Jazz whined.

"I need to let her out. When I'm showing you the rest of this...." He smoothed the prosthesis. "I'll unleg. I always have to plan ahead."

"Shall I come too?"

"Naw, stay by the fire."

He got up, and his dog followed. Carolina heard him call, "Free dog, find your spot."

When he came back in, he went down the hall and returned carrying crutches.

"Where's Jazz?"

He pointed toward the master bedroom. "She's an early-to-bed girl—although she'll leave her nest to ask for her evening treat or if she senses I need her. When I have nightmares, she wakes me right at the start. I come out here for a while to recover, and she always follows me. She's a great companion."

"After Rowan listened to the CD you sent her, she said that's service dog behavior. Maybe Jazz is a natural."

He nodded thoughtfully. "Interesting. I wonder if I could encourage and support those behaviors. I'll look into it. Maybe Row can help me." He leaned the crutches nearby and sat next to her on the couch. "Okay, next step. Ready for this?"

"Sure."

He slipped the socket off and laid the prosthesis gently on the coffee table. Rubbing his sock-covered stub, he said, "It's always a relief to take it off. Mind you, I'm grateful for it."

She reached over and rested her hand lightly on his stump. He didn't react.

"My missing leg really doesn't bother you, does it?" He sounded surprised. "People have strange responses. Especially women."

"How is it different from my missing finger?"

"Maybe because I'm a guy, and women see me as broken?"

"If so, they're crazy. Clearly, they're the broken ones."

He laughed. "Maybe so." He hunched over and rested his arms on his thighs. "You know, I thought I could sit and talk about this, but no way. I'll leg up again so we can walk outside and stare at the stars. Grab your jacket; the temperature plummets at this altitude. I'll get long pants, too."

When Moss reappeared, Jazz showed up. She was dancing and ready for a jaunt. He offered her an extra-large dog biscuit. "Free chow," he murmured. She took it gently and raced over to lie on her pad in front of the fire before breaking it apart with care and crunching the pieces. Moss closed the glass doors on the fireplace. His expression was set, as though he'd reached inside and found the starch he needed.

He gave Jazz her free command as he opened the door. She trotted into the dark as the gibbous moon appeared from behind a small cloud. As they crossed the deck, he slung his arm around Carolina's shoulders and pulled her close; she adjusted her stride to coordinate with his. He paused and turned her toward him, lifting her chin so their eyes met. "I'd been wondering if you'd ever call," he whispered. "I'm glad you've come."

She felt the words settle inside and reached up to stroke his cheek. "Me too. But what about Jessie?"

"It's clear to me—and now to her as well—she's only a dear friend."

"She wanted more?"

"She did. We'll see how the friendship unfolds. If she can't handle giving up the 'benefits' part, then we're done. I hope it doesn't turn out that way; we've shared a lot. There's so much I don't have to explain to her."

"But you do to me?"

"You've never been to war. I'm a complicated package."

"Can you leave what's in the past back there? Everything that came before has made you the beautiful man I see right now."

"You're generous. I'm far more introspective than I used to be; for sure, I know myself better." He looked up at the stars. "Let's head out to the garden. There's a great place to sit."

She intertwined her fingers with his. As they walked across the yard and down the path, she noticed he hardly limped and wondered if it was because he'd unlegged for a short while.

Moss opened the gate and turned to his dog. "Off duty," he murmured.

She tilted her head and looked at him, puzzled.

"Wait," he added.

Her ears drooped, and she sank to the ground, nose between her paws.

"She hates it when I make her stay behind, but the garden's off-limits. I added the 'off duty' part because you mentioned what Row said about her service dog behavior. I'll try to teach her that command—it'll mean she can relax and trust I'll be okay. She needs down time; we all do."

Carolina felt a rush of elation. He'd considered what Rowan had suggested.

He led her to the back and up a small rise. The moon illuminated a wooden bench swing. They sat in comfortable silence, their bodies touching. He used his foot to rock them. She enjoyed the rhythm. A few minutes later, feeling tension gathering in his body, she turned toward him.

"So," he said, and blew out a long breath. "Afghanistan." He fell silent again before picking up the thread. "I'd been there eighteen months. My buddy, Frank, and I were sent to pick up building materials in a nearby town. Some of the boards were twelve footers, so we took the flatbed truck." He shifted to meet her gaze. "I grew up with him. We enlisted together."

"A close friend, then."

"My best friend since childhood. He went to the U of O with me; we both majored in creative writing." Another silence. "It's strange how scrambled my memories were—I couldn't talk about this at all if I hadn't been writing about it and pieced some parts together." He went inside himself before speaking again. "Picking up the lumber and supplies went fine. On the way back, I remember the clouds of dust the truck raised before we reentered town. It's weird, what sticks in the brain, and what doesn't. Anyway, because of giant potholes, we had to crawl along. Near the town center, the road narrowed between one-story adobe buildings, typical construction there. I scanned the men by the side of the road—you need to develop additional body language sense—and even then, you can still get killed. We passed an open-air vegetable market; there were lots of women out shopping with their kids." He rubbed his forehead.

"This is damn hard. The puzzle still has loose pieces scattered around." He stood and paced in front of the swing. "I noticed one woman and her daughter. The mom, she wore the blue burqa covering her entirely, with blue mesh over her eyes. Her little girl, I don't know, maybe ten, had bright eyes and beautiful dark hair. She seemed curious, and we smiled at each other—a moment of real meeting. Then she pulled her hand away from her mom's so she could dash forward to wave at me."

Moss turned away. When he twisted back, his eyes were filled with tears. "Just as she waved—God, she had such a sweet, innocent smile—I was launched into the air. I have no memory of the sound of the explosion, although later, I was told about it. Something, flying debris, I suppose, slammed me." He sat back down. "When I came to, I was splayed across smashed stuff, maybe tomatoes—smelled like them, anyway. It was pandemonium, although I couldn't hear anything." He blew out a ragged breath. "People milling, faces shaped in screams, twisted bodies. Billowing black smoke turned out to be the remains of our truck, although I didn't know it then. As I tried to clear my vision—lots of grit in my eyes—I felt something." Moss choked, and tears coursed down his cheeks. "She was lying beside me, the same little girl. Our eyes locked. Then, I looked down at my body. I couldn't see my left leg. Was all the red I saw blood? I remember wondering if it was broken, bent back under me, or missing." He passed a hand over his face. "I almost fainted but lifted my head and checked again. Gone! My leg was gone." He turned to Carolina. "I squeezed my eyes shut, and a wave of relief roared up my body. I was out of there! Too injured to serve. I remember thinking, if I make it, they'll send me to Germany, and I won't have to come back. I'm so damned ashamed of that."

Carolina's heart pounded. She took his hand but remained quiet. No platitudes here.

"I don't know how the medics got there so quick. When the first doc opened his pack, I begged him—'Help her first!' I actually heard my voice, although it was muffled, so I guess my hearing was returning. I'll never forget his words—he leaned over to put a tourniquet on my thigh, and shouted at me, 'She's a goner. Triage protocol—only those with a chance.'"

Moss took a deep breath. "I blacked out from pain. When I came to, her eyes were fixed. Just staring. I touched her body—it was still warm." A sob lodged in his chest, and he turned away. "If only I hadn't smiled at her, she might have stayed close to her mom and escaped harm. I feel so responsible." He looked back at Carolina. "My smile killed that girl."

"Your smile gave her a tiny window of grace before her death," she said. "The Taliban murdered her."

He rubbed his chin. "You have a new take on it." The tears continued to slide down his face, and he touched them, but instead of wiping them away, slowly rubbed them in. "You know, *Qawwali* singers honor tears this way. I don't always remember, but I like the tradition."

"Qawwali?"

"Musicians in India. They sing sacred Sufi music." He stroked her cheek with a damp finger. "Rowan reminds me of the Afghan girl."

Carolina shivered as the memory came back: his body language the first moment he turned to greet her daughter at the library. *It hadn't been just hard. He'd paid an enormous internal price to greet Row.* She scooted closer until her arm and leg pressed his and looked at him. He was sweating, his face shiny in the moonlight.

"I was moaning—having trouble breathing. The doc put in an IV and injected meds that took the edge off. It turned out, besides my blown-off leg, I fractured my collarbone and six ribs. Those breaks weren't discovered until later—they were too busy trying to keep me from bleeding out."

He paused and shook his head. "That's not all." This came out a whisper. "I could hear the chopper, so I yelled to the doc, 'Have you seen my buddy, Frank? He was driving." The medic shook his head and said, 'Sorry, Westbury.' I wondered how he knew my name; I didn't remember him asking. That's how messed up I was. My name—all our names—are emblazoned on our uniforms. Anyway…." Moss swallowed hard. "He pointed to the burned-out shell of the truck."

"No!" Carolina's hand jumped to her mouth. The loss was carved in his face.

He shuddered. "I can't stay in the past for long. Small visits, many times, work best. And you're cold!" He rubbed his hands up and down her arms, took off his jacket, and put it over her shoulders. He fumbled in the pocket and brought out a knit hat, pulling it gently down on her head. "Let's go back." He stood up and gave her a hand. She rose from the swing and into his arms. He nestled his mouth next to her ear and murmured, "Can you bear this? Are you still all in?"

She nodded. "I am."

He kissed her ear with his trademark slow pacing, and her knees trembled. She leaned against him. "Lordy," she whispered. "The effect you have on me."

Moss made a throaty sound, although he wasn't able to smile. "I like to hear about it."

Jazz met them at the gate, jigging with delight. She knocked against Moss's hand repeatedly, clearly worried about him. He leaned over to reassure her. "She always knows when I'm upset even when we aren't physically close."

He slipped his arm through Carolina's as they walked. "War…." His voice roughened. "I don't know how people can glamorize it in movies and then joke about something as they walk out of the film. War is one shitty nightmare after another. It contaminated me."

Carolina shook her head. "The war left an indelible mark, for sure. 'Contaminated' seems awfully harsh."

He opened the front door for her. Walking into the living room, he eased himself onto the floor to bring the fire back to life. "There's more. If you can handle it, I'd rather spill it all—so I know where we stand once you've heard it. Then maybe I can look forward to tomorrow. Want some chamomile tea?"

She nodded, wondering what was coming next.

A few minutes later, Moss brought steaming mugs into the living room. She sipped in silence. For long minutes, he watched the fire. When he spoke, his words came out clipped, but quiet. "I shot kids over there."

An involuntary intake of breath caught her.

He froze. "I told you this would change everything." His voice broke.

"Don't make assumptions! I see you love kids—Rowan adores your company."

He looked down and shook his head.

She put her fingers under his chin so he couldn't avoid looking at her. "What I'm feeling is how horrible, how devastating that must have been for you."

In the flickering light, he searched her face. "Really?"

"Truly. Tell me what happened."

He focused on the fire again. "Afghanistan, it's a world of its own. Even the dust tastes different. One afternoon, I was kicking a ball around with three boys—Hadi was the oldest, then Jamal, and Abdul Rahman. Brothers, I think. At least they were always together. I'd given Hadi a soccer ball—he only had a smattering of English, some words for the sport. He would never take the ball home—too many questions, I guess— so it lived in my quarters." Moss rubbed his neck. "Mainly, I used hand signals and a few Pashto phrases I'd picked up. We played for ten minutes or so before I had to go back to work. So much joy poured out of those kids. I took the sweetest picture of them that day."

Moss pushed off the couch and paced in front of her. "Late afternoon, intel came in, solid information from surveillance. Taliban leaders were gathering in a certain family compound that evening. Their snipers picked off three of our guys that same week—friends who were also brave soldiers.

It had been the worst week of losses since we'd arrived. This info was vital to the survival of the rest of us."

He ran his fingers through his hair and settled down next to her again. "I got tapped to lead the team." He turned to meet her eyes—his, pools of darkness. The pain she saw lanced through her.

"I've never told anyone this—not even my therapist. I didn't have a good feeling about the mission. Nothing I could put my finger on, exactly, and certainly not enough to go to my C.O. What would I say? Describe my intuition? No place for that in the service." Another long silence.

She shifted to sit cross-legged, so she could see his expression more clearly.

"Once we slipped inside the compound gate, we could hear low voices and coughing from the meeting room—Afghan men are heavy smokers. On my signal, we burst through the door." He looked down at his hands, spread his fingers open. "Gunfire erupted—ours, I think; I don't know for sure. The *chuf-chuf-chuf* echoing off the walls still haunts my nightmares." He closed his eyes. Now, his hands were hard fists.

She moved closer so her leg made contact with him.

"Screams, moans, then silence. The smell. I'll never forget the smell. The rusty iron stench of blood gagged me. The light must've been blown out. I had to squint." His words spilled out, hoarse. "Hadi. Jesus, Carolina, it was Hadi. Half his beautiful face, blown away. Three men, those three boys. All dead. Right then and there, I tossed my cookies. Life as I knew it was over. Over for me. That was six days before I lost my leg."

"My God," was all she could whisper. "I'm so sorry."

Jazz crept up on the couch and pressed her body next to Moss.

"Me, too. Sorry and ashamed." He wiped tears away. "So, there you have it."

But the tears kept coming. As she reached for him, his body shook with sobs and then full-blown wailing. She cradled him and made soft sounds. Minutes passed, and gradually his weeping subsided.

"Let's go to bed," she whispered.

"I'm not good for much. I'm wiped out."

She chuckled softly. "Mossy. So I can hold you."

Chapter Thirty-two

Friday night around ten, Rowan, Seth, and Sue finished the final Scrabble game.

"I'm still amazed you can see, Rowan," Sue said. "Miracles *do* happen."

As Rowan gathered the tiles to put them away, she fingered a Scrabble "N." "Yeah—to be able to play again. Now I understand about not taking anything for granted. Most kids my age don't get that."

Seth stood up and yawned. "You won. You're so good at this. I'm headed to bed. We'll have to work on our project in the morning, 'kay?"

"Sure," Rowan said, secretly relieved. "We can play a numbers game next time. Rummikub, maybe? You're great at it. G'night." Her heart raced thinking about asking her godmother about the stuff bothering her, things she couldn't talk about with her mom. She picked her cuticle as she waited until Seth's door clicked.

Sue folded her legs under her on the couch. Zephyr flopped on the floor nearby. "What's up, kiddo?" she asked. "You seem to be chewing on something."

"Well...." Rowan hesitated. "Can I ask you anything?"

Sue looked surprised. "Of course. I might not know the answer, but I'll try."

Rowan fiddled with her hands. "You know, last week, I took a walk down near the horse farm—the one where we see the Arabian colts and fillies? And—" she stopped again. "They were trying to breed this mare,

I guess." Taking a deep breath for courage, she blew it out, and her words raced. "Four guys had ropes on the stallion, and he was going nuts. His thingy was ginormous and stiff. I mean, like two feet long."

"Horse sex can get pretty wild and because they're huge animals, scary."

Rowan splayed her toes against Zeph's spine and considered her options. She could just run off to bed. Feeling desperate, she looked back at her godmother.

"Did it bring up questions about men and women?" Sue asked.

Rowan nodded. A blush started at her neck, flaming up to her forehead. She put her hands to her cheeks and felt Sue's comforting touch on her knee.

"Are you wondering about your mom and Moss?"

Now, really embarrassed, Rowan nodded again. She slid onto the floor and pressed her face to her knees.

Zephyr took advantage of the space, leaped on the couch and settled in the corner.

"Like, you know," Rowan asked. "Do you think they're going to … do *it*? This weekend?"

Sue took Rowan's hand and encouraged her to sit in the chair facing her. "It seems like they're falling in love. They have a weekend alone. My guess? Yes." She ran her fingers through Rowan's hair. "I know this is hard to talk about, but let's try. What is it ya want to know?"

"I can't figure out if that's good, if it totally creeps me out, or both."

Sue chuckled. "Probably both. I remember feeling the same way."

"Really?"

"Yeah. My parents divorced, and Mom started dating when I was around your age." She rubbed her fingers across the top of her hand. "None of the men were as kind or thoughtful as Moss, though. He's pretty special. Think how he took care of your mom when ya fell down the stairs—driving here as soon as he heard, picking up the best dinner in town, staying with her three nights."

"Yeah, I thought so, too. And I can really talk to him. Kind of like my dad." Rowan hesitated, then dropped her face in her hands. When she drew herself up, she asked, "But—what's it like, the first time with someone?"

Sue thought for a moment. "It's different with each couple. They have ta find their way. Some talk a lot; others don't talk at all. Some men like to jump into bed too darn quick. We women, sometimes we have to slow them down."

Rowan looked at her hands and rubbed her thumbs together. She felt safe with Sue, and every day she had new questions she'd never been able to ask anyone. With her mom just getting to know Moss, no way she'd ask her. She plunged ahead. "Isn't undressing super embarrassing? You know, seeing your bodies all naked?" She didn't look at Sue. Instead, she moved to the couch and crowded in next to Zephy so she could play with her paws.

"It can be if you're self-conscious. If people feel that way, they can take their clothes off by candlelight or even in the dark. One important thing to remember: none of us has a perfect body. We've all got lumps and bumps."

Rowan chewed her thumb as she thought about what Sue said.

Sue patted her knee. "Moss seems like a good guy. From everything your mom's said, I'm pretty sure of it."

"But he's a soldier. I think he had to kill people in the war. He's missing a leg, so for sure, they tried to kill him. He must be tough."

"Yes, that was his job at the time, protecting our country. Just because he's been in the service doesn't mean he carries that toughness into regular life. Some soldiers do, it's true; some men have a hard time back home. People come back with bad PTSD, mental illness, drug addiction—they've seen or had to undertake missions they could never have imagined. It haunts them."

Rowan felt Sue's hand on her knee. She slowly raised her face to meet her godmother's.

"Getting back to the horses. Their 'thingies,' as you call them, are big because horses are big. Each kind of animal is built to that species' scale, including their penises."

Rowan colored up. The word embarrassed her. "So, it's not going to hurt Mom?"

Sue shook her head. "It feels good. Really good. Remember, Moss is gentle. Not all men are. It's important to pick the right guy."

Rowan leaned over and scratched Zeph behind the ears. "I couldn't ask Mom about this."

"I get it. Bad timing, huh?"

Relieved, Rowan nodded. "And I wanted to talk to you. Isn't that what godmothers are for?"

"You bet. Now, off to bed. Are you going to let Zephyr out for a few minutes?"

Rowan nodded and whistled softly. Zephyr got up and stretched until her chest almost touched the floor.

As Zephyr walks outside, she senses Kibble Man at the big land. He's upset and sad. But Carolina and Jazz are with him, trying to make him feel better. She sits in the field and whines. Kibble Man comforted her when she was hurting; she yearns to do the same for him.

Moss accepted Carolina's hand. She leaned back, gently tugging him up from the couch and slipped her arm around his waist. They walked in comfortable silence to his room. Jazz gave a wide, squeaky yawn as she settled in her bed near his chair.

Carolina paused at the door, and Moss watched her take it all in. It was definitely a man's space. Another of his great-grandmother's quilts— a complex diamond pattern—lay folded on the king-sized bed. The furniture and floor boards glowed blonde-red; the Pacific madrone was the one real extravagance his father added to prepare for Moss's return from the hospital. The contractor had enlarged the doors to accommodate the wheelchair he'd been forced to use for months.

Moss noticed Carolina's eyes fixed on one object: Hadi's soccer ball. It had found its final home in the built-in bookcase across the room. A small, framed picture sat beside the ball.

"It's fine—go on. It's the photo I snapped of the boys."

She walked over, picked up the frame, and studied the image. Then she set it down carefully. "This feels like an altar," she murmured.

He gave a solemn nod. "I guess it is." He felt like weeping again and watched as she grazed Hadi's ball with her fingertips. To Moss, it seemed like a silent benediction. His chest tightened. *Now she knows everything. Will she change her mind about getting involved?*

She made her way to her backpack and dug around in it for a moment. "How silly. I forgot my nightshirt. May I borrow one of your tees?" She smiled shyly at him. "I'm thinking we should keep our ... gifts ... covered up until we have the proper energy to unwrap and give them the attention they deserve. If, and when, it feels right."

At the very thought, Moss hardened. His face was still swollen from crying, but he nodded and tried to smile. He fished in a drawer and tossed her a T-shirt. "It takes me longer to get ready for bed. It's not particularly romantic, but evening stump care has to happen. Let me wash up first because after I unleg, I massage my leg out here."

After Moss was done, Carolina took her turn in the bathroom. He was still rubbing cream into his stump when he heard her footfall. On her, his white tee fell mid-hip. He could see the shape of her nipples pressing against the cloth, and below, a grand length of firm, tanned legs. She realized he was staring and flushed. This time, he managed a smile. "Do you have any idea how gorgeous you are?"

Her blush brightened.

He slipped into bed and lifted the duvet on her side to welcome her, then clicked off the lamp. She slid under the covers, reached for him, and snuggled close. Moonlight streamed across them. He rested his head on her shoulder and sighed out a long breath. "I can't believe you're here, alone with me, in my bed. I've imagined this."

"Me too. Remember how grumpy we were in the beginning? Like wary, circling dogs."

He chuckled.

She kissed his forehead and ran her fingers through his hair. "Your sharing took guts. You must be exhausted."

At the word "exhausted," his eyelids drooped. "Yeah. I'm flat-out beat. Sorry." His body released at a deeper level. A few minutes later, he murmured, "If I have a nightmare, say 'Mossy' pretty loud a couple of times. No one ever called me that in the service, so it should bring me back." He nestled in closer. "Fair warning—we could end up with a dog between us. Jazz usually jumps up when I moan." Leaning over, he ran his finger slowly across Carolina's lips. "Thanks for being here."

He kissed her. Her lips were as soft as deerskin gloves, and she tasted …
familiar.

With that, he fell sound asleep.

He awakened later with a rock-hard erection. He reached for the
lamp but lit a candle on the bedside table instead. Just after 5 a.m. He
rolled over to admire his sleeping companion. She lay on her back, hair
tousled, her mouth full and inviting. The covers had slipped off. Lifting
the bottom of the shirt she wore, he ran his lips low across her belly.
She moaned with pleasure, and her eyes opened. "Hey," he whispered.
"Welcome back. It's my birthday. Interested in helping me open pres-
ents?"

She gave a sleepy smile and arched toward him. His tongue found
her belly button and then slipped up her midline to her breasts. Lifting
the T-shirt higher, he woke one nipple with lazy tongue circles until it
stood erect, then moved to the other. After a long moment's attention
there, he eased the shirt over her head. She helped him remove his shirt
and ran the palm of her hand lightly across his chest, planting it on top of
his heart. "Moss. It's been … since Rafe died." Her voice quavered. "Go
slow with me. I'm not sure I remember how."

"Slow is my favorite pace." He took her in his arms and cuddled her
close, kissing her forehead, her nose, and lingering on her lips. "Anything
you love? Or can't stand?"

"I've … I've never felt this way," she stammered. "So I don't know."

"We'll figure it out."

She ran her finger down his nose. "What I love is how you're giving
me time."

"I need time, too."

"You're different from most guys. Why, do you think?"

"Hmmm. This will sound strange, but—" he paused. "I think part
of it comes from combat. To survive, I had to be fully present. It turns
out, I like that way of being—as it applies to everyday life, that is." He
propped himself up on one elbow. "It's a benefit from my war experience
I never considered before. Maybe it'll make me a better lover. You'll have
to report."

"I am reporting," she said. "It's an astonishing difference—quite sensual. But unsettling."

He hesitated. "There's something else you need to know."

She cocked her head and waited.

"When I was nineteen, I had a mentor, a woman twenty-three years older than I. She taught me a lot about what women like."

"How'd that happen?"

"A writing professor. A cougar, I guess. She only liked young guys. Today, she'd get in huge trouble—but I am grateful."

"You attend with such care. Did she teach you that? I feel vulnerable. Exposed, even."

"Yeah, she did. I feel exposed as well. Once we both feel safe, I bet it'll change."

"I do feel—"

He rested his forefinger across her lips. "We've barely been together. How many times have we even hugged?" He leaned down and slowly kissed her again. "Both of us are unsure. Remember, on the phone, I said I was afraid, too. It wasn't just to make you feel better." He shifted and put his arms around her; she put her head on his chest. "That's why this will be a long birthday morning. Let's just kiss and fool around. Touch each other." He nuzzled her ear. A drop landed on his chest, and he whispered, "Tears?" He felt her nod. In true Qawwali fashion, he slowly rubbed the moisture in. Tears rose in him, too. So often, he'd felt like he had to perform, to get it right. This, whatever *this* was, seemed different. He could just be himself.

Chapter Thirty-three

arolina awakened to discover she hadn't been dreaming—she was lying in Moss's arms. Feeling like a teenager exploring first love, she giggled. They had been, as her mother would have said, "necking." Well, and a little petting. She'd felt the rock-hard length of him. But that was all—just sweetly, slowly, getting to know each other.

"Want some coffee?" she whispered.

"Please. Look in the cupboard to the left of the sink." He stretched and kissed her ear.

"Sugar or cream?"

"I'll come doctor my mug. I bought some pastries. They're in a bag next to the fridge."

She slipped on his T-shirt again and headed for the kitchen. Puttering around she located what she needed—organic Sumatra beans, she noted happily—a funnel, filter, coffee grinder, and two hand-thrown mugs. She put the croissants in the toaster oven. When the water boiled, she steeped the fresh grounds, delighting in the rich aroma.

Moss limped into the kitchen; Carolina could tell from the sound he'd put his prosthesis on. He came up behind and swatted her rear end.

Eyes flashing, she whirled and dropped into a defensive karate position, fists ready. "Not that! Never. It's in the 'I can't stand it' column."

He stepped back, both hands raised, palms out. "Whoa! I'm sorry."

Still scowling, she eased out of her stance. "Be careful. I'm a black belt. No tickling, either. And no snapping my butt with a dishtowel. All three, non-negotiable."

"A black belt! Are you actually mad at me?"

"There's stuff *you* don't know yet."

"Well then," he said, smiling. "Progress."

"Progress?" she growled, still too upset to see any humor.

"Yeah. I think sharing what we don't like is hardest. Do you have an older brother?"

She nodded and watched as he tended his mug. "Yeah, but this isn't about him."

He put in half a teaspoon of raw sugar and poured cream until it was a perfect caramel color. "Do you want to tell me what set you off?"

"Not now. I'll get to it, eventually. My brother, Sam, was a trip, but he turned out to be a nice adult. I think you'll enjoy him." She pulled the pastries out of the toaster oven and set them on a plate. "Now I know how you like your java," she said.

They sat at the oak table in the corner near the window with a view of the guest house. It glowed in the early morning light. *Such a short time ago, Rowan and I stayed there, yet it seems like a lifetime.* She sipped her coffee and then bit into the flaky, buttery croissant. *Yummy.*

"Apparently, we're not quite there yet, are we." It wasn't a question. "What's still in the way?" he asked.

As she considered what to say, anxiety rolled through her. "There's something that terrifies me."

Jazz got up, went to Carolina, and nudged her arm to comfort her.

She stroked the dog and went on, "I come from nothing special. Your parents will know I'm all wrong for you. My mom was a hippie— she did astrology and tarot for a living and wasn't practical at all—so, no means and no extras when I was growing up. I was lucky if my shoes fit. I worry Rowan takes after her. She has the same strong mystical bent."

"Where'd you get the idea I come from something special?"

"Besides this gorgeous ranch? Before you arrived at the library, Gladys told me your last name. Westburys are like American royalty. Surely, you know that. She said Aston Westbury's your dad."

Moss broke in. "Let's get something straight. My parents aren't stuck up, not at all. They're just Ma and Pa. Plain folks who happen to have had success and money followed. Ma was a hippie too, for God's sake." He took her hand. "All my parents want is for me to find someone who is deeply kind and cares about me. It seems you fulfill both, and you have a world of other wonderful qualities they'll appreciate." He unrolled her fisted fingers and slowly kissed her palm. "Ma was livid when Sophie walked out. She stalked around, calling her a 'rich bitch.' I got a kick out of seeing her that angry on my behalf."

Carolina took her hand back. The sensation of his lips shot straight to her body's core. She rubbed her fingers. "I don't even have a dress."

"Who cares?"

"What about the country club? What will I wear?"

"What country club?"

"The one they belong to."

"My parents?" He chortled. "Not their style." He bit into his crois-sant.

"Really? Where does your dad entertain his financier cronies?"

"He belongs to a business club in New York City—he kind of has to—but he prefers to entertain at home, in Connecticut. His 'cronies,' as you call them, come for the weekend and Ma dotes on them."

"You mean, she does the planning, and staff dotes on them."

This time he slapped his good leg and laughed out loud. "No staff. Only a housekeeper, Anna, who comes once a week to clean, Pa's gift on Ma's sixtieth birthday. He insisted."

Carolina fell silent. She met Moss's gaze head on. All she saw was love shining. So much for sweeping assumptions about wealth. After a moment, she asked, "What about you? Is there something that's still in the way for you?"

A vein at his temple throbbed. He took a long pull of coffee.

Her heart skipped a beat, and she caught herself holding her breath.

"In my nightmares, I'm back in Afghanistan. Sometimes, I wake up flailing. Thinking anyone near is the enemy. I'm afraid I could hurt you." He paused and rubbed his fingers across his forehead. "Jesus, then what?" His voice broke. "How could I forgive myself?" When he looked up, his eyes were filled with tears. Closing them, he shook his head.

The thought had never occurred to her. *My God, for him to have to live with that fear.* A tear traced down his face, and she softly rubbed it in. "I'm glad you warned me. I'm pretty good at duck and cover; I got beat up a few times as a kid." She took both of his hands. "We'd get through it, that's all."

Under his breath, he muttered, "Damaged goods."

"Mossy," she whispered. "Picture yourself whole. The way I see you."

"I need a break," he said. His voice was hoarse. "Want to hike up Bender's Ridge as soon as we finish? I'll show you where I first saw Zephyr's eyes peeking out at me."

Jazz raised her head and stared toward the door.

Then they heard crunching gravel. Moss frowned. "No one ever just stops by. Who could it be? Some lost soul?" He limped into the living room to peek out the window, then hitched quickly back to the kitchen. "Good Lord, it's Jessie. This is awkward! I'll stall her, figure out what kind of a mood she's in. She was not a happy camper when she left."

"She was here? I thought you went to her place?"

"Long story. A fire in the area. Helicopters."

"I'll get dressed." Carolina headed for the bedroom.

Moss looked down at his torso—when he'd gotten out of bed, he'd only pulled on sweat pants. "Throw me a T-shirt," he called.

A sharp pound on the door. Moss yanked on the shirt and opened the door.

"Hey," he said. "This is a surprise."

"She's here with you, isn't she?" Jessie was quivering, her face blotched red.

"Yes." He stepped outside and closed the front door.

Her hair was wild around her face; she looked like a wounded animal. Her voice came out a low snarl. "I couldn't sleep last night, so I got up and drove instead. I'm still pissed. You intentionally misled me."

"That's not what happened," Moss said, calmly. "I don't lie. And in the future, please call before showing up."

"I want to meet her. See exactly what you've chosen over me."

"It's not like that." He reached out to make contact, but she backed away, her mouth turned down. "I need to know you'll be civil," he went on. "Carolina hasn't done anything. It wouldn't be fair to her."

"Carolina—how utterly quaint. And fair? You say it isn't fair *to her*? Jesus, Moss. This isn't fair to *me!*" Tears welled and almost spilled over.

He made his voice as gentle as he could. "Jessie, matters of the heart—you know as well as I do—they unfold in their own way and time."

"But I was here first! You were my friend and lover."

"Yes, and you're still my good friend."

∞

Carolina took a deep breath and opened the front door. Jessie stood rigid, staring at Moss.

"You must be Jessie," she said, walking forward with her hand out. "I've wanted to meet you. Moss has told me how important you are to him."

"You!" Jessie whirled, pulling her arm back, hand open and flat, and spun toward Moss.

Carolina moved smoothly and caught her arm in mid-flight. "No violence," she said, softly.

Jessie's eyes went wide. She struggled to pull away, but Carolina's grip was firm. "How'd you do that?" she hissed. "So fast? You're like a snake!"

"Quick reflexes." Carolina let her go, but watched intently—Jessie was tall and fit, but not well-balanced.

"She's being humble. She's a black belt," Moss said.

Rubbing her forearm, Jessie backed up, her face reflecting a modicum of respect.

"You've had a long drive," Carolina said. "Would you like a cup of tea or coffee?"

"No way!" Jessie snarled. "I can't bear your kindness. Just needed to lay eyes on you." She turned to Moss. "I suppose *she* wouldn't blast your chicken-killing predator, either. You two actually deserve each other. I'm outta here."

She strode to her truck, slammed the door, and tore out of the drive, her spinning tires digging ruts in the gravel.

They stood, staring at her receding vehicle.

"She's pretty rough. Did you know that side of her before?" Carolina asked. "And what'd she mean about 'blasting a predator'?"

"When she was here, we saw a red fox. I mentioned he kills my chickens, but I feel he has as much right to be here as I do. She said she'd 'blast the sucker.' She keeps a gun by her bed. I won't have one. I knew she lacked subtlety, but this surprised me, too. Let's shift the energy and take our walk?"

"I'd love it." She reached for his hand.

Moss limped back inside and sat in a chair to pull on his hiking boots. Jazz made a crooning sound and bounded to him.

"Do we need a leash?" Carolina asked when she joined him in the entry.

"Naw. She'll stay near." He patted his daypack. "I've got a water bottle."

As they walked hand-in-hand past the garden and toward the hill, Moss felt her fingers interlace his. Her stub fit neatly and safely against his palm. He rubbed his thumb along it, a friendly hello.

He said, "I want to clear something up. I haven't slept with Jessie since I met you. I couldn't; I wouldn't. It was obvious something was happening between you and me, although it took a while to sort it out."

"I guess you knew before I did, but you sure had a strange way of showing it."

"I'm not always skillful. Sorry."

His dog pranced ahead but never ranged out of sight, circling back regularly to check on them. As they started up the deer path, Moss said, "You lead and set the pace. Jazz will frighten any rattlers out of the way. Before she came to live with me, I had a close encounter. The snake struck metal."

She swung toward him, eyebrows raised. "Lucky it hit your fake leg."

"Yes, a scary moment. I'd forgotten my snake bite kit, too. But we have it today."

The path steepened and switched back. He noted Carolina slowed to measured, even steps.

"You've clearly done a lot of hiking," he said, admiring her unflagging stride.

She nodded. "I'm always hungry to be in nature." She stopped and pointed up the ridge. "There must be great vistas from the top."

"Yeah, it's a splendid view."

She shed her nylon jacket, tying it around her waist. They both sipped water.

"That's how I got into equipment repair," she said. "My gear needed fixing from camping so much. I searched, but couldn't find anyone to take it on. Affording new wasn't in my budget. My first attempts were clumsy, but I figured it out, and then hiker friends became customers. The word spread, and it turned into a home-based business.

"Jessie was seriously pissed this morning." Carolina continued, frowning up at Moss. "Could she get dangerous? Come back with a gun?"

He thought for a moment. "I don't think so."

"You don't *think* so? That's reassuring!"

"She's not going to mess with *you*. Did you see her expression when I said you're a black belt? I think she'll come around. Eventually." He closed the water bottle and stuffed it back in the pack. "It's just a little farther."

They hiked for another fifteen minutes, made their way through a stand of manzanita, then crested the top. Moss took pleasure in the full panorama. He never tired of it. All Three Sisters glowed pink in the early morning sun. He slung his arm over Carolina's shoulder. "Zephyr was there, under the overgrowth." He nodded toward a serviceberry bush. "She never let on, and I pretended not to see her. I'm sure she came here because of the spring." He pointed it out to her.

"The next day she followed you home?"

"It took three more days. She tracked my scent later—after I was back at the ranch. She's a smart one, and that's why she's alive."

Carolina turned and sucked in a breath at the bird's eye view of the ranch far below. "This *is* a different perspective."

"Now you can get a real sense of the scope." He pointed out the garden, the main buildings, the chicken shed on the side of the barn, the fields. Then, gesturing into the far distance, he indicated the approximate boundaries.

"Good heavens, this place is huge!"

"Seventeen-hundred acres of peace and quiet. Except hunting season—it's hard to keep hunters off the property. Anyone from around here respects this as private land, but we get trigger-happy tourists from Portland and Eugene."

She turned toward him, slipping both arms around his body. He kissed the top of her head and cuddled her close. Sophia had been a little thing, and sometimes the difference in their heights had been awkward. Jessie was close to six feet. Carolina, at five foot seven, fit just right.

They hugged for a long time. He could sense a thrum of tension increasing in her. "What is it?" he asked.

"What is what?"

"Whatever's going on in you—I feel it. You seem coiled up."

She looked up at him. "Well, you're pretty darn aware." She put both of her palms on his chest and took a deep breath. "What's going on—it'll have to wait. There's too much space up here."

"Yeah, I feel exposed too. It's vast, isn't it?" He lifted her chin and bent in for a deep kiss; she tasted like mint with a hint of mocha. He felt her knees go soft, and he ran his finger along her lips. "Want to head back down?"

She nodded.

He felt her trembling.

In his room, they shucked their clothes. Moss unlegged and met Carolina at the bed. With a groan, Jazz settled in her spot. Moss fitted around Carolina, pulled the duvet over them, and waited. She went deep inside herself. Occasionally, she quivered. He'd been with birthing animals; somehow this felt similar.

She finally rolled over, focused on his chest, but gradually raised her eyes to meet his. "I never told Rafe this—I realize now it was because we were terrible at intimacy." She hesitated. "But you need to know. When I was a freshman in college, before I'd ever been with a man, I was attacked and raped."

He sucked in a breath and shook his head. *How could anyone in their right mind—*

"Three guys."

"Oh, my God." He pressed his fingers to his forehead.

"They jumped me one night as I walked from the library back to the dorm. Beat me up, too." Parting her hair, she revealed a thin, two-inch scar. "It's why I'm so sensitive about being smacked from behind. It's why I became a serious karate student. No one, *no one,* is going to mess with me again."

He could find no words, so he cupped her face in his hand.

She drummed a finger on his bare chest. "I could be seen as damaged goods, too."

"You're not!"

"I'm just saying—"

"I get it," he whispered. "One way or another, we're all broken."

She nodded. "Two years later, I married Rafe. He'd been my best friend since kindergarten. We went to college in different parts of the country, so I was able to hide this from him. From everyone. We were comfortable, but not sexy—there weren't sparks between us."

He pulled her close again and felt her heart beating. "Black belt. Jeez. That really surprised me. I'll never play-hit you again. I promise. I wouldn't dare anyway."

"Thank you. That's a true gift."

Her breathing lengthened. His eyes closed.

A short while later, Moss came to. Carolina was watching him. He searched her face. Relaxed. Open. Ready.

"Hi, love," she whispered.

She guided his hand from her heart downward. He gave a low moan and went hard—she was warm down there and very wet. "Well, then." His voice was husky as he stroked her.

She murmured words against his lips. "Remember last night when you asked if I was still all in?"

"Uh huh."

"After what I told you, are you?"

"Yes, ma'am." He smiled at her. "And I'm about to be, in another way." He looked for the slightest hint of hesitation before he slipped into her hot, welcoming core.

Chapter Thirty-four

When Carolina woke, the sun was high. *1:23 p.m.? Good heavens! Slackers!* She sat up and looked back at the rumpled covers, clothes dumped, quilt tossed willy-nilly to the floor. Moss grabbed her hand. She lay back down facing him. "I need to call Rowan and check in—I said I would. I'll bet you she's figured out what's going on with us."

"Probably. She's a wise one. May I have a moment with her on the phone?"

"I don't see why not."

"Come here," he said and opened his arms.

She scooted closer and shut her eyes, felt his lips on her ear. She could spend many days—and nights—just like this.

They were awakened by screeches and upset chicken chattering.

"Something's bothering the girls. Raccoon or fox, maybe." Moss rolled into a sitting position and reached for his prosthesis. "I get so damn frustrated I can't just run out there."

"I'll go." Carolina grabbed a T-shirt and jeans off the chair.

"You don't have to do that!"

"I'm sure you'll be right behind me," she said. Pulling on her clothes, she hopped toward the door.

The ruckus worsened as she drew close to the pen. At the sight of two mangled chickens, she yelled at the unseen assailant. Then she saw a fluffy red tail scoot under the fence and the fox dart into the brush, another victim in its mouth. Carolina shuddered. The rest of the chickens huddled in the corner. "Poor girls. I'm so sorry," she said.

Moss limped across the yard. "The fox?"

"Yep. Three this time. I'm afraid she took the Plymouth Rock."

"Damn! I'm going to fix that fence. Again." He headed into the barn for supplies.

Carolina picked up the dead chickens by their feet and set them away from the coop. When Moss came back, he hammered additional stakes through the bottom of the fence into the ground. Carolina grabbed the roll of wire and wove the hole closed.

An hour later, they stood back to admire their efforts. "I don't think she'll break in again this week," Moss said. "Thanks for pitching in. It's fun working with you."

She smiled. "Yeah, it was. I set the dead girls over there; at least he didn't get your fancy white one. I have an idea that might make the coop more fox-proof. I'll draw it for you." She checked her watch. "Lordy, I'm two hours overdue calling Rowan." She started toward the house.

Sue answered the phone. "Hey! Nice to hear from you. All's well?"

"Very," Carolina replied.

"Very, huh?"

"Yes, *very*."

"Great news, Carolina, and we're doing fine on this end. Let me get Rowan."

A minute later, her daughter's voice came on the line, breathless.

"Mom, you're so late! Are you okay?"

"I'm sorry, Row. We had to scare a fox away from the chickens and repair the fence."

"Oh, no! Did he kill them?"

"Uh huh. He got three."

"That's awful!"

"And it's a constant problem with chickens. Raccoons and foxes just wait for an opportunity. But otherwise, I'm wonderful. How are you and Zephyr?"

"We're good. Zephy sticks real close; she's agitated, missing Moss. Or you. Or Jazz. Probably everyone. Seth and I got our snowflake project over halfway done, and we have all of tomorrow."

"Are the slides you made last winter still usable?"

"Yep! You should see them under the microscope. Awesome."

"I'm glad the liquid acrylic preserved the flakes. How'd your essay rewrite go?"

"I like it now. But when I read it out loud in class, will anyone believe me? It sure wasn't summer camp."

"You know the expression, 'truth is stranger than fiction'? That applies to our vacation, doesn't it? Tell them they can ask me. I'll back you up."

"After you left, I worried about you." Rowan's voice got shaky.

"Sweetheart, there's no need to. I'm relaxing—really relaxing—and happy. Just as you wanted, remember? Hang on a minute—Moss wants to talk to you. I love you so much. I'll be back tomorrow night."

"I love you, too, Mom."

Carolina handed the phone to Moss.

"Hey there," he said. "I miss you—and Zeph. I want to see you soon."

"I got worried about Mom."

"Oh, Row!"

"Are you being gentle?"

He flushed bright red. "Yes, I am. I'm taking real good care of her." He looped an arm around Carolina and pulled her in close.

"I hope to see you soon."

"It will be."

"Can't wait! Can I have my mom again?"

"Okay, until then. Here she is." He handed the phone back. "She has something else to tell you."

"I saved the best for last!" Rowan was excited. "Color is coming back! It's not super vivid yet, but I see well enough to put an outfit together."

"Yay! Fabulous news, sweetheart." When she said goodbye and hung up, she turned to Moss. "She can see color again! What a blessing. But something she said got to you. What was that about?"

"She sure is direct—she asked if I was gentle with you." He wiped his eyes. "It upset me." He frowned. "What does she think I am, anyway?"

Carolina put her hands on her hips. "Well, she knows you're a warrior. This is exactly why I wasn't going to get involved while she's at this age. Now, what are we in for?"

"Direct questions, apparently. More free fall. How do you feel about me following you home tomorrow? We might as well face this together."

"I don't think so. I need to prepare her." Carolina grimaced. "Besides, Rowan's room shares a wall with mine. After she lost her father, she needed to be close. We won't have privacy. Yet. How about next weekend?"

That evening, on Moss's signal, Jazz vacated her spot in front of the fireplace and leaped onto the couch. Carolina watched Moss light candles and place them nearby. On the way to the kitchen, he shut off the living room lamps. After rustling around, he returned with a bottle of merlot and two glasses, which he set on a small side table. "Join me," he murmured, taking Carolina's hand. He wrapped a fleece blanket around their shoulders, and they settled on the floor, leaning against the front of the couch. Jazz yawned and draped a paw over Moss's shoulder.

"She's already part of you."

"She settled right in, didn't she? I don't think her time with old Jack Lynch was much fun. He apparently ran quite the tight ship and lit into her a couple of times. A lifetime military guy—I guess he brought it home from Vietnam." Moss smiled. "She likes the 'free dog' life."

She put a hand on his knee. "She's one lucky girl." Carolina hesitated. "Moss—I need to talk about something. Something I've come to understand."

He nodded. "Sure."

"This—with you—it's so different. In every way."

"Good different, I hope."

"Rafe. I can't remember not knowing him. It turned out we were buds more than lovers—we weren't very good at it. I thought that's how sex was until I met you. I never acknowledged this before, but after the rape, I married him because he was comfortable and safe. As I said, I never told him about the—"

He touched her cheek. "He really didn't know?"

"No. Oh God, no. How unfair to him." She watched the fire and shook her head. "I didn't have the courage to let him in." Tears rimmed her eyes. "He must have been aware I was holding back." It shocked her to realize she'd never experienced true intimacy before—the no-secrets kind of trust. Her whole body trilled with both luscious satisfaction and wanting more—stupefying. Completely unforeseen.

"You look perplexed," Moss said.

She looked up at him with eyebrows raised. "Who could've thought this up? I mean really. The way we met?"

He chuckled and wrapped an arm around her. "Would you like some wine?"

Carolina nodded. "Please." The blaze snicked and snapped, warming her knees.

Reaching over, he poured two glasses and handed her one. "I want to offer a toast."

He turned so their eyes met. "To loving the complications."

"Why in heaven's name would you toast complications? Isn't that asking for them?"

"Think about it. They're inevitable. We weren't spared—look at our lives. We might as well love our way through."

A man who doesn't shrink from the hard stuff. "What does that look like, loving our way through?"

Lines crinkled at the edges of his eyes. She could admire those forever.

"This." He smiled. "Whatever this is with us."

"Ah." She smiled and clinked his glass.

They savored the merlot. He reached over and skimmed her bottom lip with his finger. At his touch, she caught her breath.

"You're going to get to meet my folks," he said.

She tried to say something, *anything* but sputtered instead. "Why?" It sounded flimsy and ridiculous. "I'm not ready," she said, more firmly. "I don't want to hurry this."

Wind scoured past the windows, pounding them with bits of debris.

"They're flying out. I told them about you, Rowan, and Zephyr. It feels so natural to introduce you."

Suddenly, she felt exposed. "What? What did you say about me? Us?"

"I said you're kind, resilient, and a great parent. Rowan is precocious and funny. Zephyr broke through my isolation." He gave a crooked grin and looked down, shyly. "And I told them I love you."

"Moss, no! So soon?"

"Yes ma'am, that's the truth of it."

"When are they coming?"

"Two weeks."

"Lordy," she said. "I don't think so. How about an introduction next spring? It feels like more appropriate timing." She pointed back and forth between them. "By then, we'll know better what *this* is. Why involve family until we—"

"Carolina. Can you truthfully say you don't trust or believe what's happening with us? If so, I want to hear you voice it."

She felt both his question and her answer in her bones. Looking away from his steady gaze, she focused on her hands and slowly shook her head. There was no avoiding their connection, nor the growing closeness. Her words came out the barest whisper. "I can't deny it."

"Exactly. This way, you won't have six or seven more months to obsess about meeting them. We'll walk through it, together."

Practical. "Why are they visiting now?"

"Because Ma could feel the change in me over the phone. She's thrilled I'm reconnecting with people and is curious what, and who, ignited the shift." He cleared his throat. "Frankly, she's earned the right. She was a terrific help after I got back from Afghanistan. I owe her a peek into my life." He patted her hand. "Wouldn't you rather face them on our turf than theirs?"

She sucked in a breath. *He's building a strong case.* "Well, if I have to meet them, yes, for sure." As she pictured an enormous family compound in Connecticut, her heart rate jumped.

"Next May is their forty-fifth wedding anniversary, and I'll need to go back East." He grinned at her. "Then I'll introduce you to my sibs, aunts, uncles, and grandmother. I didn't want to spring the whole clan on you at once."

Giggles spilled, and soon she hiccupped until tears poured. Unable to stop, the edge of hysteria pulled at her. Her chest went tight—so taut it hurt—and she gasped for air. Sweat beaded her forehead. Frightened, she looked at Moss. *Am I having a heart attack? Am I dying?*

He gripped her shoulders and forced her to look at him. "You're having a panic attack," he said. "Hang on—I'm getting a paper bag." He pushed off the floor and headed to the kitchen. Returning, he said, "Breathe into this," and handed her the small bag. "Deep, easy breaths will slow your heart down."

She followed his instructions—sucking air in and out, in and out, watching the crackling paper inflate and deflate with each breath. The squeezing pressure in her chest unwound. Her pulse gradually dropped and returned to normal. "How'd you know? It's never happened to me before."

"I had one before first combat. I'm sorry, I sprang too much on you. I didn't realize what a big deal this is."

"I'd set my life up to go a certain way. I must be attached to my plan." She traced her finger in his palm. "After being abruptly widowed, everything in my life felt out of control. To survive, I had to rebuild a sense of order. I made myself promises about what I would and wouldn't do. They worked; I felt safe and in charge." She made a face. "Now, that's all blown to bits." She shivered. "Kind of like this wind is doing right now."

Moss rubbed his hands up and down her arms. "Yeah, sounds like weather's blustering up the first big storm of the season. Darlin', you did what you needed to do. Healing from shock—well, it takes time. You've had massive traumas. I have too. It seems like we create layers of protection fast when we need them. I've learned when they stop working—or I outgrow them—I can't shuck them off all at once." He took her in his arms and cradled her so she could see his face. "Maybe peeling the onion goes on for a lifetime; I suspect so. You and I give each other a big gift—holding, and listening as deeply as we can. Without judgment."

"And you knew we could do that?"

"The first evening we talked—something about the penetrating questions you asked—you weren't impatient for answers, but you let me know you wanted them, when the time was right." He kissed her forehead. "True kindness. I fell hard." He bent down and tongued her lightly. "After noticing your mouth in the library, I couldn't keep my eyes off your lips."

She blushed. "I *thought* you were staring. When you touch me, this sensation starts in my belly."

"And when you say things like that, I get so hard it almost hurts." He kissed her softly. "Are you ready for some slow loving?"

Not trusting herself to speak, she brushed his hair off his forehead and nodded.

Chapter Thirty-five

Zephyr stands in front of the door, whining. Carolina is close, she can feel it. She wheels and lopes back to Rowan and stuffs her nose under her girl's arm. After being lost in the big land, fearful, hungry, and hurt, her people and place—with familiar smells and rhythms—bring the most comfort of all.

Rowan called out to Sue who was cooking. "Mom'll be here in about twenty minutes. Zephy always knows, and she just told me. I'll get packed."

"Do you have the snowflake project?"

"Seth'll carry it to school tomorrow." Rowan checked her watch: 5:04. She stuffed the leash into her pocket. "If he's not back, tell him 'bye' for me. And thanks for everything. Especially our talk."

Sue walked into the living room and gave Rowan a hug. "You're welcome, anytime. Don't you want to show your mom the project? She didn't get to see it being put together like I did. It's pretty darn cool."

"She can check it out after it's been graded. They'll probably display all the student work at school." Rowan went to the guest room, got her stuff together, and headed into the living room. Fifteen minutes had passed. Mom would be here soon. Sitting in the bay window with her arms wrapped around her knees, Rowan watched for the car to see how accurate Zeph was. When she saw their van pull up, she checked: 5:25.

She ran outside with Zephyr and threw her arms around her mom. "You're home! I'm all ready."

"Punkin, I'm so glad to be back with you! I'll thank Sue." Carolina patted Zephyr, who was busy nosing her for attention. "My girls," she said with a smile. "I'm ready to be home with my girls."

"I'm glad," Rowan said.

After they said goodbye to Sue and drove down one driveway and up the other, Rowan took her mom's hand as they walked toward the house.

"I'll make sleepy tea, and we can snuggle on the couch," Rowan said.

"Perfect. First, let's get our packs to our rooms and bring Zephyr's bed and bowl in. Then our chores will be done before we get tired. There was a lot of traffic today." She ruffled Rowan's hair. "I need to call Moss and let him know I made it home safely."

Rowan felt a twinge of she-couldn't-quite-figure-out-what, but nodded and went to her bedroom to dump her backpack. She lugged in Zephyr's gear and gave her a biscuit. Clicking on the electric teapot, she dangled tea bags in their favorite mugs. She loved doing this for her mom—their tradition. She touched the picture of Stormy on her mother's cup. The house still felt weirdly empty without their old dog who'd been here her whole life. She knew Zephy missed Stormy, too, but now that Jazz was around some, she'd perked up. She was lighter, even silly, with a dog her age to play with.

When the water boiled, Rowan carefully poured it and carried the mugs into the living room. As she sat on the couch, she could hear her mom giggling. Her laugh sounded different. The twinge came back—a tightening in her chest or something. She didn't like it.

A few minutes later, Mom walked—no, almost floated—into the living room.

"Mossy says hi." She sat down and nestled Rowan close. "Thanks for making tea."

Rowan scowled. "That's *my* nickname for him."

"Oh—I'm not supposed to use it?"

"Right. I invented it."

"I suspect his mom called him that when he was a little boy."

"Really?" Now she had a weird feeling about Mossy's mother, too. She frowned and blew on her steaming tea.

"How was your weekend with Sue and Seth?"

"Good. We got lots done, but we had time for fun, too. Sue took us to see *Harry Potter and the Goblet of Fire*. It was awesome."

"Was it as wild as the others?"

"Oh yeah. But there weren't any *Quidditch* games. I missed them. I'd love to have a flying broomstick."

Zephyr crawled up on the couch with them, taking her usual corner. With a deep groan, she plopped her head in Rowan's lap.

Rowan stroked her dog's ears. "Did you hike? Did Mossy cook any weird animals?"

"You mean other than rabbit or venison?"

"Yeah, like raccoon? Squirrel? Rattlesnake?"

"Nope. Just the usual suspects. But we did walk to the top of Bender's Ridge. He showed me how he laid food stashes for Zeph and where he first saw her eyes peering at him."

"Really? I can't wait to go up there!"

"We saw all Three Sisters peaks, the whole spread of the ranch, and he pointed out the boundaries. It's vast. Next time you visit, you'll be able to see it all. You'll love it."

"Right. I've pictured it in my mind, but probably it looks different than my imagination." She glanced at her mom who reached out and stroked her hair. "And then you had to clean up the chicken massacre? I can't blame the fox—he needs to eat too, but yuck! It's so unfair!"

Her mom made a face and shook her head. "I guess it's why farmers don't name chickens—they're short-lived, and stuff happens to them. We wired the fence back together and Moss hammered in some metal fence posts to hold the wire right down to the ground. They're safe for now."

Rowan picked at her cuticle. "So. Mossy. Is he like your boyfriend?"

Her mom's face went rosy.

"Mommm! You're blushing!"

Her mom pressed her fingers to her cheeks. "Am I? Yes, I guess he is. How do you feel about that?"

"I have so many feelings it's hard to figure them out," Rowan muttered. "I guess it's what older girls call 'complicated.'"

"Want to try? Whatever's going on, I want you to know you can tell me."

Rowan picked up her tea and drank. Then she looked into her cup, wishing there were magical leaves to read like Grandma did. "Glad. Mad. Scared." She checked her mom's expression, then looked down again. "Worried."

Her mom rubbed her cheek with the backs of her fingers. "I'm glad and scared, too. Can you tell me about 'mad'? And 'worried'?"

Rowan played with one of Zeph's paws while she thought. "It's been just you and me since Daddo died. Now it's different. I'm not sure. Maybe that's the 'mad.'"

Her mom nodded. "I can imagine."

"And…." Rowan felt tears spring to her eyes. She crept in closer to the warmth of her mother's body. "I think I'm jealous. It feels awful."

Her mom's arm came around her. "Aw, sweetheart."

She felt a kiss on her head and then words spoken so close to her scalp she could feel the moist, familiar warmth of her mother's breath.

"You are always my first love and priority. Always." Her mom held her close.

Rowan's tears flowed. "But you'll want time with *him*. Alone." Her voice choked at the end. "Without *me*."

"Right, sometimes I will. But I know when you're with your friends, you like space without your old mom hanging around. Besides, sometimes *you'll* get time with Moss alone."

Rowan nodded against her shoulder. "Yeah, you're right."

"So, Moss is *my* friend," her mom added.

Rowan saw it made sense, but it didn't make her feel much better. She sort of wanted things to go back to the way they had been. It was confusing because she loved Mossy, too.

That night, Carolina shifted and tossed in bed. She tried reading, which usually made her tired, but sleep wouldn't come. Rowan's discomfort concerned her. All this sexual energy had erupted at the worst time, just as her daughter was approaching puberty.

When she'd picked Rowan up, Sue intimated her daughter was thinking about sexuality. *Heavens, was she imagining us together this weekend? Did Moss and I trigger this?* It was evident Sue didn't feel comfortable sharing more. Girls need a mentor to confide in, a godmother, a wise woman—besides their mothers. Carolina wouldn't pry.

As she grabbed her body pillow and rolled on her other side, she thought about Moss and his folks. It struck her she was resisting the very change that could bring deeper happiness. Why? Probably—like Rowan—she gravitated toward the safety of the known. It wasn't just the two of them—most humans resist change.

She smacked her hands on her pillow and went to take a sleep aid. When she slipped back into bed, she thought about phoning Moss. Hearing his tender, calm voice would soothe her. 1:39. Nope, she wasn't calling in the middle of the night. He'd think it was an emergency.

The door bumped open. Zephyr padded over and shoved her nose under Carolina's shoulder. She ruffled the dog's ears. "You're incredible. Felt my distress, huh?" she whispered. "I'm okay. You'd better go keep Rowan company tonight. I'm depending on you." She trundled out of bed again, encouraged Zeph toward her daughter's room, and then pulled her door closed.

The next morning, Carolina leaned against the kitchen sink and stared out the window. Rain sluiced down at an angle, and the sky was a weary, dull gray. This wasn't going to let up. She yawned, rubbing her knuckles against her eyes. The weather mirrored her mood. Maybe after Rowan left for school, she'd sneak back to bed and catch up on lost sleep. She could feel her cozy nest tugging.

The scent of oatmeal brought her back. She turned to the stove top and absently stirred, feeling with the edge of the spoon where oats stuck on the pan bottom. Calling for Rowan, she doled the cereal into two bowls, filled a small dish with dried cranberries, and put the walnut container on the table. She whisked milk over the heat until it frothed and sat down to breakfast.

Rowan came in. "Morning. I've been thinking." She picked up her spoon. "I want to move into the downstairs workroom. It's bigger and has those built-in cubbies for my books and stuff. Plus, the Murphy queen-size is cool. Zephy's bed really crowds my room up here." She sprinkled cranberries and tucked into her oatmeal.

"When did you come up with this idea?"

"I've been dreaming about it for ages. Please?"

"I'm not sure I want to move my workspace, kiddo. It's a lot of hauling, and the upstairs room is smaller."

"You'd have a great view out your window when you're working. It's perfect! You'll be able to see clients driving up."

Her mother pursed her lips and nodded. "You have a point there."

"So, can I?"

"Let's think about it today, and when you get home, we'll decide."

Carolina watched Rowan walk down the wet path to the school bus. My God, she could be using a white cane and going to a school for the blind. *Grace! We've been gifted with grace.*

She rinsed the dishes and stacked them in the dish drainer. Then she headed back to bed. This is unlike me, she thought, as she pulled the shades and snuggled under the downy. Zephyr gave a little moan as she settled nearby. When Rowan wasn't home, Zeph looked for her next best, Moss. When he wasn't around, Carolina was comforted by the big dog coming to find her.

Rain thrummed the roof. As her body warmed and softened, she acknowledged that she retreated to her cozy nest when she felt overwhelmed. This was where she came to set her load down. To brood, to stew. To acknowledge resistance and try to parse it. Sometimes understanding came during a nap, and she'd wake up with a solution.

As she drifted off, she remembered she was taking Rowan to get her cast removed this afternoon. They had an appointment with the orthopedist at 4 p.m. She sank into the steady roar of rain, the most nourishing lullaby of all.

The musical ring of her phone dragged her from sleep. As she fumbled for it, she grabbed the clock. *Eleven? Good grief.* She tried to make her voice sound smooth and even. "Carolina speaking."

"I woke you? It's Moss."

So much for pretending. "You did. I snuck back to bed after Rowan left for school. I didn't get much sleep last night."

A beat of silence. "I sure wish I could crawl in with you." His voice was husky.

"Me too." A pause. "Moss, has Jessie contacted you?"

"Not yet. I guess that's good news."

"Maybe you need to call her? Reassure her? I'd think about it." She paused. "On this end, Rowan wants to move downstairs—switch my office for her bedroom." Her eyes went hot with tears.

"Perfect. We'll get some privacy, and she'll feel more grown up."

Carolina fell quiet. Thickness built in her chest.

"What is it?"

"I don't want to lose touch with her or feel distance between us. Not just as she's becoming a teenager. Life is slipping by so fast. I don't know if I can keep up."

"Have you ever floated on your back?"

Confused by the change of subject, she thought for a moment. "It's been a few years. Why?"

"Imagine floating now. Picture letting go, surrendering, allowing the water to carry you."

She rubbed her hand against her temple. "I don't know, Mossy. You can't imagine how I'm haunted by worries. You haven't raised kids."

"You're right; I haven't."

They both fell silent.

"I need … I don't know *what* I need. I'll call later," she said.

Chapter Thirty-six

After Moss hung up, he stomped outside into the stormy weather. Jazz stayed alongside, her nose glued to his knee. He tipped his face up and let the cold rain beat down on him. He was sure, from Carolina's reaction on the phone, she wouldn't be showing up to meet his folks in ten days, either. Damn! He wondered if she'd take back her invitation to come to Eugene this weekend. That would be a blow. He huffed out a breath. Interpersonal stuff was so bloody complicated. Maybe he wasn't ready for this.

Jazz nuzzled him for attention. Wiping his eyes, he stared down at her. "What?" he growled. She was drenched, shivering, with her tail tucked. His tone was sharper than he intended. He felt her fur. *God, she has no undercoat.* He should get her a dog coat for the winter.

"Come on, let's get you warm," he said, walking to the house. Head down, she followed. Murmuring, he carefully toweled her from her nose to her tail and built a fire in the stove. She grunted as she settled on her pad nearby. For good measure, he snuggled a fleece throw around her. She raised moist, grateful eyes and swiped his arm with her tongue. Moss shifted, warming his hands by the fire. The rain, now torrential, overflowed the gutters in front of the window like a waterfall.

He hadn't felt this lonely since the day Francie found Zephyr's microchip, and he knew she couldn't belong to him. The blues hovered like a hungry vulture. He'd gotten so tangled in his relationship with Carolina, he'd neglected writing. He knew better. He had to find his way to happiness whether she was in his life or not. He paced the room. Jazz lifted her head to watch him but didn't move from her comfortable pad and cozy blanket.

The black hole of depression made a sucking sound, dragging him close. He better get to work to stave off its gravity. He limped to the desk, flipped open his laptop. It was still strange, writing a war memoir after two novels. Fiction took playfulness. This … this wasn't fun. He blew out a breath as he thought back to one particular day in Afghanistan—a conversation he'd had with Frank—and began typing.

A few hours later, the phone startled him. His heart thumped as he walked into his room and sat on the edge of the bed. Would she break up with him?

"Can we start over?" he asked, without a greeting.

"Start over, because, why?"

"Ma? Hi! I expected you to be Carolina."

"Are you already apologizing to her?" His mother sounded suspicious. Protective.

"I pushed her a little."

She made a wry sound. "If she's going to love you, she has to get used to that."

"Thanks for reminding me."

"Is there more?"

"While we're together, it's so easy. But when she goes back to Eugene, she starts stewing and questions what we're discovering together."

"Give her time. She has a lot to consider. Her child's at a tough age for her to be getting involved."

"So she told me. You're taking her side?"

"I'm sympathetic, yes. Rowan comes first."

"Right, of course. She's a great kid. Being back in relationship flusters me; it'll take time to get used to it. So, did you call about your flight time?"

"Yes. We'll land in Redmond around two."

"Tell Pa I'll pick you up. Don't bother renting a car." He hesitated. "I can't promise you'll get to meet them."

"Ooooh. I'd be really disappointed, but don't pressure her. Mostly, we're coming to see you."

"Like I believe that. I know how curious you are. You're a mom."

She gave the earth-belly laugh he loved. "Moss, what do I hear in the background? Is it pouring there? Or worse?"

Jazz stuffed her nose in his crotch. She put her paws on his thighs and whined, then jumped up, almost knocking him back on the bed. Recovering, he squinted out the window. "No wonder Jazz launched into my lap. It's hailing—really loud on the roof."

"I want to meet her too. She sounds like a sweet dog."

"She's a terrific companion and so attuned to my moods. I'm looking forward to seeing you. A week from Friday, right?"

Moss washed up the pans and dishes from dinner and sponged the counter. He leaned over the sink and looked out the window. It was getting dark. Fast. The hail had abated, and rain fell in sheets again. Earlier, when it had let up, he'd dashed out to check on the squawking chickens. A fast-running narrow channel had cut through the pen. The fence perimeter held—bad luck for the fox, good luck for morning omelets.

His hands shook; he almost dropped a glass, and his body felt jittery. Carolina had ended the conversation saying she'd call. He would not push her by making the next move, but clearly, nerves were swamping him.

When he let Jazz out to do her business, she tore across the driveway to the weedy patch, squatted, then pinched her tail between her legs and loped back. He grabbed a fresh towel—fifth one—and wiped down her body and paws. This had been a twenty-paw-wipe day.

The night turned raw, wind whipping around the house. Since he planned to write this evening, he re-stoked the stove. Swiping bark particles from his hands, he went to the kitchen and poured a glass of wine. The phone rang while he was heading back to his computer. Three phone calls today. *I'm on everyone's radar—better get an extension in the living room.* Going to the bedroom to answer it, he took a breath before picking up the receiver. "Moss here."

"Hi," Carolina said, remorse in her voice. "I feel bad about the way I ended our conversation this morning."

"It's great to hear your voice! Ma called earlier and thinking it was you, I answered the phone with 'Can we start over?'"

"Why?"

"I asked too much of you. She agreed with me."

"Well, we've made progress here. Rowan stuck with her vision of switching rooms, and I gave in. You're right, of course; you and I need privacy." She cleared her throat. "We got most of her belongings moved except the other cedar chest. Will you heft it with me? We tried, but Rowan and I can't manage it on the stairs."

"Sure. I think my leg and I can. I've been wondering if you'd take back the invitation to come this weekend."

"Of course not. Have you been obsessing? I thought I owned that game."

Tension drained from his body.

"Moss." Her tone changed. "I can't meet your parents, though. It's too soon. Next spring sounds better."

"I know."

"You're not mad?"

"I got frustrated, but mostly at myself, for pushing." He rubbed his aching thigh. "As you said, we're getting to know each other. It takes time."

"You'll tell your mom why I'm not coming?"

"She explained it to me."

"Oh. My."

"So this weekend—I'll show up mid-afternoon Friday, so we have daylight to move the chest?"

"Perfect. I'll see you then. When you get here—consider hugging Rowan first."

Silence. "Good thought."

On Thursday afternoon, Moss drove to town with Jazz. She leaped from the car, and he gave her a pat while snapping on the leash. "You need to come in with me. I've gotta fit this thing to you. I sure hope they come in basic black." She hung back when they reached the door to the feed store. "Memories?" he asked her. "It's okay." She balked and dragged sideways on the leash but, with steady encouragement, walked in at his side.

Bob waved at him, saw Jazz, and came out from behind the counter. "So this is your girl, eh? The one you bought food for?"

Moss gave a soft chuckle. "No, that was a different dog, but we found her owner. This is my new girl, and she's got no under-layer—she shivers in the cold. Do you have any coats?"

"You've come to that, have you?" Bob grinned, his sagging eyelids almost hiding his pupils. He walked them to a far corner of the store. "Feel free to try them on."

"What size do you think she is?"

Bob squinted at Jazz and pursed his lips. "I'd try the large. She's so deep-chested."

Moss looked over the coats. There were only two in size large. "I'd prefer black. I don't think I can walk the streets with a dog dressed in pink or lime green with paw prints."

Bob guffawed. "I'm there with you. Let me check in the back—I think a box come from the distributor today." Moss heard cardboard ripping, and Bob reappeared a few minutes later. "Here's a dark brown. Fleece-lined. Cozy." He held it out. "Don't have no black in stock."

"This'll do. It'll look nice with her blonde coat, don't you think?"

Bob laughed. "I wouldn't know—never been one for fashion, and I'm colorblind to boot. Come to think, never had a dog that couldn't keep itself warm."

"She's half greyhound," Moss said, feeling defensive. "Don't you recognize her? She belonged to Jack Lynch until he died. Francine matched us up."

"Oh, yeah, now you mention it. Kind of you to take her in. He was tough on her. I remember one day—" The bell on the door jangled, and Bob lumbered to the front of the store to help another customer.

Jazz skittered and jigged on the end of the leash as Moss tried to figure out which end of this garment was which. He squinted at the instructions. It took him two attempts to get the coat on her, but when he tightened the straps properly, it was a fine fit. They walked back to the counter, Jazz stiff-legged as she adjusted to the new feeling. "I'll take it," Moss said, handing him the money. "She seems willing to wear it. I might as well get used to walking a fancy dog right now."

Bob gave a gravelly chuckle. "She's better off with you. Lynch lit into her here. Whacked her real good. When she tried to escape, she knocked over a whole display of cans. Scared the bejesus out of all of us. He was fond of her, but his temper got the best of him."

"I would never hit Jazz." *But I snapped at her.* Moss bent down, fingered her ears, and offered soft words.

As they stepped outside, fat, lazy flakes were falling. The sky had flattened to gunmetal gray. "Just in time," he said to Jazz. "Let's go on home and pray we can get through to Eugene tomorrow. I'd better throw chains in the car." He stopped and rethought his plans as the flakes continued to float down and land on Jazz's coat. "The temp could drop fast tonight; this could stick. We should leave for Eugene before dinner. We'd best head to the library and see if Gladys wants to come out to the ranch now. Looks like winter's come early," he added, shaking his head at Jazz. He pulled out his phone to call Carolina.

Rowan heard her mom on the stairs. She glanced at the clock. 4 p.m. Dinner was still a while away.

Carolina knocked. "May I come in?"

"Sure! Check it out." Rowan beamed as she looked around her new room. Her dictionaries and thesaurus sat on her desk near her laptop. Zeph lay happily in her C-bed in the corner. A poster of five-month-old Zeph, asleep, paws dangling over the top stair, hung on the wall. The photo won first prize in a national contest.

"Looking good. Did you get your schoolwork finished?"

"Done. Can we go to the movies like we talked about? Maybe Shrek 2?"

"Moss called. He'll be here a day early. It started to snow there; it was come early or don't come at all." She leaned against the wall. "I told him I'd promised you a movie. I'll leave a key under the mat. He might not even beat us home."

Rowan grinned, relieved they were still going. "Thanks. Zephy can greet him."

"He bought Jazz a jacket. She has so little fur, he said she was freezing."

She giggled. "I have to see that."

"Me too. We'd better go to the 6:15 show. School tomorrow."

Rowan shrugged. "Okay. It's a short movie, anyway."

"How's the arm feeling? Vulnerable?"

Rowan held it out and carefully rotated her wrist. "Weak, skinny, a little sore. Look how white it is."

"I remember the same thing from when I broke mine. It'll get strong pretty darn fast. You'll see. An early dinner, then?"

Driving back after the movie, Rowan thought about Mossy's visit. She knew home would seem different with him staying over. She wasn't sure exactly how it would change, or how she would feel about it. Even so, she was excited to see him.

As they pulled into the driveway, he was getting out of his 4Runner. He signaled to Jazz, and Rowan snickered at the sight of her new, fashionable coat. But his dog seemed unconcerned and bounded toward Zephy who was rounding the corner of the garage. Moss waved and limped toward the van. Rowan's heart sped up. This felt like a test.

He paused and watched them get out of the car. When he saw her mom, his face warmed into the sweetest smile. Rowan's throat caught seeing how much he loved her. Suddenly, she felt outside the special circle. Tears rimmed her eyes.

But he turned and, arms open, walked straight to her. Stunned, Rowan allowed him to wrap her in a warm hug. It felt really good.

"I've missed you and your Zephy," he whispered.

Rowan tried not to cry, but couldn't contain her hiccupping sobs, and blubbered against Moss's jacket. Then she felt her mom's arms come around her. Zephyr stuffed her nose in, too. Jazz danced around them.

Being in the middle of a sandwich is the best of all.

While they were hugging Rowan, Carolina lifted her chin. Moss met her lips over Rowan's head, ever so lightly, for the briefest kiss. "We can do this," he mouthed.

Zephyr flops on the ground, relieved to have her pack together again. Both Kibble Man and her new pack mate belong here with them. She touches her friend's muzzle and gives her a soft lick, then repeatedly noses the human cloth thing tied on her.

Chapter Thirty-seven

Carolina let them both go, and Moss ruffled Rowan's hair. "Your cast is gone. How does your arm feel?"

"Weird, but okay. It sure did stink when the doctor sawed it off."

"Yeah, that goes with the territory."

"Hey, there," Moss said, turning to Zeph. "Don't make a big deal about the coat, okay? Jazz needs to wear it. She can't handle the cold." He leaned down and stroked her. Zephyr sat and swiped his face with her tongue.

"I think she looks cute," Rowan said.

"Yeah, me too," whispered Moss. "But don't repeat it."

With her thumb and forefinger, Rowan zipped her lips.

Carolina slung Moss's backpack over her shoulder and headed into the house. "Rowan," she called, "will you bring in Jazz's stuff? Stick her dog bed in the living room. We'll find a spot for it."

"She needs to sleep with me," Moss said.

"Of course. She's welcome." Carolina walked inside, down the hall, and with no hesitation plopped his pack on the chest in her bedroom. "You're in here," she said to Moss.

He paused at the threshold and looked around her room.

"Come on in," she said. "I've cleared some space for you."

"I'm making sleepy tea," Rowan called from the other end of the house. "Does Mossy want some?"

Carolina pitched her voice to reach the kitchen. "Yes, please." She turned to Moss. "This is a tradition—she makes herbal tea, and we sit for a while in the living room."

Moss hesitated. "If this is your special time together, maybe I should get settled in here."

"About Rowan—some nights, maybe I'll need time with her alone. Not tonight."

He nodded. "Come here," he murmured. "We're standing in your bedroom together for the first time. I'd like a welcome kiss."

His eyes have that smoky look. It traveled right down inside and ignited her. She walked over to him, reached up for a handful of hair, and pulled him in. They both moaned softly when their lips met.

After a moment, she said, "Tea time." She took his hand, and they walked to the living room. The coffee table was set with the dragon teapot, three mugs, and a plate of cookies.

"Nice. Thanks for making Moss feel welcome." Carolina smiled at her daughter. "I know it's complicated for you."

"Well," Rowan said. "I've had most of a week. I have Zephy—it's only fair Mom has you. Just don't get all gushy in front of me, okay?"

"Deal," Moss said. "But let's define gushy. I plan on holding your mom's hand and kissing her, even when you're around."

They stared at each other. Carolina admired her daughter's pluck, entering this slippery territory. Moss smiled, but his tone was firm.

"Okay, then," Rowan said. "Deal."

"One other thing," he said. He grinned at her. "You'd better knock. You wouldn't want to catch me in my Easter Bunny suit."

"Right—" Her voice trailed off, and her cheeks flamed.

"Exactly." He picked up the plate like a peace offering. "Want one?" he asked. She giggled nervously and grabbed a chocolate chip cookie. He took one too.

His cell rang. He flipped it open and frowned, shaking his head. "I've gotta take this—my mom. She never calls this late." He set the cookie down without taking a bite.

"Ma? You okay? Wha—?" His color blanched. "When? Where is he?"

Carolina moved closer to him.

"Of course. I'll make reservations now. Well, I'll ask, but no promises. I'll try. When I get the trip nailed down, I'll phone. Ma—I love you. And Pa. Please tell him." He flipped the phone shut and dropped his face in his hands. "Damn." He took two slow breaths before he raised his gaze. "Heart attack. Pa had a heart attack on a flight to Washington D.C. The plane turned back to New York to get him to the hospital."

Carolina's hand flew to her heart. Rowan gasped.

"He'll be in intensive care while they adjust medications. Then he's going home because there's nothing they can do for him in a hospital that can't happen there. Pa wants you and Rowan to come with me."

Now it was Carolina's turn to feel the blood leech from her face. Anything but this. Memories erupted: Moss saying, "Are you still all in?" And "free fall."

"*Now?*" she whispered. "Us? Strangers? Why, in heaven's name?"

"Pa—he wants to be sure he gets to meet you." His voice cracked at the end. "He's asked for all his kids and their families." Then, his fingertips pressed to his forehead, he jerked to a stand. "My cell's almost dead. May I use your phone to book a flight?"

Carolina nodded. "Of course."

He started toward the telephone, but swung back, waiting for her answer. Lines were carved deep around his mouth.

She felt shredded by hesitation. She didn't have the courage, but it was clear she needed to find it. Moss's expression stiffened at her indecision.

One deep breath and a moment's beat.

"Okay. Yes, I'm coming." She turned to Rowan. "This is an emergency. It's all right for you to skip a few days of school."

Her daughter was still stunned and silent—her face a mask, her dad's final days written there. Carolina pulled her close and made comforting sounds. Then she put her hands on Rowan's shoulders and spoke intently. "We need to go. It isn't about us. The dogs can stay with Sue; I'll phone her after Moss calls the airlines."

Mute, Rowan nodded.

"Thank you," Moss said and reached for the telephone. "Thank you, both."

He booked three seats out of Eugene on Mesa Airlines to Las Vegas, switching planes to JFK. They'd be there in a day and a half, the best the airline could do.

Moss's harsh moans awakened Carolina. He pitched from side to side. "Mossy? Wake up!"

He continued to flail. Jazz jumped on the bed, nudging her nose under his shoulder.

Her heart raced. "Mossy!" she cried.

He sat up, his breaths coming in heavy gulps. "Shit," he muttered. He rubbed his face and tugged his hair.

Carolina pushed herself up against the headboard. She patted Jazz and rested a hand on Moss's chest. "How come you pull on your hair?"

"My therapist taught me—it brings me back to the present. Are you okay?" he asked. "I didn't wake up swinging?"

"No punches, just loud moaning. Jazz got here first. I said your nickname before I touched you."

"Smart move on your part. I always hope I'm done with these."

"You've never slept here before, and you've had shocking news." She pointed. "Your girl is worried about you."

He stroked Jazz and spoke softly. "I'm okay." She crawled between them and put her head on Moss's chest.

The next night, suitcases zipped and by the front door, Carolina and Moss dropped into bed after 1 a.m. They'd wrestled the chest upstairs and into her new workroom. With a squeaky yawn, Jazz settled in her space. Zephyr pushed the door open and walked over to her side. Carolina fondled the dog's ears. "All's well. You're going to stay with Sue," she said, softly. "She'll come in the morning and get you both. Now, go find Rowan." Zephyr bumped Moss, then turned to the door. A moment later, Carolina heard the dog's footfall on the stairs. Uncanny how that dog understood. She rolled into Moss's arms and promptly fell asleep.

They woke at 3:30 and boarded the flight at 6 a.m. When the sun came up, Carolina pulled down the shade to block the sharp early morning rays. On such short notice, Moss could only book two seats together, so each hour, they rotated. Carolina and Rowan, Moss and Rowan, then Carolina and Moss.

"I want to sit alone now," Rowan said. "It makes me feel grown up. Besides, you two probably need to talk." She raised her eyebrows at them and walked off to her seat six rows up on the other side.

"Your girl's maturing," Moss said.

Carolina nodded. "Any new update on what to expect when we get where we're going?" she asked, turning to him.

"I don't know if we're heading to the medical center or Connecticut. I'll call when we touch down. Pa's office wing on the first floor has plenty of room for a hospital bed and equipment. It's his domain. When he comes home, they'll set him up in there." He rubbed his chin. "I think Ma will be okay with us sleeping together. My parents need some time with me alone, I figure—family stuff, decisions to be made."

"What's there for Rowan to do?"

"My brother, Theo, has a daughter, Maggie. She's the same age as Rowan. I hadn't thought about this—they have a significant loss in common. Maggie's mom died of breast cancer."

Tired and jet-lagged, they weathered a bumpy landing at JFK. As soon as the plane rolled to a stop, Moss punched in his parents' number.

"Come home, not the hospital," his mom said. "We've brought him back. He insisted on being here. Ash speaks, and folks listen, even his doctors, although they refused to release him until I hired round-the-clock cardiac nurses. They arrived with an external defibrillator, of all things. He's not the easiest patient. You know how he is."

"I can imagine. We're renting a car right now. See you soon. Love you both." He closed the phone and reviewed all the facts from the last couple of days. Pa wanted them *all* there. Did he think he was dying? At sixty-eight? He tried to wrap his mind around the new and present reality as he limped toward the baggage claim, relaying the news to Carolina.

She and Rowan stretched their strides, trying to keep up. "This sounds serious," Carolina said.

"Apparently." He took her hand and squeezed it. "I'm so glad you're with me."

After picking up their bags, they approached the Hertz counter. Eight people stood waiting, but Moss stepped up to speak to the woman at the head of the line. "Family emergency," he said, quietly. "My dad's had a heart attack. I need to get home."

"Good Lord, go ahead," she said and waved him in front of her. People behind groused, but she stared them down. "His father's ill. I'd do the same for you. Give the guy a break."

Ten minutes later, they loaded their gear and Moss's crutches into a sky-blue van and headed out of the airport. Carolina sat next to Moss, feeling disoriented. She was seeing a whole different side of this man—his movement in the world was so capable and competent—not pushy, not snobby or entitled, but *something*. He had an air about him. Was it an aura of wealth? Or simply maturity? Could she see herself next to him, head up, shoulders back?

"I really need to unleg," he muttered. "It's been too long."

"So that's why you wore your cargo pants with the zippers. Smart. I'll drive," she said.

"Yep, I try to always travel in them. Row, will you move up here with your mom so I can stretch out in the back? I'm beat, and I need to be in cope mode when we get home." He pulled into a Shell station.

"Even if you're beat, you *have* to wear your seat belt," Rowan warned. "Mom never lets anyone ride in the car without one."

"She's right. But at least I can get this leg off for forty-five minutes. I need to stay awake to give her directions, anyway."

"They gave you a map at the car rental place. If you mark it, I can direct Mom on the big roads, and you can rest until we can get close."

"That'd be great, thanks!"

"We've taken lots of road trips," Carolina said, smiling at her daughter. "She's my map girl." She walked around to the driver's side and adjusted the seat. Rowan moved to the front.

"It's easy. We take I-95 straight up to Greenwich." Moss eased into the back and muttered with relief as he removed his prosthesis. "Then look for Arch Street."

Some minutes later, Carolina heard a rumble. Moss was snoring.

Chapter Thirty-eight

As soon as Rowan crowed, "Arch Street, coming up!" a knuckle of anxiety lumped in Carolina's belly. She remembered what Moss suggested during the panic attack—to slow and lengthen her breath. She gave a long exhale. It helped. Exiting the freeway, she pulled over when she found a safe spot and opened the slider to wake him.

Moss blinked several times and rubbed his eyes. "Here already? Okay, I'll drive now; it'll be easier. I just have to leg up."

Fifteen minutes later, Carolina peered out the window as Moss turned the van between two giant granite boulders and headed up a long, curved blacktop drive. She squinted through the dusk as she tried to take in all the scenery at once. They passed open fields studded with maples and oaks. Even this late in the day, she could tell the trees were in full autumn splendor. This place is huge, she thought. Well, so was Bender's Ridge. This family did big; she came from small. How would his parents react when they found out she'd grown up in a single-wide trailer?

A quarter mile farther, the house, a rambling two-story affair with a large wraparound porch, came into view. The home snuggled against a gentle rise on one side, and the veranda sported rocking chairs. Solar panels covered the south-facing roof. A peace pole like the one at Bender's Ridge grounded the center of the circular drive, surrounded by low jasmine bushes. It all felt big, yet friendly and comfortable.

Moss tooted the horn. A slender, older woman walked across the porch and down the steps to the drive. She had short, wiry gray hair and was dressed in well-worn jeans and a casual Irish fisherman's sweater. Her face was drawn with strain and lack of sleep, but she made an effort to offer a warm smile. "You're here," she said, throwing her arms around Moss. "Thank heavens." A tear coursed down her cheek. She wiped it away.

"I'm glad we made it," Moss said. "Ma, meet Carolina and Rowan—"

But his mother had already turned, smiled at Rowan, and welcomed Carolina into a hug. "Bless you for making the trip," she whispered.

Warmed by her greeting, Carolina squeezed her back.

Moss's mom smoothed away more tears. "Rowan, welcome! Please, both of you, call me Alice," she said.

Moss shrugged, good-naturedly grabbed the luggage, and headed into the house. "Hey, Maggie," he said to a young girl with a single blonde braid as she strode toward him. A large Doberman with unclipped ears heeled neatly at her side.

"Yay! My favorite uncle!" Maggie grinned and grabbed him tight.

"This is my granddaughter, Maggie—she's just your age," Alice said to Rowan.

Maggie gave the dog hand signals to sit and stay, and the Doberman's rear promptly hit the pavement.

After giving Rowan a small wave and a brief "Hi," Maggie turned back to her dog.

"What's his name?" Rowan asked, looking at her slantwise.

"Bender. I show him in obedience."

"He's named after the ranch?"

The girl nodded and fingered her braid. "How'd you know?"

"I've been there once."

"You've been to Bender's Ridge?" Her expression stiffened.

"Let's go inside and get you settled," Alice said. "Do you girls want to room together? Of course, it would be all three of you because Bender goes wherever Maggie is."

"My room?" She scowled at her grandmother and gave her head a swift little shake.

Carolina saw hurt spread across her daughter's face.

"Rowan, I have the Sky Room for you," Alice said, never skipping a beat. "Maggie." Her tone firmed up, and she rested a piercing glance on her granddaughter. "Please show Rowan her room and make her feel welcome. *Westbury* welcome."

She raised boys, Carolina thought. She's got spine.

Alice turned back to Carolina. "I've put Moss in his old bedroom, and you're down the hall in the Four-poster room. I've wanted to meet you since Mossy told us he had a new woman friend—but I never imagined it would be under these circumstances." She looped her arm through Carolina's. "I know you weren't ready for this family business. I'm grateful you came."

She seems friendly and unassuming—but really? We don't get to sleep together? "Moss needed me," Carolina said. "How's Mr. Westbury?"

"Call him Ash, please. He's not good. The doctors told him to get his affairs in order." She shook her head as though still not believing it. "But what he wanted most was to come home to family and meet you two. He loves all his kids, but he adores Moss," she said in a quiet aside. "His one wish is to see his youngest son happy and settled." For a moment, she looked toward the house. "You'll meet him after dinner. These nurses are fiercer than at the hospital—he only gets visitors fifteen minutes each hour—and one at a time."

Carolina froze. She would have to greet Ashton Westbury by herself? Rowan couldn't go in there alone, either. No way would she allow her daughter to be put under that kind of pressure. Maybe Moss could negotiate with these self-styled Nurse Ratched types. Suddenly, she was grateful for his capable way in the world.

As they walked in the front door, she could see the furnishings were much like the ranch—hardwood floors, oriental carpets, and a few special pieces of art. Uncluttered elegance. Family pictures hung on the wall in the entry. One of them caught her attention—a casual snapshot of Mr. Westbury with his arm around Alice. They were both wearing jeans, and she was looking up at him. He had similar hair to Moss's—but white—with intense blue eyes, punctuated by smile lines. This was what Moss would look like in thirty years. Gorgeous!

Alice stopped next to her. "It's a wonderful way to see Ash—in his prime. Hold the thought." Alice took her arm, and they walked into the sitting room. Carolina sucked in a breath when she saw Bev Doolittle's painting, *Circle of Life.*

"This same print hangs in my living room," she said. She walked closer and squinted at it. The *original*. Shame, then envy, rocketed through her.

Moss hitched down the stairs. "There you are. I lost you. Come on up, and I'll show you where Row's room is." He turned to his mom. "Hey, I'm happy to cook while I'm here."

"Thanks, but it's not necessary. I broke down and asked Anna to help out with this crowd. Of course, your dad's on a special diet, but we're having chicken soup, salad, and French bread tonight. And apple crisp for dessert—apples from the orchard. I made up the Four-poster Room for Carolina. I didn't want to make any assumptions."

"Ma, really," Moss drawled. "She's sleeping with me." He bent down and hugged his mother. "Consenting adults. End of conversation."

He stood up to her so beautifully.

Alice pinked up. "Oh my, have I just shown my age? You kids are so quick about everything."

He waggled his eyebrows. "And in the hippie days, you weren't?"

His mom gave a full-on laugh and crinkled her eyes at her son. "Hmmm, well there *is* that."

A burden of resistance lifted from Carolina. At least she wouldn't have to feel like a teenager sneaking between bedrooms at night.

Rowan followed Maggie and Bender up the stairs. Moss's niece seemed snooty and unfriendly. Angry, even. *Maybe at me, but what could I have done?* The girl's expression shifted when she mentioned Bender's Ridge. Surely, Maggie must have visited there.

"This is a really nice room," Maggie said, her tone and expression flat. "It's called the Sky Room because you can see sunrises from this window. And here's a rack for your suitcase." She unfolded it in the corner. "The bathroom's at the end of the hall."

"Thanks." Rowan chewed her lip. *Might as well face this.* She perched on the edge of the bed. Maggie was her only hope for company here. "You seem mad or maybe sad."

Bender stuffed his nose in Rowan's lap.

"He never does that. He *trusts* you." Maggie looked at Rowan and frowned.

Rowan stroked his soft ears. "It's because I trust him too. He's gorgeous."

Maggie sat cross-legged on the floor. Bender left Rowan and lay beside Maggie. "Anyone ever tell you you're awfully direct?"

"I don't know how to be any other way. Hope you don't mind." She glanced furtively at Maggie. "So, mad or sad?"

The girl looked down. "Both," she whispered. "My mom died four years ago today."

Shocked, Rowan said, "My father died four years ago next week." Her voice was almost inaudible.

"Really? You too?"

"Yeah."

"So you know what it's like."

Rowan nodded. "And now you don't even get to be alone on this day. Like you're supposed to entertain me. You don't need to. I get it."

"Thanks. My dad was going to take me to the cemetery, but then Pa got sick. Were you close to your father?"

"He's the one I ran to when I was upset. But your dad—he's Moss's brother?"

"Yep. He's the oldest. His name is Theo. He's great, but Uncle Moss is my most favorite. He treats me like an equal. My dad's cool, but—you know, he's my dad."

Rowan slid off the bed and sat on the floor across from her. "Why'd you get upset when I mentioned Bender's Ridge?"

As though deciding what to say, Maggie played with her braid. "I remember visiting there a couple of times when I was little. I loved it. Then Mom got real sick, and we couldn't travel anymore. Uncle Moss went to war and got hurt, so Dad and I still couldn't go because he needed his privacy. But *you* got to."

"Because he found my dog and saved her life." Rowan told her the story of the rollover accident, and Zephyr being thrown from the van. She recounted going blind, trying to locate her lost dog, and eventually getting a call from Moss.

Maggie's eyes were wide. "You've had an awful summer. Someday, will you tell me what that was like? Being blind?"

"Sure, maybe tomorrow. I've been to Bender's Ridge, but I haven't *seen* it. That's how Moss met my mom, and now they like each other a lot. Your grandpa asked us to come here."

"Does Zephyr get along with other dogs?"

Rowan nodded. "She loves to play. Our old dog, Stormy, got killed in the car accident. Zephy was pretty sad. But now Moss has a dog—"

"Uncle Moss has a dog? Since when?"

"A few weeks ago, I guess. Her name is Jazz. She's a mix, but she mostly looks like a wheat-colored greyhound. She's beautiful. He adopted her 'cause her owner died, and his vet talked him into it. Zephy loves her. Moss loves her too."

"I want to meet her! Want to go outside with Bender? He's great at hide-and-seek. I can show you this place."

"Sure!" Rowan patted the sleek dog. His coat was more like Jazz's than Zephy's. "Right now?"

Maggie picked one of Bender's short hairs from Rowan's jeans. "Yeah, right now. Let's go explore. I'm sorry I was mean."

Carolina awakened when Moss eased down next to her on the bed. "Dinner will be served in about half an hour. I sat with Pa for a few minutes."

She rubbed the sleep from her eyes. "How'd he seem?"

"Remarkably himself, but his color isn't good." His mouth turned down. "A bit scary, really. I've never seen him like this—he's aged."

"That's hard, I know. Hopefully, he'll look better over the next few days as he regains strength. Want to snuggle a minute? You can tell me more."

He gave her a quirky smile. "You bet."

Carolina showered and pulled on jeans and a teal silk blouse before the dinner bell rang. She checked herself in the mirror. "Are you sure we don't have to dress up? I dread being out of place."

Moss hugged her close. He whispered, "Nope. Think Bender's Ridge. Jeans are perfect. That's what Pa's friends love when they come here—how casual we are. And by the way, you look ravishing."

"Thanks." She sighed with relief as they headed downstairs. Her stomach started jumping as unfamiliar voices floated up.

Moss squeezed her hand. "It'll be fine."

An elegant chandelier lit the huge dining room. Hardwood floors gleamed. The table—Carolina was pretty sure it was rosewood—was set for seven. Yikes. New people to deal with all at once. Anxiety rolled through her.

Alice sat quietly at the far end. The seats nearest her were empty. Moss guided Carolina toward one. Maggie and Rowan were seated on the other side of the table. She was reassured to see they were chatting; they must have found their way.

Moss pulled the chair out for Carolina and slid it in after she sat. He took his place across from her, between Maggie and his mom. The table was set with sage handwoven placemats and cream-colored artisan pottery. The lump in her belly softened when she noticed there was only one fork, one spoon, and one knife to deal with. She heard a chair scraping and was taken aback when she saw a man who looked just like Moss sitting next to her. He gave a friendly nod.

Alice spoke. "I'm grateful you all came. Let me make introductions. I think everyone's met Maggie. Carolina, Theo just slipped in next to you. Theo, meet Rowan, Carolina's daughter."

"You look just like Mossy!" Rowan said.

Everyone laughed.

Alice went on, "Our daughter, Heather, is at the other end. Her husband Chas can't make it until tomorrow."

Carolina said hi to Moss's sister, whose auburn hair surprised her. Was that her natural color? She had the same deep blue eyes that ran in the family.

Alice rang a little brass bell, and a small woman in an apron padded into the room. "Carolina and Rowan, this is Anna."

The woman nodded and smiled, then spoke to Alice. Carolina caught her Jamaican accent.

After conferring, Alice went on, "We're delighted she's helping out for a while. The kitchen is her domain. She's labeled the two refrigerators—the food in one's free for the taking, the other, hands off. It holds ingredients for upcoming meals."

As Anna ladled the soup and handed it around, Alice sent the bread and salad down the table. She said, "Let's picture Ash regaining his health and thriving for years to come." There was a moment of silence, and then Alice took a spoonful of the steaming soup.

Theo turned to Carolina. "Your daughter looks so much like Moss—and me, I suppose—you'd think she was a member of the family. I guess it's mostly the hair. Does she take after her dad?"

"Not really. She's a throwback to a grandfather on her father's side."

He raised his eyebrows. "Are you divorced?"

She shook her head. "Her dad passed away four years ago." She blew on a spoonful of soup and tasted it. Delicious. Cilantro was an excellent touch.

"My wife died too. Breast cancer. Four years ago today."

She looked directly at him then. "Moss told me. I'm so sorry. I've had a taste of what you've been through, except mine was sudden."

"Single parenting isn't easy."

"Tell me about it."

"You couldn't do better than my brother. He's an exceptional man." Theo buttered a piece of French bread.

"He's won my heart, and I'd promised myself not to get involved." *Why did I just say that?*

"How come?"

"It's too complicated with a daughter Rowan's age."

He laughed. "That's for sure."

"Have you dated at all?"

Animated conversation rose at the end of the table, so Theo waited for a moment until the sound died down. "One woman. Maggie put the kibosh on it."

"Oh, no." Carolina scooped a walnut from the salad.

"It's probably for the best. My daughter's got a pretty good sense about people. She's already told me she likes Rowan—says she's very direct."

"Takes after her mama." She smiled. "May I have the bread, please? And the butter?" She spread butter thickly on the warm, seeded French bread and bit into it with delight.

Alice touched her arm. "Have you and Theo found some things in common?"

"We have. How are you holding up with all of us here? This has to be hard."

Alice set down her spoon. "It's a relief. I'm glad Ash wanted family to come; I prefer a full house. I couldn't bear the quiet with those nurses guarding him. He had a good nap after his brief time with Moss, so he'll be up for a couple of short visits. He's eager to meet you."

Carolina gulped.

"Are you nervous?" Alice asked.

"Heavens, yes."

"It'll be fine. He's a kind man." Alice patted her arm. "Let's sit down tomorrow and talk. Just you and me. After breakfast."

Carolina nodded, but the knuckle in her belly clotted up again.

Chapter Thirty-nine

He'll see you now," the stocky uniformed nurse said to Carolina. "Alone," she added, raising a blocking hand to Moss. "You can't go in with her." Her tone was brusque, and Carolina felt tacked to the wall.

Moss gave Carolina a soft shoulder cuff. "You can do this," he said.

Heart thudding, throat thick, she leaned her head against the door. Slow breaths. Feeling like she was plodding to her execution—and noting how overblown her reaction was—she pushed the door ajar. The window across the room was an inky nothing, a black hole, sucking her in.

Then she saw Moss's father in a recliner, neatly dressed in a plaid silk bathrobe over pajamas, and slippers. He still had a full head of white hair like the entryway photos, but his color had degraded, and his lips were tinged blue. Oxygen flowed through a nasal cannula, which Carolina recognized from Rafe's time in the hospital. It was all she could do not to press her fingers to her mouth. *This must be hard for him.*

"I'm Ash," he said. "Please, come sit next to me." He patted the arm of a chair.

Trembling, she made her way over and sat beside him. "Hello," she said quietly. "I'm Carolina. How are you feeling?"

"As well as can be expected. This sudden change is quite a shock for me too," he rasped, and gave a wry smile. "I've wanted to meet you because you've had quite the positive effect on my son. You, your daughter, and dog—first good things that have happened to him in a long while."

He struggled for breath. Ill or not, the man was handsome and had the same tender smile lines as Moss.

"I want to ask you a couple of questions—it's a way I have of getting to know people fairly quickly," he said.

Oh, boy, here it comes. "Okay," she said, pressing her now-damp hands on her knees.

"What do you love?" he asked.

She stared at him. Wasn't he going to ask her about her upbringing? Her parents? This seemed like safer territory. She cleared her throat to give herself time to change course. "I love my daughter more than my life," she said. "And I love the natural world—hiking, camping. Birds. Quiet. Reading. And dogs. I love dogs."

He nodded. "Do you love Moss?"

She tilted her head and looked at him. He was worried for his son. "Yes, Mr. Westbury, very much. I think he's a remarkable man. Honorable and kind. Insightful. Honest. Sweet with Rowan."

"Ash, please. And his missing leg doesn't bother you?"

"There's no question he's a whole man. I have missing parts, too." Smiling, she held up her four-fingered hand.

His chuckle turned into a cough. He pressed a fist against his chest. "Ah. Shared experience. Are you going to marry him?" His eyes leaned toward dark sapphire.

"I have no idea. We're just getting to know each other," she protested. "And for God's sake, he hasn't asked me."

"Oh, he will. He's cut from the same cloth as his pa, and I heard it in his voice the first time he told me about you. He knew when he laid eyes on you in the library."

Her breath caught. *In the library? Right after our painful phone conversation?* "You don't know anything about me—my upbringing." She found herself rushing now, to expose her failings. "Mr. Westbury— Ash—I grew up in a trailer park. I was scared there'd be too many forks at dinner tonight, and I wouldn't know which one to pick."

He touched her hand. "Just ask, my dear. No shame in that."

His words stopped her. She opened her mouth, and for a moment, nothing came out. Then, "Really? Ask?"

"Really. Our whole family's the same way. I judge people who are mean, or underhanded, or rude. No one else. You are surely not responsible for your upbringing. It's what happened."

She tried to take in what he'd said. Bewilderment skated through her. She felt like weeping as she watched her last beliefs about wealthy people crumble and fall away.

He waited quietly.

She gathered herself and said, "My brother and I were the first in our family to graduate from college."

"Trailblazers. Congratulations! Where'd you go?"

"University of Oregon." Seeing his surprise, she added, "Yes, Moss and I overlapped, but never met. I majored in biology. Different buildings."

"I grew up simply too." His voice grew gruff. "It might have stayed that way for us, but I seem to have the Midas touch. Earning money came easily. Luck, really." He fell silent for a moment. "Your Moss, he's a wealthy young man. Very wealthy. All my kids are." He raised his eyebrows and pinned her with those familiar eyes. "Does that concern you? Make you uncomfortable?"

She wasn't going to get away without responding. "I wasn't looking for that. In fact, I'd made a promise to myself not to partner at all—at least not until Rowan's in college. It's complicated with a pre-teen. What *does* matter is that I need to feel his equal."

"You are, my dear, in every way. You have quite a presence; it's clear from this short time we've spent together. It couldn't have been easy to walk in here. And you two kids appreciate the same important things in life—nature, reading, and most of all, family." He glanced at the clock. "My ball-buster nurse is about to put an end to this. May I meet your daughter?"

"Only if I can be here too. It's too much pressure on a young kid."

He smiled. "Good Mama Lion. How about you send her in with Maggie at eight o'clock? I hear they've hit it off. I think this battle ax will allow them a short visit together. If she gives the girls trouble, I'll set her straight." He took her hand and fixed his attention on her again. "Carolina, when he asks you, I hope you'll say 'yes.'"

Later that night in Rowan's room, Maggie said, "I acted stupid before. Do you want to sleep in my room like Ma suggested? Then we can talk until we fall asleep."

"Sure!" Rowan grinned, collected her gear, and then, rolling her suitcase, followed her down the hall.

In her room, Maggie pointed to the other bed, and Rowan set her bag in the corner. She came to sit on the floor with her new friend. With a cleansing groan, Bender lay beside Maggie and licked his already immaculate paws.

"What'd you think of Pa? Isn't he cool? I love having grandparents," Maggie said.

"I liked how he asked questions about stuff kids enjoy and was curious about my dog. He sure loves you. I wish he could be my grandfather. I don't have one."

Maggie raised her brows. "Maybe he'll end up your grandpa—Moss and your mom seem kind of gushy together. I saw them kissing."

"I hadn't imagined getting a whole family!"

"With us, you get the whole clan." She yawned. "Want to get ready for bed, so when we're tired, we can slide under our duvets?"

"What's a duvet?" Rowan asked. She mouthed the word trying to make it hers.

"Ma and Pa do things differently. More European style. Your bed doesn't have a top sheet—just a feather downy with a cover the French call a duvet. You were at the ranch guest house? The same as there."

"Right. We have downies at home too. I didn't know the foreign word for them." After pulling on her pajamas, Rowan crawled in and punched the many pillows so she could lean against the headboard. This duvet arrangement was much nicer than trying to squirm under a cold, tight top sheet. As soon as she got home, she'd strip off that sheet for good.

She squinted at her new buddy who had slipped under the covers. Bender leaped up and neatly settled at Maggie's feet. Clearly, this was their routine. "You could tell me about your mom now if you want to. I know when I talk about my dad, I remember the feel of his arms around me and the way he smelled. Other times, it seems like I've lost those memories. Then I'm really sad."

Maggie pulled the covers up to her neck and hugged her knees. "The same thing happens to me. My friends never mention Mom even though they knew her. When I do, they act really weird. Folks are scared to bring up dead people, don't you think? Like it's catching or something.

"My mom—her name was Phoebe—was a classical dancer, graceful and elegant. She danced with the San Francisco Ballet. People say I look like her. She'd wind her hair up in braids before she worked at the barre: you know, the dancing barre, not where people drink. She was already thin, so when she got sick, she was in big trouble. Her bones stuck out all over."

"What made her so sick?"

"Breast cancer."

"Oh. Awful." Rowan stared at the floor.

"Yeah. The surgeon took them both before she died. What about your dad?"

Rowan swallowed hard. "Flu, of all things. Four days and we lost him. Gone. I didn't even get to say goodbye because they wouldn't let kids in the intensive care unit. My mom yelled at them, but it didn't do any good."

"That's terrible."

Rowan looked at the floor, blinking fast. "And now, when Mom comes down with a bug, I get so scared. I know what can happen—even though she called it a … fluke. I think that was the word she used. I love words. Do you?"

"I haven't thought about it, but I read a lot."

"Have you read *Watership Down*?"

"Three times," Maggie said.

"It's one of my favorite books," Rowan said. "Though I love *Bridge to Terabithia* just as much."

"Oooh, if you like it that much, I want to read it."

Thinking about *Watership Down* and its intelligent animals made Rowan want to talk to Maggie about pensing with Zephyr, but wondered if she dared. Her lids felt heavy. Maybe tomorrow.

Maggie stretched and clicked off the lamp. "My eyes are falling down. G'night," she whispered.

Moss poured two glasses of wine and carried them upstairs. His room was spacious. Besides the king-size bed, two comfortable chairs sat in the corner with a lamp between. Carolina sat in one and dimmed the light.

Moss handed her a glass. "Sip on this. Want to tell me what you and Pa talked about?" He slipped off his jeans. Sitting in the other chair, he removed the prosthesis and leaned it against the wall.

"Yes, but first of all, I want to ask you something. It's personal."

"Okay. Go for it."

"Why did you enlist? It seems so unlikely. Not like the Moss I know."

"I figured you'd eventually ask." He fiddled with his thumbs. "My parents don't know about this. Please don't tell them. They don't need— it would make it much worse for Pa. He feels so responsible." He raised his eyebrows, waiting for her response.

"It's yours to share. Or not. I won't break your confidence. I'm surprised they haven't asked, though."

"They know part, just not all. Not this. Never." He twisted the wine glass slowly in his hands, staring at the deep garnet in the light. Glancing at Carolina briefly, he pulled his leg on again and paced back and forth. "My cousin, Andrea, worked for my dad. She was his protégé—so talented. He was preparing her to take over the business when he retired. We'd always been close." He eased down into the chair and ran fingers up and down his forehead. "Pa was traveling to meet new clients in Washington D.C. the morning of September 11th. The night before, he realized he forgot some papers and texted Andrea, asking her to go into the office in the morning, pick them up, and meet him at the airport. Westbury Financial had a large suite in the North Tower on the 98th floor. She lived in the city not far away."

He took Carolina's hand, but couldn't quite look at her. "That morning, Andrea called—woke me out of a sound sleep." He stopped, trying to find the grit to finish this. "She screamed, 'Moss, turn on the TV. Now!' I clicked it on immediately, although I could barely take in what I saw— crazy, billowing black smoke and a huge airliner heading straight for the South Tower."

"'I'm here,' she said, 'at our office. No one can survive this.' Her breathing was labored.

"When I saw the extent of the fire—oh, my God—that was her worst terror." Moss paused. "She went on, 'There's no way out—we tried. Can't go up, can't go down. Help me! Talk to me. *I can't burn.* You know I can't.' She was wailing now. At first, I wanted to force sense into her— there must be hope. Surely, she could hang on, I said. She whimpered, 'I'm looking at the thermometer. It's over 130 degrees and getting hotter every second.'"

He gulped the wine and sat staring at the floor. When he looked up again, he was preternaturally calm. "I told her, 'I'm right there with you; I'm holding your hand.' It's like we went into a tranquil, fictional world, and I talked her over the edge." His voice was ragged. "I couldn't look at the TV. I was terrified I'd see her falling. So I prayed and counted to thirty." He shuddered. "I shook with rage and grief for hours. The waste! My quirky, brilliant, playful friend murdered for some crazy ideology. She jumped, but they murdered her." He took a deep breath.

"The only way I could live with myself was to enlist. I signed up the next day. I had to *do* something. I had to pay, and I had to make them pay as well. You know what it taught me? Every one of us is capable of hate—I hadn't realized I was until then."

"Oh, my God," Carolina whispered. "You did the right thing, helping her. You must know it."

"I've been over those minutes thousands of times and can't come up with any other outcome. Still, I'm hard on myself. Life is so bloody unfair," he murmured. "Please, come here. I need to hold you."

Carolina crawled into his lap and laid her head against his chest. They remained there a long time. "How can you use the word 'free fall' after what you went through with Andrea?" she finally asked.

"It took a while. What she did—so much courage—I reframed the word as sacred. And each time I use it, I send a salute to her." After long moments, he took a deep breath. "Okay. I want to hear about your visit with Pa."

"After what you shared?"

"Now. Please."

"Wait, I've got a cramp. I have to move." She shifted back to her chair and massaged the knot in her foot. "Well." She paused. "Let's see. He asked me what I love, which was such a thoughtful and penetrating question—it gets to the heart of the matter, doesn't it?"

He nodded.

"I mentioned Rowan, birds, nature, and dogs. Oh, and reading. He asked me if I love you." She looked at him. "I said yes."

He watched pink bloom on her face.

"Then I told him how I grew up, but he didn't seem put off. In fact, he was kind and made me feel at ease. That's about it."

He cocked his head. "You mean it's all you're going to disclose. Your blush always gives you away."

Her coloring got brighter. "I learned early on I can't lie successfully. But that's all I'm comfortable telling you."

"Fair enough. Did you like him?"

"Very much. I bet you'll look like just him when you're older."

"Yeah, so people say—although our strengths are in such different areas." He took a sip of wine and swooshed it in his mouth, savoring the rich flavor. "You've met some of the tribe now. What do you think?"

"I took to Theo immediately. He's so easy to be with. I haven't had a chance to talk to your sister yet. Your mom and I have a date for tomorrow morning. So I guess it's going okay—better than expected. They're just human beings, aren't they."

He nodded. "Promise me you won't fall for Theo? He *always* gets the girls." He tilted his head, questioning. "I saw how you two got along at dinner."

My God, he's serious! "I've already fallen for a Westbury." She reached out and smoothed his cheek. "Fallen hard."

"Yeah, but he's the doctor. Don't women always fall for doctors?"

She chuckled. "Not this girl."

"Well, that's a relief. So coming back next year for my parents' forty-fifth—let's pray they get to celebrate it—isn't so scary?"

"I'll report back after I talk with your mom tomorrow morning." She knuckled his arm. "I'm kidding. This is difficult to admit after the fuss I made, but most likely I'll be fine."

"Well, you do rise to emergency situations. Come here again," he said gruffly. He took her hand and snuggled her back into his lap. He buried his nose in her hair, breathed in her scent, and kissed the crook of her neck. "I don't think you have any idea," he murmured.

"Any idea of what?" she whispered.

Instead of answering, he slowly kissed her.

Her breath quickened. She pulled away. "Uh, who's sleeping in the rooms on either side of us?"

"Only my sis," he said. "Her room is there." He pointed. "With a walk-in closet and bathroom between."

"So, limited privacy."

"She's a sound sleeper, and we're consenting adults." He grinned and kissed her again. "And she's not so innocent herself."

"Mossy…."

"Sweetheart, I'm aching to make love with you. It's been days, and I need the connection tonight. I'll be very quiet." He ran a finger slowly across her breasts. "You open to that?"

"Lordy," she said. "One touch and I'm on fire."

Chapter Forty

Carolina woke early and hoping not to disturb Moss, slid out of bed. She watched him—early morning stubble, hair askew. Adorable. She snugged the covers around his shoulders. Morning sun poured in the window; she pulled the curtain closed. Perhaps he could sleep in this morning. He had become such an important part of her life so quickly. Was this an out-of-control freight train?

She pulled on jeans and a long-sleeved forest-green knit shirt and headed downstairs to find java. What revelations would the day bring? The scent of cinnamon and brown sugar floated on the air. Anna must have been up for a while making breakfast cake.

"Good morning," Carolina said, as she walked into the kitchen. "It smells fabulous. May I make some coffee?"

"Ms. Graham, would you rather have a latte? I'd be happy to make you one."

"Yes, please! And call me Carolina. A mocha, with just a splash of chocolate in it. May I help?"

Anna gave a throaty laugh. "Ms. Carolina, this is what I love to do. Care for folks. You head into the sitting room—I lit the fireplace— I'll catch you there. A couple of today's newspapers are waiting. The coffeecake'll be ready in a bit. What's 'just a splash' of chocolate? Ours is powdered."

"An even teaspoon would be perfect."

She found the sitting room, sank onto the leather couch, and perused *The New York Times*. A bomb plot on the city subways had been foiled. More of this terrorist stuff—first the twin towers, now this. This period Rowan was growing up in was far scarier than the time of her own childhood.

She rested her head back and pondered what Moss had divulged the night before. What an impossible, unbearable—she couldn't find words to accurately describe his experience. None did justice to what he and Andrea had faced. Did his cousin's photo hang among those in the entryway? She wanted to spend a quiet moment honoring Andrea's astonishing bravery.

A few minutes later, Anna appeared with a mug. "Is Mr. Moss up yet?"

"He was still sleeping when I came downstairs." A creamy leaf design topped the mocha. "This is beautiful. Thank you. Have you known him a long time?"

Anna pursed her lips, thinking. "Since I started cleanin' this home, come six years ago next month. My services were Ms. Alice's sixtieth birthday present. Two years back, after he got out of that Walter Reed Hospital, Mr. Moss stayed here while Mr. Ash was gettin' the ranch ready, so I got to know him close-up. I helped out more then—did cookin', cleanin', and laundry too. I saw him struggle through all that awful physical therapy. So much pain, but no complainin'. Just bearin' up."

"He's a courageous man, that's for sure. What time does Mrs. Westbury usually get up?"

"Seven a.m., like clockwork. We'll see her any minute now." She turned to the kitchen. "Cake smells done. I'll slice it up and be back in a couple of minutes."

Anna was right. Five minutes later, Alice walked in, stifling a yawn. Carolina rose to greet her.

"No need to stand for people in this house," Alice said. "You're up early; I thought you might sleep in. I hope the bed was comfortable. Come, sit down."

"I slept well, thanks."

"I checked in the kitchen. Anna's cutting the coffee cake. Did Moss sleep all right?"

"He's still out, at least he was when I left. I'll be delighted if he can sleep late today. He's so worried about his dad."

"Me too. Any nightmares? Are they better? They were bad when he stayed here."

Carolina felt a flush rise. It seemed like an awfully personal question. "I don't know. We..." She fiddled with her fingernails. This was awkward. "You need to ask him. We only spent ... last weekend...." Now she could feel the blush crawling around the back of her neck. She must be flaming red. She pressed her hands to her face.

"Please, don't feel uncomfortable." Alice patted her on the knee. "I understand the boundaries you've set. They make sense. I have other questions, though. I'd love to know more about you."

Carolina relaxed, just a little. "What are you interested in? I don't think I have any secrets."

"Your parents—what are they like?"

Carolina paused and considered. "They loved each other. My dad was killed in a motorcycle accident—I was thirteen, and my brother, Sam, was fifteen. A drunk driver. It turned out Dad hadn't planned well. No life insurance. We'd lived simply, but after his death, we were truly dirt poor, lost our little cottage, and moved into a trailer park. Mom had no skills in the real work world. She did, and still does, astrology and tarot readings. She's airy-fairy—that's how I always describe her—more interested in the realms she can't see than the one she can. It's not my favorite side of her."

"You lost your dad young; I'm so sorry. Your mother's work helps to guide people. She must be interested in and care about her clients."

"She does. But it didn't put food on the table or buy the books or the sewing machine I so desperately wanted. Or shoes, for that matter."

Alice nodded.

Carolina's voice dropped to a murmur. "As a girl, I was ashamed of her. She dressed flamboyantly, and I could never be sure she wouldn't embarrass me in front of my friends."

Alice put her hand on her arm. "Oh, my dear, people are who they are. I'm not sure we get to choose our predilections. And obviously, she raised a daughter whose priorities are straight. Your sound parenting shows. Rowan is quite something—smart and personable with good manners."

"Thank you. Her dad had a strong part in that. He was a good man and a terrific father."

"Maggie embarrassed me yesterday, the way she treated Rowan."

"I watched you set her straight. Apparently, she took it to heart because the girls are sharing the same room. Don't be hard on her. Kids make mistakes."

"You're right, they do. So, back to you."

Carolina waited, anxious about what Moss's mother might ask next.

Anna walked in with a platter, set the coffee cake on the table, and slipped out of the room. Alice reached for a piece and offered the plate to Carolina. Glad for something to do with her hands, she took a square and bit into it. Warm, melt-in-your-mouth delicious.

"Have you thought about having more children?" Alice asked.

Carolina almost choked on her cake and felt perspiration prickle her neck. It was all she could do to not get up and run. After she swallowed, she said, "Well. Huh. No, I haven't thought about it—we-we're … it's … premature. We need time—time to get to know each other."

"Look. I'm matter-of-fact, and I'm not going to apologize. Feel free to say, 'You need to back off.' I can take it. I ask because Moss wants kids. He's been quite open about it."

Bombshell. "He hasn't shared that with me yet. But I'm pleased how wise he is with Rowan."

"She won Ash right over, by the way."

Here was a way to turn this conversation in a different direction. "I'm not surprised. She's a light, for sure. I call her my wordsmith. She's interested in veterinary medicine, but she's also a good writer."

"It's something she'll have in common with Moss." Alice took a sip of her latte. "Have you read his books yet?"

"Books? What books?"

"He hasn't told you he's a published author?"

"*Really?*" Carolina frowned. "No. He writes, I knew that."

"He has two books out—novels he wrote before the war. The second one did quite well. It was on *The New York Times* best-seller list for twelve weeks."

"What are the titles? I read a lot; maybe I'll recognize them."

"*Cancelled* was his first one, then *Drive-by.*"

"The dickens," Carolina muttered. "He's so darn modest."

Alice laughed out loud. "Usually that's considered a positive quality. Ask him about them."

"I should be learning this stuff from Moss. Ash pulled the same stunt. Worse. Much more personal."

"Yes, he told me. Way over the top. Forgive him; I think it's because he's concerned he might die without saying what's important." She sighed. "Some folks might call me nosy, but I'm deeply curious about what moves people. Welcome to the Westburys. We're all outspoken."

"No kidding. And I thought *I* was direct." Carolina folded her arms across her chest. "I don't know how I feel about this. I'm uncomfortable."

"Good for you; speaking out is hard. Here's the upside: with this clan, you'll know where you stand. I guess it requires gumption. It's not for everybody."

They ate in silence, taking measure of each other.

Moss limped into the room. He took one look at Carolina's taut expression and, resting a comforting hand on her, swung on his mother. "You've been grilling her?"

"Apparently, you haven't shared with her that one, you want a family—and two, you're a published author. So we've had a frank talk. I told her not everybody can handle our bluntness."

He sank into the chair next to Carolina and wearily rubbed his fingers across his forehead. "We've spent exactly one weekend together where we had privacy. One weekend! It was hard enough telling her about losing my leg and sharing war experiences. Jeez," he muttered, shaking his head. "Lay off, Ma."

He reached over and took Carolina's hand. "I'm sorry, sweetheart. I'm not withholding anything—we hadn't gotten there yet." He felt her hand relax. He moved next to her on the couch and put his arm around her. "You're welcome to read my novels," he said softly. "But I feel like a different man from the one who wrote them. As for children, you've seen how much I like Rowan—she's such a great kid. She even looks like she's my daughter."

He saw tears leaking down Carolina's cheeks. He touched them with his thumb and gently rubbed them in. "What is it?"

"I wanted to hear these things from you."

Alice stood up. "I can see I've caused trouble. I'm sorry. My curiosity gets the best of me. I'm going to see Ash."

"Leaving me to clean up your mess, are you?" Moss growled.

"Yes. You're the one Carolina wants right now. You'll make it right."

"You don't get to drop this all on him," Carolina said. "I have things to say. Will you come back after you visit Ash?"

Alice nodded, acknowledging the mess she'd made, and left the room.

Moss held Carolina while she wept on his chest. He agreed with her; he'd have preferred they find their own timing. But Ma was Ma, and what was done was done. He stroked her hair and waited until her tears stopped.

She snuffled and said, "I need to collect myself, maybe take a walk. Any special direction?"

He pointed. "There's a sweet little pond over there." He indicated the entryway. "Go out the back French doors. If you like, ask Anna for bread to feed the ducks."

"I'll be back in half an hour." She touched him on the cheek and left the room.

Carolina stopped in the downstairs bathroom and splashed cold water on her face. Her eyes were somewhat swollen. After patting herself dry with the towel, she headed to the kitchen to see if Anna had stale bread.

With crusts in a sack, she slipped on a jacket in the hallway, opened the French doors onto the patio, and followed the path Moss had suggested. The crisp air braced her. Aflame with color, the sugar maples stood bold and red against the cornflower-blue sky. The moist air felt wonderful in her nose. She could smell the humus. How big was this property, anyway? It felt immense; she could see no other homes. Carolina heard ducks before she saw the pond, which wasn't small—more of a lake. It curved around a corner and out of sight. A carved wooden bench overlooked it, and she ran her fingers over the detailed surface. As soon as she sat, three mallards headed toward her, curious and hopeful. Then a raft of wood ducks showed up.

Tearing pieces of bread and venting pent-up energy, she launched each chunk over the water. The birds paddled and scrabbled for their share. She closed her eyes, sat in silence, and considered the morning's events. She and Alice were more alike than she'd realized. She'd been trumped, that was all. Thinking back, she wasn't sure it had ever happened before. Suddenly, she saw how others might experience her, and her sense of self shifted.

She felt a presence. Two mute swans made their way toward her, clearly a mated pair. They were attentive to each other, as though they had a private, intimate language.

"This is what you've always wanted," she whispered. "People who aren't covert, who say what they mean." She hadn't realized how scary it would be to open up and trust, to put her hopes and desires—her truth—out there. Did she have the courage? If she didn't reach down and find the strength, she'd lose Moss. The thought pierced her like a sharp, steel wedge, and she flattened her hand against her heart.

Dawdling near the pond, she was relieved to have alone time. These people were relaxed and laughed a lot. They obviously loved and appreciated each other. Wouldn't it be wonderful to be enveloped in big family love? It would be good for Rowan too. You have one life, she thought. Pull yourself together, girl; it's a strange new map.

Discovering one more small crust at the bottom of the bag, she pitched it to the swans. The female—with a slender neck and smaller knob at the base of her bill—nabbed it. Carolina smiled, pulled the jacket close against the chill, and walked back to the house.

Moss was still sitting on the couch reading *The Wall Street Journal*. He looked up.

"It's okay," she said. "This upfront family stuff. I'll get used to it."

He smiled as he set the paper down. "You astonish me."

"Did I upset your mom? Will she come back?"

"Oh, yeah. She's always game for Round Two."

"I'd like more coffee cake."

"I'll get it," he said. "I want some. And a latte. Fortification for what's to come."

She giggled. "Exactly. I'd love another mocha as well. Anna made a perfect one for me earlier."

After Moss left, Alice walked back into the sitting room. "Those nurses," she said. "They must sit at the door with a stopwatch."

"How's Ash this morning?" Carolina asked.

"His color seems better than yesterday. We took a little stroll." She pressed her lips together before going on. "I'm not ready to lose him. Not yet. It turns out life is unbelievably short. It speeds right by." She dropped into an overstuffed chair and wiped her fingers across her brow; the gesture reminded Carolina so much of Moss.

"I learned that when Rafe died. Right afterward, I wanted time to stop, to honor what had happened. But it kept plowing relentlessly along."

"I get it. Remind me, how long has it been? I think you might have told me last night, but I'm not tracking well."

"Four years, same as Theo. Parenting Rowan has kept me together and forced me to be grounded."

"You're lucky to have her—a living piece of her dad. You're too young to have faced such a significant loss."

"I'm not alone. Both your sons have had profound losses."

Moss limped back in with a goodie-filled tray—more coffee cake, but also cheese and crackers in addition to the drinks. "I thought we needed protein."

She recognized Jarlsberg but wasn't familiar with the others. Moss sliced and set some on crackers. "This is the Ewe Bloom," he pointed to a wedge of cheese. "That's Manchego, and this one is smoked Gubbeen."

They ate for a few minutes quietly.

Carolina spoke first. "Now, it's my turn. To answer your question, Alice, I'd figured there'd be no more children for me because I promised myself not to even date until Rowan went to college—I'd be over forty, too late for more kids. But then I met Moss, and there went the no-dating plan. He's the only kind of man I can imagine raising a child with—kind, engaged, a sweet sense of humor. And he treats Rowan with such respect." She sipped her mocha and then stared pointedly at Alice. "This could work. So please back off. Give us the opportunity to make our way together."

Alice's mouth circled into a surprised "O."

Moss reared his head when she said "back off," so she added, "Your mom gave me permission."

"Yeah, but I bet she didn't expect you would!"

"Welcome to my world," Carolina said. "I'm a quick study." She straightened her shoulders and looked from one to the other. Alice seemed chagrined. Moss beamed.

Rowan came in. "Morning everyone. Yum! Coffee cake. Can I have a piece?"

"May," the three adults said in unison and then all laughed together. "Sure," Alice said. "Grab a plate and help yourself. Have some cheese, too." She pointed to the Jarlsberg. "This one complements the cake."

"So, Row," Moss said, after the girl took a piece and some cheese. "It's good you're here. I have a question for you." His eyes were unusually bright.

Rowan dropped into a chair and looked at him expectantly.

"You know I like your mom a lot."

"Mossy, it's like, sooo obvious. It's clear to everyone."

Moss reached for Carolina's hand. "Would it be all right if I asked her to marry me? It would have to be okay with you."

Alice gasped. Carolina's heart lurched and she gawked at Moss. Had she heard him correctly?

Rowan squinted at him. "You're serious, right? It'd be so mean if you joked about this."

"I've never been more serious."

Fingers of her other hand pressed to her mouth, Carolina watched her daughter carefully. The girl frowned, considering the implications. Hesitating, Rowan spoke. "Well ... I'd need to feel included."

"That's why I'm asking you first."

"Maybe...." She chewed her lip. "Would you adopt me? Then we'd be a real family." She rushed on. "But I can't ever call you Daddo. I couldn't. I couldn't do that to my dad."

His eyes filled with tears. "I'd be honored to be your father. And 'Mossy' is just fine."

"One more thing. I need a promise."

Curious, Moss waited.

"I want Maggie and Bender to spend the summer at Bender's Ridge with us. Then it'd be like I have a sister. Almost a twin sister."

"I'll have to check with Theo, but I bet we can pull it off. In fact, you could ask him; it might be even more convincing." He turned to Carolina and murmured, "So, will you have me? Of course, I come with this blunt clan of good-hearted people." He smiled. "We're both a package deal."

Carolina's impulse was to laugh and cry simultaneously. "Yes," she whispered. "It feels inevitable and right, just seven years early. Then again, as your mom says, life is short. Are you sure?"

"Oh, yeah, I'm sure. I knew early on, and then you stood up to Ma just now. You have to be able to, and you can." Grinning, he flung one arm around Carolina, and the other around Rowan. "The dog members aren't here, but meet my human family, Ma."

"Ash will be delighted, as am I. Shall I look for your grandmother's engagement ring?" Alice asked. "Perhaps Carolina will like it." She turned to her. "Of course, it's fine if it's not to your taste."

Moss looked over at Carolina, questioning. She nodded.

"The dogs can be together! They're going to be so happy!" Rowan crowed. She sent a blast of love toward Zephyr and Jazz in Oregon.

Zephyr rises, and for the first time, crosses the room and lies pressed against Jazz. Receiving Rowan's pense and bathed in her love, she sees her pack taking a new and beautiful shape. She yawns and rests her nose on her new buddy's hip. She sends a picture to her girl of all five of them living at the big land, where she first found Kibble Man.

If you enjoyed this novel and got involved with the characters, Skye is working on the second in the series, *Must Like Dogs,* which takes place four years later.

Yes, a third is planned!

Thank you for taking time to read *Unleashed*. If you enjoyed it, please consider telling your friends and posting a review on Amazon and/or Goodreads. Word-of-mouth referrals are an author's best friend, and I appreciate them deeply.

About the Author

Skye Blaine writes short essays, memoir, fiction, and poetry, developing themes of aging, coming of age, disability, and awakening. In 2003, she received an MFA in Creative Writing from Antioch University.

Bound to Love: a memoir of grit and gratitude, was published in 2015, and has won three prizes, including two firsts from Pacific Northwest Writers Association and Bay Area Independent Publishers Association (BAIPA)

Skye has had memoir, fiction, and poetry published in seven anthologies, and personal essays in national magazines: *In Context* (now known as *Yes!* magazine) and *Catalyst.* Other essays have been published in the *Register-Guard* newspaper, and the *Eugene Weekly.* She also presented radio essays on KRML 1410 AM in Carmel, CA.

Skye is adjunct faculty at Santa Rosa Junior College where she teaches fiction and memoir in the Older Adults Program.

She can be reached at skye@skyeblaine.com, and welcomes comments.

Colophon

This book is set in Minion Pro, 11.5 point.

Minion is a serif typeface designed by Robert Slimbach in 1990 for Adobe Systems and inspired by late Renaissance-era type.

…

As the name suggests, it is particularly intended as a font for body text in a classical style, neutral and practical while also slightly condensed to save space. Slimbach described the design as having "a simplified structure and moderate proportions." (Wikipedia)

Made in the USA
Monee, IL
09 August 2021